COMING HOME TO LOVE

Lakeside Porches Series Book Two

KATIE O'BOYLE

Pearl, a woman I
admire so much!
Enjoy—
Katie O'Boyle

SOUL MATE PUBLISHING
New York

COMING HOME TO LOVE

KATIE O'BOYLE

Cover Design by Niina Cord

Published in the United States of America by
Soul Mate Publishing
P.O. Box 24
Macedon, New York, 14502

ISBN: 978-1-61935-838-6

ebook ISBN: 978-1-61935-566-8

www.SoulMatePublishing.com

I am indebted to Dr. Ellen Horovitz

who has worked miracles

through Yoga Therapy,

and to Dr. Bonnie Cronin

the intrepid Naturopathic Physician

who tracked down gluten as my number one enemy.

Acknowledgements

Heartfelt thanks to the anonymous contest judges of the Golden Claddagh and Golden Rose who freely shared their expertise to improve the telling of Justin and Gianessa's story. Warm hugs to my test readers—Kathy, Jackie, Debbie, Anne, and Martha. Respectful bows to the authors who critiqued sections of this novel: the Lilac City Rochester Writers and the Sunday Afternoon Critiquers. I couldn't have done any of it without the Early Birds.

Chapter 1

Gianessa jolted out of her meditation as her roommate pounded down the stairs.

With a breathless, "Later," Sara slammed the front door, but not before frigid wind swept in a few snowflakes.

Gianessa pressed her fingers to her forehead and chuckled. "Ohmigod, I'm living on the polar ice cap." She tugged the lavender pashmina from the ottoman behind her and wrapped herself in its soft warmth.

"Breathe," she told herself and tried again to find her center. It grew harder every day, and she knew her galloping roommate and the arctic blast were not to blame.

She was stuck. *I hate stuck. I'm tired of stuck. Coming here was about getting unstuck.*

Joel had brought her to Tompkins Falls to redesign the spa at his luxury Manse Inn and Spa, but the week she arrived he'd been horribly injured in a car accident. Two weeks in a coma, and he was still in a hospital in Rochester and faced months of rehabilitation.

Now here she was, three thousand miles from home, broke, with no car, and stuck giving massages at the spa until Joel got back on his feet. *Thank the universe for Sara.* The spa's one-off hair stylist was letting her share her townhouse, in exchange for great meals every day.

There was only one downside. Sara was determined to find Gianessa a husband. *I will not tell her that my marriage ended in a shameful divorce, and that I lost custody of my beautiful baby daughter, Isabella.* It was far too painful and private to share. For now, the plan was to get her career on track and make a new life in Tompkins Falls. *No dating. No husband.*

With her body heat restored, she loosened the pashmina, opened her arms, and rested her hands on her thighs, palms up. Back in her meditation pose, she spoke her mantra, adding positive thoughts and images.

"Breathe." *I know my professional life will be back on track once Joel recovers.* Big, shimmery worry bubbles floated away with her breath.

"Breathe." *I will buy a toasty warm winter coat*. Frosty bubbles vanished from sight.

"Breathe." *I will get a car*. This time, the bubbles were circles of exhaust from a cartoon car that putt-putted across her vision.

"Breathe." *I will make wonderful new friends and be part of my new town in the Finger Lakes*. Champagne bubbles rose in crystal flutes. "No!" Her eyes popped open. *No champagne! What am I thinking*?

She closed her eyes and replaced the bubbles with the faces of sober friends at her very last AA meeting in Northern California—old and young, men and women, some in suits, some in jeans and T-shirts. Was it a month ago she had boarded the bus for Upstate New York? No, six weeks already, six weeks without a meeting. *No wonder my energy is blocked.*

That was a problem she could fix. In one fluid motion, she stood up from the floor, let the shawl drop from her shoulders, and bowed. "Namaste" brought her meditation to a close.

Cell phone in hand, she found the number in her contacts for the local AA office. Joel had written it down for her when she met him at the conference in October, and something had made her program it into her phone before she'd even made the decision to come east to work for him. *Why did I wait so long*?

"AA Central Office," a woman answered on the third ring.

"Yes, hi, I'm Gianessa and I'm an alcoholic. I live in Tompkins Falls, and I need a meeting today or tonight. Thank god you picked up the phone."

"Right back at you, honey. My name's Carol, and I'm an alcoholic. Are you sober today?"

"Yes, but I'm a little crazy. It's more than a month since I moved here, and I haven't been to a meeting."

"We've got just the thing, the Top Shelf Women's group. We meet tonight at seven at the Presbyterian Church downtown. Do you need directions?"

Gianessa gave her the address of Sara's townhouse, and Carol told her how to navigate the five short blocks to the church.

"It's less than ten minutes. We're around back and down the stairs. Will I see you there?"

"You will see me there tonight, Carol," Gianessa committed. As soon as she ended the call, her phone chirped and displayed the number for the spa.

Oh no. Had she been scheduled to work today and forgotten? "Hi, Remy," she said with a quaver in her voice.

"Remy just went home sick. We need you," Grace the unflappable implored her. "I know you were counting on a day off, and I'm sorry but—"

"I'll be there in twenty minutes."

How am I going to pull this off? Her uniform was in the laundry hamper under her sweatiest sweats. Still, if the spa manager was out, no one would care what she wore. A call to her neighbor Linda netted her a ride in return for an hour of babysitting later in the week.

She grabbed a quick shower and dressed in a clean white T-shirt, one of a dozen she'd brought in her little duffle from the West Coast. She added a cheerful skirt and her favorite sandals. The weather had turned frigid this week, and she desperately needed a coat and warm clothes. Truthfully, she needed more money than a few extra hours would give her.

I can't put it off any longer. She had to sell the necklace her ex-husband, Les, had given her when Isabella was born. With a decisive nod, she took a lumpy blue pouch from her top dresser drawer and shook out a heavy necklace. *Someone besides Joel has to know where I can sell this.* She placed the double strand of platinum and gold hearts around her neck. It fit as if it had been made just for her. *Maybe it was made for me.* Les had spared no expense for his girls. She fussed with the elaborate closure and arranged it so the big, round amethyst rested in the hollow of her throat. Surely she could get five thousand for it.

She grimaced in the mirror at the show of wealth, the last token of her old life with Les. She would invest the proceeds in her life going forward: get a coat, put something down on a used car, look into getting her physical therapy license in New York State. She vowed she would never again hook up with someone like Les who pampered her out of her independence. *I swear*.

As she struggled to undo the clasp, a horn sounded. Giving it up, she raced, coatless, out to Linda's waiting car.

"Brr. You'll catch your death, girlfriend. I'd have loaned you a coat if you'd asked. Pretty necklace."

"You wouldn't happen to know where I could sell it, would you, Linda?"

"Other than that seedy pawnshop on the way to Rochester, I have no idea. But they'll cheat you, so forget that."

"Thanks anyway, and thanks a million for the ride." Gianessa rubbed her arms and watched the passing scenery to distract herself from the cold. "Those white houses with the gingerbread trim that look like they're marching up from the lakeshore—what street is that?"

"Aren't they sweet? That's Lakeside Terrace. Your boss, Joel Cushman, owns them and lives in that last building, way at the top of the bluff."

"Must be a fantastic view of the lake."

"They're apartments, two or three flats in each building. I understand his grandmother Bridey Tompkins built them many years ago. Her idea was for the young faculty at Tompkins College to rent them during the school year, and then tourists would rent by the week or the month during the summer. She was a romantic, the way I heard it. She wanted every young professor to find his or her true love in their first year, marry in the summer, buy a home and start a family."

Gianessa responded with her musical laugh—two notes, low then high—that sounded like the start of a happy song. "How funny that her name was Bridey."

"I love your laugh. They say, while Bridey was alive, most of the professors who rented at Lakeside Terrace married quickly and happily. She brought her magic with her from Ireland and built it into every apartment."

"What a way to see the world. How sad that she died."

"It was a terrible accident, drunk driving."

Gianessa shivered, although Linda had turned the heat as high as it would go. "Was she an alcoholic?"

"Nope, not Bridey. Her son-in-law, Josh Cushman, Joel's dad, was driving. The whole family was killed, except Joel who was just a boy then. Joel's uncle Justin—"

Gianessa laughed. "They were into names starting with 'J' apparently."

Linda nodded. "Family tradition. Anyway, Justin came back from Europe and did his best to raise his nephew. Poor Joel was traumatized, though, and took years to straighten out." She sighed. "And now Joel's been injured again. Not drunk driving this time. Just black ice and bad luck. Have you heard how he's doing?"

"They say he's out of the coma and will need one more surgery and months of therapy, but he will recover. Joel's a hard worker and very strong in himself."

"I heard yesterday his Uncle Justin is back in town to manage Joel's affairs. He's an international financier, so he'll be glad it's not forever."

Gianessa froze. *What if he's going to manage the Manse? And the spa?*

"Tell me the secret," Justin coaxed with a whisper. He cupped a hand to his ear, half-expecting an answer.

"Where do I need to look?"

Something told him the answer to all his problems was in Joel's apartment. He wanted what his nephew had gotten for himself the last few years—vigorous good health, the respect of his community, personal integrity, and a high-spirited, beautiful woman to share his bed and his future.

Justin's life's work the past two decades had been successful beyond all measure, but it gave him no satisfaction. It was founded on values he no longer espoused. Six years ago, the woman he thought he would spend his life with had cheated on him, and every relationship since then had been shallow and pointless. And for the last two years he'd battled a mysterious illness that continued to sap his strength.

He was a shadow of his former self, and his high-priced doctors were still unable to agree on a credible diagnosis. Lately he wondered if they were just in it for his money, milking him for donations while they ordered one expensive test after another and argued about the results.

Is there anyone I can trust? He had reached out to four long-time colleagues and friends over the past year, asking what they thought his fundamental problem was.

His mentor in London told him to see a psychiatrist for his "bloody anger issues." Justin had protested that he thought of himself as jovial, and wasn't he entitled to a good rant from time to time, especially when someone crossed him? His mentor had snapped, “You bloody think the whole world is trying to cross you, starting with every woman you meet.”

Justin had laughed. “Poppycock,” he’d told his mentor. He stroked his chin now. *When did we last talk*? Surprise registered. *Not since then*.

He’d also asked Bhaskar, the international negotiator who facilitated several of his multi-million-dollar deals in Asia. “How do you see my problem?” Bhaskar had chastised him for making deals that benefited no one but himself and told him his digestive problems were karmic payback. “I can believe that,” Justin had acquiesced, “but surely karmic payback comes with a diagnosis and treatment?”

Bhaskar had shrugged and turned away.

Third on Justin’s list was his Swiss banker. Jean-Claude advised him to forgive his old lover, Alexa, marry her, and have a bunch of children to keep her at home. “That makes no sense,” Justin had argued. “Even if Alexa agreed, she’d just hire nannies for the children and continue to do what she pleased.” Jean-Claude knew as well as he did what Alexa wanted. “You mean, spend your money and run around with any man who catches her eye? What’s wrong with that, my friend?” Justin seethed, even now.

Fourth and last, his old lover from Chicago had put her hands on her hips and told him to try an AA meeting. “Ridiculous, Syd! I haven’t had a drink in six years.” A hollow laugh escaped him now. *My life’s a bigger mess sober than when I downed a pint of Absolut every night*.

If his trusted colleagues and friends didn’t have the answer, any more than his doctors, who did? *Joel. Joel has the answer*.

Justin eyed his nephew’s plush, serene living room. Pale gray sofas and chairs with big, soft pillows in shades of blue and gray, sleek ebony tables, a wall of windows with French doors to a porch with a lake view.

“Give me a clue, nephew.”

Wind pummeled the doors behind him.

Justin jumped. "You old fool." He goaded himself with a chuckle, as he checked that the doors were secure. His gaze wandered to the gray, windswept lake, and a long-forgotten memory tugged his mouth into a smile.

He had come here for tea with Joel's grandmother Bridey O'Donohue Tompkins when he was twenty-four, just over twenty years ago. It was Bridey's private, getaway place, but she issued a special invitation to Justin and her grandchildren to join her. Joel was eight then, Christie eleven—both of them full of mischief.

Bridey served them on her delicate Belleek china and pretended to read their tea leaves. How he missed Bridey! If he could share his desperation with her, she'd point him to the answer. *What did she read in our tea leaves?*

Christie's fortune was, "You will shine brighter than the sun." Christie loved that. She tossed back her blond hair and puffed out her budding chest. Christie perished five years later in the fiery crash that killed Joel's parents and Bridey, too. He sighed heavily at the memory.

Bridey had been accurate in her tea-leaf prediction for Joel: "You will kiss many women before you find The One." At the time, young Joel had screwed up his face and told them, "I'm not kissing anyone until I find her. And maybe not even then." They'd all laughed, but she was right. He had become a womanizer.

It was only a few years ago that Joel had sworn off women and moved here, to Bridey's old apartment. Alone. He was "on a quest," he'd told Justin, to redeem himself, after a mindless bed-them-and-leave-them tear that followed the demise of his engagement to a wealthy heiress named Lorraine.

To hear Joel tell it, he'd been without sex for two or three years when he met the irrepressible Manda last winter. Joel had known immediately that Manda was The One. And now they were engaged. *Or will be if I can find the engagement ring and take it to him in the hospital.*

Justin turned away from the lake to resume his search for a two-and-a-half-carat sapphire set with white diamonds. But what *did* Joel mean by "the usual hiding place"? He'd already searched the inlaid ebony box with Joel's cufflinks, his sock drawer, his desk, his safe, and the bedside table.

"I need another clue, Joel," he said aloud.

The wind rattled the doors again, this time accompanied by a howling Justin hadn't heard since he'd gathered with his brother's family around the tree on Christmas Eve. The ancient fireplace in the great room at his brother's home—now the Manse Inn and Spa, with Joel as proprietor—was famous for setting a mood on a stormy winter night.

Justin snapped his fingers. *Christmas presents.*

The parents had always hidden the smaller gifts where children dared not go—behind the crystal. He turned to the wall of cabinets next to Joel's dining area and found the one that still held Bridey's Waterford crystal and Belleek tea service. Sure enough, on the top shelf in back, perched on the lid of a Belleek sugar bowl was a tiny blue Tiffany box with a perky white bow.

Justin pocketed the box in his suit jacket, grabbed his overcoat, and started for the front door. The porch doors rattled one more time and compelled him to take another peek at the lake. White caps tossed, and waves pounded the bluff forty feet below. To his left was the marina and beyond it the city of Tompkins Falls, founded by Joel's ancestors and financed by generations of Cushmans. To his right, the long, silver finger of Chestnut Lake stretched twenty miles to the south, nestled between fertile hills planted with vineyards. Justin's forehead rested for a moment against the cool glass of the French door. *How I've missed this*!

His mouth curved in a smile. *What did Bridey read in my tea leaves? Something about a storm, something about my heart.*

Suddenly Bridey's words were so clear he could almost believe she was here with him. Her strong fingers gripped his arm and she told him in her musical brogue, "*At the center of the storm there's a stillpoint, Justin, and that's where your heart is.*"

Just for a few seconds, the turmoil inside him ceased. "*Find the stillpoint, and you'll find your heart.*"

His throat ached as he whispered, "Bridey, I need your magic back in my life."

A thought popped into his head. Why not swing by Joel's spa and get a massage before driving back to Rochester?

Tension emanated from the spa's reception desk. Gianessa edged along the hallway to take in the scene. A well-dressed man struck a casual pose, one arm resting on the high counter, his face set in a scowl.

Grace insisted, "Sir, we have no cancellations. Every treatment room is booked for the remainder of the day. I am sorry." Her voice was hoarse, and Gianessa guessed she had given the same message several times. "We cannot help you today."

His frown darkened dramatically.

Gianessa would have smacked the guy, Armani suit and all. The Armani was custom-tailored, she could tell, probably fitted by the best tailor in one of the shops in her father's hometown outside of Milano. *Why do wealthy men think they're entitled*?

"We have an opening tomorrow morning at eight-thirty. Would that suit you?"

The man shifted on his feet, and Gianessa saw pain crease his eyes. Maybe she was wrong about him. He swallowed hard and composed his face in the familiar frown.

She peered closely at his body. The fit of his suit told her he had been ill for some time, probably not cancer, since he had a full head of brown hair, with a hint of gray at the temples. He leaned heavily on his left arm that rested on the reception desk, as though his lower body was in pain. Maybe he didn't feel entitled to a massage, so much as desperate for relief from his pain.

Desperate and used to getting his own way.

She stood tall and strode toward the desk. "Just arrived, Grace. How can I help?"

As the man examined her, she realized why he was so certain he would be accommodated. His eyes were the same gray-green as her boss Joel Cushman. Despite the frown that marred his handsome features, she saw an unmistakable resemblance to Joel.

So this is the international financier? She wondered why he hadn't given his name to Grace. Or introduced himself as their new boss. Must be he wasn't planning to run the show. Regardless, if Grace had known he was Joel's uncle, she would have fit him in him somehow. *What game is he playing?*

Gianessa stood behind Grace's left shoulder and made her a quiet offer. "Grace, I'll take care of Mr. Cushman."

His eyes brightened.

Grace let out a strangled moan. "He's—?"

Gianessa gave her shoulders a reassuring squeeze and asked, "He wanted a massage?"

Justin Cushman nodded, a satisfied smile on his face.

Grace took a deep breath. "Gianessa will take excellent care of you, Mr. Cushman." She added under her breath, "I have no idea how."

"Come with me please," Gianessa said. She waved a delicate hand in the direction of the treatment rooms, then turned with a swivel of her hip that she hoped would make him swallow.

He cleared his throat.

I've got his number. She headed to the only available treatment room, one never used with customers. The staff shunned "the closet" because it was barely large enough for a massage table. Gianessa's voice carried back to him, "We'll be cozy, but we'll manage."

Grace coughed to cover a laugh.

Justin rarely met anyone better at manipulation than he was. *Until now.* Gianessa had been politic and inoffensive when she'd granted him an appointment and magically freed up a treatment room just for him, with no threat to Grace's authority. As he tossed his coat on a chair, he admired her elegant bearing, the way she held her head and swayed her hips.

This was a woman he wanted to know.

Her name, Gianessa, rang a bell. Wasn't she the guru Joel had brought from the West Coast? Why was she giving massages, if Joel's intention was for her to redesign the spa?

With a speculative "Hmm," Justin strolled down the hall, admiring the view. Gianessa posed in the doorway to the treatment room, her head tilted at an alluring angle.

Sexy. But anyone would say she appeared to be wholesome and pretty. The thin grosgrain straps of her simple sandals crisscrossed up her shapely calves and disappeared under the wide ruffle of a faded pink cotton skirt. An immaculate white T-shirt caressed her breasts and showed off her sculpted arms. Just for a second, he imagined his hands roaming over that T-shirt and under to those breasts. He hadn't felt a rush like this in months, maybe longer. *Give it a rest, old man. You have no business fantasizing about this young goddess.*

His gaze shifted to the double strand of alternating platinum and gold hearts fastened with an amethyst at the hollow of her throat, a perfect match for her smoky violet eyes. Justin knew all the right gifts for women. The necklace was, unquestionably, a Jacques LaFave worth on the order of thirty thousand dollars.

She wore no wedding ring. Her fingernails were short and buffed, and her toenails were bright pink and expertly polished. Honey-colored hair, fashioned in a French braid, and minimalist makeup gave her a clean-faced, focused look, fitting for a massage therapist. Just a hint of fragrance. *Chloe*.

Gianessa stepped aside as he brushed past her. She drew in a deep breath, preparing to take charge, but his scent threw her off—cloves and sandalwood and something she couldn't identify. Justin Cushman had a force field nearly as strong as hers, and she didn't like it one bit. His eyes were all over her, appreciating and assessing at the same time. *That's* my *role—to evaluate* his *body.*

When his gaze fastened on her necklace and one eyebrow rose, she forgot to breathe. Okay, she was out of uniform, she had led a client to a shamefully tiny treatment room and she was wearing outrageously expensive jewelry. *Is he making a case to fire me?* Nonsense. She was doing him a favor.

Gianessa squared her slender shoulders and tapped her foot in protest.

He met her gaze, and a smile tugged at the corner of his mouth.

She blushed. *Enough. No more games.* She was in charge here, and he needed her finest care.

"You've come home to support Joel's recovery, I assume. Do you—?"

Both eyebrows arched in surprise. "And I assume you are the physical therapist and healer my nephew brought to the Manse to reconceptualize his spa. Aren't you overqualified as a massage therapist?"

"—know what illness is wasting your body?"

His eyes flashed a warning. "I asked for a massage."

He's more vulnerable than I thought. She soothed him with her voice and her smile. "I will give you a massage, but we will talk about your body, Mr. Cushman, if not today, then soon. Joel would expect it, and I'm sure I can help you. I see from your reaction that you're not in denial about being very ill."

He shrugged one shoulder. "Maybe I've lost a little weight."

"Forty or fifty pounds."

He looked around the treatment room. "What is this space? Ten by twelve?"

Testing. "Seven by nine. Which is why it's never scheduled."

"Yet you're slender enough to move around the table." His gaze softened. "And kind enough to go the extra mile for me."

She admired the way he had shifted his energy, from defensive to open. She relaxed her shoulders and gave him a warm smile.

His gaze penetrated. "You know, Gianessa, I've been seen by experts in three countries, but if you can figure out what my doctors haven't figured out, I'll be glad to hear it."

Her face flushed with pleasure. "Let's get started. There are hangers on the back of the door. I'll give you a few minutes to undress. Please lie face down with your head here," she instructed, even though he'd probably had a thousand massages. She placed one hand on the padded frame that would cradle his head and face and still allow him to breathe. "Cover yourself with the sheet."

"And this will be the massage of a lifetime, you say?"

"I'll do my best for you and let you be the judge."

She left the room and nearly tripped over Grace in the hall.

"Thank god." Grace exhaled with relief.

"What's wrong? Why do you have your cell phone?"

"I thought you might need me to call 911 or bop him over the head or something."

"You are the best." Gianessa chuckled and lowered voice. "He's a teddy bear."

Grace looked at her doubtfully. "Well, get him naked and show him your stuff."

"Shush. What if he hears you?"

Grace switched to a whisper. "I want to know everything you do and everything he says. Especially if he's going to be our boss."

"Stop worrying. Go, you have a customer." Gianessa laughed as Grace hurried back to the desk.

She found Justin Cushman face down, as she'd requested, with the sheet thrown carelessly across his bare backside. They said nothing to each other while she surveyed his body. Judging by the way his suit had fit, he'd been overweight before his illness but had carried it well. He'd lost at least forty pounds, and his muscle mass was depleted. Even so, he had a powerful torso and a tight butt.

Gianessa took a moment to visualize him well again—lean this time and strong and fit. Well-muscled legs, strong shoulders, and a powerful pelvis to match his personality. Her face flamed. *Easy, girl. Don't complicate your life by getting the hots for this one*. She drew in a deep, cooling breath and exhaled to channel her best professional self.

When she kneaded his shoulders and his back, he seemed to fight her touch. *Wound tight with tension.* She shimmied around to the other end of the table, straightened the sheet and folded it to mid-thigh. She kneaded and stroked his feet, then his ankles and his calves. As she worked on the backs of his thighs, her healing touch induced a deep, restorative sleep. Only then did she turn her full attention to his back, shoulders, neck, and arms, using slow, deep, skillful moves.

After thirty minutes, she woke him. He sat on the edge of the table and they talked for a few minutes. Gianessa listened to his symptoms and heard how desperately he suffered.

"The symptoms you describe are just like mine ten years ago when I was a sophomore in college," she said.

His eyes brightened with hope. "But you're so well now."

She nodded with a kind smile.

"What was it? How did you recover?"

"It was celiac disease," she told him. "My symptoms were severe indigestion, bloating, gas, chronic constipation, fatigue, loss of appetite, headache, shortness of breath, muscle weakness, joint pain, general malaise, and unexplained weight loss."

"Almost exactly like mine." His eyes were wide with surprise. "But you couldn't have lost forty-eight pounds, like I have, without disappearing."

Gianessa laughed. "Not quite. I was down to eighty-six pounds and sick of doctors by the time a naturopathic physician suggested I be tested for food intolerance and celiacs."

"And then what? Pills, surgery . . .?"

"Not at all. The treatment is low-cost and fully in my control. I adopted a strict, gluten-free food plan, one I'll have to maintain for life. And then I became a terrific cook, so eating wouldn't bore me to death."

"Why didn't my doctors look at food intolerance?"

"Western practitioners don't always think that way. Just as your first thought was drugs and surgery, that's often how physicians are oriented."

"Well, we can see where that's gotten me. Bunch of pill-pushers."

"And that anger just made you tighten up. That is in your control." Gianessa touched his arm, and a warm current flowed between them.

Justin relaxed.

"I'm not suggesting you self-diagnose, and I'm not telling you that's what you have. I'm not qualified to. We'll talk more about it after I finish your massage, if you like."

Justin agreed and lay on the table, face up this time.

She stood at the crown of his head and made tiny circles with her fingers on his forehead, working toward his temples.

He murmured something before he slipped into a deep sleep.

When Justin awoke, he found the room dark. The nagging tension and bone-deep aches that had plagued him for months were gone. The naked fear remained, but on its heels came the knowledge that Gianessa had overcome the same symptoms. *I will, too.*

As soon as he sat up, his head pounded. He had just swung his legs over the edge of the table when a quiet knock sounded at the door. He realized he'd heard it a minute earlier, too. *Probably woke me up.* "Come in," he croaked.

Gianessa carried a liter bottle of water and a short plastic cup with two round pills.

He cracked a smile. "I thought you said no drugs?"

"Tylenol, in case you have a headache."

"You know I do."

"You'll need plenty of water for the rest of the day."

He took the pills without comment and drank a few inches of water in noisy gulps.

"Take it easy," she advised.

He wiped his mouth with the back of his forearm. "How long was I out?"

"You've slept about two hours."

"Thank you, I needed it," he acknowledged. "It's fortunate this room wasn't scheduled."

"Tell me what tests you've had." She leaned against the wall and folded her arms across her breasts.

"Every test money can buy."

"Was there any time this past year when you did not have the symptoms?

He thought for a moment, and his eyebrows shot up with

surprise. "Indonesia. I was there for nearly three months last spring, and I felt much better, almost instantly, and for the duration of my time there."

"You had none of the symptoms while you were in Indonesia?" She smiled widely.

"Some took time to dissipate, but eventually they were gone." His voice took on new energy. "I even got my appetite back and some strength, though I didn't put on any weight."

"That's very encouraging. Tell me everything you ate while you were in Indonesia."

Justin thought back and slowly gave her the list. "Rice. Fish. Chicken. Lots of vegetables, all kinds of vegetables. Spices. Delicious fruits. That's all."

"Sweets? Desserts? Alcohol?"

"I don't drink alcohol any more. Haven't for years. For sweets, we had ices—fruit ices, sorbets."

"Breads, rolls, biscuits of any kind?"

He shook his head. "None."

"No pastries, cookies, cakes, tarts, tortes, scones, muffins?"

"None."

"My guess is the sensitivity is to a combination of grains used in abundance in the West but not in Indonesia. Almost certainly wheat, and probably the gluten in wheat, barley, rye, and a few other grains. But remember I'm just speaking from my own experience. I'm a Doctor of Physical Therapy, not an M.D."

"What should be my next move?" Justin narrowed his eyes, expecting some kind of con—purchase twenty massages, or some such.

"I think the next right move is to be tested for food allergies, followed by some trial eliminations to identify your intolerances. I would recommend starting with gluten, and I wouldn't put it off. Your symptoms are unrelenting. You're losing weight for no reason; your muscle mass is being depleted because you are not getting nutrients from the food you're eating. You must stop what you're doing and focus on recovery."

He nodded, bringing himself up to his full, seated height, and snatched the sheet as it slid away from him. He threw one end over his shoulder like a royal sash and then chuckled when he saw her smile.

"I feel like a damn fool. I've spent a fortune on tests at the best hospitals and come up empty."

"In other words, your high-priced doctors eliminated the stress-related and most-dreaded illnesses, starting with garden-variety ulcers and running the gamut to parasites and exotic cancers?"

Justin let his silence confirm it.

"Those are the test results I'd want," she told him with a smile.

His eyes twinkled. "Thank you for putting a positive spin on it."

"I can recommend someone at Clifton Springs who will do a blood test for gluten and a needle biopsy of the intestine. She is very familiar with celiacs and with food intolerances. You might want to be tested for additional food allergies, if you can stand a dozen or so needle pricks."

He shuddered at the sound of that.

"Then"—she lightened her voice, and he took hope that the rest might be more palatable—"I recommend that you try a gluten-free food plan for two weeks, starting after the tests. I'm betting it will help, just as it did when you were in Indonesia."

She added a smile, and it was the first time he'd seen the dimples. Surely the best was yet to come.

"You were obviously in great shape before this happened, and you can be again. In fact, you should plan on it and work toward it, as your energy returns."

The little sparkle in her eye made his body respond in a way it hadn't in a very long time. He glanced down to be sure the sheet was in place.

"That's my advice to you. I'll let you get dressed now." Gianessa turned to leave.

"Wait." Justin grabbed her arm, and she turned back to face him.

Her amethyst eyes looked deep inside him. He imagined himself unfastening her necklace and freeing her honey hair from its braid. He started when the amethyst at her throat winked at him. Then he realized she had simply blinked her eyes. He shook off the whim.

"You wanted to ask me something?"

"Ah, yes." He recovered his sanity. "Can you tell me how to know what has gluten and what doesn't? And what to eat to rebuild my body?"

"When you're dressed, I'll meet you back at the desk with an information sheet about eating gluten-free, plus menu suggestions and the physician's name." She gave him a slow, sexy smile. "I can give you cooking lessons, if you're interested."

Before he could pursue the offer, her cheeks flushed. She lowered her eyes, put her professional face back in place and slipped out of the tiny massage room.

She can't possibly be interested in an old wreck like me. He made a mental note to ask Joel about her.

When he arrived at the reception desk, Gianessa handed him half a dozen sheets of paper and gave him a friendly wave. "Call anytime for an appointment, Mr. Cushman," she sang out.

He laughed heartily at the artful rebuke for his rude imposition on them.

"Justin," he corrected her. "Since we're going to be cooking together, let's be on a first-name basis."

Grace's head swiveled toward them.

Justin winked at Grace and scribbled his cell number on the back of a business card for Gianessa. "Let me know if Sunday afternoons work for you. We can use Joel's kitchen."

Chapter 2

Stupid, stupid, stupid! Gianessa punctuated her words with sharp raps of the wooden spoon on the edge of the counter. Whatever had possessed her to flirt with Justin Cushman? He probably liked wealthy, sexy, sophisticated women, and she was none of those. Throwing in those hip swivels, *what was I thinking?*

I do not want a relationship. The spoon rapped against an empty wooden salad bowl. *I want to be a professional.* And if she had to be unprofessional, why hadn't she asked him where to sell the amethyst necklace?

Gianessa squinted at the kitchen timer, willing the strata to be done. *Just enough time to make the salad.* She grabbed the head of romaine lettuce from the colander, threw it on the cutting board and whacked it into bite-sized pieces.

As she mounded the lettuce in two salad bowls, her mind went to Joel in the hospital. Where exactly had Uncle Justin been for the two weeks after Joel's accident? Evidently, his business took precedence.

She pitched six olives, one at a time, onto each mound of romaine. Why had he left it to Joel's sweet girlfriend to bear the responsibility of visiting Joel in intensive care? The poor girl had been worn to a frazzle when she indulged herself in a spa day last week, finally able to breathe after Joel regained consciousness. *What's her name? Amelia, Amanda, something like that. Sara will know.*

Gianessa sprinkled on sunflower seeds, then added figs and bright green scallions. She squeezed fresh lemon into a glass dish with olive oil, vinegar and herbs, whisked it all together and drizzled it over their salads.

What delayed Justin's arrival?

"Aha!" she realized just as the timer buzzed.

"Food," Sara chortled. She pounded down the stairs and burst into the kitchen. "What are you aha-ing about?"

"Food's ready." Gianessa evaded the question with a bright smile. "Make way, this is hot." She carried the steaming glass baking dish to a trivet on the dining room table and returned to the kitchen.

"Another amazing meal." Sara lounged against the counter. "What can I do?"

"You're letting me live here rent-free. The least I can do is keep us in good meals."

"My clothes fit way better since you came. I'm so glad you're not a pig."

Gianessa let out a laugh. "I've never resembled a pig."

"You're more the gazelle type," Sara said with a dramatic undulation of her arm. She bumped a jar filled with cooking utensils, which, mercifully, came to rest on a stack of towels. "Or is it the springbok that leaps effortlessly and is delicately beautiful?"

Gianessa chuckled as she righted the jar and picked out what she needed to serve the strata. "You take the salads, I'll bring the water. That's everything."

Sara grabbed their overflowing salad bowls, made it to the table without a spill, and set them carefully next to each plate. "So, 'Aha!' What?"

"You said it. Aha, time to eat." Gianessa put on her Mona Lisa smile. It always worked with Sara.

"Are you really only twenty-nine?"

"Please tell me I don't look thirty." Gianessa speared a forkful of salad.

"Of course not, you're beautiful. It's just that you know so much about cooking and nutrition. And check out this table. It's like living with that *Everyday Italian* person—what's her name?—Giada." She waved her loaded fork to make her point, and the piece of strata wobbled. "Oops. Almost trashed your linen tablecloth."

"It's your linen tablecloth."

"Really? Who knew? My mom must have snuck it into a drawer last time she came." Sara savored another bite. "This is to die for. What is this?"

"Strata. Fresh eggs, roma tomatoes, low-fat ricotta, and eggplant. It puffed up just the way it's supposed to." Gianessa smiled with pride.

"It would go really good with Italian bread, wouldn't it? We should have some next time."

"You're welcome to it, and I'll be glad to put it on the grocery list."

"Oh, come on. I know you eat healthy, but what's wrong with Italian bread?"

"I can't eat wheat."

Sara's fork stopped in mid-air. "That's tragic. How do you live without bread?"

"Lots of people can't tolerate the gluten in wheat." She was not going to divulge Justin's problems to gossip-queen Sara. "Haven't you noticed all the 'gluten free' food in Wegmans?"

"You're serious? I thought that was just the latest buzzword, like 'low-carb' used to be."

Gianessa shook her head and gave her a one-minute spiel about gluten intolerance and celiac disease. "I have celiac disease."

"Tragic," Sara said again. "No wonder you eat so healthy and stay so thin."

They ate in silence for a few minutes. Gianessa's thoughts wandered back to her conversation with Justin.

"So, spill, what's Mr. Cushman like?" Sara watched her with an eagle eye.

"He's actually a smart, funny guy."

"Grace told us you had him naked in the closet."

Gianessa burst out laughing and rescued the olive that flew from her mouth. "There was no treatment room available and he was not going to go away." She took a sip of water and said with dignity, "So we used the closet. I really don't understand why we don't schedule that room, especially this time of year when we're so busy."

"Everyone else hates it. Was he naked?"

"Don't be silly." Justin hadn't had to disrobe completely for his massage, but he had chosen to. Gianessa fought down a flare of heat at the memory of that thin sheet draped carelessly over his cute butt. She needed a distraction. "His name's Justin, by the way."

"Justin and Gianessa. Has a nice ring, don't you think?"

"Stop, he's almost old enough to be my father," Gianessa protested.

"How old do you think he is really?"

"I don't know. Probably forty-five."

"That's not too old for you."

"I'm not in the market for a man right now." Gianessa wanted to clang her fork on the side of the plate to emphasize the point, but she kept her voice calm. "You know that." She needed to distract Sara. Inspiration struck. "And I would never get involved with anyone I work with." She stole a look across the table.

Sara paled. "You think he's going to be our boss while Joel's out, don't you?"

Beautiful. "Possibly."

"What do you know? Grace was, like, totally freaked today."

Gianessa shrugged. "You know the rumors. Justin's probably just home to support Joel until his recovery is well under way, and then he'll go back to his world-traveling, high-finance life. End of story." *Why does that make me sad?* "I'm looking for a career, not a man.

"So, is he cute?"

Gianessa squelched her first thought: Justin Cushman was a handsome man, and, if she had her way, he would be buff again in the coming year, leaner than before. If this weren't Sara she was talking to, she might open up a little about Justin, so she could get him out of her head.

She concentrated on her food while she decided how to answer. "Justin's cuter than Joel, in a mature sort of way," she conceded, "and if you tell anyone I said so, I'll cook you Brussels sprouts and liver for a week."

"Oh barf!" Sara made a show of pushing her plate away. "You're disgusting. I don't know why I asked you to room with me."

"Because you're lonely." Gianessa gestured at the spacious living-dining room. "I'd have gone crazy by myself in this huge townhouse."

"It's not my fault my parents own it and want me to live here and take care of the place."

"But I'm right, aren't I? It's too big for you. And you were lonely by yourself?"

"I could have gotten a cat."

"Cats can't cook." She pushed Sara's plate back to her. "Finish that while I get the dishes started."

"Yes, Mom," Sara said with a smirk.

Glad for a break from a conversation that centered on Justin Cushman, Gianessa hummed along with Adele on the radio while she put leftovers in the fridge and scrubbed the baking dish.

A glance at the clock told her it was time to leave for the AA meeting.

Sara slid her dishes into the soapy water. "I'll do the rest later, roomie. I'm going to watch TV."

"Enjoy."

She wanted to borrow a coat, but she knew if she asked,

Sara's response would be, "Oh, are you meeting Justin?" A sweatshirt under the pashmina would have to do.

Justin stood at the door to Joel's hospital room and watched his nephew. The pain showed on Joel's face as he slept. That was what he got for refusing narcotics to ease the discomfort of a skull fracture and broken bones. As a sober alcoholic, Joel was determined to use as few drugs as possible through this recovery.

Maybe Joel wasn't asleep; maybe he was just doing one of those Celtic meditations he was so fond of. Justin rather hoped so, hoped Joel felt relief from the pain when he slept.

Joel's devotion to all things Celtic came from his grandmother Bridey. Looks aside, Joel had little in common with the Tompkins or the Cushmans. Unlike his WASP ancestors on both sides, Joel Tompkins Cushman seemed to be ninety-percent good Irish stock, as resilient as the best of them, with the warmest of hearts.

"Is that your stealth mode?" Joel asked, his eyes still closed. Justin stood smiling until Joel caved, opened his eyes and said, "Good to see you, Uncle."

"Back at you."

"Found any women yet?"

"As a matter of fact—"

"It took you three days longer than I thought. No, you can't have her."

"Have who?"

"Gianessa."

"We'll talk," Justin demurred.

"We won't. It's not negotiable."

Is Joel interested in her? Involved with her? He shook off the thought, certain that Joel was devoted to his fiancée, Manda.

"What else is on your agenda, Justin?"

"Why do you think I have an agenda?"

"Because you're in stealth mode," Joel answered with a chuckle. "You stood at the door a long time, studying me, sizing me up for something."

"I was standing respectfully." Justin blustered comically. "Merely debating whether to wake you or go downstairs for a cuppa."

"Stop, it hurts." Joel laughed, holding his ribs with his good hand.

Justin pulled up a chair and placed his hand on Joel's good arm. "I'm glad to see you haven't lost your sense of humor. What can I do? What can I get you?"

Joel's gaze was fixed on Justin's hand on his arm. "That's all I need. I'm so relieved you're here. Tell me you weren't joking about staying in Tompkins Falls for a decade or so."

"Well, no, I wasn't joking, but I'm finding it damned disorienting. That's my agenda, in fact. I don't seem to know who I am here."

Justin studied his nephew's face, so much like his own.

"It was like that for me when I came back to town eight years ago. Do you remember how much I whined about living down my old reputation as a wild child?"

"I don't recall you whining. I was very proud that you opened the inn and furious that you got engaged to that frigid rich bitch Lorraine."

"Now, now," Joel said, his voice playful, "Lorraine was not frigid."

"But you're not denying the rest, are you?" Justin laughed.

"She had her moments."

"She had you wrapped around her finger, the one with the three carat diamond on it."

"She did."

"So I was right to protest your engagement?"

"You were right. Are you going to tell me not to marry Manda?"

"Nothing of the kind. I'd make her mine if she weren't already betrothed to the best friend I have in the world."

Joel beamed. "So what's my best friend doing about getting the sapphire ring into my hand so I can put it on her finger?"

Justin stood up and patted his pockets. All of them. Several times. Joel smiled indulgently at the little drama.

"Ah!" Justin said at last and drew out the blue Tiffany box with the white ribbon. He fussed with the squashed bow, making it perky again. "It's a mystery to me why she accepted your proposal without a ring."

"It was the world's worst proposal, believe me. I owe her a much better one. This will go a long way." Joel took the box Justin offered, set it on his chest and shook Justin's hand. "Thank you. And when I can shake with my right hand, I'll do that again."

"Just see that you're good to the lass." Justin heard his British accent come out.

"I plan to be."

"Bridey would have loved her." Justin's voice caught. "Having Manda in our lives is a little like having Bridey back with us."

"I believe you mean that." Joel studied his face.

"Indeed, I do."

"There's that accent again. Do you even know when you're doing that?"

Justin had lived in London several times, but the accent came and went randomly. He barked a laugh, "Some psychologist would love to analyze it, I dare say."

"Seriously, what is this illness that kept you away while I was in the coma?" Joel's voice was light, but Justin saw the worry lines in his forehead.

"Funny thing. Not one of my doctors has offered a believable diagnosis, but our goddess Gianessa believes it's a food intolerance. Wheat or gluten. She's given me two pages of instructions, plus menus, a list of cookbooks, and an offer of cooking lessons. She wants me to have some awful tests at Clifton Springs." He shuddered for effect.

"How did Ms. Dupioni come to that conclusion?"

So she's Gianessa Dupioni? "Dupioni as in 'silk' or as in 'duplicitous'?"

"Gianessa, duplicitous? Maybe you *should* see a psychologist. It's Dupioni, like naturally flawed silk, stunning in its beauty, artfully arranged as only a Northern Italian woman can be. Her father came to this country from the heartland of the Italian fashion industry."

"He's in fashion?"

"He has a restaurant."

"And is Ms. Dupioni married? Divorced?"

"She's doing her best to recover from devastating personal losses, and I'll thank you to consider her off limits." Joel's tone left no room for argument.

"I heard that." *Maybe it's temporary. I'll check back.* "As for the gluten thing, she nailed my symptoms, including the weight loss and muscle depletion and fatigue. And when she learned that my symptoms stopped and reversed themselves during my months in Indonesia, she suspected grains we used in the West, such as wheat and barley and rye."

"Perhaps that's why you gave up beer."

Justin guffawed. "Never thought of that. It did make me puke. Whiskeys as well. And now I'm done with alcohol, just as you are. Haven't had a drink in six or seven years."

"You're not saying you're an alcoholic?"

"I don't know. I lost myself out there somewhere in the world of high finance, and I thought I'd find myself again when I stopped drinking. But I haven't yet, and I need to quit high finance, too. It holds nothing for me anymore. I need to be here, to learn from you."

Joel's open mouth and furrowed brow told Justin he hadn't seen that coming. "Learn what from me?" Joel probed.

"Learn how to care about people the way you do. How to feel with my heart without it being too painful to bear. And anything else you have to teach me." He stood abruptly and shoved his hands in the pockets of his overcoat. "You're getting tired. I should go."

"Bullshit. You're getting to the truth. Take your coat off. Stay a while. Let's get room service and catch up with each other."

Justin chuckled.

"You think I'm kidding? I've bribed one of the aides. Shauna will make a run on demand to that coffee shop near Mt. Hope Cemetery I told you about."

"Good place. Manda and I ate lunch there. Great salads. My favorite is the Frederick Douglass. Without the croutons now, I suppose. You?"

"The Susan B. Anthony. You make the call. I'll page Shauna."

Once Shauna was dispatched for their salads, Joel found a comfortable position, and Justin settled back in the armchair.

Joel spoke first. "Why quit the work you've done for decades? You thrived on it. Making deals, sniffing out opportunities, financing new ventures, getting appointed to corporate boards, raking in millions. Billions for all I know."

Justin confirmed it with a nod.

"Are you really quitting or just pulling my leg?"

"I've shut down my office in London. You know my arrival here was delayed."

"Yes, but not why."

"I was in a research hospital in Chicago for a week, trying to understand what had gone wrong with my body. The two weeks after, I was in treatment in Arizona to build up my blood—something about electrolytes, minerals, vitamin levels.

"I did a lot of soul searching and decided to quit my venture capital business entirely. I flew back to London, tied up loose ends, logged on to Facebook, and found Manda's pleas for help."

"Didn't the hospital make an effort to contact you?"

"Yes, but I had turned off my phone and closed my office. The doctors had no way to reach me, except through Manda's ingenuity with social media. The timing could not have been worse, and you have my most sincere apology."

Joel steadied himself with a deep breath. His voice wavered when he asked, "When you said you were tying up loose ends, did you think you were dying?"

"No. I meant I needed to be done with empty pursuits. Don't laugh, but on the flight to London, I thought about becoming a Buddhist monk, if there is such a thing. Then I saw Manda's messages and knew what I needed—to be here with you and get right with myself."

"You used to thrive on your work," Joel persisted.

Justin nodded pensively. "I did thrive on it. Ten years ago, I was enjoying the good life in Switzerland with Alexa. We had some good years together. Then I saw she was betraying me. I moved back to London, drank heavily, dated smart, beautiful women, and worked. On the road I had my pick of women offered by my business partners. I became disgusted with myself, I won't say why.

"I took stock of what I had accomplished and saw that I wasn't benefiting anyone but myself and the companies I represented. That's an empty existence, Joel. I—"

Justin jumped from the chair as the door to the hospital room burst open.

Shauna juggled a heavy bag and a drink caddy with two tall espresso drinks.

"Good woman!" Justin said heartily and offloaded the drinks. Shauna set down the bag on the tray table by Joel's bed. Justin's generous tip netted him a million-dollar smile from Shauna and an eye roll from Joel.

"Since when is giving a tip cause for an eye roll?" he asked after the door closed.

"She's already been well compensated."

"Which I should have known, *mea culpa*."

"Just eat."

The salads consumed, Joel proposed, "Let's hear more about this 'disoriented' feeling. I'm good for about fifteen minutes."

"I'll sum it up in two sentences. I'm not who I was when I left here in my twenties. I'm not sure who I am now, and I don't have my work." He brightened. "But I have a challenge in front of me. You've entrusted me with cleaning up the mess at Tompkins College, and I will do my utmost in your place as trustee."

"You know what you're dealing with." Joel had already filled him in on the embezzlement at the expense of students, with collusion in high places. Plus the sexual exploitation of students by a few professors, and its widespread cover-up. "All of it needs to be cleaned up for the college to continue. Or those persons need to be fired and the college closed down."

"Agreed. But, Joel, what I do about the college will define me in Tompkins Falls. I'm sincere about wanting to live here long term. Closing the college is the simplest solution, but the worst for the town and for my reputation in Tompkins Falls."

Joel muttered, "Wish I'd never inherited the damn college."

"It's been run by scoundrels from the day it opened. If you hadn't the integrity you have, and if you hadn't insisted on an investigation, it would go on as it always has."

"It has to stop, Justin. You have to stop it." Joel's distress alarmed Justin.

"I will," Justin said forcefully, laying a hand on Joel's arm. "And you have to heal. If I took your blood pressure right now, it'd be off the charts."

Joel managed a weak smile. "I can picture you wrestling with a blood pressure cuff."

Justin barked a laugh. "Let's try it! Where can I find one?"

"Seriously, don't make me laugh," Joel pleaded. "You can play it out however you want with the college. I know you have the skill. Remember, money is not the object."

"And what is?" Justin folded his arms across his chest.

"Two things. The economic health of the town. And your own principles."

"Imagine me having principles," Justin mused.

"You know you do."

"Maybe I'll get in touch with them now." He opened his arms and raised his hands.

"Bet on it. Use them, and it will be fine, however it turns out."

"If you could have any outcome, Joel, what would it be?"

"I want the criminals out of there, along with the people who covered it up. That amounts to about one third of the employees, as far as we can tell. Is it possible to rebuild a college with just two-thirds of its people? I don't know, but I'd prefer to have the good people protected and jobs saved for the sake of the town."

"That's what I thought. I will not involve you further, you have my promise. Now get some sleep."

Joel's eyes had already closed.

Justin stood by the bed, watching Joel's chest rise and fall, hearing his breaths deepen and lengthen. *How can I resolve this without Joel as a sounding board?*

When Joel's face relaxed in sleep, Justin left the room and ambled down the hall, hands deep in the pockets of his overcoat.

Who can I trust that has no stake in the college? At the elevator he thought back to his recent dinner in New York City with his old lover, Sydney Shorey. They'd been hot and heavy during their graduate studies in Chicago. She was now happily remarried to her first husband, Danny and, more importantly, was now president of a small college in New York City. *Perfect sounding board*. He'd give her a call tonight.

The elevator dinged.

Justin cracked a smile, remembering what Sydney had predicted at dinner, after her second vodka martini: that Justin would marry within the year.

Chapter 3

Gianessa wrapped her arms around her middle and willed the shivering to stop. She silently intoned a litany of affirmations. *I'm getting warmer. I'm right next to the heater. The scalding tea will cool enough to drink. I will buy a coat as soon as I get paid.* She added out loud, "And gloves."

"Gianessa?"

Gianessa opened her eyes and locked with a pair of sapphire blue ones.

"I'm Manda. You gave me a massage at the Manse last week."

"Of course." Gianessa recognized the woman's artless black curls and sculpted cheekbones. "You're Joel's fiancée, right?"

"And you're freezing." Manda draped her coat over Gianessa's shoulders and sat down next to her.

Gianessa nodded. "Thank you for not saying 'crazy'. I don't own a coat or a car." A sob rose in her throat.

Warm hands covered hers, and she felt the heat spread all the way to her troubled mind.

She took a deep breath and let it out. "I ran five blocks. I just needed a meeting so badly."

Manda picked up the cup of tea next to Gianessa's chair. "Hold it with both hands. Drink."

Gianessa felt warmth all the way to her belly.

"Don't do anything that foolish again. The cold is dangerous, and people die of hypothermia. I'll drive you home tonight and loan you my coat until you get one."

Gianessa started to protest but saw the wisdom. "Thank you. My denial will kill me. I'm so glad I came."

Someone nearby whispered, “Quiet.”

The Tuesday night Top Shelf Women’s meeting of Alcoholics Anonymous started with a moment of silence and several standard readings about the twelve steps and the promises of the AA program.

Gianessa heard the words—so important to her, so familiar—but from another place and time. She let tears run down her face. It had cost her dearly in peace of mind to be away from meetings for so long, and she hadn’t fully realized it until she sat on a folding chair at a meeting in a church basement.

When the chairperson asked if anyone had thought about a drink today, her hand lifted automatically. She told them about the champagne bubbles that shocked her out of her meditation this morning. And she laughed about “a new customer at the spa today” that she couldn’t get out of her head. She promised not to bore them with the hundred little things in the past few weeks that had made her cranky and discouraged.

“That is all so unlike me. I haven’t even tried to make friends because I feel so vulnerable. How stupid is that? Instead of screwing up my courage, I’ve been standoffish.” Gianessa sighed. “I’m my own worst enemy. What’s that phrase, ‘My mind is a dangerous neighborhood to visit alone’?”

The women laughed and nodded.

Gianessa accepted the box of tissues someone passed to her. She smiled her thanks, used one to wipe away her tears, and set about blowing her nose with the rest.

“I’ll get you some more tea,” Manda whispered.

Gianessa nodded.

She knew her AA program could restore her to sanity if she got back in the habit of meetings and got connected to a group here in Tompkins Falls. With a heavy sigh, she admitted that, by herself, she couldn’t get Justin Cushman and his cute butt out of her head. The last thing she needed was involvement with a client. Who was also the boss's uncle. And, by the way, fifteen or so years older. And sometimes arrogant and demanding.

Manda set the scalding mug of tea between their chairs just as Gianessa muttered, "Screw Justin Cushman."

Manda gasped.

Gianessa shook her head. "Sorry, bad choice of words."

Manda leaned closer and confided, "I feel that way sometimes, too."

Gianessa covered her mouth to smother a giggle.

When she'd finished her tea and set down the cup, she whispered to Manda, "You're an angel."

Manda snorted, "As if."

"So," Manda said into the silence in the car, "where did you get sober?"

"California. Palo Alto originally, and then I made a total mess of my life about four years ago—drunk driving with my baby daughter in the car, both of us injured. Then a pill addiction and divorce. I got clean and moved north of San Francisco, because it was the only place I could find work in my field. I've been clean and sober since, but I haven't been to meetings since I left the coast, and I've been trying to handle everything by myself. Today I . . ."

Manda just nodded. She had no idea what to say next. She wasn't going to touch the "Screw Justin Cushman" line. Justin was difficult. And manipulative. Hell, he was obnoxious sometimes.

He must have been poking around the Manse. Maybe he was the "new customer at the spa" and he'd gotten a massage from Gianessa, which he'd probably loved. Whether Gianessa was angry at Justin or had the hots for him, Manda didn't want to know.

She cranked up the heat as high as it would go. She was shivering without a coat. "You had to be desperate to walk without a coat in this weather. It's gotten a lot colder this week. It must be twenty degrees tonight." She poked a button to display the outside temperature. "Twenty-eight."

"Yes, I was desperate, you're right."

Manda's memory kicked in, and she heard herself say, "When I got sober last winter, my life was a disaster, and I had no idea how to get out of the jam I was in. Some asshole professor was stalking me, and one night he slashed a razor right through my warmest jacket, which also made it a bloody mess. I had to wear every layer of clothes I had when I went outdoors, until spring. So I understand about needing a coat."

"How awful. Our disease takes us to terrible places."

"Amen. I'd be dead without the program."

"When I get away from meetings, I get crazy; when I'm working my program, I'm calm and serene and focused."

"I know. You were serene when you gave me a body wrap and massage last week. It freaked me out to see you have a meltdown tonight."

"I'm sorry," Gianessa said. "I remember you. Remy told me you were Joel's sweetheart, and then he said, 'Ooh la la. Such a story *ma petite* has to tell.'"

Manda laughed at her perfect imitation of the spa director's French accent. She'd been a little worried that Gianessa's tone was flat, but suddenly her laugh was musical.

"But then he wouldn't tell me your story." Gianessa turned toward her with a sunny smile. "Sometime I want to hear more about your story and about you meeting Joel and falling in love."

"I'll probably speak at the Top Shelf meeting in March when I have a year. Where do I turn?"

"Left at the next block. I'm sharing a townhouse with another woman who works at the Manse. Do you know Sara?"

Manda grinned. “I sure do. We’re thrift-shop buddies.” She made the left turn. “Is that how you get to work every day without a car?”

Gianessa nodded. “I’m lucky she’s willing to cart me around. But she’s not in the program, and I wouldn’t ask her to drive me to meetings.”

“AA people will give you rides to meetings if you ask. How about going with me to Happy Hour tomorrow right after work, and I’ll introduce you around? Carol will be there. She’s the one who talked to us at the end of the meeting.”

“She’s also the one who answered my phone call this afternoon. I recognized her name and her voice. That was nice of her to give me her phone number and offer to be my temporary sponsor.”

“We’ll pick up a phone list at Happy Hour, too.”

“Perfect, thanks.”

“I’m an accountant at the Mansa, and I know you get paid this week. Just a suggestion, if you’re free Saturday or Sunday, I’m going to Rochester to visit Joel both days. You can meet him, and then we’ll go to Eastview. There’s a huge sale at L.L. Bean’s. Unbelievable discounts on winter coats and stuff.”

“What is L.L. Bean’s?”

“Seriously?” *Maybe they don’t have duck hunting on the West Coast*. “It’s a big outdoor-wear, sportswear and sporting goods store that a lot of people on the East Coast swear by. Good quality, and a good match for our weather.” As Manda stopped the Volvo in front of Sara and Gianessa’s townhouse, her teeth were beginning to chatter. “Some of the coats are good to forty below.”

Gianessa turned to her with wide eyes. “Forty below . . . zero degrees?”

Manda backpedaled. “It doesn’t get that cold here. I think the worst I’ve seen is twenty below.”

Gianessa took a deep breath and whispered, “I’m okay. I can do this.” She cleared her throat. “I’m working Saturday but I’m free all day Sunday, so anytime that works for you. I really appreciate it.” She scribbled her cell number for Manda and dashed to the front door.

Tony Pinelli let out a whistle. “Slick,” he pronounced, tapping his fingers on the plans spread out in front of him. He’d had his doubts about turning the ugly old garage at the Manse into a therapy suite for Joel’s recovery, but now that he saw the plans he knew it would work. It might even become a destination suite after Joel moved out.

The project foreman, Ralph, gave a grunt of agreement. “Only problem, they need it done yesterday.”

“No way. Joel’s still in the hospital, and he’s having more surgery Monday morning.” He examined the cavernous, multi-bay garage. They’d already gutted the structure, power-cleaned the concrete floors and insulated the floor on the far side, beyond the load-bearing columns. And he’d seen the hole they’d dug last week, behind the garage, for the therapy pool.

Ralph’s gaze sharpened. “How do you know that?”

“Joel’s a buddy, and I was the one driving when we had the accident.”

Tony watched Ralph’s face for any sign of blame or censure.

Ralph grinned. “So that’s how come you got that shiny new red truck in the dead of winter?”

Tony let out a breath of relief. “Yeah, the old white one was totaled. I’d been saving to get one next summer. The insurance money gave me enough extra to get what I wanted right away.”

Ralph clapped a hand on his shoulder, the one that had been steadily improving through physical therapy. “So you got your own red rider wagon for Christmas?”

Tony grinned. “That’s what my girlfriend said, too. She even made me a Radio Flyer pilot’s license. I guess her little nephew got one with his red wagon, and she found out how to get one for me.”

“She sounds like a keeper.”

Tony beamed. “Yes, sir, she is.”

They returned their attention to the set of construction drawings spread out on a sheet of plywood on saw horses. Ralph explained the aggressive schedule. “Crew’s coming this morning to finish insulating the floor. This afternoon they’ll start the laminate flooring and finish it overnight. It’s faster than hardwood, and we can’t go with carpeting because he’ll be in a chair for a while.”

Tony felt that in his gut. *Joel in a wheelchair*.

“You okay?”

Tony gave up a prayer to get his emotions under control. Maybe other people didn’t blame him for skidding on black ice and plummeting into the trees, but he blamed himself for the accident. This was his big chance to help Joel’s recovery, and he meant to do all he could on this construction project. He nodded for Ralph to continue.

“Framing crew will put up the studs tomorrow morning. Insulation goes into the walls tomorrow right after. Dry wall starts tomorrow night. Kitchen and bathroom—”

“There’s plumbing already?”

Ralph nodded. “We roughed it in last week, when we dug the hole for the pool. We’re just lucky the ground hadn’t frozen yet. The real cold snap started this week. This time of year, you don’t expect a break like that.”

“You got all the worker bees you need?”

“Depends on how much you can handle yourself. I know you got banged up in that accident.”

Tony showed him his doctor’s release with the current restrictions. They talked about his tasks over the next two weeks, and Ralph drew up a schedule.

"Looks like we could use another carpenter who can also do the heaviest lifting in the kitchen area," Ralph concluded.

"I know a guy. Needs some supervision, but he's good."

"Bring him around this afternoon."

Tony hesitated.

"Something else on your mind?"

"Yes, sir. I know you're the foreman and you're my boss, which is great. But how did you happen to call me for the job?"

"Justin Cushman is calling the shots here. He recommended you, gave me your cell number. You know him?"

"Joel's uncle? No, sir." Tony wondered who had given his name and number to Justin Cushman. Must have been Joel or Manda. He remembered telling Manda he was ready to build anything Joel needed for his recovery. She'd probably passed that along. That felt really good. "Never met the man."

Ralph grunted. "You will, soon enough. It's an experience."

"As in . . .?"

"He could get St. Peter to redesign heaven, if he wanted."

"Are you sure Joel's up for a visit from me?"

Manda took her eyes off the road for a second and smiled at Gianessa. "Absolutely. He's been starved for company, and I know you won't tire him out. You'll know how to handle it."

"I can just wave from the doorway and wait for you two in the café."

"Well, I have an ulterior motive."

"Which is . . ."

Manda's laugh was self-conscious. "I want you to help Joel recover, and I think if you can spend some time talking to each other you'll know what he needs and he'll have confidence that you're the right person for the job."

Gianessa shifted on the seat to get a better view of Manda's face. "Why do you think I'm qualified to do that?"

Manda shrugged. "I just know when I came for my spa day—remember what a wreck I was? You totally got what my body needed, and you got me into healing mode in, like, ten minutes."

"You don't know anything about my credentials, do you?"

Manda shook her head. "I just know you're a healer. Joel needs a healer."

Gianessa was unsure how much to say. Joel had asked her to keep a low profile until she'd worked with the staff as one of them for a while. None of them knew about her alternative healing certifications or her physical therapy degree.

"I know you'll like meeting him. He's in recovery like us."

"Yes, I know," Gianessa said quietly.

"You do?"

"Joel hired me."

"Duh, Manda. How did I not get that? So, you met him at a meeting?"

"Joel came to a conference and retreat for spa managers at the spa where I worked in northern California. There were about fifty people, discussing different business models and innovative practices for spas and retreat centers. I think, from what we talked about, he's got an idea that the Spa at the Manse can be more than it is, and the conference let him explore ideas and meet people that were doing cutting-edge things with their facilities. He got some cool ideas, and he asked me to come here and help make it happen."

"Are you sure it was the spa in the current facility he was thinking about?"

"I just assumed it was. Why?"

"Well, last summer Joel and I talked about different ways we might want to use a beautiful piece of land called Cady's Point on Chestnut Lake. He was actually checking out the land when he had the accident."

Manda shuddered, and Gianessa instinctively reached out to calm her.

"God, I'm so glad he's going to be okay."

"He is going to be better than okay, Manda. We'll make sure of that." She squeezed Manda's arm. "What did you think the land should be used for?"

"Well, this may sound weird, but Cady's Point is a place with healing energy. The Indians knew that. I felt it myself when I lived there for a year." She glanced at Gianessa. "Do you think that's crazy? That a place can have healing power?"

"I've been to places that are spiritual, holy, that have the power to heal and redeem certain people. Usually people who believe healing is possible and who are willing to suspend their normal lives for a time and enter into a new way of praying and living. A healing path, I'll call it."

Manda smacked her hands on the steering wheel. "You know exactly what I'm talking about."

Gianessa laughed. "Manda, we must have been sisters in a previous life."

"That is so cool. Anyway I told Joel I thought Cady's Point should be the site of a rehabilitation center slash retreat slash spa. A place for people to take time out of their lives to change in ways that would promote their recovery from serious illness—like heart disease, severe arthritis, traumatic injury, yada yada. Maybe he had that in mind when he came to California. Anyway, fast forward, you won't believe what happened when Joel was in the hospital."

"What happened?" Gianessa was glad Manda wasn't driving as fast as she was talking.

"Well, Justin, Joel's uncle—"

"Oh yes, we've met," Gianessa said with a little chuckle.

"You probably know he has more money than god. Anyway, two things happened really. One was that the doctors didn't have any recommendation for us about a rehab facility for Joel in Tompkins Falls. That was awful.

But the good news is, Justin and I were talking over dinner that first night, and he asked me what I wanted to do, what my passion was—besides Joel, of course—and I started pitching this rehab slash retreat idea to him, and he knew it was exactly what *he* needed for his own healing. Long story short, he wants to put up the venture capital for it. That was, like, a week ago, and now when I'm driving back and forth to Rochester, I'm planning it in my head, and I seriously want to do it."

"Of course you should do it. It's stunning. I wonder if that's why Joel brought me here."

"We should talk more about it. I mean, if you're interested."

"I am. It's fascinating." Gianessa's heart did a happy dance.

"Good, we'll talk on the way home. But we're getting close to the exit. Let's plan how we want to organize our time. We don't want to tire Joel."

"Okay, I'm going to be late if I stay one more minute. I have to meet with people about your surgery tomorrow," Manda told Joel. "I won't be long, I promise."

She gave Joel another kiss and waved to Gianessa. "I know you and Gianessa have a lot to talk about."

"I'll take good care of him." Gianessa gave her a quick hug and closed the door behind Manda.

Joel reached out with his left hand.

Gianessa sandwiched his hand between hers. She smiled warmly and stood peacefully beside him. When his shoulders had relaxed and his breathing steadied, she pressed and released his hand.

"You're the calm after the whirlwind," he told her with a tired smile.

"You love her so much."

"She is the love of my life. I'm grateful to be alive and to have a future with her."

"What's tomorrow's surgery?" Gianessa asked brightly. She repositioned the chair and sat where he could see her face without straining his neck.

"The lower leg. They weren't able to set the tibia and fibula the way they wanted during the emergency surgery, so they're going back in. I hope they finish the job this time. Plan B is to go in again a week later."

"I believe they'll succeed this time. Is your skull up to the surgery?"

Joel nodded. "Still hurts, but my brain is functioning the way it should. My eye was out of whack, but it's improving, they tell me."

"The right one. I can see there's still some wavering when you track movement in the room. If it's improving, it will continue to, and they won't need to correct it surgically."

"I need that encouragement. The fewer surgeries, the less I'm anesthetized. And I'm trying not to use narcotics for the pain."

"I understand, but are you sleeping okay?"

"Well enough. If the surgery goes the way we hope, I may be out of here in two weeks."

Gianessa chose not to disillusion him about that. "The suite at the Manse is going to be excellent. They've dug the pool, and I hear they've gutted the garage already."

"I need you to review the plans and make sure the place will accommodate my recovery start to finish, and it also needs to be a comfortable place for Manda and me to live for a few months. Tony Pinelli will be showing the place to my uncle around six today, and I'd like you to be there."

"I'll have Manda drop me at the Manse after we shop, and then Sara can drive me home."

"Good. I hear you've met my uncle?"

"Uncle Badger, yes, I have." Gianessa had forgotten Joel's trick of engaging someone in light chatter and then nailing them with hard question. *I walked right into that.*

"Who was he badgering?"

"Grace. He was desperate for a massage. I took him to that tiny room no one else uses. Did he complain about it?"

"Not at all."

"He's seriously ill, you realize."

Joel nodded.

"He may have celiac disease or gluten intolerance or some other food allergy. I have celiac disease, did you know?"

Joel's eyes narrowed to slits.

She explained the disease process. "When a person with the disease ingests wheat or another food with gluten, the villi that line the small intestine are damaged. We're unable to absorb nutrients for the rest of the body. Justin told me his symptoms, and they're almost identical to mine before I was diagnosed and treated." She stood and did a muscle-man pose that made him chuckle. "Now that I'm gluten-free, I have no symptoms. I'm normal weight, and my muscle mass and strength have come back. He should have a gastroenterologist do a needle biopsy to—"

"Is it cancer?" Joel grabbed for her arm, and she sat down, leaning close to him.

"No. Biopsies can help diagnose a variety of conditions, not just cancer."

He let out his breath. "I'll work on him about that."

"If it proves to be gluten intolerance or celiac disease, he would need to observe a strictly gluten-free diet. Does he cook?"

Joel cracked a smile. "I understand you've offered to teach him. He's taken over my place, which has an awesome kitchen. He's a beast for appropriating it."

"If he's living in your place, where will you live after rehab?"

"Justin is renovating the first floor flat at 14 Lakeside Terrace for Manda and me. I intend to keep an eye on that construction. If he doesn't give me an equal, or better, kitchen, I'll shove him off the porch onto the rocks below the bluff."

"You boys play rough," she chided. "That's not good for your stress level."

Joel shut his eyes and nodded. "You're right. Old behavior. The Cushman men have always been aggressive with each other, and it was never healthy. First things first: can you send me some information about gluten-free diets, and I'll study up? Manda, too."

Smiling, Gianessa produced the information from the depths of her tote bag. "Done."

"I should have known you'd come prepared."

Following the direction his finger pointed, she set the papers on his rolling tray.

"But, before we get to my agenda, what else did you want to cover with me?"

She took a deep breath and plunged ahead. "I understand Manda and Justin are brainstorming a rehab and retreat facility on the lake. Katie's Point?"

"Cady's Point. C-a-d-y. Tell me what you know." Joel plucked the bed covers while she talked.

"Manda's apparently been thinking about it for a while, and your injuries made it gel for her. Justin has offered to back it."

"I wasn't aware it had gone this far, or I'd have brought you into it right away. You should be the brains of this." He raised a hand and flipped it over and back. "Unless you think it's insane?"

"I think it's inspired. And I want to be involved. Thank you for your trust in me."

"You know I have absolute faith in your ability and your credentials."

"Even though the state of California has revoked my PT license?"

"That was for drug charges that you're addressing through your recovery program. We need your talent here.

I asked you to come here because I had some vague idea that the Spa at the Manse could be more than it is, and I wanted your ideas to shape it. And down the road there's a connection between the spa and the new facility. You'll know what that should be, when the time is right. For now you're the brains behind both. Did I just blow you away?"

Gianessa's hands covered her warm cheeks, and her mouth was open. She recovered her breath with a laugh and beamed at him. "Yes, and you made me very happy."

"Good." He reached for her hand. "You looked stressed when you came in. How's it going for you in Tompkins Falls?"

"It'll be much better now that I'm back at AA meetings. And I'll get a warm coat at L.L. Bean's this afternoon. I have Manda to thank for both. She's an angel."

His grin was soft with affection. "May I ask a favor for my angel?"

"Anything, Joel."

"Manda does not have any confidence with fashion. She needs help finding a wedding gown. I know you're a fashionista at heart. Will you help her find the dress of her dreams? Money is no obstacle."

Gianessa let out a squeak of delight. She tried to put the words "thank you" together but just babbled.

"Good." Joel laughed. "And now the rest of my agenda."

Gianessa closed her eyes and got herself back to center. "Ready, boss."

"I need significant physical therapy, and there is no facility convenient to Tompkins Falls. Are you willing to take on that job and make it your highest priority for at least six months? Even though it means delaying the redesign of the current spa or the facility on Cady's Point?"

"Of course, Joel. Your health and wellness are paramount."

He let out his breath in relief and raised his eyes to the heavens.

"I'll leave it to you to propose your fee. Do you have a computer so you can prepare your budget, get online, check comparable rates for your expertise in New York State, *et cetera*?"

Gianessa shook her head.

"Manda will lend you her old laptop until you have your own. Regarding benefits, we can cover you on the Manse's health plan, if you continue to work part-time at the spa."

Gianessa nodded enthusiastically.

"Good. Done. Any questions?"

"Yes. Is anything stressing you that might affect your recovery?"

Joel's gaze clouded. "Justin has agreed to take over my responsibility at Tompkins College, which is a huge relief for me. He's trading that responsibility for management of the charitable foundation he helped me establish twelve years ago. He's been managing it for me, mostly through benign neglect, and in confidence it's probably a mess. I'll need to dig into the books and the staffing and procedures, and I'll also need to rethink the whole thing. It never had a good focus, because I didn't have a good focus when I started it."

"Joel." Gianessa spoke quietly and remained still until Joel gave her his full attention. "That's the kind of work you should be doing. Even though it's a challenge right now, I'm confident you'll find your way with it, and I can't believe there's any rush."

Something passed, unspoken, from Gianessa's eyes to his.

His body relaxed. "I believe that. Yes, I know all of that is true."

He was thoughtful for a moment.

Gianessa remained still.

"How do you do that?" he asked.

She cocked her head.

"How do you see what I'm struggling to believe in?"

"It's a gift," she said simply. "My grandmother had it, too. It used to scare me."

A shadow passed over Joel's face.

"What's worrying you?"

"Justin has come back here to find his purpose. I don't know if he'll succeed. I don't know if he'll stay."

Gianessa averted her gaze. She didn't want to talk about her attraction to Justin. Or admit how sad it made her that Justin might not stay.

"He's intrigued with you. Be careful, Gianessa."

Chapter 4

Tony hustled onto the site Sunday evening ten minutes before the big boss was due. The sun was down, but floodlights lit the perimeter of the construction. *Lots of changes in a few short days*. Footers were in place for the glass-walled structure that would house the pool, and a slab had been laid for the heat pumps for the pool house and the suite. The pool was no longer just a hole in the ground; it was ready for a liner and then a lot of warm saltwater, as soon as the pool house went up and the heat was connected.

Why does warm saltwater appeal to rich people and sick people?

Tony shrugged. As long as it helped Joel recover, he was fine with it.

"Mr. Pinelli," a deep voice from behind him said.

Tony did an about face and then a double take. "Joel?" he croaked. For five whole seconds he thought he was seeing his buddy Joel, standing tall and taking charge the way he usually did. Same eyes, same brown hair, same proud manner, like he owned the place.

But this man was older than Joel by fifteen years. Plus, Tony didn't think this man ever let down his guard to be one of the guys, and that was one of the things Tony liked best about Joel. Underneath his inheritance, sharp clothes, college degrees, and smarts about money, Joel was a down-to-earth, fun-loving guy who never put anyone down. The guy before him seemed pretty buttoned up, and he was definitely looking down his nose.

"Sorry, wishful thinking."

"I'm Joel's uncle, Justin Cushman." The man smiled and held out a muscled, manicured hand.

Tony liked his firm handshake. "Call me Tony."

"Thank you for meeting me this evening, Tony. I'm glad you've recovered enough to be part of this construction project."

"Yes, sir. It's a privilege, sir. I'll do anything for Joel." He paused then continued. "I'm so—so sorry about the accident. There was no way to prevent the crash once we hit the black ice. If I'd had the new truck then, with the side air bags . . ."

"Can't be undone. Joel is focusing on the good that's come out of it. Let's both of us do the same."

"Yes, sir." And it was true, there was some good in his own life as a result of the accident—his new girlfriend Sunny and the new red truck.

"A few people are working here that were unemployed a week or a month ago. They're not home worrying how to pay the bills. And this eyesore garage is becoming a luxury suite with a lot of potential for the Manse Inn and Spa."

"Ralph showed me the plans. There's a lot of work to be done in a short time."

"Show me the progress. I haven't been inside for a few days."

"Sure. Do you know this lady?" Tony pointed over Justin's shoulder to a slender, toffee-haired woman making her way across the parking lot toward them. Her long down coat might be off the rack at the mall—probably Bean's—but on her it looked silvery and sleek, like a hot runway item.

Justin's eyes softened and his mouth struggled with a smile.

"Ms. Dupioni," Justin greeted her. "Meet Mr. Pinelli."

"Pleased to meet you, ma'am." Tony stuck out his hand.

For a moment, the woman kept her hands in her pockets and only had eyes for Justin Cushman. Tony withdrew his hand. Obviously these two knew each other. She flirted with her eyelashes and Justin reacted with a silly smile.

Finally Ms. Dupioni favored Tony with a smile that outshone the sun. "Hi, Tony."

How does she know my name?

"I met you last night at . . ."

"Oh, right," Tony said quickly. He recognized her now. She'd been with Manda at the Hot Dog AA meeting in Canandaigua. "Jessica, right?"

"Gianessa. Is this the right place for a tour of Joel's therapy facility?"

"Yep. Are you ready for the tour, Mr. Cushman?"

"Justin," Justin corrected him. "Glad you could join us, Gianessa"

"What's your interest in the construction, Gianessa?" Tony asked.

"I'm a physical therapist by training, and I'll be handling Joel's therapy once he's out of the hospital."

That statement put a scowl on Justin Cushman's face. While Tony wrestled with the padlock, he tuned into their murmured exchange. Justin seemed peeved that Joel had picked Gianessa for the job without consulting him. Gianessa's frosty reply sounded like, "Be glad Joel is taking charge of his recovery."

Tony flipped the wall switch and went ahead of them into the old garage. The space was lit by a string of caged lanterns that crisscrossed the beams of the garage. The flooring was complete and the drywall was taped and curing.

"The flooring will do nicely," Justin remarked. "We wanted hardwood, but high-quality laminate was faster. The walls are ready for paint?"

"In a few days," Tony said. "They need some drying time. We've started on the kitchen, and the plumbers will be back tomorrow to finish the fixtures in the bathroom. Then tiling."

"Are you planning a roll-in shower?" Gianessa asked, her tone professional.

"Right, let me show you." Tony led the way and pointed to marks on the floor for the boundary of the shower. Drains and pipes were already in place.

Gianessa nodded her approval. "Plenty of room in here for a chair."

Tony let out his breath all at once.

"He won't need the chair very long, Tony." Gianessa pressed his forearm with her firm, gentle hand, and the knot in his stomach let go. "Once his arm heals, he'll use crutches and then a cane. He's determined to stand for the wedding."

"Thanks," Tony mumbled. He felt better than he had in a month. *How did she do that?*

Back at the makeshift table where the construction drawings were spread out, Gianessa studied the plans, touching the dimensions of each doorway and tracing the path of Joel's wheelchair between the living spaces, in and out of the kitchen and into the pool area. Justin stood across the table, watching her.

When she had traced every possible path of the wheelchair, she pointed to an unlabeled area between the pool and living space. "What's this going to be?" she asked.

Before Tony could answer, Justin said, "I thought it might serve as a workout room. I'm curious what you think."

Gianessa favored him with a smile. "Thanks for asking. It's a good size for a couple of machines and some weights. Is that in the budget?"

"It is now."

"Good. Joel will be ready for it about a month after he comes home."

"He does like working out in the spa with his guests," Justin said amiably. "Is it better for him to work out over there?" While he talked, he circled around the table to stand beside her.

"Not at first. Having this facility," she said, pointing to the unlabeled room, "will give him the freedom to stay indoors during the worst weather and also give him privacy for his workout until he feels ready to mingle with the guests in such a physical setting."

Justin put his hand on Gianessa's back, and reached over to brush an invisible speck of dirt from the plans.

Gianessa smiled at his touch and his proximity.

"Good thinking," Justin said.

"About the kitchen." Gianessa circled her finger over the area on the drawing. "Since you haven't decided about the cabinets—where, how many, and so on—keep in mind Joel will want to cook as much as he's able. It's good therapy for him. He'll need one counter, or perhaps an island, at the correct height for a wheelchair. And we'll need to be smart about the appliances. Have they been ordered?"

Justin shrugged, and Tony told them, "Not as far as I know."

"You'll choose those for us, Gianessa?" Justin's tone was brusque.

To Tony, it sounded an order. *Uh-oh.*

Gianessa's suddenly stiff posture was the only indication she'd heard Justin. She moved away from him to a section of the plans that showed the pool structure. Instead of getting huffy, she responded in a musical tone, "Justin, your vision for this place is stunning. And I can tell that your crew is fully on board, including Tony. You're a strong leader."

She favored both of them with a smile. "Of course, you won't hear 'yes, sir' from me because I work for Joel as a physical therapist. Nevertheless, I support the project and will help out where I'm needed, when I'm available."

Justin cleared his throat. "I'm sure Joel will appreciate having your expertise brought to bear on the selections for the kitchen, Gianessa."

Tony closed his eyes. If Justin was playing the Joel Card, he knew he'd blown it.

"Since I don't have a car and don't know the stores around here, I'd need to team up with someone."

"Tony?" Justin barked.

Tony had seen that coming. "I'm your man."

Gianessa graced him with a dazzling smile. "Perfect, thank you. And, gentlemen, I'll need shelving and cupboards near the pool for the weights and noodles and so on. I'm thinking they might fit along this wall." She ran her finger along the line on the drawing. "This faces the Manse, correct?"

Tony nodded, but he knew not to say "yes, ma'am." He worked for Ralph, who worked for Justin Cushman.

"If we can place the shelves and cupboards on the side toward the Manse," Gianessa continued, "it will give Joel and Manda some privacy in the pool but still admit most of the light from the glass wall. May I have a copy of the pool plans to sketch it out while there's still time?"

"Good idea," Justin said.

Tony flipped through a manila folder and produced a photocopy of the plans for the pool structure for her to take with her. "Mark this up any you want, and Ralph will go over it with you tomorrow."

"Perfect."

Justin's eyes held a measure of respect when he asked, "Gianessa, I wonder if you're available to go with Manda to the furniture showroom tomorrow to make sure she approves the furnishings. She may wonder at the handicap-friendly styles I chose. They'll give you fabric samples, and you can see how they work with the paint colors. If we can determine her satisfaction with the colors before the final coat of paint goes on, we'll save time."

"Unfortunately, Manda and I are both working tomorrow, but I'll arrange a time with her soon." She smiled at both of them. "I'm all set here, gentlemen. Thank you."

Justin studied Gianessa's face. *Probably sizing her up for vice president or something.*

"Everything meet your approval, Mr. Cushman?" Tony asked.

"I like what I've seen so far."

Tony was pretty sure he meant Gianessa as much as the progress and plans.

"If you folks are ready to go, I'll finish up here and lock up on my way out."

Justin gave him a decisive nod and a firm handshake before shepherding Gianessa to the door.

Justin said, as they left the garage, "Now about those cooking lessons you offered, Ms. Dupioni." Gianessa's musical laugh was cut off when the door shut behind them.

Tony took measurements and found there was just enough room for an island. He had forgotten, until Gianessa mentioned it, how much Joel liked to cook. He could picture Joel and Manda starting their life as an engaged couple under this roof while Joel got stronger a day at a time. He imagined them cooking together in this kitchen, hanging out in the master suite, reading together side by side, and using their private pool.

It was funny, as soon as Gianessa touched his arm back there, the knot in his stomach left and it hadn't come back. He wasn't worried about Joel anymore or beating himself up about the accident. *How does she do that?*

Like Ralph had said, maybe their new boss could manipulate St. Peter into redesigning heaven, but Tony was sure Justin Cushman couldn't manipulate Gianessa Dupioni into anything she didn't already want to do.

Sara sighed and hung up the phone. She understood why Manda wanted to spend every possible day with Joel, especially weekends, but Sara missed her Saturday day trips with Manda to the thrift shops and boutique back rooms around the Finger Lakes. In a couple of weeks, Manda's graduate program would gear up for the spring semester, and

Sara wondered if they would ever jump in the car and go like they had last year.

She needed a buddy. Someone who liked clothes but didn't have money. Someone who had Saturdays off, like she did. She eyed Gianessa, who was up to her wrists in dough.

I'd love to get her out for some fun and get to know her. Like personally.

"What are you making?"

"Gluten-free shortbread, I hope. This is my first ever attempt. I don't eat many sweets."

Sara watched as Gianessa formed the crumbly dough into balls and press them flat on a waiting cookie sheet. As soon as she took her fingers away, the little rounds fell to pieces.

"It's a lost cause, roomie."

Gianessa straightened up, let out her breath all at once, and brushed a lock of hair out of her eyes.

Sara giggled. "You've got dough in your hair."

To her surprise, Gianessa blushed. Then she cracked a smile. And giggled.

Cool.

"Okay, that's it. I'm just going to shove it in the oven and see what happens. Stand back." Gianessa threw open the oven door, letting out a blast of heat. She put on oven mitts, maneuvered the two cookie sheets onto the hot racks, and slammed the door shut.

"Take that!" Sara proclaimed.

Gianessa laughed from her belly. After untying her apron and balling it up for the hamper, she lobbed the baking utensils into a dishpan full of sudsy hot water, rinsed her hands and reached for a towel. "What a mess."

Sara surveyed the countertops. "You think?" Open bags of rice flour, hazelnut flour, millet flour, and sugar rested on a dusting of spilled ingredients. Butter wrappers and measuring spoons lay where Gianessa had tossed them. Cans and boxes and bags sat open, and a bottle of vanilla lay on its side with a brown puddle under its mouth.

"There are better ways to have fun, you know." Sara watched the frown lines melt away from her roommate's forehead.

"You are right, Sara. Please teach me how to have fun in Tompkins Falls."

Perfect. "Do you think Remy will ever give you a Saturday off?"

"As a matter of fact, since I filled in when he was out with the flu, he's giving me this Saturday off."

Double perfect. "That could work. Manda's classes start the first of February, and I keep telling her she needs a break from the hospital. Don't you agree?"

"What are you planning?" Gianessa eyed her roommate. "A chick thing?"

"Yes, and it would be great if you'd come with us."

Gianessa's eyes brightened. "Where? What? Tell me."

Sara held her arm in front of her and wiggled her hand, setting four bangle bracelets jingling.

Gianessa came closer to finger the bracelets. "Gorgeous."

"I want to resume the Great Thrift Shop Adventures that Manda and I started last year."

"These are enamel, hand-painted, worth a bundle. You got them at a thrift shop?"

"A buck apiece."

"No way." She stepped back and gave Sara a skeptical look.

"Way. In Ithaca."

"I'm in." Gianessa held up her hand.

"I figured." Sara gave her a high-five. "We went all over the Finger Lakes and ended up with four favorite destinations."

While she helped clean up the kitchen, she told Gianessa about their biggest finds and how little they'd spent. "Bottom line, we figured about ten bucks each for lunch, and both of us put a personal limit on what we could spend. Manda's limit was twenty bucks, and usually she didn't spend it all. Mine was ten, but whatever I didn't spend one week, I'd roll it over to the next."

"My limit will be the first tip of the week."

Sara hummed with excitement. "I'm so glad you want to do this. It's no fun alone. Manda was crazy busy her first semester of grad school. And then Joel's accident. She said something the other day about missing our adventures, and when I said 'soon' she said 'maybe'." Her eyebrows arched impossibly high. "Let's both work on her for this Saturday, okay?"

"Absolutely. I can't drive, obviously, but I can spot a bargain and I might have two bucks to spend by then."

"That would get you two of these." Sara jangled her bangles one more time.

"I love the butterscotch one with the—"

"Hah. Not for sale." She sniffed. "Is something burning?"

Gianessa turned in alarm and opened the oven door. Smoke wafted toward them. "Totally burned." She muttered, "Why didn't I set a timer?"

Sara opened the kitchen window a few inches while Gianessa turned off the oven. They both fanned the smoke toward the open air.

"You know," Sara said without thinking, "usually you've got it all together, but sometimes lately you're a total scatterbrain."

"I know. I'm overwhelmed with getting my work back on a professional track and trying to . . ."

"Trying to what?"

From the way Gianessa's eyes shifted and the little smile on her face, Sara doubted she was going to get a totally honest answer. *What's she hiding?*

Gianessa busied herself putting away the bags of flour and boxes and cans. "Just trying to fit in here," she said evasively. "You're a sweetheart to include me in the plans with Manda."

"Are you kidding? I'm thrilled you're joining the fun. Listen, I hope the shortbread cookies weren't super important?"

Gianessa cleaned the layer of flour off the counter. "Justin and I will just have to make do without shortbread with our coffee tomorrow."

"You were making these for Justin Cushman?"

"It was a stupid idea."

"And you're having coffee with him tomorrow?" *Romance in progress?*

Gianessa carried the flour-coated sponge to the sink and turned on the water so hard it sprayed her T-shirt and jeans.

Sara clapped her hand over her mouth to stifle a laugh.

Gianessa glared at the faucet. "The man makes me completely crazy," she muttered.

Sara took pity on her. "Listen, why don't I clean up here, and you take a nice relaxing bath? We'll take turns doing laundry tonight. Sound good?"

"Heavenly. I'd hug you if I weren't dripping wet."

"Go. Soak. Relax." *So Justin Cushman is making her goofy?*

At that moment, her usually graceful roommate tripped on the sill to the dining room.

"Get it together, girl," Gianessa said under her breath.

She's got it bad. Baking cookies didn't go with a casual cup of coffee at Starbucks. *What are they cooking up?*

"Poached salmon with dill, roasted red potatoes—with your rosemary and fennel—and a salad of field greens and beets tossed in a lemon vinaigrette." Justin stopped reading his menu and fiddled with the pencil.

"I like it, Justin." Gianessa beamed a smile. "And it's all gluten-free. Let's get to it."

Justin set aside the pencil and posted the menu on an upper cabinet. "I'll start the poaching liquid," he proposed.

"You work your magic with the fennel and rosemary. Let's make the vinaigrette together so I can learn."

"It's a plan."

Justin removed items from the refrigerator—one brown-paper-wrapped salmon, one sprig of fresh thyme, assorted dried spices, one sweet onion, one fresh lemon—and lined them up on the counter beside Gianessa's fennel bulb and rosemary. He turned to find Gianessa squatting next to a cabinet with the door wide open. "What do you need?"

"Fish poacher." Her voice echoed into the cabinet.

When she moved to the next cabinet, her skirt hiked up showing plenty of thigh. Justin enjoyed the view.

"Pop taught me everything I know about cooking. He loved poaching a chicken on the stovetop in a big pot, big enough to hold the whole bird without cutting it into pieces. Good for Sunday dinner, a jug of soup, and sandwiches for the week. There it is." She wrestled the elongated poaching pan from the back of the cabinet and handed it up to him. "Mauviel."

"Which is?"

"French. A respected name in copper cookware, very exclusive." She stood up and tugged her short skirt back into place.

Justin watched the procedure.

Gianessa flashed a smile. "You're not too ill to enjoy a little leg."

He examined the Mauviel copper pot. "Very impressive," he said, without admitting he meant her legs. He raised his eyebrows at her.

She smiled her thanks and got back to business. "Time to unwrap our salmon. Do you want the honors?"

Justin wrinkled his nose.

"Tell me you didn't buy a whole fish—scales, head, eyes, and all?"

"Not intentionally."

She unwrapped the brown paper to find a perfectly prepared slab of pink flesh. "*Magnifique*! Justin, you chose well."

"I take no credit. I asked the fish department for a magnificent salmon for poaching, one that would impress my cooking teacher."

She threw up her hands in celebration. "And they don't even know me!"

He laughed and saw a knowing look come over her face. "You schemer! You know perfectly well how to cook, don't you?"

"Do I?"

"Justin Cushman, you bought a perfect salmon and assembled every ingredient I could ever want for poaching liquid—thyme, bay leaf, clove, onion, and lemon—without a single hint from me."

Justin blustered. "The fish department—"

"Nonsense." She planted her hands on her hips. "They'd have given you wine suggestions and coached you to pick out two of their ready-to-bake salmon steaks." She tapped her foot with an agitated rhythm.

Justin enjoyed the display. He folded his arms and raised one eyebrow.

Gianessa pushed out her chest with a sniff.

Justin took slow steps in her direction. "So," he observed, "two imposters have revealed themselves."

Gianessa stood her ground. "I'm not an imposter."

He smiled disarmingly. "Nor are you an entirely cool, reserved, disinterested professional."

Gianessa's eyes opened wide. They stared at each other.

Justin savored the moment of truth. He could see by the set of her cheeks and mouth and jaw that she would never blink first, but he also detected a glimmer of fear in her violet eyes. He was going to blow it with her if he didn't back off.

"Full disclosure." He shifted his weight to his back foot and let his smile soften. "I am a decent cook, but I don't know the first thing about planning a week's worth of menus that represent good nutrition and that are strictly gluten-free."

The tapping continued—nervous, hesitant.

"You do, Gianessa, and I need to learn." He spoke with all the humility he could muster.

She huffed.

Justin spread his hands in surrender. "And I have the social skills of a bull in a china shop."

She snorted at that and struggled against a smile.

Justin sat on the nearest stool and rested one elbow on the island. "I asked you to come today because I wanted to know you better, yes, but I also need to learn to cook regularly for myself, without gluten, ever. And I enjoy cooking with a partner, much more than by myself. If you'd like to go home, I will accept that, and I'll give you a ride."

"Oh, shut up. We're wasting a good salmon." She executed a dazzling hip swivel, reached across the sink for a handful of paper towels, and set about preparing the salmon.

Justin muffled a laugh.

He moved to the counter a few feet from her and measured the ingredients for the poaching liquid. Gianessa pre-heated the oven and scrubbed the potatoes. Justin set the beets on the stove to blanch and assembled ingredients for the salad. Gianessa thick-sliced the potatoes and fennel and tossed them with olive oil on a baking sheet.

While the potatoes roasted and the salmon poached, she demonstrated the simple art of making vinaigrette.

"It's not as tricky as I thought," Justin concluded. "But then, you're a good teacher."

"Thank you. I'll let you dress the salad with our vinaigrette."

When the oven timer rang in the middle of tossing the salad, Justin calmly set down the salad utensils, pushed his hands into big oven mitts, slid out the roasting pan, and set it on the range next to the poacher.

Gianessa cocked her head. "You're very comfortable in the kitchen. And fun to cook with." That got her a smile. "I'll finish the salad if you'll set the table." She watched Justin while she tossed the salad.

He selected plates and salad bowls from a cupboard and prepared the table for them, humming as he worked.

She smiled at his happy, slightly off-key tune. At last she identified it. "'Anticipation?'" she said with a laugh.

He turned and saw her watching him. "Carly Simon, right?"

"Yeah."

Justin held her eyes. "We need music. What do you like?"

"Surprise me."

"No. I want to know what you like."

"This afternoon, a quiet, slow jazz would do it for me. Does Joel have anything like that?"

"Joel is not a jazz fan, but he has satellite radio." Justin flipped two switches and adjusted the volume on a sexy, slow jazz quartet. "I found this station last night. Does it do it for you?"

"Perfectly. You have good taste."

Seated at the table by the French doors, they toasted with Waterford goblets and tucked into the meal. Justin exclaimed at the zing of the citrus vinaigrette, and Gianessa complimented the way the poaching concoction enhanced the salmon.

"It's the bay leaf that makes it, I think. I like your fennel and rosemary with the potatoes."

"What would you have done if I'd left?"

"Fixed our meal and felt very bad about eating it alone. What would you have done?"

She raised her chin and shook her head.

"You're not going to tell me." With a twinkle in his eye and a nod of his head toward the radio, Justin challenged her, "What group is this?"

Gianessa shrugged but smiled at the game. As the meal continued, Justin scored more of the groups, but Gianessa knew more of the titles.

"I never figured you for jazz," he told her. "I was sure you were a classical devotee. Debussy. The Romantics."

"Not me."

"Or perhaps bluegrass."

"Bluegrass!" she burst out and covered her mouth, too late to stop a leaf of lettuce from escaping. "Bluegrass, are you crazy?"

"I'm teasing. I just wanted to see you react."

"You wanted to see tiny red romaine fly out of my mouth. Confess!"

"I was hoping for a beet."

She smiled into his eyes. "Seriously, you're on some kind of quest, aren't you? One that has brought you back to your hometown, which surprises me. Where do you think your quest is leading you?"

Justin thought for a moment, his gaze on the table. The situation was so unfamiliar to him. Gianessa wasn't here as his date. She was coaching him back to health, and her question, however uncomfortable, was relevant. He forged ahead. "At the risk of putting a damper on our afternoon, I have the answer to your question."

"It's not anything bad, is it?"

"Not bad, but it is quite serious and quite sensitive. Are you sure you want to know?"

She set down her fork. "Yes, I do, Justin."

He set aside his fork and knife and sat back. "There is a passage in the Bible that I thought about all the way across the Atlantic, both directions. It may be from Hosea. It's about being in the wilderness and learning to listen with your heart."

She sat back and studied him. "Are you done with the

'wilderness,' do you think? And now you're learning to listen with your heart?"

Justin's voice was hard when he answered. "I believe I'm done with meaningless accumulation of wealth."

She blinked in surprise. "I had a different impression of what you were doing out in the wide world."

"Which was?"

"You were using your wealth as venture capital to launch businesses and other endeavors. And build additional wealth."

"True."

"I don't see that as meaningless," she persisted.

"I don't see it as meaningful," he countered. "Perhaps in the beginning, yes, you're right. But it became a sickness, evaluating each possibility by its potential return or its probable yield, without regard for the people or resources involved. I lost my soul, Gianessa."

Gianessa's mouth dropped open. She took a calming breath. "So it's a quest to find and heal your soul as well?"

"Yes." Justin placed his hands flat on the table and drew strength from its solid surface. He had no idea what to say next.

"You know that I'm a healer. Tell me some things I can use to help you heal."

"You intend to help me?"

"Of course I do. That's why I'm here."

Was that her only motivation for coming today? "What things do you want to know?"

Gianessa sat up straight and gave him a bright smile. "I'll start with questions," she proposed. "How old are you?'

He chuckled. "I feel like an old man. I'm forty-six."

"I guessed exactly."

"Joel told you."

"No, he didn't. So how old were you when Joel lost his family and you became his guardian?"

He did the math on his fingers. "Twenty-nine or thirty."

"About Joel's age now. And when did you lose your own parents?"

Sadness punched him in the gut, as it always did. He breathed through it. "When I was in London gathering data for my Ph.D., on a project out of the Center for Entrepreneurship at the University of Chicago. I was twenty-six."

"Let me think for a few minutes," she proposed, and he nodded.

Gianessa picked up her fork and returned to her salad.

Justin gave his attention back to the meal.

After a few minutes, she rested her fork on the side of the plate. "Having done that without anymore flying lettuce leaves," she said, and he laughed, "may I follow the money story for a minute?"

"I've nothing to hide."

"Your brother was Joel's father?"

"Joshua, yes. Josh was seven years older than I."

"When your parents passed, Josh and you both inherited?"

"Correct."

"You never had any need to work or to accumulate wealth."

"Financially, no. I'm not sure what drove me to work, except that the Cushmans always worked in finance. I suspect work was the way I found to keep functioning after my parents' deaths and, later, Josh's death."

"How did your parents die?"

"Plane crash. They were on their way to visit me in London."

"That's horrible. I'm sorry."

The sympathy on Gianessa's face reminded him of how gutted and guilty he'd felt after the crash.

"I saw a therapist for a time, finished my degree, taught at the London branch of the university for three years, and then moved to Switzerland as my home base. My plan was to make money as a venture capitalist."

"Which you did very successfully."

Justin nodded wearily.

"Were you and Josh competitive?"

"With each other?"

Gianessa nodded.

"Yes, I suppose we were, although we took different paths in life. He married young and had children and was superficially involved in his wife's family ventures—Tompkins College, and various industries that they off-loaded when manufacturing moved offshore. Josh was focused on the children—Joel and his sister, Christie—and didn't have the drive I had to amass wealth." He sat back for a moment and regarded her. "Are we going anywhere with this?"

She squinted in frustration. "I'm searching for a key, and I'm not finding it."

"A key to what?"

"For one thing, a key to why you're so competitive with Joel, even though you say you've come back here to learn from him. I can't make any sense of that."

"Am I competitive with Joel?"

Gianessa eyed him as though he might be joking.

He shrugged, genuinely puzzled. *Am I competitive with Joel?*

"Maybe it's just the nature of the Cushman men. I guess that's something for you to think about."

"On my quest," he said with an easy smile. "I'll add it to my challenges. What other questions do you need answered as the healer of my lost soul and my depleted body?"

"Here's one you can answer easily, and I have no clue what you're going to say."

"Let's hear it."

"What do you consider your most important accomplishment in your forty-six years?"

He thought for a moment about various deals, startup ventures and collaborations. Then he smiled into her eyes. "Joel. Pulling him back from where his addiction had taken him. He was young and out of control. Fourteen when he smashed a car into a building, fifteen when he got hooked on crack cocaine. I sent him to a place where he could get the help he needed, if he was willing to make the choice and do the work. And thank god he was. He's been clean and sober for a dozen or more years. I don't take credit for his hard work, but bringing him back from the brink was by far the most meaningful work I've ever done."

"I had no idea. That's a side of you I didn't know existed."

That hurt. "Why does that surprise you?"

"Of all the accomplishments you could have chosen, you singled out Joel's recovery. And now it's your turn to recover," she said quietly, "to heal your body and your heart and your soul." When she raised her empty goblet, he filled it with water from the pitcher. She smiled her thanks.

"Yes. Is that an illness? I've heard of being 'heartsick'. Is there a 'soulsickness'?"

"Absolutely. We talk about soulsickness all the time in the rooms of Alcoholics Anonymous. Most of us come into recovery with soulsickness."

"You're in AA?" He topped off his own water.

She nodded. "A few years clean and sober."

"Tell me, how does one recover from soulsickness?"

"In AA, we do it through the twelve steps. I suppose you could use them yourself, even though you're not an alcoholic."

He blinked his puzzlement. "How would I go about that?"

Gianessa gave it thought. "I suppose you'd find what we call a sponsor, someone who understands the process and the steps and who can help you apply them to your own life."

"Couldn't you do that?"

"If you're not in the program, I wouldn't know how." She offered, "I'm new to AA here, but I know there are a couple of good therapists who are also in the program. They might structure their work with you around the twelve steps. I can get you a couple of names."

"I'd appreciate that."

She nodded. "What I can do, Justin, for your recovery, is teach you to cook delicious, gluten-free meals and prepare menus and make good choices at restaurants and in the grocery store. And I can help you rebuild your body. I'll be glad to do that with you."

Now he understood the reserve he had seen in her at the spa. There was no flirtation in her voice or her face or her body, because this was her profession, and she was making a professional commitment to him. Those hip swivels at the spa were probably thrown in to appease him for having to beg for an appointment from a receptionist who didn't recognize him, and having to put up with the tiny little treatment room.

He asked her, without any trace of impropriety, "And what is your fee for a job like that?" In her eyes, he saw a flicker of unease. *What's that about?*

She sat up straighter and drew her hands closer to herself. "In this case, it would be my way to repay Joel for what he has done for me—bringing me here, giving me a chance for a new start."

He could tell she was prevaricating. He drummed his fingers on the table. "Let's leave Joel out of this. I can pay you well, and you're not in a position to turn it down, are you?" This time, Justin saw anger in her pinched-together eyebrows.

"Was that a put-down or an incentive? Either way, I don't care for it."

"My apology." He tried again. "What I meant was that this is a business arrangement, and I need to pay you for your professional services."

"It's my choice, Justin. I won't take your money."

He saw her firm resolve in the line of her jaw but not the reason for it. Evidently the confusion showed in his face.

"Justin, I don't want to walk away from this challenge. In truth, it's not about repaying Joel, but I won't take your money."

He smiled disarmingly and shifted in his chair. "I can't help wondering what's in it for you, Gianessa?"

"The satisfaction of seeing you well. Fit, strong, lean, and full of energy."

He smiled. "So you don't want me to regain all the weight?"

"Maybe ten pounds, no more."

"I'll be buff?"

Color rose in her cheeks.

So she is interested. "Busted," he said, teasing her with his eyes and voice.

She laughed. "You are, without a doubt, the most skillful negotiator I've ever dealt with."

He grinned. "One way or another, I find out what motivates my business partners."

"But I don't want to be your business partner." She leaned slightly forward, her chin held high, a little tilt to her head. "For me, this got personal right around the time you started humming 'Anticipation.'"

How did I miss that? His eyes traveled from her lush breasts, up the curve of her neck, to her gentle smile. "I can see I'm out of practice." He met her eyes and saw them sparkle. "How would you describe this relationship of ours?"

Gianessa raised one eyebrow and moved her breasts closer to him. "I'd say we have a promising friendship."

Justin stroked the crystal stem of the goblet and gave it a quarter turn. *Very promising.*

Chapter 5

Manda stopped at the door to the half-finished suite. She peered left and right, her brow furrowed.

Gianessa guessed she was nervous about living with Joel in the early stages of his recovery from serious injury. It was one thing for a sweetheart to imagine nursing her man back to health; it was another to confront the physical reality.

"What did you think of the furniture Justin picked out?" Gianessa said brightly. Manda had made no comment at the showroom when they'd examined Justin's selections.

Manda shrugged. "It's cool."

"What I liked were the clean lines and firm surfaces of the furniture—very handicap-friendly. I also liked Justin's taste in colors and patterns. But maybe you didn't."

"It's fine. He has good taste." She sounded sure, even pleased, but she still had the frown lines, and she hadn't moved even an inch into the room.

"Good match?" Gianessa held up the fabric samples next to the just-primed walls. "It's okay to tell them to change the paint color, you know. This is just the first coat."

Manda took a few steps and gave a cursory glance at the swatches and paint color. "I'm okay with it." She stuffed her hands in her pockets and looked up at the short windows, high up on the old garage-door walls.

"Come see the plans," Gianessa called cheerfully. She sat down at the makeshift table where the drawings were laid out. "I have little cutouts we can use to arrange things on the plans and see how the furniture will work best. Bring over that stool, okay?"

Manda dragged a stool across the space, and Gianessa held her breath, but no drag marks sullied the new flooring.

"Come close. Let me show you what I'm thinking."

Manda dutifully moved her stool and sat.

"It's a little hard to get oriented," Gianessa began. She pointed across the room to the right while planting one finger on the drawing. "That's the bathroom, which is plenty big for Joel to swing his chair around. He'll be able to roll right into the shower, and there will be grab bars to help him on and off the toilet."

Manda swallowed. "I won't know how to help him."

"We'll have a visiting nurse nearby for a few days to help out. She'll teach you anything you need to know. And Joel will want to do most things himself. You know Joel."

"I want to help him," Manda insisted.

Gianessa squeezed her arm. "Good. That's something you and Joel will negotiate. He's stubborn, you know."

That brought a smile. "You think?"

Gianessa moved her finger on the drawing and pointed ahead and to the left. "Over there is the passage to the workout room and the pool. The pool is only fifteen by thirty, so you can't do endless laps, but it'll be perfect for water walking, aqua-therapy, short laps, and just floating in warm salt water."

"Sounds great."

"Do you swim, Manda?"

"I love to swim. It would be so cool to do some easy laps after work. Am I allowed?"

Gianessa did a quick mental reset. Manda wasn't worried about Joel's care so much as the living space she and Joel were moving into. "Of course you can use your pool. This isn't just a place where Joel gets therapy. It's your home. That's why it's important for you to give input during construction. It needs to suit you and Joel."

"Cool, I didn't know I could say anything."

"Really?"

Manda shrugged and teared up. "Justin and Tony have been telling me how wonderful it's going to be, and I thought they didn't want anyone's input. I mean I'm really grateful they're doing this, don't get me wrong."

Gianessa closed her eyes. "Justin can be overwhelming when he takes charge, can't he? He does have great taste and a clear vision, but I know he very much wants your input, Manda."

"Wow. Okay." Manda stood up and circled the table to the section of drawing for the pool structure. "In that case"—she traced the lines representing the walls—"isn't this going to be all glass? I'm worried we won't have any privacy in the pool."

Gianessa pointed to one wall after another on the drawing. "The side that faces the Manse is all cabinets and benches and shelves, so there's no way anyone can see in. The wall that looks out on the lake is glass, but it's the short wall. You'll have a beautiful view of the water, and no one's going to stand there peering in at you. And the other long glass wall faces the woods and the fitness trails, which are not lit. No one has a legitimate reason to be out there at night, and you know how tight security is around here. During the day, people might get a glimpse as they come back from their exercise, but they're not going to stand gawking. We can always get screens if you decide you need more privacy."

Manda's shoulders relaxed. She went back to her stool and perused the drawing. "So this is the living room?" She pointed.

"Yes, it's just fifteen by twenty, which is why we need to be careful with furniture placement. Let me show you what I'm thinking." Gianessa placed the paper-cutouts for the sofa, two chairs, narrow coffee table, and rack of folding tables. "Your lighting is all in the ceiling, and each fixture can be remote controlled—on, off, dim, and swivel to a new direction."

"That works." Manda reexamined the new windows, high in the wall behind her. "That wall used to have half a dozen garage doors, right? Now I see why the windows are up high. It's neat that they give us privacy from the parking lot."

"Exactly. And Justin wanted them to give you a nice view of the treetops, which will be pretty as spring starts to show itself."

Manda sighed. "Spring. Joel will be getting stronger, and my semester will be winding down, and the wedding won't be far away."

"Exactly. All the hard work will be paying off."

Manda sat taller.

"Manda, your biggest job with Joel's recovery—besides loving him, of course—is to make sure Joel eats really well. The kitchen is tight." She pointed to the area on the drawing. "But it will be fully functional, so you can cook all your meals here if you want. Justin is arranging for someone to keep the kitchen supplied with fresh produce, lean meat, and lots of healthy ingredients."

"That's a huge help to have someone do the grocery shopping."

"Justin says he'll arrange for a cook if you want."

Manda waved her hand in dismissal. "We both love to cook. Will Joel be able to?"

"He'll work up to it. It will be good for him."

Manda shifted on the stool with excitement. "So, where will we eat?"

"Tell me what you think. Tony has figured out how to install an island between the living room and the kitchen." She showed Manda on the drawing. "Joel can roll up to it from either side. He can use it for cooking, and the two of you can use it as a table. Or there's space for a slim table between the front door and the passage to the pool."

"Or both," Manda said firmly. "But both of us need

to use our laptops, sometimes at the same time. Did anybody think of that?"

Good, she's owning this. "Justin did. He's been using that alcove at Joel's apartment for his laptop, and he's planned two workspaces here—one for you, one for Joel." She put her finger on a section of the drawing, an area beyond Manda's view.

"Where is all that?"

Gianessa pointed to the cavernous space beyond the weight-bearing pillars that marked the midpoint of the garage.

Manda crossed to one of the pillars and peered into the dark.

Gianessa found a switch. Lights came on overhead. "Welcome to your master suite."

Manda's eyes brightened with interest.

Gianessa led her on a quick tour, starting at the wall closest to the lake. "You have a walk-in closet that adjoins the bathroom with a door between and a door to the bedroom. It will have built-in drawers and shelves and a bench so you and Joel can dress in private."

Manda laughed. "This closet is bigger than my whole kitchen and dining space."

Gianessa pointed to the line of chalk on the floor, as they entered the master bedroom. She gestured to her left and straight ahead. "In your bedroom, you'll have windows to the lake and to the woods, with shades that open from the top and the bottom. I thought two chairs for reading and conversation could face the windows. What do you think?"

Manda smiled and let out a sigh. "Joel will love it. He can read and meet with Phil, and we can talk in the evenings."

"The bed could go in the center. King-size? There's room."

Manda nodded her agreement.

They traversed the length of the room and stood under the high, wide windows. "And here are the workspaces Justin had in mind." She drew imaginary boundaries for the side-by-side alcoves. "He has requested that this wall have its own power circuit, so you can load it up with electronics."

Manda moved into "her" alcove and pretended to use her laptop for a few seconds. Then she turned and contemplated the whole space. She made her way back to the windows that faced the water, carefully stepping around the imaginary bed. She sank to the floor, cross-legged, with her back to the room.

Gianessa heard a whimper. Worried, she came up beside her.

Manda had tears on her cheeks.

Gianessa knelt on the floor and lay her arm lightly across Manda's shoulders.

"Do you think it will work for you and Joel?"

"It's going to be really good. We could never have done this without you guys. Justin's thought of practically everything, and you've thought of the rest. You're a great team."

Gianessa's stomach took a dive. *Les always said he and I were a great team. And look how that turned out*. She didn't ever want to repeat that nightmare. "Thank you, Manda."

"I know Justin's going to make a great dad. And I think you're going to be a wonderful mother."

Gianessa swallowed. "Why did you say that?"

"That sounded like I'm matchmaking." Manda laughed at herself. "I'm not. It's just that he makes me feel so protected, and you make me believe that my opinion and my ideas count. I always wanted that from my parents."

Gianessa rubbed her back. "So you and Joel will both be okay here for a couple of months?"

"Hell, yes. We might want to live here until we build a house."

Justin surveyed the well-heeled clientele at Sydney Shorey's favorite steakhouse in the theater district. No one had a suit that could match the ones he'd just ordered. He tapped his fingers on the tabletop. "Good choice, Syd."

"Tell me this, Justin." Sydney swallowed her olive and set down the toothpick. "Why are you being fitted for new suits if you're just going to gain back the weight?"

"Perhaps I'm not."

"Not which?"

Justin sat back with a satisfied smile. Bantering with Sydney always gave him a lift. "Not putting the pounds back on. My plan is to stay at this weight, perhaps one or two pounds above or below."

"You're a lean, mean, money machine, you mean?" Sydney inspected him from a couple of angles. "Very sexy on you."

"You think?"

She nudged his foot under the table. "I'll tell you what I think. I think Justin's got a woman."

He felt his cheeks grow warm.

Sydney pointed her finger and smirked. "I knew it the minute you came through that door."

Justin found himself smirking right along with her. "I haven't got her yet, Syd."

"She's young and beautiful, am I right?"

"She's young and beautiful, and at the moment she's my cooking teacher."

"You schemer. You're already an accomplished cook."

"She's teaching me to cook gluten-free. And I'm learning to plan menus so I can cook my own meals regularly."

Sydney folded her arms under her voluptuous bosom.

Justin leaned closer and whispered, "I love that view."

"Spill. What's the story?"

Justin explained his food intolerance and the dramatic improvement in his health in a matter of weeks, similar to the improvement when he'd been in Indonesia the previous year. "I'm still weak, but I'm eating without difficulty, sleeping soundly, no more headaches or nausea. I feel like a new man."

Sydney nodded and swallowed the last of her vodka martini. "You look younger, fitter, and happier than you did in December."

"Not fitter, not yet, but I can work on that now that I have some energy back. Let's talk about the college."

"Mine or yours? Mine's not very interesting. Yours was a disaster, last I heard. Decided yet who you're going to fire?"

Justin raised his hand to signal the waiter for another round of drinks.

Sydney stilled his hand.

"I've had enough vodka. Make mine Perrier, too."

"I've been meeting with the Provost and one trustee who's local to Tompkins Falls. I'll meet two more trustees when I come back for my suits next week. Syd, there's a to-be-fired list that's shocking. The corruption went all across the campus, nearly every department."

"So you'll fire a few from everywhere?"

"Not my decision alone, as you know, but I suspect we will. I'm feeling out the other trustees, letting them sniff me."

"You definitely need world-class suits if the big boys are sniffing you," Sydney said dryly.

"And you definitely don't need any more vodka, my dear."

"I need food, dearest. Let's order."

Justin chose filet and salad, no croutons, to Sydney's prime rib and baked potato.

"Danny expects me to bring home half my meal and make a complete report on what we talked about."

"Is he jealous?"

"Just protecting his territory."

"And is he behaving himself?"

Sydney smiled tenderly, her eyes on her wedding band. "He's being a thoughtful, attentive, faithful husband, and I love him for it."

Justin drummed his fingers on his glass of Perrier. "You're happy?"

"I'm happy, Justin."

"It's as it should be."

"I expect the same from you. If not with this cook then with another lovely woman. Tell me"—she fixed him with a look— "where did you find your women in London? You don't drink, and I can't imagine you pub crawling now that you don't drink."

"At the university, of course. We had a smashing faculty club and soirees and dinners and holiday bashes. And there were coffee houses around the area. A very lively social scene."

"And you had your pick of women."

"Smart, attractive, unattached women. Every one of whom reached the conclusion that I am a workaholic with a heart of stone." Justin put his hand on his heart and let out a heavy sigh.

"Well, the nerve." She rolled her eyes. "I don't suppose they were right?"

Justin laughed at himself. "Perhaps they were. About the workaholism anyway."

Sydney appraised her friend and said gently, "You protect your heart fiercely, don't you, Justin? Is it all about that Alexis person you knew in Switzerland?"

"Alexa." Justin was surprised to hear his voice catch. He coughed and took a swallow of Perrier.

"She hurt you deeply, my sweet." Sydney patted his hand. "Don't let it make you paranoid with this fair maiden of yours. If there's love between you, she'll be true to you, but she won't stick with you if you're suspicious or jealous without cause."

"Why do you say suspicious and jealous? Do you think that's the case with me?" The pucker of his forehead betrayed his hurt.

Sydney nodded sagely. "I have heard it in your voice over the years. I heard it long before things blew up with Alexa. Perhaps it's the nature of your work not to trust your partners any more than your enemies. But after Alexa betrayed you, you carried that suspicion into your love life, too. No wonder your London ladies said you had a heart of stone." She raised her eyebrows. "Suspicion is a huge turnoff, you know."

"You've had too much to drink."

"Mark my words, Justin. I'm not being mean. You know I want your happiness."

Before Justin could reply, their dinners arrived.

The waiter set heavy plates in front of them. "Can I get you folks anything more just now?"

"Two coffees," Justin growled.

Sydney smiled, and the waiter left the table. The aroma of sizzling steak enveloped them. "Mm." She patted Justin's hand. "Eat, growly bear. You know I'm right."

Gianessa talked with her hands and with anything her hands happened to be holding. At the moment, she was holding a half-full mug of coffee, and Carol watched its movement carefully, prepared to move out of the way as needed.

"Joel is coming home to the new suite at the Manse very soon, and we'll be ready for his treatment." She set down her coffee mug, brushed a splash of coffee off her hand with a napkin, and continued. "You should see the treatment pool and the equipment room. It's a first-rate setup, and I know Joel will make progress quickly."

Carol warmed to the happy tone in Gianessa's voice, the lightness of her smile. When she asked for details of the setup, she heard more than she could ever understand. Gianessa wound down after a few minutes, and Carol told her, "As your AA sponsor, I am so glad to see you embrace this exciting change. You've worked long and hard for this opportunity. I see one of the AA promises coming true for you. Would you agree that you have a new freedom and a new happiness? I think you're breaking free of the past, Gianessa."

To Carol's surprise, Gianessa's face lost its sparkle. *What's that about?* She waited a few beats for Gianessa to take the lead, but Gianessa seemed lost in thought.

"Gianessa, when you told me about your new opportunities, you seemed so happy and excited about your work. And now you're not. What did I miss?"

Gianessa came back with a false smile. "Maybe I'm just realizing all the work ahead of me."

"Want to know what I think?"

Gianessa picked up the empty wrapper from Carol's sugar packet and ripped it in half. "Of course. That's why I have a sponsor."

Carol ignored the tone of dismissal and told her, "I think you were hoping the fulfillment of work would blot out the sadness from the past, and maybe it hasn't."

Gianessa's face darkened, and her jaw hardened. Carol wasn't sure what was coming next. Tears or an angry outburst.

Neither. Gianessa calmly shredded the sugar packet. When she had reduced it to eight thin strips, she picked up each strip in turn and tore it into four tiny squares.

Carol marveled at her concentration and dexterity.

Gianessa nudged the thirty-two tiny squares into a neat pile, sat back and sighed. "I totally failed my daughter and my husband, when what I really wanted—more than anything—was to be a mother and a wife."

"Yes, we've talked about that, and it's very sad. Do you still want to be a mother and a wife?"

"It's not possible." Gianessa's voice was hard.

Carol lightened her tone. "What are you planning to do with that pretty pink pile of torn paper?"

Gianessa huffed and squirmed in her chair, pursed her mouth, and finally met Carol's gaze. "It's not that I don't want to have a career. I do. I'm a healer, and I want to share that gift.

I'm a talented physical therapist, and I want to use that skill. I'm happy Joel will be home and in therapy very soon."

"But?"

Gianessa looked around the coffee shop, swallowed hard, and brought her gaze to rest on the tiny squares that used to be a sugar packet. "I can't forgive myself for what I've done."

"You mean the drunk driving accident?"

Gianessa nodded, and her eyes filled with tears.

"I'm pretty sure you know how to forgive yourself," Carol corrected. "I think you just can't let go of what you've lost."

The tears spilled over.

"How can I possibly let go of my little girl?" she whispered. When her teardrops hit the tabletop, Gianessa reached into her tote bag for a pack of tissues.

To Carol's surprise, Gianessa made no effort to dry her eyes or take care of her runny nose. Instead, she wiped the teardrops from the table and methodically put the thirty-two tiny squares of paper into the tissue and folded it neatly.

If she puts that into her tote I'm going to make her see a psychiatrist. At times like this Carol wished she still smoked.

"I am so torn," Gianessa said in a whisper.

Carol eyed the tissue with the torn paper. *No kidding*.

"If I let them go, Les and Isabella, what do I have left?"

Carol said gently and with conviction, "Yourself. Your gifts, your skills, and all the warmth and love that made you want to be a wife and mother in the first place."

Gianessa shook her head. "I've destroyed that part of me."

"No, Gianessa. Your addiction destroyed your life with Les and Isabella. But I believe, deep inside, you still have the love, the instincts, the desire to be a wife and mother. The question is, do you have the courage to let go of what's gone and open yourself to love and commitment in the present and the future?"

Gianessa squinted at her as if she were speaking another language. Slowly, comprehension dawned. “Is that why I’m fighting so hard to hang on to them, even when I know they’re lost forever? Because I still want a loving relationship and children?”

“I think so.” Carol waited a beat. “Of course I’m not a therapist, and I’m not you.”

“I am so afraid of failing again. I couldn’t live with myself if I destroyed another marriage or lost another child due to my addiction.”

“That’s honesty. Good for you.”

“I have so much fear and anger toward myself.”

“And you will work through that one day at a time, as you explore new relationships and take on new challenges.”

Gianessa’s eyes were dark with doubt. “That is scary. It’s easier to beat myself up about my failure than to . . .”

“Than to what?”

With a secretive smile, Gianessa picked up the neatly folded tissue with the neatly torn sugar packet, and made her way to the trash.

When she came back to the table, the soft smile was gone. Back in place was the apprehension.

What the hell? “How did it feel to let go of that?”

“Scary.”

“You know, you had a sexy little smile going before you left the table.”

Gianessa gaze met hers and then darted off, seeking but not finding a safe place to focus.

“Fess up, kiddo. Is there a nice man in your life? Is that where all this is coming from?”

Gianessa’s laugh was tentative. “I’d say ‘interesting.’ There’s an interesting man in my life, and he’s interested in more than cooking together.”

Carol shifted in her chair. “And that scares you. Tell me about this man. What are you cooking up together?”

"Gluten-free meals. He's made a commitment to gluten free, and he's learning strategies for eating out and meal planning. We've seen each other a few times. He's slowly getting well and strong again."

"So this is a professional relationship that he wants to become personal?"

Gianessa's mouth opened, but no words came out.

"Or it's already personal, and he wants it to be sexual?"

Gianessa's face flamed. "You know, you're very good." She laughed.

Carol probed, "Is this someone you might want to get serious about?"

"Heavens no. He's . . ." She sighed and her brow knit with bafflement.

"Tell me about him. Is he cute?"

"Handsome. He's too old for me, and anyway he's just a temporary thing. I think."

"That's an odd way to describe someone."

"He's had a whole life away from here, and he came back for a specific purpose, and I don't trust that he's going to stay."

Carol cocked her head. "That's different from what I was envisioning for you. I'm not suggesting you have a meaningless fling."

"It wouldn't be meaningless."

"How so?"

"I don't know why I said that."

"Sounds like we're in unexplored territory here." Carol glanced at the clock. "How about 'Easy Does It' as your guideline for now. We'll talk again as things unfold. Meanwhile, can I trust you not to do something foolish?"

"Such as?"

"Oh, I don't know. Get your heart broken. Get pregnant. Run off to Morocco with Mr. Wrong."

"I'd rather be here, see where this new work leads, and keep making friends. Besides, I've got the ultimate winter coat, good to forty below."

Carol laughed. "So I see. It takes up a whole chair by itself."

"It's light as a feather and toasty warm. I love my coat. Don't disparage my coat."

Her voice was teasing, and Carol was glad to hear Gianessa's enthusiasm for life in wintry Tompkins Falls. As they bundled up in coats and mittens, she wondered what the next meeting with Gianessa would bring.

"I need an answer here," Justin said in a tone she'd never heard.

Gianessa wouldn't call it bullying or badgering or bossing, but it left no room for evasion. She raised her eyes from the sheet of phyllo dough.

Justin's smile was disarming. "You're prickly around me. What's that about?"

"Prickly?"

"I walk behind you, you press against the counter to avoid contact."

"No way. I'm being polite and moving out of your way."

He nodded as if he'd expected that. "I brush against your arm, you jump a mile."

"I don't jump a mile."

"A foot," he amended with a practiced smile.

She could see he'd played this game before and, of course, won. She gave him a dimpled smile of surrender.

"And now you're distracting me with that dimple. Where does that come from? What does that mean?"

Gianessa averted her gaze, gave one last roll to the sheet of gluten-free phyllo, and began cutting strips to make the mushroom roll-ups. "It means you've *got* me."

"*Got* you?"

She peered at him from under her eyelashes. “Figured me out.”

His chest swelled. “Perhaps a little.”

Gianessa continued the expert pastry cutting. When he didn’t press her, she took a deep breath and said, “I’m almost ready for the mushroom stuffing.”

“Ready any time.”

Of course, he’s a step ahead of me. He’d been working out his strategy since she came in the door, arms loaded with flour, herbs, and fillings. Justin had agreed to use his kitchen for the preparation of the hors d’oeuvres she was taking to the staff party at the Manse, on three conditions: she allow him to contribute the fresh produce and cheeses, teach him to make the hors d’oeuvres, and take him as her escort.

Gianessa cleaned her hands and swiveled into a provocative pose against the counter. He raised an eyebrow and brought the bowl of fragrant herb-mushroom mix up to her. She placed a finger on the counter, and he placed the bowl so it touched her finger.

She instructed. “Now you scoop one-fourth of the mix onto one strip of dough and spread it evenly the whole length of the strip, leaving just a little dough free at one end.”

“You trust me with this?”

“You’re a very accomplished cook, Justin.”

He feigned surprise. “Why would I ask for a cooking lesson if I already knew how to do this?”

“I cannot guess.”

“You think I am an opportunist?”

Her eyes sparkled, and she nodded.

“Perhaps.”

She laughed from her belly and touched his arm.

“You’re right,” he admitted. He spread the mixture as directed and stepped aside. “Your move.”

Gianessa rolled the strip and sealed the end. Holding the edges to prevent a spill, she deftly transferred it to one of the baking sheets already prepared with parchment paper. They worked in tandem preparing the other three strips, arms touching, hips occasionally bumping "accidentally."

"And now?"

Gianessa reached for the knife. "Now we make them bite size."

Justin stepped back and watched her slice the rolls and tip each piece onto its side.

"If you'll finish cutting this sheet," she invited, "I'll cut the rest, and we'll let them bake until they're golden and bubbling."

After Justin slid the sheets into the oven, she handed him a towel for his hands. "And we will eat a few delicious samples ourselves," she told him.

"But phyllo has wheat." He looked puzzled, and then the light dawned. "So you made this dough from other flours."

"Exactly, and I've only done it once before, so we need to sample."

"You've gone to a lot of trouble."

"I wanted to take something special, and my name was on the list for hors d'oeuvres."

"Is the After-the-holiday Staff Party at the Manse a bring-your-own or a pot-luck or some such?"

"A combination, I think. People who are really good cooks are encouraged to bring appetizers or desserts, and the rest is catered. I don't know the history, but everyone's excited about it, and it should be a good time."

"While these bake, let's get back to my question."

Gianessa leaned back against the counter. "The one I thought I'd sidestepped?"

He grinned.

"But we had a nice detour, didn't we?" she said with a bright smile.

"An unprickly detour." Justin dried his hands and set aside the towel. "I still don't know why you're prickly today, and the mixed messages you sent on our detour didn't clarify anything."

"You're a patient strategist."

"And persistent."

Gianessa bit her lower lip, her eyes down, and nodded.

Justin pressed, "Seriously. I enjoy our flirtation, but I want to know if you're interested in more with me."

Gianessa blurted, "I don't want to fall in lust with a Sugar Daddy." She met his gaze and cringed.

Justin's head tipped back, as if he'd been slapped. "And that's all that could happen here?"

"No." She shut her eyes and apologized. "No, that came out all wrong."

"I think that was loaded with truth, wasn't it?"

"It was loaded with fear, Justin."

He stepped back and reconsidered. "Now I'm even more confused."

"Justin, you're the most interesting, exciting man I've met in a decade, but I don't trust my feelings right now. I've screwed up my life. I think the right thing is to focus on my professional gifts and to become self-sufficient. But then I see you and you get me. And I know I'm at my best in a loving relationship. But I feel so conflicted, I don't know what I'm doing. You're rich, and I wonder if I'm just flirting with you so I won't have to do the hard work of rebuilding my career. You're handsome and funny and getting more buff every day."

Gianessa smiled as Justin drew himself up taller and squared his shoulders.

She swept an admiring gaze over his lean hips and the very interesting bulge in his jeans. When their eyes met, she blushed.

Justin stroked her cheek, and heat spread all the way to her toes.

"My self-esteem thanks you. There was a 'but' coming, I feel sure."

She pressed her fingertips to her forehead. "But I worry that you're just a distraction at a time when I should be—"

"—focusing on your professional gifts, yes. I don't understand why the two have to be at odds with each other."

"That's the thing. They shouldn't be, but they are at odds. When I gave you that first massage, I couldn't set aside my attraction. I couldn't be strictly professional with you, and—"

"Ah. That's why you always insist on handing me off to another masseuse?"

Gianessa nodded.

"And why you won't let me pay you for the cooking lessons and the coaching?"

They could smell the herbs and the just-baked dough. Justin suggested, "Think they're done? Let's see."

Gianessa moved to the oven and opened the door halfway. Heat and mouth-watering smells rushed at her. She reached for the top pan.

Justin grabbed her hand.

She looked at him, startled.

Justin fitted an oven mitt on her hand and gave her the second mitt.

Gianessa stared at the mitts. She'd reached into the oven with no protection. "Where is my head?" She stuffed her other hand in the second mitt, drew the pans out of the oven, and set them on the cooling racks.

Her hands shook when she removed the mitts. "And that's what I mean. I'm a little insane about this attraction to you." She gave a little kiss to each mitt before placing it on the counter.

"It scares you?"

"A lot." She got her breathing under control. "Thank you for keeping me from a serious burn."

Justin reached around her to switch off the oven. He rested his hands on her shoulders.

Gianessa did not jump this time.

"Let's have lunch and talk this over."

She put her hands on his chest and felt the warmth and softness of his cashmere sweater, pressed a little to check the firmness of his chest muscles. His gaze was on her lips. She placed a gentle kiss beside his mouth and let him draw her into a warm embrace. "Yes," she told him. "A good meal with you is just the thing right now."

She let him hold her until she stopped shaking.

"And we'll talk about whatever is going on between us?" he tested.

"We will." She gave him a dimpled smile. "You know, I think I am starting to get you, Justin."

"There's a lot to get," he said, eyes twinkling.

Gianessa closed the front door as quietly as she could, slid the deadbolt home, and let her hand linger there for a moment. She was deliciously happy. Justin had been a funny, charming companion at the party. She hadn't laughed so much in a long time.

The Manse staff party must have been a challenge for him. What did he have in common with hairstylists, masseuses, receptionists, security guards, waiters, chefs—well, chefs, that was obvious. In fact, he'd spent quite a bit of time with Louie and Alicia, probably talking about gluten-free menus.

He was a dancer, too, something she hadn't guessed. He'd had every one of the spa women out on the tiny dance floor at one time or another. He'd timed it so he danced just a minute or so each time and only for the slower dances. His body had a long way to go before he could handle a whole night of dancing. He'd been caught by surprise once when the band switched to a hot rhythm midway through a slow number. Justin had feigned ignorance of the steps and let his partner "teach" him the moves while he acted out a comically slow version of her lead. Everyone enjoyed the show.

They'd left the party early. Justin wanted to enjoy a coffee with her, so they'd gone back to his apartment and talked for an hour. Or was it longer?

"And where have you been?" Sara asked from the living room in a sleepy imitation of a stern parent's voice. Her cheek was creased from the pillow.

Gianessa hung up her coat with a laugh. "Don't tell me you waited up for me?"

"Are you kidding? Of course I waited up. My assignment is to get all the juicy details. Where did you and the hit of the party go after the party?"

"Ohmigod, Sara, are we the hot topic now?" Gianessa pretended a groan. "We had coffee at his place and talked."

"Talked?" Sara drew out the word with a knowing smile.

"Talked." Gianessa drew it out with a 'Duh' look on her face. "We're just friends, Sara. I keep telling you." *But those kisses at the door . . .* A delicious shiver ran through her.

"Maybe you were friends before, but tonight you were On A Date for all of the Manse and a pretty good chunk of Tompkins Falls to see."

"Are you serious?"

"Think about it." Sara drew her legs to her chest and wrapped the afghan around her.

Gianessa slid onto a slipper chair, kicked off her heels, and massaged her tired feet. "He's quite a dancer, isn't he?"

"He's a hell of a dancer. And you're the queen of changing subjects."

"You're catching on, roomie. So you really believe Justin and I were on a date tonight?"

"Everyone at the party thinks you were on a date tonight. Especially when he called you 'Darling.'"

Gianessa muttered, "I hate that word. I wish he'd stop. He knows I don't like it."

"He's crazy about you. So, what's the scoop? You asked him to the party, and he said, 'Sure,' just like that?"

"I didn't ask him."

"Gianessa, it was *your* party. *He* couldn't ask *you*."

Gianessa moved her attention to her left foot.

"Or did he?" Sara laughed. "I have a feeling he can do whatever he wants and people will just go along with it and think it was their idea."

"That's the truth. I remember now. I asked him if I could use his kitchen to make the hors d'oeuvres, and—"

"They were delicious. Those mushroom thingies especially, and the cheese puffs were so light and really delicious."

"Thank you. Justin helped make the mushroom roll-ups, and he provided the cheeses for the puffs. Grated the cheese, too, and did all the heavy mixing."

"But—wait—why did you need to use his kitchen? You have a great kitchen here."

"We have an adequate kitchen here. Justin has two ovens, one of them generous enough for two pans of hors d'oeuvres at a time. We prepared everything in less than two hours start to finish."

And in between we had lunch and talked very seriously about our relationship. Gianessa was not about to tell Sara about that discussion. She wasn't entirely sure herself what they'd concluded. *But those kisses at the door were more than friend kisses.*

"So you asked to use his kitchen and, somehow, he wrangled an invitation to the staff party?"

"He agreed to my using his kitchen, but only if I'd teach him how to make the recipes and let him contribute some ingredients and take him to the party."

"Hah. He's good."

"I never thought twice about it." Gianessa frowned at her roommate. "But you're right, we looked like we were on a date, didn't we?" Another thought followed. "And as if *I* was pursuing *him*."

Sara wiggled her eyebrows, and they both burst out laughing.

"That schemer." Gianessa made tiny fists and beat the air.

"And you had a great time, didn't you?"

"I did. He's a fun date."

"Are you going to get jealous if he starts dating the other women he met at the party tonight?"

"What?" She stood up and planted her hands on her hips. "Is that why he did this? To meet other women?"

"Don't get crazy, Gianessa. He may have been working the room, but he only had eyes for you."

"No, he did not. He was pretty tight with Mireille and Alicia out there on the dance floor."

"You're jealous. You're crazy about this guy."

"Stop it. You're making me crazy. I'm just . . ." her voice trailed off.

"You're just miffed because he manipulated you into a date and now everyone thinks you're an item, and no other guy will dare ask you out."

"That is so not fair. You're being mean."

"Lighten up, roomie." Sara laughed. "You're out of practice, and he's smarter than you are.

Gianessa stamped her foot. "I don't like that."

"I can see that."

She turned on Sara. "And when did you get so smart about dating politics?"

"Dating politics?" Sara chortled. "You made that up."

"Well, yes, I did." She collapsed onto the slipper chair. "I had a perfectly wonderful time tonight, and now you've gone and spoiled it."

Sara rushed over and gave her roommate a hug. "I'm

sorry. I was just teasing." She sat cross-legged on the floor next to the chair.

"But you're right," Gianessa pouted. "He manipulated me into taking him as his date, and everyone saw us and assumed I'd asked him. And now every eligible woman in Tompkins Falls knows he's on the dating scene."

Sara squeezed her hand. "You know what I think he *really* intended by coming with you tonight?"

"You already said." Gianessa huffed.

"But you heard it wrong. I think he wanted everyone to believe you and he are an item. He has staked his claim on you."

"I don't like that. I'm nobody's claim."

"So what are you going to do about it?"

Patrice LeBlanc came late to the village coffee shop. She spied George in a booth in a quiet section. Good, they could talk freely there. As she approached the booth, she sized up the man he talked with. He looked remarkably like Joel Cushman, but older and somehow more powerful. No wedding band, but he had the aura of a man contented in his relationship. *Good.* She didn't want another sex scandal at Tompkins College. They were in enough trouble as it was.

Joel had blown the whistle on an unbelievable mess of exploitation, abuse, and embezzlement. She loved her alma mater and did not want to see it fail. But without someone with vision and the balls to fire the hundred or so offenders, her college was going down the tubes.

She announced herself with a crisp, "Gentlemen, don't get up. Booths are barriers to old-fashioned manners. George, thanks for finding the booth in the back with no listening devices."

George's eyes crinkled in a smile, and he returned Patrice's firm handshake. "Latte, Patrice?" he asked and, at her answering nod, headed for the coffee bar to let her talk privately with the new guy for a minute.

She slid onto the bench on George's side of the booth and extended her hand across the table. "Patrice LeBlanc," she introduced herself.

"Justin Cushman. Thank you for joining us on short notice." He pressed her hand in both of his. It was not a come-on, she knew, but acknowledgement they needed to join forces quickly to solve serious problems.

"How is Joel doing?" she asked him.

"My nephew is healing well, thank you, and hopes to be out of the hospital very soon. He's asked me to assume his place on the board indefinitely, and I take the role very seriously."

"You're from Tompkins Falls yourself, aren't you?"

He nodded. "And I fully appreciate that the loss of the college would be catastrophic for the city. I trust, as an alum, you're also interested in saving the college?"

I like a man who doesn't waste time. "How do you propose we do this?"

"What followed," Justin told Sydney later, over tuna steaks, "was a hard-hitting strategy session. George is not a power player, but he's discerning and thoughtful, a good balance for Patrice. She's fiercely loyal to the college and quick to defend. And excuse. George has a way of breaking through her denial to the truth of the matter."

Sydney folded her hands. "He's a data person and a realist. She's emotional and forceful."

"Exactly. And they're the two longest serving and most influential board members."

"Did they like your suit?" Sydney fingered the sleeve of the jacket of his new, custom tailored Italian wool suit. She gave a sexy growl of approval.

Justin grinned. “Neither of them noticed. They heard my ideas, though, and I believe we’re very close in our preferred strategy. Our session in Tompkins Falls next week with the full board should be productive.”

“And very tense,” Sydney said.

“There’s a lot riding on this, for a lot of people.”

“And you’re up for it?”

“Yes.” Justin reached for Sydney’s hand and held it with both of his. “Your support and guidance mean a great deal, you know.”

Sydney layered her free hand on his. “I’m in your corner. I may sound flippant when we talk about your college, but I want you to succeed. To be honest, Justin, I think you have a great deal to offer higher education.”

“Really?”

“Think about it. You have faculty experience, you’re a visionary leader, and you have a financial network that you can activate in a New York minute.”

Sydney took a swallow of sparkling water. “Now tell me more about your woman. I like what I’ve heard so far. I have a hunch she can be a confidante for you with this college business.”

“You’re serious?”

Sydney raised both eyebrows. “Yes, but only if you involve her.” She leaned forward. “And remember ‘involve’ does not mean ‘talk at’.” She offered a smile to soften the sting of her criticism. “Mark my words, Justin.”

Chapter 6

"To me, Justin, putting your name on some buildings is different from being the leader of a college where you'd be proud to send your kids for their degrees."

Justin opened his mouth, frowned, and closed it again. *She's right.*

He'd bent her ear long enough about upgrading the networks throughout campus and renovating the library, perhaps putting the Cushman name on the library and on a new laboratory sciences facility.

"You're right, Gianessa. That's a completely different perspective. I haven't thought of myself as a leader of this college. And that's the real need, isn't it?"

Gianessa shrugged.

Justin recognized that shrug. It was the shrug smart partners used when they had reached the truth first and were graciously giving the slower partner time to catch up. He smiled at the irony. He was usually the one giving the gracious shrug. *Sydney was right.*

"From what you've said, yes, there's a big problem at the leadership level," Gianessa said. "Good facilities are important, I don't deny that, but without leadership . . ." She shook her head, as if pretending she didn't know where to go with the thought.

"Without strong leadership the college can't move forward. I must say you're a perceptive listener. My ego and my tendency to think in dollar signs have been blinding me."

Gianessa tipped her head and answered with her Mona Lisa smile.

"Let's think out loud together. How did the college get into this mess?" He stepped to the porch doors and gazed at the choppy water of the lake on this gray afternoon.

He answered his own question. "Until now, the president has been just a fundraiser, and the provost has simply focused on faculty satisfaction, not on curriculum or standards." He pressed his forehead against the cool glass. "A college is no better than its curriculum and the quality of its faculty. At Tompkins College the curriculum is hopelessly disjointed and out of date. I think if I asked the faculty, each one of them would tell me about their favorite course, but no one would be able to tell me what the college curriculum is or what its purpose is."

Gianessa touched his arm. "So what do you *really* think needs to happen?"

Suddenly he knew. "The best possible outcome is for the faculty to rally around a new, meaningful curriculum they believe in, that we can sell to potential students and their backers—the parents that are supporting them through their four years of undergrad and the workplaces supporting their grad programs. And to the companies and businesses that will hire them." He turned to her with a confident smile.

"That's clear and exciting." Gianessa gave him one of her dimpled smiles.

His heart raced.

"It is, isn't it? And we don't have to be traditional about it. Why not let students finish in three years, take summer classes, go abroad, and continue to take classes online?"

"Brilliant, Justin. How are you going to make all that happen?"

Justin studied her face. *She's really good for me. Very different from Sydney. Together, she and Sydney are my sounding board.* "First, I need to bring a consultant in to stir the pot, make the faculty realize they have the answer."

Gianessa cocked her head. "You're serious? If they have the answer already, why involve a consultant? Does the consultant have a better answer?"

"Excellent question. I think—no, I think none of us has the complete answer at this moment in time. I think we'll find it together—the faculty, the best thinkers in the field and, to some extent, me."

"But not the consultant?"

He shook his head. "He's going to stir the pot."

She looked puzzled. "Then why do you need him? Or her. Can't it be a her?"

Justin shook his head. "He needs to be a stuffy, obnoxious, highly credentialed know-it-all. Young and ambitious."

"I don't understand."

"You'll see."

"You've got a plan?"

"I do now, thanks to you."

"Can you share it?"

"Yes. While the consultant is stirring the pot—and by that I mean proposing an absurd concept for what a college is and does—I'll get current with the best thinking and sit down with the faculty one-two-three at a time, perhaps with the provost initially to see how that goes. I'll ask questions and listen to their ideas. I'll ask what's most effective about their program, their curriculum, their teaching. It's important, don't you think, to have their strengths as part of the foundation for any innovation?"

"Of course it is. In physical therapy we don't just ask what's not working. We also assess range of motion and observe what's working well. We use the client's strengths when we define the baseline and prescribe treatment."

"Yes, I remember, when you first gave me a massage at the spa, you commented on my investment in fitness, and you encouraged me to work toward that again as part of getting well."

"Exactly." Gianessa's eyes danced with excitement. "That was a big asset for your recovery, and you didn't seem to realize it."

"I've never seen that particular smile." He moved into her space, stroked her cheek, and drew her into a powerful hug. "You're my muse, are you?"

She wriggled into a more comfortable position in his arms. "We are good together, Justin."

"In so many ways," he said with a sexy growl.

"You have vision, and look at the energy you've brought to the new therapy suite at the spa."

"The entire team has pulled together to make that happen. I think it's more than my vision and the dollars behind it. I think their dedication to Joel is motivating them most of all."

"Sometimes lately you have flashes of humility that I never expected from you."

"What do you mean?"

"I mean your awareness that you're not the only force making things happen. When I met you I wondered if you were an egomaniac, but you're not."

Her words hurt, but they had the ring of truth. "Perhaps I was then. I'd like to think I'm changing."

"Tell me about the big picture for your college. Or don't you have a vision yet?"

Justin frowned.

"Do you see it as an ivory tower? Do you expect your students to interact with the world they're going to work in and contribute to for the rest of their lives? Or something else?"

"You're right. I'm an educator, and I need to be weighing in on the fundamental nature of a college. It won't do to just have the consultant to propose something stupid. As I'm delving into what the experts say, I have to develop my own vision, and, of course, see what the faculty are thinking. And revise the vision using their input." He brought her closer, too close, and she wriggled away again. "And I hope I can talk it over with you as we progress?"

"I want that, too. I want your strategy to work. I want to know what you and your faculty choose as your vision."

Justin caressed her cheek. "You're sure you can't get out of those massages tonight and come with me to the faculty dinner? I know it's a weeknight, but . . ."

She glanced at the grandfather clock and gasped. "No, and I've got to leave for the spa right now. Another time, I'll come with you to one of your shindigs. Will you drive me please?"

She grabbed their coats while Justin found his keys.

"I'll hold you to it, and we'll have brunch tomorrow as planned? You can do it even though it's a Friday, yes?"

"Yes." She beamed at him, and his heart soared. "I have Friday and Saturday off."

"What are you doing Saturday?" he asked as they started down the stairs.

"We three chicks are going on a thrift-shop adventure."

"Tony's giving us a little time to ourselves." Phil closed the door to Joel's hospital room.

"He's a wise man sometimes," Joel said to his AA sponsor. "What's on your mind?"

"The entire drive to Rochester, Tony told me about the construction that Justin is masterminding. Something is setting off alarm bells for me. I need to talk about it to know if it's a problem or if I'm overreacting."

"Let's hear it. Tell me about the construction."

"No, I'll let Tony do that. It's your uncle I want to talk about."

Joel smiled grimly. "What's he doing that's setting off alarm bells?"

"He's dropping a bundle on this garage makeover. According to Manda, he's also got a suite indefinitely for the two of them at that ritzy boutique hotel in downtown

Rochester so they can use it anytime they visit you and don't feel up to driving all the way back to Tompkins Falls. Plus he's driving a rental BMW two-seater. He's having suits custom made in New York. And I understand he's completely stopped his life's work. How long is his money going to last?"

"One minor correction: he just returned the rental and bought a new, top-of-the-line, four-door Saab. But why are you worried about all that?"

"Because I don't want you taking responsibility for him when he goes broke. That's the kind of thing you would do, Joel."

"It is the kind of thing I would do, but it's not going to happen. He's not going to go broke."

"I also want to know if he gambles."

"No, he doesn't gamble. He's deliberate with his money."

"Ease my mind, Joel. I don't need to know the details of his finances, but the last time I saw someone spend money like that, it was a high-roller in AA who had a drug problem and a gambling problem, too. It wasn't pretty when he killed himself a few million dollars in debt. Am I overreacting?"

Joel nodded and motioned for Phil to come closer. "Get comfortable. You're making me nervous standing there wringing your hands."

Phil chucked his coat on the back of a chair and shoved it closer to Joel's bed.

Joel reached out a hand and gave his AA sponsor a proper handshake.

"You're right," Phil said. "We should have started with a handshake."

"That alone told me how upset you were about whatever was on your mind. Now I understand what and why." He waited until Phil was settled in the chair before telling him, "Justin's net worth is measured in billions. I don't know how many, but I know he's smart in how he manages it. He loves his money. He loves spending it on himself and on the people and causes he cares about. He hates gambling.

"He's making a huge shift right now, from piling up more to figuring out how to use his money to benefit other people. At least that's what I intuit from what he's said about closing his twenty-year-old venture capital business. Without the business, his current income is limited to return on investment. That annual figure, even in an off year, is way more than the income of everyone in Tompkins Falls, including me and you, put together."

Phil laughed from his belly. "I contribute heavily to that equation."

"Justin's biggest financial problem right now is when to establish residency in the U.S. and what that will mean for taxes, which is why he's squatting in my apartment at the moment."

"But he does intend to live here, you think?"

"Yes, I've come to believe that."

"What's he going to do here?"

"His first big project is this therapy suite for me at the Manse. And I understand he's doing it in a way that has potential as an accessible luxury suite for future guests. Once a strategist, always a strategist. His second big project to benefit mankind will be a holistic rehab center for those with chronic illness, to be built according to Manda's vision, possibly located on Cady's Point, but that's on hold right now because Lorraine has changed her mind about selling. And third, he might decide to pour money into Tompkins College if he believes it's a viable institution. Personally I'd rather see him exercise leadership at the college, if it turns out to be viable. But he hasn't asked me, and he probably won't ask me."

"Good. So you're not worried about him?"

"I'm plenty worried about him. I'm just not worried about his money."

Phil gave a dry laugh. “Then I’m right to hear alarm bells going off around him?’

Joel nodded. He turned his head to look at the pictures on his rolling table. A framed photo of his sister taken a few months before Christie was killed, and a snapshot of Manda.

Phil cleared his throat. “Are you going to explain that statement or keep me in suspense until something terrible happens?”

“Did I ever tell you about my sister, Christie?”

“Many times. You were very close to her and she died in that horrible crash when you were a teenager. And that triggered your drinking and drug use, I believe.”

“Yes. Justin’s brother Josh was Christie’s and my dad. Josh was driving that day, and he was drunk when the SUV went off the road.”

Phil leaned forward, resting his forearms on his knees. “You never told me that detail, Joel. Why not?”

Joel choked on the answer. “I guess it’s too much to bear, even now. I think people knew, but I never saw the papers or the news around then because I was in bad shape in the hospital for a long time. But I was in the car and I could smell the booze on him. Bridie was worried and Mom was yelling about how erratically he was driving.

“When Justin came home to bury them and to make sure I was taken care of, no one took care of Justin. He and I never talked about the accident or my dad’s drinking. Even when I was out of control with drinking and using, even when I crashed a car into a bowling alley at three in the morning, he never said, ‘Your dad was an alcoholic. You are, too, and you need help.’ I don’t think he ever accepted that Josh was an alcoholic, even though there was more than enough evidence. Denial is powerful.”

“And you think Justin is one of us, too?”

Joel nodded. “He’s been dry for quite a few years. But I’m seeing some craziness that worries me.”

Phil sat back. "Give me specifics."

"I can't explain it very well, but I think he's got some really toxic thinking that's affecting his relationships. Manda's ready to kill him half the time, but she chalks it up to his personality and says she needs to practice tolerance. You're sensing something, too, something 'off.' He's acting like a dry drunk, and you know how insane that can get."

"Any chance we can entice him into recovery?"

Joel plucked at the bed covers with his good hand. "He wants what I have, so I take every opportunity to pitch the program to him."

"You can't prevent him from hitting bottom, Joel, but we can hope it's an emotional bottom, that he doesn't start drinking again."

"I know you're right. He's got to be ready or it won't work."

"Or if he gets really bizarre, some of us could do an intervention." Phil's gaze was on Joel's nervous picking at the bed linens.

"Good thought, thank you."

Phil patted Joel's forearm, and Joel stopped fussing.

"So tell me about you, Phil. Catch me up."

They talked a few minutes more until Phil had assured Joel he was taking care of his health and getting rides to enough meetings without him. A noisy knock at the door got their attention.

Phil motioned Tony to join them.

Tony gripped Joel's good hand and grinned from ear to ear. "I hear you're coming home soon, pal."

"It's about time you found your Big Book and got back here with it," Phil's gravelly voice chided Tony. "Were you chasing nurses on the way or what?" He winked.

"As if. I've got all the woman I need."

"Wait a minute. Someone told me you and Roxanne broke up." Joel gave Tony a sly wink. "What's the story?"

"We did. Long story. Right after we broke up, I fell for my physical therapist, Sunny."

Phil grinned and continued. "You'll like her, Joel. She's a cute blond and a very nice girl. She told me she's almost finished with her doctor of physical therapy degree."

"Yeah, she was interning here when we had the accident, and I got lucky. She was assigned to my case. Thanks to her, my shoulder's almost one hundred percent now."

Joel grumbled and kicked at the covers with his good foot.

Phil and Tony looked at each other.

"Didn't hear you, pal." Tony insisted. "What's up?"

Joel admitted, "Feeling sorry for myself. I think I should be one hundred percent by now, but I'm only about twenty percent."

"Unrealistic expectations, Joel," Phil told him. "They'll take you down every time."

"Yeah, you need a meeting, pal. You need to focus on what's going good."

Tony pushed his copy of *Alcoholics Anonymous* at Phil. "Listen to your sponsor read about how it works and then we'll have a meeting about the promises of the program." He pointed a finger at Joel. "Especially the one about uselessness and self-pity disappearing."

"Wise guy."

"Tough love."

Joel nodded. "You guys and a meeting are exactly what I need."

"We'll begin with a moment of silence," Phil said, and the meeting began.

After the readings, after twenty minutes of discussion about the AA promises, Phil asked Tony to fill them in on the progress at the Manse.

Phil endured another round of construction details, while Joel pounded Tony with questions. The more Joel heard, the more he perked up.

"I've got the best friends in the world."

"You bet you do, pal."

"And I need to say something else," Phil chimed in. "I am really impressed with what Justin's doing for Joel and Manda. He's given careful thought to their lifestyle and their happiness."

"Manda is beyond excited about the new suite," Joel said. "She thinks we should live there until we build a house and start a family."

"And think about what the project is doing for me and the crew," Tony said. "These are guys that were out of work and going stir crazy."

"Justin's got his faults," Joel said, "but he's been there for me at my worst, every time." He shared a look with Phil. "I hope to return the favor very soon."

Phil took his cue. "Joel, you say that as if you're expecting a crisis?"

Joel locked eyes with his wise sponsor. "I am. Justin's not drinking, and he's doing a lot of things right, but he's carrying too much baggage."

"Is he an alcoholic?" Tony asked him.

"Maybe. It's for him to say. And he's not saying." *That's enough to plant the seed with Tony.* He wanted someone at the site who could observe Justin and talk about the principles of the AA program.

"Here's what I want to know," Tony said impatiently. "Are Justin and Gianessa an item?"

Joel's head swung toward him. The pain made him suck air through his teeth.

"Take it easy, Joel." Phil rested a hand on his arm. "Do you need a nurse?"

"No, I'm okay," he croaked. "Just can't turn my head that fast, I guess."

"What's this about, Tony? And let's remember Joel needs to lighten up, not to worry."

"Have you met Gianessa, Phil?" Tony followed the question with a suggestive whistle.

"I've seen her at a few meetings. Manda has befriended her."

"Gianessa's going to help Manda find her wedding gown."

"That chick knows how to wear clothes."

Phil chuckled. "I hope she doesn't pick something all crinoline and poufy. I'm walking Manda down the aisle, and I might have to lean on her a little. You can't lean on a hoop skirt."

"Poufy? Manda?"

"Yeah, Phil," Tony teased, "I think petticoats went out with Scarlet O'Hara."

"No they didn't. You see these magazine covers—celebrity weddings with the big princess gowns." Phil's hands pantomimed puffed sleeves and yards of skirts layered over hoops.

Tony whooped.

Joel let out a belly laugh. "It's only been a few days since laughing hurt. I thought I'd never be able to let loose again."

"See, you're getting better? They're gonna kick you outa here, pal."

"Let's hear it," Justin said with quiet authority. "What happened between last night and this morning?"

The face Gianessa turned to him was bereft. Her lips parted, as if she wanted to tell him something, but she didn't speak.

Instinctively, Justin reached out a hand to her, but something told him not to touch her just yet.

"I'm sorry," she said with a shake of her head. She flashed a smile at him. "I didn't sleep well, that's all."

"No, that's not all. I'm concerned."

"Thank you" was all she said.

"Would you rather cancel our brunch?"

The question shook her.

Justin backpedaled. “Darling, I think we both need a good meal. And god knows I need a lesson in omelets.”

She didn’t even flinch at his slip of the tongue calling her *darling*. He didn’t know why that endearment bothered her, but she’d admonished him several times in the past couple weeks. Still, he hadn’t been able to stop thinking of that word when they were together. For her not to comment when he used it was another indication that she was in pain or in crisis or something just as serious.

He lightened his voice and gave her a warm smile. “What do you say, Gianessa? We’ll stay in and make our own omelets. What do you like on yours?”

That brought a weak smile. “Lots of spinach. Avocado.”

Justin rubbed his hands together. “Let’s see what we’ve got in the refrigerator.” He bounded across the kitchen and threw open the double doors. “Eggs,” he announced and handed the carton to her.

Gianessa ferried them to the island without faltering.

Justin rummaged in the vegetable bins. “Fresh spinach, loaded with sand. This will take some washing.”

“I’ll take care of that,” Gianessa sounded more cheerful with a job to do. She took the bunch of spinach to the sink on the island.

He heard water splashing into the sink. “One perfect avocado,” he continued.

“You don’t know if it’s perfect until you cut into it,” Gianessa reminded him.

“How could I forget? Roma tomatoes?”

“Good choice.”

Glad to see her back in the role of cooking teacher, he asked, “What should I do first?”

“Peel the tomatoes, remove the seeds, and dice. Then do you remember how to open the avocado?”

“Um, I’ll be thinking while I’m dicing.”

That brought a big smile.

Justin finished the dicing as Gianessa started a third bath for the spinach. He came up behind her and touched her shoulder. “I shouldn’t have bought a bunch so loaded with sand,” he said apologetically. “Is there hope for it?”

Something in his question made her lean forward over the sink. She dropped a fistful of spinach and brought trembling hands to her face. Her shoulders shook with sobs.

Justin reached past her to turn off the faucet and drew her close. She didn’t pull away. Instead she turned and let him wrap her in his arms. He felt her hands clutch at his sweater as though she desperately needed to hang onto something.

Justin remembered what Joel had told him in the beginning, that she was recovering from devastating personal losses. He thought about his joking words just before she doubled over the sink, asking her if there was hope for the spinach. “There’s always hope,” he told her.

Gianessa cried harder at that, but her hands opened and she slid her arms around his waist.

Justin was unaccustomed to intimacy, aside from sex, but this felt like intimacy to him. It felt right to search for a way to comfort and to share a dear friend’s pain. He’d only ever done that with Joel, and theirs was a joking, manly exchange. This was, well, he didn’t have words for this.

“There’s always hope,” he said again and bent his head so his cheek rested against her hair.

She nestled her head against his shoulder with a hiccough.

When her crying subsided, he led her to the sofa and grabbed a box of tissues on the way.

“You’re very kind,” Gianessa said tearfully. “I shouldn’t have come, knowing this could happen.”

“Nonsense. Do you think you should be alone with your pain? Where’s the sense in that? What are friends for?”

She blotted her eyes with a tissue and touched his arm with her other hand. “Thank you for understanding.”

He blustered comically. “Well, I’m not entirely sure I do understand.” She didn’t explain. “Just tell me, is this something I precipitated? Or did something happen between last night and this morning?”

“Oh, good god, no, you didn’t have anything to do with this.” She shook her head and plunged ahead. “I got a phone call from an old friend last night telling me . . .” She exhaled, at a loss to continue.

“It might help to share it.”

Gianessa bit her lower lip and made a decision. “You know that I was married.”

“Yes.”

“Les was, *is*, a good man, very principled, very successful in high tech. A major geek.”

Justin guessed she needed to talk a bit before getting to the heart of the matter. “Major in what way?”

“Brilliant, worked his way up to corporate consultant and into top management in one of the research and development firms in the Bay Area. He’s highly respected, and he didn’t deserve the fallout from my addiction.” She didn’t wait for him to ask. “I was an alcoholic—am an alcoholic—and drove drunk one night with our baby girl in the car, Isabella. I had an accident. Isabella was unhurt, thank god, but traumatized. I was injured, arrested, terrified of what I’d done. It was shameful, not just to me but to Les, and it had repercussions in his job. The main thing, of course, was the damage to Isabella, and I couldn’t forgive myself for that.

“Les, of course, immediately filed for divorce and full custody, which he was granted. Unbelievable as it sounds, I was not yet done with my addiction. When I was released from the hospital, I was sent to rehab for a month, rather than jail, thank god. But I had been prescribed Oxycontin for the pain from my injuries, and I got hooked on it. After a few months my physician would no longer prescribe it, so I stole it from work.”

"Where were you working?"

"I was a physical therapist on staff at an exclusive spa and fitness club on the coast below San Francisco. I was caught and fired and had my PT license revoked in the state of California.

"I finally got clean and sober in AA and have maintained that, but it was hard to find work—any work—in the Bay Area. For a while, all I could do was go to meetings, but I needed to support myself."

"You had no alimony?"

"No. I knew some of the staff at a high-end, New-Age retreat and spa in northern California. I moved there, worked a little job at the spa and sometimes was asked to do follow-up treatment for a client. I did okay, and I worked a strong AA program. The puny income didn't matter. I was able to live with a woman friend and cook for her—the same arrangement I have with Sara. I was grateful that I had work in my field.

"That's where I met Joel, you probably know. He was there for a meeting of spa owners last fall, and he liked our set-up. We saw each other at an AA meeting the second night and realized we had a lot to talk about. When he suggested I come east and help him redesign the Spa at the Manse, I didn't know if I could leave the coast. But I already had no way of seeing Isabella, my beautiful baby girl. I had no hope of seeing her." Gianessa choked on the word "hope."

Justin stroked her back. "I'm so sorry."

"And this has turned into a long story, I'm afraid."

"Keep going."

She took a shaky breath and plunged ahead. "A friend of ours in Palo Alto agreed to let me know from time to time how Isabella was doing and to tell me if she needed anything. She has been good about sending me pictures and updates at the holidays."

While Gianessa took a deep breath, Justin interjected a question. "How long ago did you move to northern California?"

"Three years. Isabella is four now."

"And you haven't seen her in all that time?"

Gianessa shook her head. "It was a stipulation of the divorce, and I honored it."

That must be hell. No wonder she's so private and protective of her feelings. A growl in his throat alerted him to his own anger, and he made himself breathe through it. He would not burden Gianessa with that.

"And last night?" he prompted in a calm voice.

"She, my friend Tracey, called to tell me Les got married yesterday. I had no idea. But I know the woman he married. She's lovely, and she will be a good mother to Isabella." Her hand fluttered toward her eyes and then reached for a tissue.

Justin rested his arm across her shoulders.

"Tracey wanted to tell me all about the wedding. Isabella was their flower girl, and Tracey kept saying how proud I would be, how graceful and sweet she was, walking down the aisle like a princess." A sob rose in her throat. "Scattering rose petals and smiling at everyone."

When Gianessa dissolved in tears again, Justin drew her to him.

"I couldn't make her stop saying it." She choked on her words. "I wanted to hear every detail about my little girl, but it hurt so much, Justin. I've never wanted so badly to drink or drug." She ripped at the soggy tissue, balled the entire mess, and frowned at it. Her chest heaved as she drew in one cleansing breath after another.

"And did you drink or drug?"

"No. I called people, and someone took me to a late meeting in Canandaigua, and they made me eat ice cream and talk about it."

"*Brava*, Gianessa."

"Thank you. Thanks to my friends in the program." She snuffled then nodded as she let out a noisy breath.

"And I'll bet you didn't get any sleep?" He nudged a long strand of toffee hair away from her face.

"Pretty much. I'm sure I look awful this morning."

"Not up to your usual, extraordinary beauty, but, except for the red eyes, you'd still fool a lot of people."

She squeezed his arm and smiled at him with her liquid-amethyst eyes. "Thank you for being so kind, Justin. I know I'll be better with an omelet in me."

He spread his hands. "So, we'll continue, shall we, or would you prefer to go out somewhere?"

"Cooking is always good therapy," she said. "And especially today. I promise, no more waterworks."

"You can cry if you need to. The good news is that spinach has cleaned itself by now."

He was glad to hear her musical laugh.

"You're a nice man."

"Hah! I never thought I'd hear that from a woman."

Gianessa poked him in the shoulder. "I never thought I'd say it about you and mean it. You're changing."

"In ways you like?"

"It's all good." She gave him a peck on the cheek along with a dazzling smile. "One omelet lesson coming up."

Justin did all the work, with Gianessa's coaching. They ate at the table by the window where they could enjoy the lake in the morning light.

The omelets, while not restaurant-worthy, were delicious. "You snuck some seasoning into this," Gianessa challenged him. "What is it? I can't tell."

"There's some basil," he told her.

"There's more than basil."

"It's Joel's secret. He always puts some cilantro in his omelets. I thought I'd try it. Do you like it?"

She considered. "Yeah, I think I do."

Justin frowned.

"Don't you?"

"I'd like it better with just the basil. Maybe a little oregano. Maybe some mozzarella, too. Can you eat cheese?"

"I can, and I like it. Next time," she proposed.

"It's a date. Next Sunday. How are you feeling now that you've had an omelet?"

"Much better." She dimpled when she smiled this time. "Maybe you're a healer, too."

"I like seeing your dimples." Justin reached across the table and touched one dimple.

"They only come out when I'm happy." She tossed back her hair. "Can we talk health for a minute?"

Justin drew his eyebrows together, unhappy with the change of direction.

"It's important to me. I want to know how you're feeling after a few weeks of gluten-free eating, and I want to know if it's been onerous."

Justin sat back, contemplated the lake for a moment. "It's been a challenge. It's hardest when I'm rushing from one appointment to the next or eating in restaurants. I don't have much confidence I can do this consistently, out there in the real world, without putting myself in jeopardy."

"We'll work on that. Judging by the contents of your refrigerator, you're becoming a good gluten-free cook, competent for the challenge ahead."

He corrected her with a self-effacing laugh. "To be honest, I'm becoming a competent grocery shopper. But cooking is a pleasure, especially when we do it together."

"When we're not cooking together, how well do you eat?"

"Better than I would, thanks to your menus and our grocery store's prepared foods. The fact that they label everything makes it deceptively easy."

"That's a good strategy when you can't do better. I do want you to work toward fixing most of your meals. If you're eating prepared foods, you may be getting more fat and sodium than you should."

"I'll keep that in mind." He resisted reaching for Gianessa's hands. "You asked how I'm feeling. I feel good on the whole. Most of the symptoms are at bay. I'm sleeping well, getting some energy back. I can handle a mile on the treadmill, up from half a mile two weeks ago. I tried lifting weights yesterday, and it was not a total embarrassment. I know they'll open Joel's pool next week, and I'd like to make use of it when it suits you both."

"Good. I have a couple of routines for you to try in the water. Did you ever hear back about your tests?"

"I do have celiac disease, and the doctor explained why it is so serious."

"I'm sorry, but, as you know, it's treatable. It's why I am so faithful to my food plan and so committed to cooking for myself."

"Enough serious talk." He pushed back from the table.

Gianessa jumped up and gathered the dishes from the table.

He offered to help.

"Nonsense. You cooked, I'll take care of the dishes."

Justin followed her movements in the kitchen—rinsing plates, sorting mugs and silverware into the various compartments of the dishwasher, whooshing the sponge along the countertops with a happy smile on her face.

He had a flash of how it could be every morning and evening, the two of them starting the day like this, fixing an evening meal together and talking over the day. *What is happening to me?* He drummed his fingers on the table and glanced at the lake, but his gaze came back to her—that delicious, graceful body. He wanted her in his bed, not just now, this morning, but every morning.

Gianessa finished the cleanup and dried her hands on a towel. He imagined her barefoot and pregnant, her curves rounder than now, her wavy, toffee hair falling around her shoulders.

Amusement made her voice musical. “Justin, what in heaven’s name are you thinking about? You look like a little boy caught with his hand in the cookie jar.”

His face flamed. He threw back his head and laughed. “Just thinking about a half-mile stroll along the lakeshore. Is it too cold for you?”

“Don’t be silly. I have my L.L. Bean, good-to-forty-below coat with a hood and a wool hat and mittens made of Gore-Tex, whatever that is. Oh, and space-age lining. I’m not a California girl anymore.” Her smile dazzled him.

“Then let’s do it,” he declared and stood from the table. Anything to get away from the lure of the mattress. He handed her the long down coat and put on his own storm coat. Even with her nose red from crying and dark circles under her eyes and her body wrapped in layers of downy warmth, Gianessa was a stunning, sexy woman.

For god’s sake, I’m too old for her. And he had no business taking advantage of her vulnerability. Wasn’t it enough for him to get well and start his work at the college? Of course it was enough. He just needed to get a grip on his libido. *Bad image, old man.*

“Coming, Justin?”

“I vote for Skaneateles,” Manda’s voice sang out.

Sara and Gianessa traded looks.

“I think we’ve reached a decision,” Sara said.

“Without even asking the question,” Gianessa quipped.

“And Sara’s driving, right?” Manda pushed it too far.

“Now wait a minute, Little Miss Bossy.”

Gianessa challenged them. “Manda, did I hear you say you’d treat the driver to lunch?” She opened her hands to signal a brilliant compromise.

Manda and Sara nodded at each other.

“Cool,” Sara said with a satisfied smile.

"I'm glad you could come," Manda said grudgingly to Gianessa as she trudged to Sara's passenger door.

Sara gave Gianessa a quick hug. "Thanks for handling that. Do you mind sitting in back? I know it's a little cramped."

Gianessa shook her head. "I'm small."

After they buckled up and got underway, Manda wanted to know, "When are you going to get a car, Gianessa?"

"I was actually going to ask your advice about that, Manda. I know you're the queen of budgets."

"Says who?"

"Your almost Uncle Justin. He thinks you walk on water."

Manda eyed her suspiciously.

"I think I should save a lot before I spend a lot on a car, right?"

"Well, you should have an emergency fund."

"And how much would that be?"

"Equal to three or even six months living expenses—groceries, rent, all the things you have to spend on every month."

Gianessa felt her eyes grow wide. She exhaled a laugh. "So maybe I'll get a car in a couple of years."

"No, listen, when you're working fulltime as Joel's therapist, you could do something like . . . make a car payment every month and save the same amount toward your emergency fund. It doesn't have to be either-or."

"I can see that. You're a good teacher, Manda. Do you mind if I ask you money questions?"

Manda shrugged. "I guess, if it would really help."

"It would really help, thank you. I was married and taken care of for a bunch of years, and then I was broke for three years, so I have no money skills. It's a little scary, and I don't want to be foolish."

Sara chimed in, "I keep telling Gianessa she should marry Justin."

"Oh please, don't start. I'm trying to focus on my career right now."

Manda twisted around and looked Gianessa in the eye. "If you can deal with his personality, he's a good catch. It took me a while, but I really like him, and basically he's a good guy."

Gianessa was stunned. "Justin doesn't want to be caught."

"I wouldn't be so sure."

"Don't you think he's just going back to Europe or wherever in a few months, after your wedding?"

"I really think he's going to stay in Tompkins Falls. I know Joel's hoping for that."

Gianessa watched the scenery roll by. Joel had warned her away from Justin for a reason, but she wasn't sure what was behind that. One thing she knew for sure. She could handle Manda well enough to take her shopping for a wedding gown. That was one less stressor for Joel. She'd firm up a shopping date with Manda today for the coming week. *For now, enjoy the journey.*

When they arrived in the lakeside village of Skaneateles, Gianessa fell in love. "This is gorgeous. The gazebo, the park, the lake, all the shops and pretty houses. Good call, Manda."

Sara drove in behind a building across from the park and tucked her little car into a tight spot. "Isn't it pretty here? We always have lunch on the porch at this inn." She led the way up brick steps to a lakeside inn that dated from stagecoach days. "And I'm starved."

For the next half-hour, Gianessa's eyes were riveted on the lake. Beyond an ice-covered area close to shore, the water was navy blue, dotted with whitecaps. In the park between the inn and the lakeshore, families played in the snow, walked their dogs, and stopped to chat with each other, apparently oblivious of the biting wind. No one had a down coat as long as hers. How could they stand it? Were they used to it? Would she grow used to it?

She listened with half an ear to Manda and Sara as they caught up on their lives. Sara was starved for girl talk, and

Manda was stressed about starting classes in a few weeks. Maybe she had something to offer each of them. She could trade girl talk with Sara each evening. Being in Sara's confidence might give her better protection from the Manse rumor mill. And she could work on Manda's stress as they shopped for her gown. A few hints here and there might help shift her self-centeredness and take some pressure off Joel.

After they ate, Manda's mood brightened, and Sara was more relaxed, too.

"Ladies, a good lunch goes a long way, doesn't it?" Gianessa declared as they sauntered along the main street.

"Yes, Mom," Sara teased.

"Maybe it's just me," Gianessa said, "but I get cranky when I'm hungry and I get hungry too fast when I don't have protein at every meal."

"What are you and Justin cooking up in Joel's old kitchen?" Manda asked with a sly smile.

"Gluten-free meals. We're both gluten intolerant, and he's learning what that means and how to live with it."

"Is that why he was so sick when he got here?"

Gianessa nodded. And that was all the information she was going to give about Justin's health.

"He looks a million times better," Manda stated.

Gianessa blushed, pleased at the compliment. "Where's the thrift shop?"

"Next block." Sara pressed her palms together in a prayer. "I hope it's not an off day for us."

"Three pairs of eyes will find the gems."

"What are you hoping to find, Gianessa?" Manda asked, her tone easy-going.

"Today, for me, the joy is in the journey." Gianessa gave her a megawatt smile. "I'm so glad to be doing a chick thing with you two."

Manda beamed. "Me, too."

And it wasn't an off day at all.

Manda turned up a blue and white striped T-shirt for three dollars.

"Cute," Sara and Gianessa chorused.

Gianessa found almost-new skinny jeans—dark indigo—that fit with no room to spare. "Five bucks." She opened her arms.

"Sexy." Sara made her voice low and sultry.

"Hot." Manda shook her hand.

Sara hit the jackpot. An above-the-knee, fuchsia, cowl-neck dress showed off her slender legs, hugged her hips, and flattered her diminutive chest. "Twelve-fifty. Do I dare?"

"You will score in that dress, roomie. Trust me on this."

"I trust you. I'm doing it. If this doesn't get Randy hot, I'm going to give up and find someone else."

"Who's Randy?" Gianessa asked.

Manda explained, "Reliable Randy has been Sara's boyfriend for two years. He'll be back from winter break next week and you'll finally meet him."

"Why do you call him reliable?"

Sara rolled her eyes. "He's always on time, always picks up the check, always asks what movie I want to see, always gives me a little kiss good night, always calls the next day to see if I had a good time."

"Reliable sounds good," Gianessa said.

"Yeah, I just wish he was a little more, you know, randy." Sara's face flamed, and she giggled.

"So, wear this dress on your next date. And don't let me cramp your style. I can be invisible, and I have noise-canceling headphones."

"Good to know. I'll work on that."

Chapter 7

"Nothing." Manda threw herself onto the chair. "How many shops did we hit? And after everything we saw and all the dresses I tried on, how could we end up with nothing?" She shrugged out of her jacket and let it fall behind her on the chair.

Gianessa fitted her good-to-forty-below coat over the back of the chair and slid gracefully onto the seat. "I only know one thing."

"What?"

"I know it's not possible to tuck a full-length down coat under one arm. I was roasting half the time wearing this."

"Hah. You rookie. That's why I wore a jacket."

"So good of you to warn me." Gianessa reminded herself she was doing this because Joel—her savior—had charged her with shepherding Manda to the perfect wedding gown. She rallied a smile. "Okay, let's review. You don't want flounces or chiffon or puffy sleeves."

"I must be an alien. How could I not like a single dress I saw today?"

"Turn it around. When you picture yourself processing down the aisle toward Joel, what are you wearing? How do you look?"

Manda closed her eyes, and Gianessa saw a smile bloom on her cover-girl-perfect face. "I'm beautiful. I have flowers in my hair. My dress is elegant silk—something long and sleek—that swirls around my ankles, with maybe some beads or sparkles at the top and the bottom." Manda opened her eyes. "That's how I want to be for my wedding to Joel."

"Gorgeous! It's perfect for you." Gianessa pressed her hand. "Big sigh, Manda. 'Sleek and elegant' is not in this year in Rochester."

"Justin wants us to go to New York City. He says he'll set it up and have someone cut through the fluff."

"Justin? What's his interest?"

"He's buying my gown. It's his wedding gift to me."

"How generous of him." That was another side of Justin Gianessa had never guessed. Maybe he was just making sure Manda wore a gown fitting for a Cushman wedding, but Gianessa sensed it was something different, something more personal.

"I thought you knew that."

Gianessa's laugh lightened both of their moods. "You thought I knew not to wear this monster coat. What else do you know that could make our lives easier?"

"I know the espresso drinks in this place are to die for. And every single salad is great. What would you like?"

"You're buying?"

"Of course."

Gianessa scanned the choices on the blackboard and gave her pick to Manda. "My tummy thanks you." Before Manda could dash off to place their orders, she pointed to Manda's iPad. "May I? I'd like to find something sleek and elegant in New York."

"Why didn't I think of that?"

"Because you're hungry. So am I. Order already." Gianessa poked the on button, typed in the password for the coffee shop network, and brought up pages for the major designers whose names she knew. She had eliminated four designers by the time Manda returned.

"Fifteen minutes for the salads, and he'll bring our drinks right over."

Manda scraped her chair close to Gianessa's, and they

bent their heads over the screen. "That one." She pointed. "You're a genius. That's better than anything we saw today."

"It's a mere fifteen thousand, twenty with beading on the bodice, thirty with beading and sparkles top and bottom."

"You're joking."

Gianessa chuckled. "I'm guessing." She stretched her arms overhead and wiggled her back to work out the kinks. "They don't publish their prices. But it's a high-end designer and hand-sewn beading. I'm probably close."

"Justin has more money than god."

"He'll say we're contributing to the economy, right?" That was what Les had always said when they spent an outrageous amount on something they didn't need.

Manda giggled. "I've never done anything like this. This is fun." She hugged the iPad to her as the barista approached.

Gianessa accepted her peppermint hot chocolate, and he set down Manda's snowman latte. Mint and vanilla and chocolate permeated the air.

"Enjoy, ladies. Salads are in the works."

Gianessa gave him a big smile of thanks.

"Have you ever been to New York?" Manda asked in a scared voice.

"Yes, have you?"

"No. It's scary to think about going alone. You'll go with me, right, if we don't find anything around here?"

"I'm very sure we're not going to find your gown around here. And I'll go with you to New York, but only if Justin comes, too."

"Why?" She gave Gianessa a sly look.

"He's writing the check for your gown. And by rights it should meet his approval. Plus, we don't want to pay for the hotel by ourselves. And he'll know where to go, who to ask, where to have dinner, and how to get tickets to a show if we want to do that."

"Show?"

"Broadway play. Or a concert."

"I've never traveled anywhere."

"So you haven't flown?"

"On a plane? No. That scares me a little, too."

"It's definitely time for you to go to New York. You and Justin and I. We'll let Justin make all the arrangements."

They bookmarked the first perfect gown and browsed a few more websites. In ten minutes they had four possibles and three perfects.

Manda let out a sigh, and her whole body relaxed.

"New York will be fun," Gianessa said. And Les had brought her amethyst necklace back from a business trip to New York. *Justin will know where I can sell it.* Maybe she could get enough for a little used car. *I'll bet Tony could advise me about the car.* "Yes, we'll go right away—next week—plan a couple of days for shopping, see a show, and act like tourists for a day. Sound good?"

Silence.

Gianessa studied Manda's face. She appeared paralyzed by fear, just as she had been last week on her first visit to Joel's therapy suite. Maybe Gianessa was guilty of the same mistake Tony and Justin had made, not letting Manda have a say in the planning.

"It's important that we do the things you want to do, Manda. Have you thought about what you'd like to see and do in New York?"

"I'd like to go to Ellis Island, but not in the dead of winter. Maybe Joel and I can do that sometime."

"Two salads at the bar for Mandy."

Manda glared at the barista.

He consulted the order. "I mean Manda." He gestured at the two salads and shrugged an apology.

Manda claimed them, and Gianessa tucked the iPad back into Manda's tote bag.

As they finished their salads, Gianessa asked brightly, "So where are you and Joel going for your honeymoon?"

Manda's gaze turned dreamy. "Ireland. We both want to go to Ireland. Did you know Joel's grandmother was from Ireland, and my ancestors were, too? Do you think Joel will be able to travel by June?"

Gianessa squeezed her arm. "We'll make sure Joel is well enough by June to stand with you at the altar and maybe do a slow dance at the reception. Ireland is a stretch, even with a wheelchair, but certainly within the year you'll be able to do that together."

"I have to remember it doesn't matter if things can't happen all at once."

"That is great advice. I have to remember it, too."

"You mean, with your romance with Justin?" She looked sideways at Gianessa.

"I do not have a romance with Justin." Gianessa enunciated clearly. "I was thinking about my career when you said that. I want everything to fall in place—and honestly I think it is falling in place—but it's going to happen slowly. I just need to cooperate with the pace the universe has in mind."

"But you like Justin, right?"

Okay, what will satisfy her? "I enjoy cooking with Justin, and he's been a really good support for me as I adjust to life in Tompkins Falls. And did you know he likes jazz?"

"How did you find that out?"

"When we cook, we also eat the meals we prepare, and it's customary to have music with a nice dinner. It turns out we're both jazz fans."

"So maybe you and Justin should go to a jazz club in New York one night."

"Maybe we should all go together."

"Or I could come back early, and you and Justin could explore New York together."

Give it up, Manda. "Justin and I are friends, nothing more."

"But good friends, right?"

Gianessa had to admit that was true, and she hadn't expected it to be. She nodded without commenting. *I've acquired a taste for Justin.*

She liked what she was learning about him—things he didn't flaunt. Like buying Manda's gown when Manda's strict budget would not pay for the dress of her dreams. And his photography. One afternoon she'd noticed an older digital camera connected to his laptop, and the latest shots were on the screen. They were artful, skillful—shots taken from his porch looking out at the lake in unusual lighting, sometimes focusing on an island, sometimes a cloud formation, sometimes a moody or misty scene.

There was a side to him that sought beauty and enjoyed it. She smiled at a sudden intuition. Justin was feeding his soul, working on that soulsickness he'd spoken of at their first meal together. She might ask him about that. *Or not.* It was something he was keeping private, and she respected that.

Manda had taken out the iPad again.

Gianessa brought them back to her point about New York. "If you're scared to fly, this trip to New York will get you over that."

"I just thought of something. If Joel and I are going to Ireland, I should get a passport, too, right?"

"Good thinking, Manda. And you'll need extra ID to get on our flight to New York." She pointed to the iPad. "Let's check the details. And, listen, since we're not going to find a wedding dress today, let's stop at Eastview on the way home and shop for lingerie for your honeymoon."

Manda groaned.

"You're not worried about . . ."

"Sex? Hell, no. I just never thought about wearing slinky and silky and peek-a-boo. Can you help me find some things Joel will like that don't look trampy?"

"I'll be delighted. What are you thinking you'd like to wear for Joel?"

"Well what I really like," Manda told her, keeping her voice so low Gianessa had to lean closer to hear her, "are boy shorts and skinny tank tops made of cotton and cashmere. They make me feel sexy and 'me,' but maybe they're not hot enough for a honeymoon. What do you think?"

Gianessa flashed a sexy smile. "On you, with your curvy figure and long legs, they are plenty hot, Manda."

She'd distracted Manda, but now she couldn't stop thinking about Justin. She thought back to the conversation with Carol, who urged her to be open to a relationship. Sometimes taking the next baby step helped her know if a new direction was right for her. It had been two years since she'd slept with anyone. After the divorce, in early sobriety, she'd had a couple of flings, but the sex was empty. She wanted sex to be linked with intimacy and deep caring about a man. *And Justin and I do care about each other.*

Flawed as they both were, they were good together in everything they did—cooking, talking things over, laughing, dancing. And he stirred her passion. Her face flamed at the memory of him naked under the thin sheet in the tiny massage room, and she could almost smell his scent, just thinking about it. Cloves and sandalwood and—*what was that other ingredient?*

The night of the party, when he asked her if she wanted to take their relationship to the next level, she'd held him off. Was she ready now for sex with Justin? Her eyes softened, a smile spread over her face and she nodded.

But not without silky, lacy lingerie.

"Before I come in," Gianessa said from the doorway, "I need you to catch me up here. Is this a date?"

Justin dropped his keys on the hall table and turned to face her. She smiled, but she did not budge. The door was open for everyone to hear their discussion.

He struggled to keep a straight face. "Yes, this is a date."

She tossed back her hair.

His laugh brought a matching laugh from her. She kicked the door closed behind her, hung her coat on the coat tree by the door and joined him in the kitchen.

"Why did you ask if we're dating?"

"Because according to the rumor mill at the Manse—and who knows where else—we were on a date when we went to the party at the Manse."

"Of course we were."

"I see. And today, when we were seen shopping at Wegmans together"—she lifted her shopping bag full of produce onto the counter—"did your friends from the college perceive us as being on a date?"

Justin raised his eyebrows. "I carefully considered the ramifications of our public appearance. Grocery shopping together is serious. We were undoubtedly talked about as An Item. Do you object?"

She tipped her head. "I just want to be clued in about these things."

Justin set his two bags on the counter with a rattle and a thump. "In my mind all our cooking dates have been dates. What did you think they were?"

"Cooking lessons."

Justin's brow furrowed. "But I'm already an accomplished cook. Didn't we establish that the very first time?"

"We established that, you're correct. And I'm clueless about dating, okay? I got married in college, and I don't have much experience dating." Gianessa folded her arms across her chest and set her mouth, as if she dared him to make fun of that.

He teased her with his eyes. "And we've now established that you and I are dating?"

Gianessa gave a single, firm nod.

"Publicly. And that's okay with you?"

She winked. "I'm good with that." With a swivel of her hip, Gianessa sashayed around him and poked her nose in the first of Justin's shopping bags. "What have you got in here? Cod"—she read the labels—"halibut and tilapia."

She investigated the other bag. "A sack of mussels and some cooked crab."

"Look good?"

Gianessa flashed a smile. "I think you've done this before."

"That's why the recipe is so colorful." Justin pointed a finger to his bouillabaisse recipe taped to the front of an upper cabinet.

"I see smudges of tomato, saffron, and—what's that, wine or lipstick?"

He peered at the stain. "Blood. I remember nicking myself with a knife once, bearding the mussels. Read me the spices and I'll set them out on the counter for us."

Gianessa read off the spices as she removed leeks, tomatoes, fennel, celery, and onions from her bag. She sniffed the air. "You've already started the *rouille*."

Justin put his hands on her slender shoulders and she leaned back into his chest. Her scent filtered through the smells of the ingredients. "I have, yes. I'd like to take the lead, for a change, since this is my very favorite weekend dish. I believe it's gluten free as long as we don't add a hunk of bread at the end."

Gianessa read carefully through the list of ingredients and the instructions as he took up his position at the soup kettle. "Gluten free, yes, and I'm glad you're taking the lead, because it's complicated."

"Does that mean I can boss you?" Justin wiggled his eyebrows at her.

"Not if you're bossy." She carried a few vegetables to

the sink on the island. "Am I preparing the leeks and onions and celery, boss?"

"Now this will be interesting."

"What?"

"Watching you pretend to give up control to me."

Gianessa laughed.

After the vegetables had been sautéed and the spices and herbs imparted their flavor, Justin added the cut-up fish fillets and some water to the big copper pot. He held the lid off to the side, and they peered in, contemplating the mix of ingredients.

"This is one thing I enjoy about cooking," Justin said.

"What?"

"That every ingredient plays a part, but they all give up their individuality to make the dish what it is—something new and unique and bursting with flavor."

"Sometimes, Justin Cushman, you blow me away. Who knew you were a contemplative at heart?"

Justin smiled, set down the spoon, and let the lid rest on the pot with a little crack for the aroma to drift out to the kitchen. "We'll let this simmer and get the table ready for our feast."

They set the table together and spent a few minutes enjoying their birds-eye view of the whitecaps on the lake until the aroma of the soup called them back to the stove.

"Time for the crustaceans." Justin added the crab and mussels.

Gianessa leaned a hip into the counter. "Who were the women you made bouillabaisse with before today?"

"Suppose I won't tell you?"

"I'll always wonder."

"The truth is I've made bouillabaisse many times, and shared it with friends but never actually shared the cooking with anyone." Justin watched her face. "You seem a little disappointed."

"Sad, not disappointed. You enjoy cooking so much, and you're so much fun to cook with, I'm sad that the other times were solo. I hope the eating was great fun, shared with excellent friends."

"Yes, it was, without exception."

"Do you prefer making this recipe solo?"

He shook his head. "Not at all. Are you still jealous?"

Gianessa dimpled when she smiled and shook her head. "I know there were many women in your past, and I trust you to tell me whatever is relevant if it becomes relevant."

"Such as?"

"I can't imagine."

"Well, I'm very jealous, and it's time I said something."

Her forehead creased with puzzlement. "Why are you jealous?"

"You're wearing the necklace."

Her hand flew to the double strand of hearts around her neck. "Yes, I've been wanting to talk to you about it, and we always get so caught up in whatever we're doing I forget. I'm wearing it today so I won't forget to ask you. So thank you." She squinted. "Why does my necklace make you jealous?"

Justin turned back to the fragrant pot on the stove and took out one mussel that refused to open for them.

"Tell me the story of the necklace."

Gianessa gathered her thoughts. "Les, my husband—"

"Your ex-husband?"

"Of course." She seemed even more puzzled.

He let it go.

"Les gave it to me just after our daughter Isabella was born. He said the side-by-side hearts were symbolic of his love for his two women—the Bennett Girls, he called us—wife and daughter. I think he had the artist add the amethyst in the center because my eyes have violet in them."

"And are you in need of money? Is that why you're thinking of selling?"

Gianessa blinked a few times, but her face was calm, no sign that she'd taken offense at the question. "I am making enough now to support myself, but I would like to have a cushion. Manda calls it an emergency fund. And I want a little car. But mostly, I don't want or need the necklace. And when the trip to New York City came up, I hoped it would be possible to sell it there. I think that's where Les bought it. I hope you don't mind my asking you for advice about finding a buyer."

Are you kidding? "Not at all." He added the final few ingredients to the pot.

"What bowls would you like to use?"

"Third cabinet, middle shelf. Those dark ones."

Gianessa put two of the bowls next to the stove and poured tall glasses of water for them. While he stirred the pot, she extracted a ladle from the jar of utensils. "Do you need this?"

"Thank you." He reached for it without taking his eyes from the bouillabaisse.

"What are you contemplating?"

"Come look." He traded places with her. "It's splendid, isn't it? The mussels are open to the rich broth. The fish pieces are swimming around with the chunks of tomato. It's a fascinating pot, don't you think?"

"It is." She inhaled. "And fragrant."

"Please take off the necklace."

She met his gaze. "It bothers you?"

He nodded. "I promise we'll talk over dinner about how and where to sell it. Please take it off now."

Gianessa fumbled with the clasp and finally succeeded in opening it. She slid the heavy piece off her neck and dropped it carelessly onto the counter.

Justin studied her as she turned back to the pot of swimming seafood. Her eyes never strayed to the necklace.

She watched the bouillabaisse cook for a while, inhaled again the intense fragrance and gave him a smile.

"Think it's soup yet?"

Manda stepped onto the pedestal to view the gown in multiple mirrors. It was the fifth gown at the second bridal shop, but it was the first one Gianessa considered a possibility.

"Shoulders back, head high," Penelope, the saleswoman, reminded her for the fifth time.

Manda watched Penelope, who demonstrated. Manda imitated her.

"It's lovely," Gianessa said.

Manda's smile was tentative. Gianessa saw her steal a look at Justin. He sat across the room with one eye on the *Wall Street Journal*.

"What do you think, Manda?" Gianessa pushed her to voice her opinion.

"I really like the top, and I like how it skims my body. I like how swirly it feels." She swiveled in place, and the fabric floated by her legs. "But I don't like these layers." Her fingers teased the translucent silk layers that flowed downward from the waist.

They heard the newspaper rattle. Justin studied Manda in the champagne silk gown with the filmy layers.

Gianessa hoped he wouldn't insist on this one. It was too ethereal for Manda and the wrong color.

Justin voted. "Not her best color, but I like the sleek lines."

"Good, we're getting closer," Penelope said with a perky smile. She signaled her assistant and made a number with her fingers. Ten plus one.

Were they were skipping over six others? Gianessa wondered how anyone had the patience and tact to do Penelope's job.

Justin went back to his newspaper, and Manda climbed off the pedestal.

While Manda changed into gown number eleven, Gianessa helped herself to another cup of herbal tea.

Justin joined her at the refreshment table. "I agree with Penelope that we're starting to find Manda's style."

Gianessa touched his arm. "Manda is the first to tell you she has no confidence about clothes, but I'm seeing a change in her as we do this. She really wants to find the perfect gown for her wedding to Joel, and it's a learning process for her."

"She's not a princess, is she?" he observed.

"Not even close."

"I hoped one day I'd be helping my niece Christie find the perfect gown. Christie was a princess." He chuckled, but his eyes were moist.

Gianessa remembered the story of the fiery accident that took Christie's life as a young teen. *So that's why he's giving Manda the gown of her dreams*. She touched his arm and smiled. "Are you disappointed that Manda isn't a princess?"

"Not at all. And I'm sure Joel wouldn't want to marry one."

"He was engaged once," Gianessa mused and tried to remember.

"To the wealthy and beautiful Lorraine. The woman everyone expected him to marry."

"Was she a princess?"

"Ah, no, Lorraine was a queen." He poured tea for himself.

"Sounds all wrong for Joel."

"Indeed. We had a fierce fight about it. I flew back to London, sure he was going to go through with the biggest mistake of his life."

"What changed his mind?"

"I don't know. I think Lorraine was pressuring him to have children, and he wasn't sure he wanted any. The next thing I knew, Lorraine was married to a handsome professor. They had two or three children right away, and then divorced. She and the children are ensconced in a country estate outside of London."

"If I can read between the lines, you're still in contact with her?"

Justin gave her a startled glance. "How discerning of you. I'll tell you the story sometime."

Penelope came to join them, shaking her head. "I was sure eleven was the one. Mandy stuck up her nose and wouldn't even consider coming out to show you."

Gianessa said pointedly, "Perhaps if you call her Manda, you'll get more cooperation."

Penelope's face flamed. "You're right. I apologize." She hurried away.

Justin touched Gianessa's hand. "You did that so graciously. I was about to snap her head off."

"I can't imagine doing her job." She gave Justin her full attention. "Tell me the story of your connection to Lorraine."

Justin drew himself up, as if debating how much to tell her. "You know Manda and I want to build a holistic rehabilitation center on Cady's Point on Chestnut Lake."

"Yes, Joel and Manda have both urged me to be part of that."

"I think you should be the brains of it, personally, but that's a discussion for another setting."

Evidently Joel had planted the seed, just as he'd promised. Gianessa coughed to cover a shout of excitement.

"What's pertinent here," Justin said, "is that Lorraine owns Cady's Point. When Joel approached her about selling it to him, he let slip that he and Manda are marrying. That killed any chance of Joel purchasing Cady's Point."

Gianessa gave him a slow smile. "So you're approaching her as an interested buyer?"

"How discerning of you. Again." His tone was inexplicably angry this time. "If you breathe a word of this to Joel or Manda, I will cut you out of the deal."

He might as well have hit her in the face. Gianessa stumbled backward two steps. "You play too rough sometimes, Justin Cushman," she said, her voice hard when she rebuked him.

Justin studied her face, and Gianessa let him see her flashing eyes. "I don't deserve suspicion and harsh words." To her surprise, Justin looked shocked himself at his own behavior.

"Manda would like you to see this gown." Penelope interrupted the exchange.

While Gianessa was glad that Manda had regained her composure, she had totally lost her own. Her face still flamed, as if she'd been slapped on both cheeks. She gave the saleswoman a bright, false smile and moved back to her chair.

Justin came close behind her and hovered. Her shoulders stiffened.

Manda glided out of the dressing area as though she were walking down the aisle to Joel. Her smile was radiant, her shoulders back, her head high.

Penelope offered a steadying hand as Manda stepped onto the pedestal and admired herself in one mirror after another.

Gianessa caught her breath. *This is the one*. The single-shoulder style sparkled with beads that cascaded across Manda's breasts. The cascading beads repeated from the top of the knee-high slit all the way to the hemline and around the dress. Manda did a little twist and watched the beads sparkle and the silk swirl at her ankles.

"*Bella*," Gianessa said with a little clap of her hands.

Manda's eyes connected with Justin's in the mirror. His face glowed with affection for this young woman, and his eyes were bright with tears that tugged at Gianessa's heart.

Justin nodded, and Manda's smile brightened.

"I think Joel will like it, too," Manda said tentatively.

"Indeed he will." Justin's laugh was pure joy.

"You're going all British on me, Justin." Manda teased him about the sudden appearance of his accent.

Gianessa felt Justin's hands on her shoulders.

"You make me very proud, Manda." He bent his head, his lips close to Gianessa's ear. "She would never have come without your intervention. I owe you for this."

Gianessa shook her head, too flustered to reply, still smarting from his harsh words. She left her chair and circled around the pedestal away from him.

Penelope fussed with the hem and the waist of Manda's gown. "We'll do a proper fitting in the morning, shall we?"

"I think it's perfect," Manda complained.

Penelope gave the bride a practiced smile. "And it will be. Just a few tucks along the waist and a little shorter in back so you don't trip during that first waltz with your husband. It won't take but an hour when you're fresh in the morning. And perhaps your friend will find a dress she likes for the ceremony." She gave Gianessa an engaging smile.

"Oh no," Gianessa said in protest. "I'm just—"

Justin jumped on it. "You're an honored guest, and I insist on finding a dress that's suitable for the occasion."

As if I can't find a dress myself that's 'suitable for the occasion.'

Penelope pressed the issue. "We have one that is nearly a match for your eyes. What can it hurt to try it on?"

"Please, Gianessa," Manda implored.

Gianessa said firmly, "Tomorrow maybe. Not today."

"Let's relax now," Justin said, his good humor restored. "Radio City Music Hall, followed by the best steak in the city with a crisp salad. We'll pop back here tomorrow morning and then do whatever you both want for the afternoon."

Justin directed the driver to Radio City and, when they arrived, pointed to the box office. He told the two women,

"Your tickets are in Manda's name. Reservations are set for our dinner. The car will pick you up in front of the box office after the show and take you to Gallagher's, where I'll meet you."

While Manda madly texted Sara, Gianessa asked the obvious question. "Where are you going, Justin?"

"College business."

He could see from Gianessa's raised eyebrows that she didn't buy it.

"Syd is an old friend and president of a college not unlike Tompkins. We've been talking for a month, and she wants me to meet a possible consultant."

"How good of her," Gianessa remarked with emphasis on "her."

Discerning and pissed. Justin said as professionally as he could, "I rely on her expertise and her support, just as I appreciate your support every time we talk about college affairs."

Manda chimed in, "We'll be checking you for perfume, Justin."

He hadn't thought she was listening.

"Let's go, Manda," Gianessa said snappishly. "The show won't wait, and Justin has business to take care of."

"We'll talk later," Justin said, but the noise of the street drowned his words.

Sydney Shorey watched Justin enter the bar and scan the crowd for her. She'd chosen one of the cocktail tables for four with a bench under the mirrors and two chairs facing the mirrors. She wondered if Justin would choose a chair or cozy up beside her on the bench.

What's he perturbed about? That scowl had nothing to do with the little niece he'd been shopping with this afternoon. She would bet the man had woman troubles. *How delicious.*

Justin spotted her.

Sydney gave a come-hither smile and leaned forward to show a little cleavage for his viewing pleasure.

He winked. "Devastating."

She gave him a sultry laugh.

"You have no right to look so sexy at this hour of the day. At least not in public."

"You hush." Sydney raised her cheek for his kiss.

Chatter swirled around them, glasses clinked, and laughter rose from a table across the room.

"What's got you all hot and bothered, my sweet?"

Justin draped his coat over one of the chairs and joined Sydney on the bench. "Shopping for wedding gowns," he said with a weary sigh.

"Ah, the young lady marrying your nephew. Did she find the perfect gown?"

"She did, and it's stunning. You'd approve."

"Don't tell me you sent her back to the hotel? You could have brought her."

"Nonsense, she and Gianessa are at Radio City. I'm meeting them in a couple of hours for dinner."

"Gianessa? Would this be your young and beautiful confidante? She's got you in a tizzy, doesn't she?"

Ignoring the question, he rubbed his hands in anticipation. "Tell me about the consultants you have in mind. Did you bring one?" He craned his neck.

"You know perfectly well I didn't. I'll discuss their credentials with you in a minute. Right now, you need to tell me about Gianessa, whom I already know is not the maid-of-honor or the bride's little friend. Spill, Justin."

"Don't torment me." Justin signaled for the waiter.

"Oh, is Gianessa tormenting you?"

"Yes, sir, what can I bring you and the lady?"

"I'll have . . . Good lord, I almost ordered a vodka martini."

"I'll take one of those," Sydney said.

"Yes, a vodka martini for the lady, and I'll have a *doppio con panna*." Justin dropped a twenty-dollar bill onto the table. "Make that decaf. Good man."

The waiter slipped the twenty off the table and hurried away.

"I haven't heard that British accent in a long time, Justin. And I thought you'd stopped drinking vodka years ago."

"I did," he snapped.

"Calm down, Justin. What's this about?"

He huffed and did not give her an answer this time.

"You've fallen hard for Gianessa, haven't you?"

"I have, and I don't like the way I just treated her."

Sydney studied her old friend carefully. Deep worry lines told her he was unhinged about whatever had happened. She dropped the flirtatious tone. "What did you do?"

"I spoke to her so harshly, you'd have thought I hit her in the face. I don't know what got into me. I don't know if I can make it right."

Sydney half turned to him, braced one shoulder against the wainscoting and raised both eyebrows at him. "Well, I can tell you right now you'd better make it right. You're in love with this woman. I've never seen anyone get under your skin like this. And, by the way, who exactly does she think I am?"

"I told her who you are, and I don't think she believed me."

"She's in love with you," Sydney said.

Justin huffed.

"Mark my words, Justin."

"That's preposterous."

Sydney saw his mouth struggling against a smile.

"And she's young and beautiful, am I right?"

Justin nodded.

"How young?"

"Not quite thirty. She married a Bay Area techie and lost custody of their child in a wretched divorce."

"Good god, what had she done to deserve that?" Sydney

gave her toothpick a half turn and studied the changing face of her vodka-coated olive.

"Drug addiction and a drunk-driving conviction. Husband cut her out of their lives. She's been clean and sober a few years and is doing well."

Their drinks arrived. Sydney put her uneaten olive in her half-empty glass and nodded for the waiter to take it away. Justin hunkered at the table and contemplated the whip on his espresso.

Sydney nudged the side of his foot with hers. "And what set you off that you punched her in the face?"

"I didn't punch her," Justin said, his teeth clenched.

"Lighten up, Justin," Sydney cajoled him. "I meant that as a figure of speech."

"Sorry. You're right, Syd."

Sydney chuckled. "I declare, I've never heard you say that." She picked up her new olive and twirled it so the droplets of vodka spun off. "Say it again, Justin."

Justin laughed.

"There, the tension just flew right out of you."

Justin shook his head and chuckled. He turned to face her.

"It's silly. I made a big deal out of something."

"What exactly?"

"I'm trying to buy a beautiful piece of land for my nephew and his bride, ostensibly as a wedding gift. We mean to develop a holistic clinical retreat for boomers and others, and it's proving to be . . ." He sighed.

Sydney waited a beat and then circled her hand to urge him to continue.

"The landowner was Joel's fiancée at one time, and she's apparently caught wind of the coming nuptials. She's making the purchase impossible, asking millions more than its market value."

"Why not just walk away?"

Justin scowled.

"I mean it. Make her come to you with a reasonable offer. She can't have other prospects."

"You may be right."

"Of course I'm right."

"It means so much to these young people to have that land. Joel was checking on it when he had the accident."

"Do they know you're angling for it on their behalf?"

"No, that's the thing. I let it slip to Gianessa and then realized she would naturally say something to Manda and Joel, and I couldn't have her do that, particularly since I may fail. I *ordered* her not to tell them. It was stupid and—"

"You ordered her?" She smacked the table with her hand. "Yes, that was stupid. Haven't you been confiding other things to her?"

Justin toyed with his cup of espresso. "Quite a lot. And she's not betrayed a confidence."

"You're confiding in her about the college?"

"Yes." He looked at her sideways. "Why, do you think that's unwise?"

Sydney gave a secretive smile. "Not at all, Justin. I think you're treating her like a trusted spouse. Except in two matters—the land purchase, which is fraught with tension for you. You don't like failure, and you're emotionally involved, since you adore Joel and Manda. The stakes are very high on that one."

"Agreed. And two?"

"You've told her nothing about me. I'll bet you just sprang it on her, didn't you? About the same time you snapped at her about keeping the land purchase a secret?" She sat with her eyebrows raised, waiting for Justin to see her point.

"I'm an ass."

"Yes, but fortunately you have a very cute ass. That's in your favor."

"How can I make it right with Gianessa?"

“Now that’s a sweet response. That tells me you want to work things out to her satisfaction.”

“You do couples counseling on the side?”

“I’m sure it would be more fun than administering a college.”

“I’d like your advice, Syd.”

“Tell Gianessa what you’ve told me about the land purchase and ask her advice.”

Justin toyed with his cup.

Sydney stilled his hand with one touch of her finger. “And for god’s sake, drink that before the whip flops.”

The moment Justin sat down at their table in Gallagher’s, Manda announced, “I want to go home after the fitting tomorrow. You guys don’t have to come with me.”

“You don’t want to see more of New York?” Justin asked.

Gianessa’s eyes studied the table, and he could not read her expression.

“I want to be with Joel. Thank you for everything, both of you. But I have my gown now, and I love it, and I need to be with Joel.”

Justin took out his cell phone and called the airline. The aroma of grilled beef permeated the dining room. He watched Gianessa’s face as he negotiated with the agent, wondering if she would ask him to rebook her flight as well. Instead, she carried on a light-hearted conversation with Manda about flowers and music for the wedding.

He interrupted them to say, “Early tomorrow evening is the only possibility. Shall I book one seat on the six-thirty? We would need to be at the airport no later than five.”

Manda nodded, thanked him, and turned back to her conversation with Gianessa.

Justin confirmed the reservation with his credit card. He would let the women decide how to spend the time between the fitting in the morning and the cab to the airport. Apparently Gianessa intended to stay in New York with him. He decided not to read anything into it just yet. Hungry and rattled from an emotional day, he signaled the waiter to place their order.

Over juicy steaks and crisp salads, they talked about the history of the Rockettes, the Christmas show, and their options for the next afternoon. Manda and Gianessa decided to window shop on Fifth Avenue then meet Justin back at the hotel by four o'clock. Manda agreed to be packed and ready to go before she left the hotel in the morning.

"And I will follow up with our three jewelers for the following day, if you're still interested in making that exchange," Justin said cryptically to Gianessa.

Manda turned to Gianessa, and some silent communication passed between them.

"Excuse me, you guys." Manda left them and headed toward the ladies' room.

Justin studied Gianessa's face. Her eyes darkened and her lips twitched with unspoken anger.

She drew in a steadying breath while avoiding his gaze. Evidently she was waiting for him to go first.

"I was beastly to you about the land purchase." Justin heard his own British accent and knew it sounded pompous. He breathed out and retired the accent.

"Yes, you were."

"Can you forgive me?"

"I don't know." She flashed angry eyes at him. "I *won't* be spoken to that way or held in contempt for *no reason* or suspected of *betraying* your confidence or—"

"I apologize. I had no basis for accusing you that way. You've been a tremendous support about the college, and I value your involvement. I would hate to lose that, and I'm afraid I have done exactly that with my behavior this afternoon."

"How is the land purchase any different?" She tapped her foot under the table, and the linen tablecloth rippled in time.

He swallowed. “In several ways. For one, it’s not going well, and it may fail completely. I don’t like to fail, and I would actually like your advice about it. Also, it’s very important to Joel and Manda, and I’ve already disappointed them terribly by not being here for them for the two weeks immediately following Joel’s accident. Finally, it’s important to you, since you’ll be an integral part of the center we want to build on the land, and I cannot stand the thought of failing you before we even begin.”

Gianessa’s nostrils flared, but her voice was calm. “When you say it’s not going well, what do you mean?”

Justin leaned closer and resisted the desire to capture her hands in his. “You know Lorraine, the owner, is Joel’s former fiancée and—”

“Yes, so you said. Go on.”

She would not give an inch, he was sure. This discussion was on her terms or not at all. “Lorraine is asking millions more for the property than its market value.”

“She doesn’t want to sell,” Gianessa said.

“You may be right.” Justin sat back. “That never occurred to me.”

“Why not? What made you believe she was serious about selling?”

Justin read her face. She was not mocking him. She was simply bringing a fresh perspective, asking a pertinent question. *A good one.* “I assumed she was serious about selling because she asked Joel to advise her last summer about developing the land as a gated community. I thought she had abandoned that foolish venture and was searching for another way to offload the land.”

Gianessa gave him a knowing smile. “Last summer she was probably trying to keep Joel on the hook until she could get Manda out of the picture. It was never about selling the land.”

“That’s interesting.” Justin drummed his fingers on the table. “I believe you may be right.”

"Women know these things."

"And men don't," he admitted. "I'm out of practice negotiating with women. I believe I said that to you shortly after we met."

Gianessa dropped her eyes. "Manda is coming."

Justin caught Manda's gaze and held up his hands in a time-out sign. At her eyeroll, he opened the fingers of his right hand to buy five minutes.

Manda put her nose in the air and redirected her steps to the wall of photographs of famous visitors to the steakhouse.

He would thank her later for pretending an interest in the dignitaries she'd never heard of. "She's okay for a few minutes. Suppose Lorraine really is willing to sell the property. How would I get her to sell at a fair price?"

Gianessa moved the salt and pepper shakers into the middle of the table and added a bottle of hot sauce. "Right now it's a triangle. She touched the salt shaker, "you," then the hot sauce, "Joel," and finally the pepper shaker, "Lorraine." Gianessa paused, sat back a little, and told him, "You can convince Lorraine that Joel is terribly damaged by the accident and that Manda is resigned to being his nursemaid for life. That's not a role that would appeal to Lorraine." She moved the hot sauce to the edge of the table by Manda's chair. "Then let it go. Pretend you've given up purchasing the land, although it's very appealing to you personally as a piece of lakefront that might be of interest down the line, if you decide to stay in Tompkins Falls." She moved the salt shaker in front of Justin. "Break off communication."

Justin sat silently. It was not unlike Sydney's take. The women's thought processes were intriguing. He waited for the next installment, but none was forthcoming. "That's it?"

"Give it a month. If she wants to sell, she'll suggest a figure. You can negotiate." Gianessa moved the salt and pepper shakers close together. "Make a deal that's generous without ignoring the market value. Did someone say there's a home on the property?"

"The home she built for Joel and lived in with her husband until they divorced. It's probably worth a million or more by itself."

"Acknowledge the value of the house by adding it to your final figure to seal the deal. What had you planned to do with the house?"

"Raze it. It's brought nothing but unhappiness."

A smile tugged at the corners of Gianessa's mouth. "Just think, Justin. You could demolish two houses in the same year. The Cushman mansion and Lorraine's."

To Justin's surprise, she reached for his hand and gave a gentle squeeze. "Then you'd have two clear sites to build your future—your own house on the Cushman grounds and the holistic healing center on the land for Joel and Manda."

Justin looked at her in wonder.

Gianessa gave him a slow, sexy smile. "You see how easy that was?"

"Remind me often that I need you in my life."

"I will."

Chapter 8

"Did she get off okay?"

"She wouldn't let me stay with her. I asked her to call when she was on the plane. We got her bag checked in at curbside, and I made sure she headed in the direction of security."

Justin flipped through the room service menu and reached for the phone.

Gianessa prompted, "And did she call from the plane?"

"What?" He glanced up in mid-dial. "Yes." He gave her a big smile. "You were as worried as I, weren't you?"

She blushed. "I guess I was."

"She really is very young and inexperienced," he remarked.

"In surprising ways, yes." Their eyes held for a moment.

Justin broke the silence. "Care for something from room service? I'm wanting decaf and strawberry ice cream."

"I'll have ice cream, too. You're wearing your British accent tonight," she teased.

"Am I?" He chuckled. "I wonder where that came from."

"It probably gave you better cooperation from airport personnel. 'Wealthy British gent putting his daughter on the plane' and all that."

"That is the worst British accent . . ." He got a better grip on the phone as a voice crackled from the receiver. "Yes, room service, we need a pot of decaf and two dishes of strawberry ice cream. There's something in it for you if you get it here before it melts." He winked at Gianessa. "Good man! We're ready for it as soon as you can manage."

He balanced the receiver on two fingers before replacing it. "Retiring the accent now." True to his word, he continued in his normal voice. "How did you get so relaxed in the half hour I was gone?"

She shifted a little on the sofa and tucked her feet under her. "It was two hours and a half, enough time for a leisurely bath and some yoga. You might want to try it after the ice cream."

"Make mine a hot shower and—" He paused as the door buzzer sounded. "Our ice cream already?"

He tipped the waiter outrageously.

She laughed heartily after he closed the door.

"What?" He looked comically at his front.

"The tip. You don't do 'moderation,' do you?"

"Nonsense." He wheeled the trolley next to her, slid over an ottoman for himself, shed his suit coat, and rubbed his hands together. "Strawberry ice cream is as moderate as I get. Enjoy."

Gianessa put a spoonful of ice cream in her mouth. "Cold!" She waved her hand helplessly. "Icy cold!"

"See there," Justin said. "He earned that tip, didn't he?"

Gianessa's musical laugh made him smile.

His eyes roamed over her mouth, the spoon, her lips as she savored the silky ice cream loaded with strawberries.

Justin finished his, put down his spoon and asked, "If I take a very fast shower, will you still be up?"

"I will. Take your time."

"Is there a robe that will fit me?" he asked, with an eye on the Trump logo over her left breast on the terry spa-style robe.

"I'm sure there are a couple to choose from in your closet." He tossed aside his napkin, and she saw a smile tug at his mouth as he turned away from her.

Gianessa found a sexy jazz station on the radio, put the ice cream dishes and the trolley in the hallway and tucked the coffee pot under its cozy. She loosened the tie of her robe just enough to show the lace trim of her camisole.

"When does Manda's plane land?" Phil asked Joel for the third time and he and Tony prepared to leave the hospital room.

"Seven-thirty. You're only about fifteen minutes from the airport."

"She'll have her cell turned on?"

"And you both have her number, right?"

Tony nodded. "We've got it covered, Joel. You sure you can handle a visit from her before we take her to Tompkins Falls with us?

"Actually, I'm going to have you drop her here, and she'll get a taxi back to the hotel. Justin booked a suite for both of them when he flew home in December, and he's keeping it until I'm back home."

"That's costing a fortune."

"He's got a fortune, don't worry. It's what's happening in the hotel suite in New York that I'm worried about."

"What do you mean?" Tony asked and then clunked himself in the forehead. "Duh."

"Tony, aren't you the one that said Gianessa's won't be manipulated into anything she doesn't already want to do?"

Tony nodded. "What they do is out of our control, guys, right?"

"Makes me crazy. My uncle is old enough to be her father."

"He's not," Phil scoffed. "And Gianessa is a divorced woman. She can make her own decisions."

"And her own mistakes," Tony added with a laugh.

Phil lifted his hands in surrender and said sternly, "And Joel needs to manage his stress level."

"You're right, Phil. Joel, buddy, we're out of your hair." Tony zipped up his jacket. "We'll return with the lovely Manda and then take off for home."

"Love you, guys," Joel told them. "Thanks for all of this. We'll do it again at the Manse as soon as I'm out of here."

Gianessa was so wrapped up in the music she didn't hear the shower stop. She was swaying to a sensuous sax solo when Justin came up behind her.

"Dance?" he asked with an old-fashioned tap on her shoulder.

She turned with a happy smile and moved into his arms. He smelled of soap that was nothing like the one the hotel supplied in her bathroom. The mingled scent of cloves, nutmeg, and sandalwood made her melt into his body.

At first they made slow circles in time with the music. Then as Justin's arm tightened around her waist and her head nestled on his shoulder, they made their own rhythm. His right leg found its way between her legs, and her arms tightened around his back. His lips caressed her neck, and she sighed. Gianessa immersed herself in all the sensations—the soulful saxophone, the spicy soap, the warmth of his body, the touch of his hands and his lips, the pressure of his leg as it moved between hers.

When the music ended, Justin told her, "That was better than any kiss could be."

She smiled into his eyes and touched his lips with one finger. "I wouldn't be so sure." She invited with a lift of one eyebrow.

His mouth was on hers before she could take a breath. Demanding. Deep. She felt a thrill between her legs, and she shifted tighter against him where his leg touched her sweet spot. When his mouth was too much for hers, she pulled back, startled.

"You don't like it rough, do you? I apologize."

"You're right, I don't," she said. "But deep is good." She laced her fingers at the back of his neck and told him, "Deep is very good."

He got it very right with the next kiss.

She laughed breathily. "I want more like that," she told him.

"And I want to spend the night making love to you."

"Let's." She said it with a dimpled smile.

She couldn't read his expression. "What is that suspicious look about?"

"I am, you're right. It's from wheeling and dealing with unscrupulous people. My question is, did you two women arrange for us to be alone together?"

"God, no, there's no conspiracy here. When Manda wanted to be with Joel, I welcomed the chance to be with you."

"I see," he whispered. His mouth captured hers, and she loved the way his tongue slid over hers and probed every sensitive surface inside her mouth.

She was breathless when he paused to watch her face, perhaps studying the passion she knew was written there.

"What's under your robe?"

"Something I brought especially for this," she said, her voice shaky.

"You were so sure?"

"I knew what I wanted."

"And I thought I was the one doing the seducing tonight."

"Oh, you were," she said with a chuckle. "We did that very well together, didn't we?"

He tugged at the tie of her robe and slid his hands inside, pressed his forehead to hers and invited her. "Come to bed with me, and we'll find out what else we do very well together."

At the foot of his bed, he slid the robe off her shoulders and let it pool on the floor. His breath came out in a rush as he observed the sheer, lace-trimmed camisole and lacy thong. "Especially for me?" he asked her, his voice husky.

"Exclusively for you," she said. "Do you like it?" She modeled the view from all sides.

He unbelted his robe and tossed it on a chair. Her eyes made an admiring pass over his lean body, the firm, well-developed muscles and the erection that promised what she'd been dreaming about.

His eyes devoured her as she sat on the edge of the mattress and used one shapely foot to push herself to the center of the bed where she stretched out on her back. Opening her legs, she slid her left foot up the inside of her right calf.

Justin picked up her left foot and kissed the inside of her ankle. Her juices rushed as his gaze traveled up her inner leg. She walked her trembling fingers to the bottom edge of the lacy thong to tell him where she wanted his mouth to go next.

He knelt between her legs, edged aside the thong and planted kiss after kiss on the inside of her thighs until she tangled her fingers in his hair and urged his mouth to touch her where she ached for him. He licked and teased her until she opened herself completely, arching her back and crying out as waves of pleasure swept over her. His kisses made their way up her belly to her mouth, and she tasted strawberries and cream and her own sexy liquid.

Strong hands scooped and lifted her buns. When he thrust into her hot, wet core, she squeezed, and he grew harder and thrust deeper and faster. She gripped the pillow above her and her breaths became moans of pleasure. His rhythm quickened until he emptied himself inside her, and she held him there for an exquisite moment before relinquishing him. His withdrawal excited her again, and she mewed in surrender.

Justin rested on his side, watching her, his eyelids heavy.

As her breathing eased, she touched his cheek with the back of her hand. "You're magnificent."

"Just think, if I were twenty, we could do this all night."

She gave a breathless chuckle. "I'm not sure I could take it." She placed both her hands on her belly.

"Why so pensive? What are you thinking?"

"It feels like you just healed something in me that I didn't know was broken." She turned to smile at him, but his eyes had closed, and she drifted with him into a peaceful sleep.

When she awoke some time later, he had covered them with a blanket, and his hand was on her belly. He snored softly and twitched when she touched his cheek. She smiled, turned on her side, and snuggled back against him. His arm tightened around her, but he didn't awaken.

It was nearly dawn when they both opened their eyes and made slow, sensuous love, accompanied by a different, equally skilled saxophone quartet in the next room.

Manda teased Joel. "I told you last night when I got back, it's bad luck for you to know what my gown is like."

"Phil's hoping it isn't poufy."

"Phil will approve. In fact, it will knock his socks off."

Joel raked her curls with eager fingers and brought her closer for a kiss that he knew would knock her socks off. "Am *I* going to like it?" Her sigh was an intoxicant for his sore body.

"You will be so proud, Joel. And I will be beautiful. And the garden will be blooming—our garden, Joel." Her eyes sparkled like the lake in the early morning sunshine. Sapphires on fire.

"Your garden," he corrected.

"And Harold's and yours. He showed me the plans again last week. There's a rose arbor. Did you know?"

"I asked him for one. I want us to stand in the archway when we say our vows."

"You are so romantic." She snuggled closer on the bed.

"You didn't know that about me?"

"Of course I knew it." She smiled into his eyes, and he felt a tug that made him know he was getting better every day.

"What kind of romantic entanglement are Justin and Gianessa having in New York without you?" He heard the worry in his own voice.

"Romantic?" Manda snorted. "Not. Justin went off to see some woman after we bought my gown, and Gianessa was fuming."

"Really?" He chuckled. "Who's the woman?"

"He said she's some college president he knows who's been advising him. When I saw how pissed Gianessa was, I told him we'd be sniffing him for perfume. He ditched us at Radio City and met us later for dinner. He and Gianessa had it out at the table while I went to the ladies' room for, like, half an hour. And then, when we went for a fitting yesterday morning, she wouldn't let him buy her a dress for the wedding, even though it was gorgeous on her." Manda squinted, trying to remember something.

"What?"

"They've got something planned for today, something that involves jewelry. I think maybe Gianessa wanted to sell something and Justin set it up. I don't really know."

"Her necklace?" Joel wondered.

"What necklace?"

"Maybe you haven't seen it. Gianessa has a necklace from her marriage that is worth quite a bit."

"I know she wants to buy a car. Is it worth a car?"

"It might be."

Manda whistled and ran her hand back and forth across his chest.

"And Justin would know how to find a jeweler to give her a fair price."

"Is there anything Justin doesn't know?"

Joel laughed. "Apparently he doesn't know how to get Gianessa to accept a beautiful dress as a peace offering."

Manda shrugged. "Gianessa may be broke, but she has

principles. She was beautiful in it. It was the exact color of her eyes—kind of smoky violet."

"Gianessa would be beautiful in a flour sack."

"You're making me jealous." She sat up with a playful scowl, and he trailed his fingertip down her cheek and jaw, onto her neck.

"And, although you'd be beautiful in a flour sack, I prefer you naked."

"Still want to do this?"

Gianessa nodded, though she looked everywhere but at him.

Justin waited for her to say more, but she didn't. "I called our three jewelers again yesterday, and two of them were still enthusiastic about the piece. Both gave me estimates this time, and they were miles apart. I recommend we start with the better estimate. Henri might have a buyer. How does that sound?"

If she said, "Whatever you say," he would know she'd had second thoughts.

"It sounds right," she agreed, her voice firm. "It helps me so much that you've done this footwork, that you have the contacts to make this so easy for me."

He touched his finger to her chin. "I don't think this is easy for you," he said gently.

"Emotionally, no, you're right. I've been going back and forth with 'what to do about the necklace?' for three years. I don't know why, but it's only since I came to Tompkins Falls that I've known the right thing is to sell it and invest the proceeds, whatever they may be, in my life going forward."

"Even though it's your last link with Les and Isabella?"

Her eyes filled up.

"I have no link with Les, not even in my heart. This necklace is really about him, about how he once valued the two of us, mother and daughter. My link with Isabella is in my heart, not in this beautiful necklace."

Justin felt his heart glow with warmth and hope. "Then, we'll proceed. Henri will see us anytime this morning."

Gianessa reached for her coat and said with finality, "It's time. Thank you for helping me to move on. I couldn't do this on my own."

"You're stronger than you think."

Gianessa shook her head. "For me, it's overwhelming, the thought of waltzing into a jewelry store in New York City and trusting someone to give me a fair deal. You are guiding me and protecting me.

She patted her hand over her heart and rested it there for a moment. "I like the way that feels."

"If we don't go now, we'll back in bed for the day."

She burst into a laugh. "See how wise you are?"

Henri greeted Justin with a practiced bow. "Monsieur Cushman."

"Henri, meet my dear friend Gianessa Dupioni."

"You are Italian, Madame?"

"My father grew up near Milano. I've never been, but it's on my list."

"You must go!" Justin said in chorus with Henri, and the three of them laughed.

Henri gave Gianessa a little bow. "Monsieur Cushman tells me you have a LaFave for me to consider. Did you bring the piece with you today?"

Gianessa nodded.

Henri ushered them to a nearby jewelry counter, where Gianessa drew a blue pouch out of her pants pocket and loosened the strings.

If Henri was aghast at her scheme for protecting the necklace, he gave no indication. "Allow me, Madame, to place it here," he said formally, indicating the black cloth-covered square on the glass counter top.

Gianessa handed the piece to him. He hefted it, and his eyebrows shot up. Evidently the weight of the metal pleased him. He drew out his instruments and set to work.

Justin explained to Gianessa, "Henri is testing the weight and integrity of the platinum and the gold and examining the jeweler's mark."

Gianessa watched the procedure without comment for a few moments before asking Justin, "You've done this before? Sold pieces of jewelry?"

"Yes, several times. My mother had no interest in most of her family jewels but knew they were collector's items or otherwise of interest on the market. Henri handled those pieces for us."

Henri held up his hand for silence, and Justin touched his finger to his lips.

Gianessa gave him a conspiratorial smile and let him look into her eyes. Her face radiated calm and determination about this transaction.

It made him happy beyond all reason that she was, at last, letting go of the necklace and all it symbolized. As she turned back to watch Henri, a whiff of Chloe suffused his senses. He wanted more.

What's happening to me this weekend? He'd swallowed his pride to make amends for the way he'd treated her at the bridal shop, something he'd never done with a woman. He'd let her see his affection and concern for the young bride Manda, feelings he barely realized he had. He'd taken this beautiful, desirable woman to bed with him and made passionate love to her. Now his heart burst with joy that she was divesting herself of the last, high-priced token of her marriage.

This was not the Justin Cushman he'd seen in the mirror a year ago—or ten years ago for that matter, when he'd lived with Alexa.

Henri cleared his throat. “Madame, the best price for this item will come at auction, as you may know, but I am prepared to make you an offer today, if you are interested.”

“I am interested, Henri. I would prefer not to go to auction, if we can agree on a figure.”

He raised his eyebrows, perhaps surprised that she was not pushing for the ultimate return.

He glanced at Justin, who gave him the most discreet of shrugs.

“Very well. Let me say this necklace is a genuine LaFave, as you no doubt know. It is unique among his two-hearts necklaces. To my knowledge, he never fashioned two complete strands with a jewel closure, except in this piece. He occasionally placed a gemstone or a pearl at the closure of a single strand, never such a large stone as this and never encircled as this stone is by bands of gold and platinum. This is, indeed, a unique and exquisite piece.” He glanced at Justin. “You knew that, no doubt, Monsieur?”

Justin smiled. He actually had no idea. He had simply recognized the alternating gold and platinum hearts of LaFave.

Henri went on, “LaFave is enjoying attention right now, and, of course, Valentine’s Day is upon us. I have confidence I can sell this piece. For all these reasons, I am prepared to offer you today, Madame, fifty thousand dollars.”

Justin inhaled reflexively and looked quickly at Gianessa who stood with her mouth open. She swayed a bit, and he reached out a hand to steady her.

“You—you’re offering me fifty thousand dollars for my necklace?” she asked in disbelief.

Henri nodded.

“Thank you.” She reached out her hand. “I accept your offer.”

Henri, Justin saw, was stunned. It must be he had a buyer who was prepared to pay a good deal more than that. Justin, however, had never imagined the piece was worth more than thirty thousand. An uneasy thought crossed his mind.

"A word, Henri?" he said quietly. "In private."

Gianessa eyed him, troubled and a little annoyed.

"Sorry, darling, there is one small point I need to discuss with Henri first. I beg your indulgence for a brief moment." The fire in her eyes said she was peeved at him. He'd not only interfered, he'd called her darling.

Their eyes held for a long moment before she brought out a beautiful smile and said brightly, "I'll just look at the watches a moment, gentlemen."

As she floated past him, she gave Justin's ankle a sharp kick.

Justin sucked in his breath, and Henri closed his eyes in sympathy.

Henri discerned, "Your concern is with the buyer? I cannot share the gentleman's identity with you, as you are aware."

"Indeed. I will watch your face as I tell you that Ms. Dupioni's former husband Les Bennett gifted her with the necklace when their daughter Isabella was born."

Henri's face flooded with relief, and he gave an almost indiscernible shake of the head.

"*Merci*, Henri. I could not have allowed that."

Henri gave a slight bow. "You are a gentleman."

"As are you, Henri."

"Now, will the lady prefer a check in hand or an electronic fund transfer?"

"You'll need to speak with Ms. Dupioni on that matter, Henri. At the risk of another ankle chop, I'll see if she's ready to address that with you."

Ms. Dupioni preferred an electronic fund transfer to her money market account, which she and Henri arranged in the privacy of Henri's office while Justin looked at the watches.

A saleswoman strolled up beside Justin, pointed to an exclusive French ladies' watch with a mauve crocodile band. "I believe that is the one the lady asked to see."

Justin regarded the heavy piece with skepticism. "And did she like the way it felt on her wrist?"

"I believe she found it too weighty. It was the color of the band that caught her eye, sir."

"Did she inquire about the price?" Justin probed, wondering if that was the real turnoff.

"She did not, and as you know our items don't have price tags."

"Have you anything lighter weight with a similar look that we might bring to her attention?"

"I'm afraid not, sir." She gave him a wide smile. "Believe me, I wish we did."

"And I as well," Justin said. "You've been very helpful."

Justin knew he was in trouble with Gianessa for interfering with her transaction, and a gift might have helped. But then, she'd refused the silk gown at the bridal shop yesterday. He must remember he could not buy his way back into her good graces. Full disclosure seemed to be the better strategy.

Henri emerged from the back, looked around for Justin, and made his way across the room.

"Done to your satisfaction, Henri?"

"*Mais oui*. The lady is powdering her nose, I believe."

Henri shook Justin's outstretched hand. "You are a very lucky man, Justin Cushman."

Justin's eyes lit up as Gianessa came toward them. She wore a megawatt smile, which he tested with a scowl and asked, "Am I in trouble?"

She laughed, shook her head, took Henri's arm, and planted a kiss on Henri's cheek. "Now, I'm starved. Henri, where can Justin and I find a salad with fresh seafood and a quiet table for two?"

Henri signaled the saleswoman to hail a cab for them, scribbled an address and the name of a restaurant, and bid them a hearty "*Bon appetit*."

"My brain's not working," Manda groused.

Gwen Forrester laughed. "As your AA sponsor, I've been listening to you process things for a year now. Take it from a psychologist, your brain's perfectly normal. You just get stuck sometimes, like all of us do. You're not thinking about drinking?"

"I'm not going to drink."

"Good. What's got your brain all befuddled?"

"The wedding date."

"June twentieth, right?"

"Well, it could be May thirtieth."

"Really? An earlier date has opened up?"

Manda nodded. "I got a call this noon as I left Rochester. Joel and I are so ready to be married. And I have the gown. Wait till you see it! The thing is Joel wouldn't be ready for a honeymoon in Ireland that early."

Gwen reached out a hand to her favorite sponsee and gave it a squeeze. This had been a tough courtship for Manda and Joel. They had agreed to hold off on sex until Manda got a full year of sobriety, but Joel had been critically injured about nine months into Manda's sobriety. Gwen had gone through at least a case of tissues on her lakeside porch for Manda alone as they talked through all the agonizing twists and turns. Gwen doubted Joel would be ready for a trip to Ireland anytime this calendar year. No wonder her little chickie was fretting. She probably knew Ireland was out for now, and she didn't know how to get Joel on board with a realistic plan.

"Let's think about this," Gwen said gently. "There are really three things wrapped up in this honeymoon in Ireland. There's a dreamy, romantic honeymoon. There's hot sex. And there's a trip to Ireland. Remind me, what is the possible new date for the wedding?"

"May thirtieth instead of June twentieth."

"So you'd be moving it up three weeks, basically?"

"Yes." Manda sat at the edge of the chair.

"Will moving it up three weeks mean you and Joel are less ready for sex or for romance or for a trip to Ireland or all three?"

Manda scrunched up her face and looked out at the lake.

"You don't have to tell me all your secrets. I'm just pointing out that the demands of a trip to Ireland are vastly different from tender lovemaking in your own little love nest."

From the dreamy smile and the hot blush on Manda's cheeks, Gwen figured there were no reservations in the sex department. That would be a huge gain for Joel's recovery, as soon as he was able. Moving up the wedding date could also give him a mental boost.

"Let me ask some ridiculous questions."

Manda swiveled her head, and Gwen was glad to see a conspiratorial smile.

Gwen sat back and sagely folded her hands in front of her. "What are the pros and cons of postponing the trip to Ireland for a whole year?" This game always worked for them.

Manda's face fell.

"Ridiculous question, I know, but go with it for a minute."

Manda squirmed, glanced out at the lake and took a deep breath. "Cons. We're both really excited about this trip, and it would be a real downer for Joel's recovery if we had to delay it."

"He's using the trip as a marker for recovery, you mean?"

"Yeah."

"Pretty high stakes, don't you think?"

Manda shrugged.

"Is anyone other than Joel saying that this June is realistic for him to travel to Ireland?"

"Like . . .?"

"His doctors, his physical therapist?"

"Um, I don't know."

"Do you have reservations already? Flight reservations, hotels, a driver?" Gwen doubted that would be a problem anyway. Joel could afford to blow off a trip around the world if he had to.

"I don't think he's talked to anyone about details."

"No brochures lying around his hospital room? No map of Ireland? No Irish music playing when you visit him?"

Manda shook her head, her forehead wrinkled in puzzlement.

"Sounds like he may not be so sure about it himself." *Good thing we're having this conversation.*

"He's adamant about going to Ireland," Manda said insistently. "We're both wild about it."

"And Joel's adamant about having the new suite ready for him very, very fast, right? Yet he's on top of every detail about that. So, if he hasn't been on the phone daily with a travel agent, he may know in his heart it's too soon to lock in a date." When Manda didn't burst into tears, Gwen said, "Maybe moving up the wedding date to May is a way to plan an alternative honeymoon, postpone the trip to Ireland, and save face for Joel."

"You're brilliant." Manda's eyes radiated hope and joy, like sun bursting through the clouds on a stormy day.

That's why they pay me the big bucks. Gwen smiled. AA sponsors did the work for free, but the rewards were beyond measure. She segued the conversation into suggestions for a low-stress, handicap-friendly honeymoon—free of security lines, long waits, and uncomfortable vehicles. But very, very big on romance.

Within minutes, Manda took ownership of the honeymoon plans. She claimed first-hand knowledge of some outstanding inns around the Finger Lakes. "We always have lunch at an inn on a lake when we do our thrift shop adventures," Manda said. "Some of them are unbelievably romantic."

"Like . . .?"

"Belhurst Castle on Seneca Lake, the Sherwood Inn on Skaneateles Lake, the Aurora Inn on Cayuga Lake. And there are more."

"You'd better make some phone calls fast and see who's got an elevator and a spectacular suite available, don't you think?"

Manda nodded with a happy smile.

"So who's your maid-of-honor? Sara?"

"No, my sister, Lyssa."

Gwen, who prided herself on her professional mask, felt it slip. A shrill voice—her own—said, "Lyssa who you haven't seen in six years? Who's not in recovery and needs to be?"

"I can't wait to have her come for a weekend so we can get her gown and—"

"You know, you might want to have a backup plan, sweetie."

Manda waved aside the suggestion and focused on the exact shade of blue she wanted for the flowers and Lyssa's gown. "Periwinkle. And we saw a gorgeous cake at a bakery in Ithaca one trip. It was decorated like a present with a creamy wide pink bow. Wouldn't that be pretty with a periwinkle bow and the frosting the same shade of white as my gown?"

One big change at a time, Mother Hen Gwen. "Gorgeous. And is your wedding cake chocolate or vanilla?"

"Are you kidding? Chocolate, of course."

The cab dropped them at a café that brought a smile to Justin's face.

"Good memories?" Gianessa asked him, silently hoping he hadn't been here with That Sydney Woman.

He nodded and placed his hand on her back as they climbed the steps. "I came here with Joel to celebrate his graduation. I'd forgotten the name of the place."

"Where did he study?"

"He had just finished his MBA at Wharton—Penn—and he wanted to spend the weekend with me in New York. I flew over from London. We saw plays, went to concerts, visited Ellis Island, all the tourist things. We had fun. And at this restaurant, our lobster was caught that day and prepared simply and deliciously." He ushered her through the door, caught the *maître d's* attention and pointed to a table in a quiet corner.

When their tea arrived they placed their orders for lobster salad. Gianessa reached across the table for his hand. "I am dying to hear what that was about—that outrageous interference of yours at Henri's."

He smiled. "Forgive me. I knew he had a buyer, and I had a horrible thought. What if the buyer was Les?"

Gianessa paled. "He is vindictive enough to do exactly that," she said. There was hurt but no bitterness in her voice.

"It wasn't Les. Henri couldn't tell me who it was, of course, but it clearly was not Les."

"I would have died."

"I would not have let it happen."

"Thank you." She smiled brightly. "Let's imagine it was a darling sixty-something gentleman looking for a special anniversary gift for the fifty-something woman he'd been married to for twenty-five years."

Justin started to say, "That could almost be us twenty-five years from now." He wondered where that thought came from. Surely neither of them was thinking about marrying? He pushed aside that rogue thought and, instead, smiled into her eyes. "You are a romantic at heart, aren't you?"

"I never thought so until now. I'm not sure where that idea came from, but it's a lovely story for the necklace, don't you think?"

"I do. What are you planning to do with your fifty thousand?"

"Buy a car, certainly, and start an emergency fund."

Justin sat back and folded his arms. "How level-headed and fiscally smart of you."

Gianessa drew herself up to her full height and leaned

toward him, leading with her breasts. "I know a little about money management. Manda has been teaching me."

He swept his eyes over her curves and gave her a wink. "I have no doubt she's giving sound advice. What kind of car do you fancy?"

"Something small that will handle well in snow and ice."

He tested, "Planning to stay in the frozen north for a while?"

"Tompkins Falls is my new home," she asserted.

That pleased him.

"Any recommendations?"

"For what?"

"A small car that handles well in snow and ice. Where did your thoughts take you?" she teased.

"Homes," he confessed. "You have enough for a nice down payment, if you're interested in a home for yourself."

She dipped her head from side to side. "No. Too much work. I'll rent."

She thanked the waiter who put two entrée-size salads in front of them, each with a mound of fresh lobster on top. Gianessa teased the lobster with the tines of her fork, took a bite and moaned with pleasure. "There is nothing like fresh lobster. Do you know how hard it is to find it on the West Coast? And it never tastes like this."

Justin's eyes roamed over her mouth and her breasts.

She reached for her water glass and asked, "You never told me what kind of home you want, Justin."

"I still don't know. I did tell you the Cushman estate is still up for grabs?"

She shook her head and forked up another bite of the lobster. "Delicious. Fresh. Do you have to sell it before you can do anything else?"

Justin laughed. "No. Are you interested?"

She joined his laughter. "I probably can't afford one bay of the garage."

"You wouldn't want the garage, or the house either. Nor does anyone else, apparently. It's been on the luxury market for a few years now."

"Where is the Cushman estate?"

"If you know where Overlook Park is," he began and paused to see if she did.

"Next to Lakeside Terrace where you live, isn't it?"

"Yes. The park was part of the Cushman grounds at one time. Lakeside Terrace is the north border of the park. The grounds of the Cushman estate are the south border. The mansion is past the bluffs, so its lawn slopes down to the water's edge."

"Must be a beautiful setting," Gianessa commented.

"It is, actually. The mansion, on the other hand, is a pink elephant, and it's time to tear it down."

"Pink elephant?" Gianessa let out a laugh and, with it, a mesclun leaf.

"Hah! Give you a salad, and lettuce leaves fly out of your mouth."

Gianessa dissolved into laughter and let her fork fall from her hand.

Justin watched her, glad the tension she'd been carrying all morning was gone. He loved seeing the high color on her cheeks, the sparkle in her amethyst eyes, the touch of salad dressing at the corner of her mouth.

He handed her a handkerchief. "There's a little dressing on your lower lip."

Instead of dabbing at it, she asked him, "Where?"

He liked this game. He stroked her lower lip with his finger. She followed his finger with her tongue. He lifted off the dab of dressing and offered it to her. She licked it off his finger.

"Do we still have the room?" she asked.

"Check out is at noon." He consulted his watch. "Let's stay another night." He pulled out his phone.

"Let's. Do you have more consultants to interview?"

Justin shook his head. "I saw all three while you and Manda did your window shopping. My work is done." He paused for a moment to call the hotel and secure their suite. "You never said. Did you and Manda buy anything?"

"Nope. That's one of the rules of window shopping. Look all you want, but don't buy a thing. Did you hire a consultant?"

"I picked one that I'll ask the board to approve. I think they'll agree."

"So today is just for us." Gianessa retrieved her fork and speared another mouthful of salad. "What shall we do?"

"It's barely noon. Would you care to see a play?"

"Yes, a matinee, something light, maybe a musical."

"Followed by an early dinner and a cozy evening in our room, perhaps."

"We have a fireplace, don't we?"

"We do. It would be a shame to let it go to waste."

"You know," Gianessa said, as she stroked his palm with her thumb, "I was prepared not to like you. Look how that turned out."

He blustered. "Not like me?" He winked.

"The first time I saw you, you were badgering Grace." She leaned forward, leading with her breasts. "That ticked me off."

"And you wore your hair in that French braid, which ticked me off."

She gathered her long, toffee tresses behind her shoulders. "You never said you didn't like my braid."

"I wanted from that first moment to get my hands in your hair. I plotted six ways to Sunday to get rid of the braid."

"My braid is perfect for work. It feels elegant and simple, and it makes me feel put together and focused."

He caressed her cheek and jaw and neck with eager fingers. "But you're elegant and complex, and I prefer you undone."

Gianessa looked into his eyes. He saw happiness and wonder in hers.

If I demolish the Cushman mansion, we could make a life together on the shore of Chestnut Lake. The thought warmed and excited him.

"Is everything all right, sir?" the waiter asked.

Justin did not respond, his eyes focused on Gianessa.

Gianessa smiled at the waiter. "The salads are delicious," she told him. "We're ready for more tea." She lifted her full cup, drank a sip, and he went away.

Chapter 9

Tony set down the hammer and caught the look of relief on Gianessa's face.

"Hey, I didn't know you were here. I wouldn't have barged in to work on these cabinets if I'd known. I thought you went with Joel to his doctor's appointment."

"I stayed because I wanted to talk to you. These will be great, Tony. Thanks a million." Gianessa surveyed the doors Tony had just installed on the cabinets beside the pool. "I can put most of the paraphernalia out of sight."

"I'll paint them today, if you want."

"Sure."

"I've got the bucket and brushes in the truck. Will I be in Joel's way if I do it today?"

Gianessa shook her head. "Joel will probably just sleep when he gets back. I doubt if Justin will hang around, so it's the perfect time."

There was something about the way she said Justin's name. *Soft*.

"What did you want to talk to me about? Need more cabinets?"

"I want to buy a used car."

Tony whistled in surprise.

"And I need to learn to drive in snow and ice."

"I can help you get a car, no problem. But are you sure you want me as your driving instructor? I'm the one that landed Joel in a wheelchair, you know."

"I asked three people, and they all said you're the best winter driver they know. It would really help me out, Tony."

"Well, sure, I guess. Do you have a license?"

"I got back my California license right before I came east."

Tony didn't need an explanation for that. Plenty of others in AA had lost their licenses for drunk driving.

"Driver's license, that is," she muttered to herself.

Tony didn't want to ask what she meant, but he'd heard her say she was a physical therapist. He'd really like to introduce her to his new girlfriend, Sunny, who was just finishing her Doctor of Physical Therapy degree.

Gianessa didn't offer any more information, so he shrugged and said, "Let's do it. Tell me what you want in a car."

They brainstormed for the next half hour, and Tony made a few phone calls. He located several gently used, front-wheel-drive cars for sale by people he trusted. "We can check them out this week if you want."

"Wonderful. I'd really appreciate your opinion about them, Tony. I have no idea what to watch out for or what questions to ask."

"I'm your man," he agreed. "What day's best?"

"Tomorrow."

"Morning?"

"Sure, why not. I'll buy us lunch."

"Now you're talking. These places will want cash." He looked at her skeptically. "You come into some money?"

"I did," Gianessa said with a big smile. "Justin helped me sell a piece of old jewelry in New York last weekend."

"Must have been big for you to get a car out of it."

Gianessa just nodded, her eyes soft.

Maybe she'd been married before and they sold her diamond. Must have been a big one. None of his business, he decided. She was still standing there with a dreamy look on her face.

They've done the deed.

A knock at the front door startled them both. "Need help with Joel," Justin called, his voice stern.

"I've got you covered, Justin," Tony yelled. He grabbed his jacket.

Gianessa opened the front door wide, and Tony barreled through the force field that had suddenly materialized between Gianessa and Justin.

Joel had maneuvered himself out of the front seat of Justin's car into the wheelchair. His face was white, and he gripped the arms of the chair. Tony shouted encouragement, and Joel looked up in relief. He shook his head as if shaking off a nightmare.

Tony put his jacket around Joel's shoulders, turned the chair around, and hustled it up the short ramp and across the threshold.

"Right to bed, pal?"

Joel managed a nod. "Please."

Tony expected Gianessa to help him out, but she was locked in murmured communication with Justin.

"Gianessa?" Tony said as he crossed the living room. When she didn't respond, he paused at the bedroom door, called her name sharply and waited for her to make eye contact.

"Can you help, so I don't do damage out of stupidity?"

Gianessa came back to reality and followed Tony into the bedroom. Together, they got Joel onto the bed, removed his shoes, and covered him with the down comforter.

Gianessa stayed at Joel's side, tucking the comforter close to his body, touching his forehead, murmuring reassurance.

Tony sensed her channeling something. Whatever it was seemed to be working. The color come back into Joel's face.

"Tony, can you make some hot cocoa? There's a sandwich in the fridge, too."

"Coming up."

Justin was already busy in the kitchen warming milk and mixing cocoa and sugar. *What, does he have elephant ears for Gianessa's voice?*

"Rough trip, Justin?"

"I'll never do that again without a nurses' aide along. Did you see his face?" Justin's voice shook worse than his hands.

"Yeah, Joel seemed pretty pale to me, but he's got a little color now. What happened to the nurses' aide?"

"She canceled at the last minute."

"I'm surprised Gianessa didn't go along when that happened."

"I insisted she talk to you as planned. But I was foolish to try it alone."

Tony arranged the sandwich on a plate. He thought it was pretty grandiose of Justin and pretty irresponsible of Gianessa not to step in as medical backup.

Asking for advice about a car could have waited. Tony felt like a pawn in this fiasco, and Joel had been the one to suffer. Joel had suffered enough, and Tony was ticked off.

If everyone weren't so shook up, he'd probably make some wiseass remark about their poor judgment and get himself fired for it. "Sweet Jesus," he prayed silently, "don't let me make it worse."

"What did Joel's doctor think?" he said instead.

Justin paused, took a breath, and calmed down a bit. "The doctor's says Joel is doing really well. Everything's healing. His eye is tracking correctly now. No evidence of cognitive problems. No need for further surgery."

"So no real harm done today?" Tony said with more generosity than he felt.

Justin gave a hollow laugh. "Other than all of us being nervous wrecks, no. But his face was absolutely white coming in from the car."

"Gianessa will see to him, and if there's a problem, she'll call the docs right away, right?"

"Thank god for her." Justin had an adoring little smile on his face.

They have definitely done the deed.

Tony rummaged in the cupboard for a mug. "Almost ready with that cocoa, sir?" Tony wondered if Joel was on to Justin and Gianessa. That could be an interesting conversation.

The next morning, Tony pumped Gianessa for an update on Joel's condition.

"He's excellent now. After you left he got something to eat and then slept for a few hours. Manda came home, and he perked up."

They drove into the used car lot where Tony expected to find the first of the three cars. He drove down the second row as instructed, and *voila*.

"What are we seeing first?"

"Four-year-old subcompact. Low mileage, very good condition." He stood on the step of his red truck before jumping down, spotted the manager of the lot and waved to him.

After a spin around the lot and around the block, Gianessa decided she didn't like the way the car handled. Tony liked it fine, and he wondered if the color—boring beige—was the real problem. Gianessa crossed it off the list.

He and Gianessa piled back in his truck and made their way out of Tompkins Falls to a lot halfway to Canandaigua. "This baby is only three years old and has a little more mileage. I hear this style is really hot with the younger crowd. I've seen these on the highway, and all the drivers are smiling."

"You don't have to sell me Tony," Gianessa said with laugh.

He blushed. "Just telling you what I know."

"What kind of maintenance record do they have?"

"Very good. No recalls, good resale value, very reliable car."

They took a spin in the little red car, around the lot and out onto the nearby country roads. Gianessa liked the way it handled and liked the pep it had climbing hills, but she fussed with the seat back every time they came to a stop sign.

"Can't find a good position?"

Gianessa shook her head. They asked the dealer if there were more controls for the front seats, and his face fell. "That's why the lady who owned it gave it up. Her sister got a backache every time they went somewhere. Sorry."

"Who knew?" Gianessa shrugged.

"That's why we do test drives."

Gianessa thanked the dealer and stuffed her hands in her pockets of her down coat. Tony turned his truck toward Canandaigua and navigated through the city to a new housing development overlooking the lake. The snow was coming down hard when they arrived at their final address.

Tony stayed close to Gianessa on the gravel driveway, not happy about her footwear. Sandals had no traction on snow. "We should get you some boots on the way home. There's a great family-owned shoe store on the main street in town."

"Maybe."

The first car in the turnaround was a black BMW sedan. "Oh, baby, see that? What a beauty," Tony sang out.

Gianessa took one look and blanched.

"You all right?"

She shook her head. "I mean, yes. Yes, I'm fine."

"Wait a minute. You're not fine. We can come back after a warm up or lunch."

Gianessa shook her head. "Bad memories, that's all. I totaled a car just like that with my baby girl in the back seat. The car seat saved her life."

"Geez. Is that why you lost your license in California? DWI?"

"Yeah, that's why."

"I'm sorry. That's a hell of a memory to hit you out of the blue."

Gianessa brushed away a tear and gave him a weak smile. “When I’m sober, I’m really a very good driver.”

“I’ve seen that, and here’s our third option.” He pointed to a seven-year-old hybrid with an inch of snow on it. He wiped the driver’s side clean with his arm and headed to the passenger side to finish the job. “Nice color. You like blue?”

“I like it. Let’s try it.”

“It’s going to be slippery going. You sure?”

Gianessa squared her slender shoulders. “No time like the present. I have to learn how to handle these conditions.”

Tony gave her a few quick pointers and was impressed with the way Gianessa backed the car around in the snow, eased forward on the slippery drive and drove with confidence and caution on the messy roadway.

“You’re a good teacher, Tony.”

“You’re a quick study.” He pointed to an empty parking lot just ahead on the left. “Let’s get in there. They haven’t plowed today. We’ve got two to three fresh inches with some good drifts. I want you to get a feel for how it corners in snow, how to recover from a skid, and what it feels like to maneuver on ice.”

“The owner can’t see us out here, can he?”

“Nope. And if we get stuck, I’ll get us out, so don’t worry.”

Gianessa face was fearless as she slipped and slid down the access ramp. “It’s like sliding down a sand dune.”

“Hah. Spoken like a California girl. We usually say it’s like being on skis.”

With Tony’s coaching, Gianessa did figure eights, learned to handle a skid, and maneuvered out of a snow bank without needing a push. At every success, her face lit up with a smile.

“A-plus, honey,” he declared at the end of the exercises. “You can drive in a Finger Lakes winter.”

“I am ready.” Her voice rang with exhilaration. “I can do this.”

"Just let me brush the snow out of the grill and the wheels before we head back."

When Tony had eliminated the evidence of their adventure and examined the exterior for rust, dents, and dings, he climbed back into the warmth of the car. Gianessa sat studying the packet of service invoices and gas receipts the owner had provided.

"So, what do you think?" she asked Tony. "Should I buy it?"

"Hell, yes, if you like it."

"I love it. I want it."

"It's older than the others, but it's probably good for another hundred thousand miles."

"It's still getting good mileage, according to the records."

Tony tucked the packet of receipts back in the console. "You okay with the dent in the back fender?"

"I didn't see it. Show me when we get back."

Back in the turnaround, Gianessa dismissed the dent with a wave of her hand.

"Let's wrap this up. I'm ready for lunch."

Gianessa wrote the owner a check.

Tony agreed to handle the registry and insurance paperwork for her, and they arranged to pick up the car that Friday.

"I can't wait." Gianessa grinned and shook the owner's hand.

Over lunch, Tony asked her, "Got some hot plans for your new car over the weekend?"

"I'm working both days. It'll be nice not to drag my roommate out of bed for a ride to work."

He threw in the next question without warning to see how she'd handle it. "You think Joel's doing all right?"

"He's frustrated by how weak and exhausted he feels, but, yes, he's doing really well. That determination will move him forward, as long as he doesn't get down about how slow the progress is in the beginning."

"When can I get him out to a meeting?"

"Give him another month. But there's no reason a few of you can't bring a meeting to him. Phil has come by a couple of times already, and Joel does well with that. He's able to sit up in a chair for an hour."

"Riding in a car's a lot harder, isn't it?"

Gianessa exhaled something between frustration and disgust. "A lot. He should have gone in medical transport for that doctor's appointment yesterday. Joel insisted he'd be fine, and Justin went right along with him, and neither of them would let me come because they knew how much I wanted to talk to you about a car. They're a mighty force when they combine."

"Couldn't talk them out of it?" Tony still thought she should have stepped in.

"I stopped trying when I sounded like a shrew, even to my own ears." She shook her head. "Apparently they had to learn that lesson the hard way. No harm done to Joel, but he won't make that mistake again. And Justin was really scared. I was surprised at how much it affected him."

"Why?"

"Justin's larger than life. It's easy to think he doesn't have feelings."

Tony decided they'd gotten personal enough. "You going to have dessert?"

"Just coffee." Gianessa grinned at him. "You've got your eye on that pie, don't you? Go wild. Ice cream, too."

"You've cured me," Justin praised.

Gianessa pressed her head back, deeper into the pillow, and teased him. "I didn't know there was a cure."

"Correction, I know there's no cure, but you've made my body strong again. Are you pleased with that?"

"I'm very pleased with your body and pleased that you

share it with me. I'm sure all your lady friends are excited and delighted about your body."

"No, I have only one lady friend," he said, tracing his finger down her bare breast and watching the nipple pop up. He sucked it for a moment and relished her intake of breath. "I like giving you pleasure." Justin buried his face between her lush breasts.

She gave a throaty laugh. "How do you feel about giving me a break for sustenance?"

Justin groaned.

"I happen to know there is a box of chocolate-covered strawberries in your refrigerator. And I'll fix us salads with that cheese you like."

He licked her other nipple and reluctantly sat back on his heels. His eyes roamed over the feast before him. "If we must."

Gianessa twisted and reached for the robe on the floor beside the bed, and he planted a kiss on her backside.

"While I'm fixing salads," she said with a sly wink, "you can fiddle with that new espresso contraption of yours."

Justin laughed. "I'll make us *doppio con panna* to pair with the strawberries. How does that sound?"

"Delicious. I'll reward you in some decadent way once I am fed and jazzed on your espresso."

Gianessa assembled ingredients for their salad. Lettuce and peppers. Avocado, poached chicken, and a container of goat cheese. Justin went into the cupboards for rice vinegar and olive oil. Gianessa snipped some fresh basil. Justin reached for the salad spinner and handed it to her, then selected a knife and started cleaning and dicing the peppers and the avocado.

After the salads, after the strawberries, while they lingered over the sweet espresso drinks, Justin asked her, "What do you like best about a weekend like this?"

"You mean dinner and breakfast and a day we spend together?"

He held his glass mug with both hands and nodded. "For example, I like sharing the Sunday *Times* and time for sex and time for cooking and anything else we think of."

"I like that you're easy to be with and fun to do things with." She dimpled when she smiled. "I like the way we move together. Not just the sex, which is glorious, but when we cook, too, and in everything we do. And I like the way you study the crowd at a restaurant and tell me what you see. It's always different from what I see. And you care about what I think and what I need." She sipped the espresso. "Tell me more about what you like."

He set down his mug and reached for her free hand. "When we're out together, I like the way you study people's bodies. I imagine you're thinking how you could help them be well. Is that what you're thinking?"

Gianessa nodded and rewarded him with an appreciative smile.

"That's extraordinary for me, to be with someone whose orientation is giving. And you tell me what you need so I can give to you, in my own way." He touched the dimple that still showed on her face. "And I like it when that dimple comes out."

She chuckled. "Why?"

"Because it tells me you're happy."

"You're right. How did you find the restaurant we went to for dinner last night?"

"I had a meeting recently with two college administrators, and I asked my secretary to find a classy restaurant with gluten-free choices. She found Gusto's, and I liked it. I thought you would, too."

"So what did these college types talk about?"

"Financial concerns, mostly, and the marketability of new programs and the fit with jobs and professions."

"Did they like your ideas?"

Justin chuckled. "They think my consultant is a clown. But when I spoke my mind, told them my ideas, they listened and agreed."

"What is with you and this clown consultant?" Gianessa asked with a musical laugh. "You always smile when you say how lousy he is. Did you hire him to fail?"

Justin raised his eyebrows. "I didn't say that."

"I'm right." Gianessa raised her hands in triumph. "You're setting something up, and he's the fall guy."

Justin blustered comically. "Why would you even think that?" He placed both hands flat on the table and leaned toward her.

She jabbed a playful finger at him. "Because you're a master strategist, and you wouldn't tolerate a fool in your employ, would you? Unless he's serving some purpose. Justin Cushman, what are you plotting?"

He laughed. "You'll just have to wait and see, darling."

She pointed the finger again. "There, you did it again. You knew I would go off on a tangent about 'darling,' and you deliberately slipped it into the conversation so I wouldn't ask you any more questions about this chess game you're playing at the college. Right?"

Justin laughed.

"I'm right, I know it."

"What do you have against 'darling,' darling?"

"You know perfectly well." She sat back in the chair and crossed her arms.

He shook his head with a look of pure innocence. "You have yet to tell me. Is it all about me being a chauvinist?"

"You are, but that's not what bugs me about it."

"Tell me."

"No, it's too hurtful. I don't want to spoil our lovely time together."

Justin's eyes narrowed and he watched with dismay as the happy sparkle left her beautiful face. "Les called you that, didn't he, and it's too painful to remember your marriage. Is that it?"

"He never used it as a term of endearment. He used it sarcastically throughout the divorce, and it was like a slap in the face every time. I hate it."

Justin felt like he had been slapped himself. "I'm sorry, Gianessa. I had no idea. I won't do it again."

"Thank you."

"What would you like me to call you?"

She shook her head and reached a conciliatory hand across the table. "I'm sorry, Justin. I hate when that bitterness comes out, and I apologize for taking it out on you."

He captured her hand in both of his and pressed it gently.

She put on a smile. "What do I want you to call me? I don't know. We'll find something."

"Sexy lady? Chickadee?"

She was laughing now, pushing away his suggestions by waving her free hand.

"I know. Dimples."

"Oh god, no, Justin." She tossed her hair and scrunched her face at him.

"Perhaps sweetheart. I've always liked sweetheart."

Gianessa tipped her head from side to side.

"I'll work on making sweetheart part of my vocabulary." He brought her hand to his lips for a kiss. "What will you call me?"

The dimples were back now. "Dude."

"Yes, now that's dignified for public gatherings of college administrators."

Her eyebrows peaked with interest. "Are you planning to take me to such gatherings?"

He sat back, his face serious now. "I'd like to, Gianessa. Er-sweetheart."

"Very cool, dude."

She dissolved into laughter, and he joined in. When they had laughed themselves out, Justin made a proposal. "I've been wanting to go over to the Cushman grounds with you. It's about half a mile, through Overlook Park, and this is a good day for it, with the sun shining and the snow packed down to a few inches. If the groundskeeper is around, we can take a turn through the mansion and identify some items to keep before I open it to an estate sale. Are you game?"

"Yes, I can try out my new boots."

"I want to know what you think of the place."

Gianessa laughed. "I'm not going to make you an offer on it, dude."

"You're getting good at snow tromping," Justin teased.

Gianessa took her eyes off the snow in front of her feet and laughed up at him. "Tromping. Is that what we're doing?"

"Keep up this pace and you'll break a sweat in no time. We're crossing onto the grounds now."

"Good, because I'm dripping." She stopped for a moment.

"It's because you're wearing that down coat."

"So cross-country skiers don't wear down coats?"

"You're a quick study, Ms. Dupioni."

"And hot." She took one more step.

"And how. Or did you mean your coat is too hot for tromping?" He turned toward her. "You can unzip, you know. That's a two-way zipper—top and bottom."

"How do you know so much about my zipper?"

"Hello, folks," a voice called, and a man emerged from a border of shrubs uphill from them.

Gianessa turned quickly and lost her balance. Justin caught her and stood firmly beside her as the groundskeeper approached them.

"Marcus, always good to see you on the job."

"Mr. Cushman. Nice sunny day." He nodded to Gianessa. "Miss."

"I've decided to have an estate sale within the month, Marcus. I'd like to go through the place before that to mark items for the family."

"No problem. I can let you in shortly, if you give me a few minutes to check the lights and clear the snow off the steps."

"We'll be somewhere on the grounds."

"Nice view up by the birches. Always thought that'd be a good home site." He pointed diagonally uphill a hundred yards. "There's another site beyond the house where the tennis court is." Marcus touched his hat and trod toward the house.

"A man of few words," Justin said quietly.

"He lives on the grounds?" Gianessa unzipped and flapped the front of her coat to cool herself down.

"He and his family. There's a gatehouse along the drive." He pointed vaguely toward the trees to the southwest. "Marcus patrols the grounds, monitors the security system and troubleshoots the house. Old houses spring leaks, in a manner of speaking, and Marcus is always on the lookout."

They trudged uphill to the grove of birches. From this vantage point, Gianessa saw the old mansion, a little downhill toward the lake, squatting behind its windbreak of evergreens. She shivered and wrapped her coat tight around her.

Justin chuckled. "Ghastly, isn't it?"

"I was expecting it to be like the Manse."

"Joel was lucky with his family home. It has grace and charm. The Cushman mansion is the heaviest of Romanesque style, ugly pink sandstone exterior and depressingly dark inside."

"You were right. A pink elephant."

"It's coming down." His thunderous voice conveyed how a momentous decision it was for him.

He has struggled with this. "That sounds like a final decision. Are you comfortable with it?"

He nodded and moved away from her. She watched him pace off fifty feet before he turned back to her. "There's a beautiful view up here, and Marcus is right." He came beside her and touched her hair. "What would you think about a home situated on this spot?"

What is he asking? Was he thinking about them living here together? Marrying and spending the rest of our lives together? *Yes, Justin, yes.* But she took his question at face value for now. She looked out at the lake, deep blue in the afternoon sun. "It's breathtaking, isn't it? Now I can really see why they call it a 'finger lake.' Even from your place, I hadn't seen how far to the south it goes."

"It's about twenty miles from Tompkins Falls to the south end. Two miles wide at its widest point."

"Is there a town at the south end?"

"A pretty state park and waterfall, and a seasonal town with shops, ice cream, and a service dock for boats. We'll go there when the weather improves."

"You'll take your camera," Gianessa guessed.

"How do you know about my photography?"

"I saw the camera hooked up to your laptop. You've never shown me your work."

"I will. It's just for fun." He waved toward the pink mansion. "Marcus is giving us the all-clear. We'll check out the other house site first and then go in by the front door."

When they reached the old tennis courts, Gianessa asked, "Are you thinking Joel and Manda will build a house here?"

"I like that thought. Both of us, Joel and me, living on the grounds, the old pink elephant cleared away."

"Which site do you prefer?"

"Up there, near the birches. I always loved that view of the lake."

"This view is not as striking, but it's a gentler slope." Gianessa stood with her hands in her pockets. "I can see Joel and Manda's children playing on the lawn."

He stroked her hair. "It warms my heart to think of that."

"You've really come home, haven't you, Justin Cushman?"

He nodded. "I'm working on it."

"I think you already know what kind of house you want."

Instead of answering, Justin drew her to him, fisted her hair and kissed her hard. Gianessa welcomed the embrace. He plundered her mouth. She felt his heart pounding, even through the layers of their clothing. When he released her, her cheeks were on fire and her eyes danced with happiness.

"You take my breath away, Justin."

He touched his forehead to hers. "If the house weren't forty degrees, we could find a bed for ourselves."

"Brrr. Let's check out the antiques and tromp back to Lakeside Terrace for hot cocoa and hot sex."

"Let's."

"Ten weeks or twelve to the wedding?" Gianessa asked Joel. "I've lost track."

"Ten and a few days. I'd like to stand for the ceremony. Maybe hold Manda for a slow dance, pretend we're moving on the floor." He grinned at the thought.

"You're on track for that. I don't want you overdoing it between now and then."

"Do you think I'm overdoing it?"

"I think you're feisty." She teased and then sobered. "That tells me you're impatient, and that worries me."

"So you're saying I could overdo it and it would push me backwards?"

"Exactly. You've had two serious leg injuries in the past. Each has taken a toll. This accident compounded the damage. And you're not a teenager this time. Bodies heal slower at thirty than at fifteen."

Joel pulled himself up the steps from the pool, grabbing the railing with his good left arm. He took the towel she handed him and sat on a teakwood stool she'd placed by the steps. "So it was completely unrealistic to think Manda and I could go to Ireland on our honeymoon?"

"Only if you were content to go in a wheelchair."

Joel nodded thoughtfully as he rubbed his legs dry. "Not that there's anything wrong with that, but it's not how I want to do it. I want to hike with Manda on a country lane and brace myself against the wind on top of a rocky cliff and maybe climb a hill together."

Gianessa handed him a bottle of water. "Do you use those images in your meditation?"

Joel nodded.

"You're on target to do the lane and the cliff top in a year or so. Maybe the hill, too, if you pick a gentle one."

"Manda will finish her degree a year from May and sit her CPA exam that summer. So fall next year might work for us?"

"Sounds just right, Joel."

Joel reached for her hand, and she squatted down beside him.

"What is it?"

"You're gifted. And skilled. I want you to go after your physical therapy license from New York State."

Gianessa's eyes went wide with fear. She dropped down on her butt in a puddle of pool water and hugged her knees.

Joel pressed her. "It may take a couple of rounds, and it may be uncomfortable, which is why you should start now. The holistic rehab center you create with Manda and Justin will require a licensed therapist in the lead. Obviously that's you."

"Joel I wouldn't know where to begin."

"I don't buy that. Get online and research it, like anything else. And network. The docs in Rochester will support you. I'll support you. But you have to do the footwork."

"Scares me to death, you know?"

Joel chose a dry towel from the stack on a cart to his left and wrapped himself in it. "There's a reason one whole line of the Serenity Prayer is 'Courage to change the things I can.'"

Gianessa nodded slowly, not in agreement, he sensed, but in thoughtful consideration.

"You should ask Tony to introduce you to his girl, Sunny. She's in the program and is finishing her Doctor of Physical Therapy, same degree as yours. She could be a sounding board and might introduce you to a few good people." He nudged her knee with his elbow. "She'd probably appreciate your support with her exams and boards and whatever else she has to do this year."

Gianessa lifted her smiling face to Joel. "I've been scared and selfish, and you're a genius."

He sat up straighter.

She quizzed, "So, boss, how are you handling all the stresses in your life these days?"

Joel let out his breath in a laugh. "It's a challenge living with Manda in close quarters like this, especially since I can't get out much. It helps that the weather's improving. And Phil and Tony bring meetings here."

"I'd like you to get out some. If you don't want to be seen in the chair, put it in the car as a backup and take your walker with you."

Joel grinned. "Busted. I've also been scared and selfish. When will I be ready for the cane?"

Gianessa eyed the mahogany cane with the ebony handle Justin had brought back from New York on one of his trips. He'd had it made to the specifications Gianessa provided.

Joel had hung the cane from one of the cabinet door pulls as an incentive.

"It's really very classy," Gianessa said. "A few weeks, probably. Getting out now with the walker will help your recovery in several ways, you know. And people will be thrilled to see you out and about."

"You don't think I look scruffy and weak?"

"I think you need a haircut and a really classy pair of pants that will slide over your knee brace."

Joel paused in his effort to fasten the brace. His eyes bored into hers, and he challenged, "So, you want to go shopping with me?"

She winked. "Now you're talking. I'll see if Sara will come over first to cut your hair. What do you think?"

Joel reached for his chair and maneuvered it closer. "Give her a call. I'll get dressed. Then we'll swing by your place for dry bottoms for you," he teased.

She gave his arm a playful swat as he wheeled by.

"Bridey would love this scene." Justin hadn't realized he'd said it aloud until Gianessa tapped her cards on the table and cocked her head.

"I know who she is, don't tell me. Your grandmother."

"Bridey was Joel's grandmother, on his mother's side."

"She came from Ireland?"

Justin beamed. "She did, and she loved romance."

"And read the tea leaves, right?"

"She was a fey one," he answered with a nod.

"What do you mean?"

"She could see the future."

Gianessa's eyes opened wide. "Do you believe that?"

"I'm beginning to."

"Tell me what she saw in your tea leaves."

Justin straightened the haphazard pile of winning tricks in front of him. *Why did I bring this up?*

"Spill, Justin."

"Spill?"

"Spill. It's the short form of spill the beans."

"Suppose I don't want to spill?"

"Why did you bring it up?"

"I think you brought it up."

"Because you brought it up, and, you're right, it's a romantic scene we've got going here." She gestured to the kitchen, the table, and the porch as she talked. "Irish stew simmering on the stove. The two of us warm and cozy playing honeymoon bridge, wind rattling the porch doors and rain hitting the panes. And Bridey popped into your mind, because she would love what's going on here this St. Patrick's Saturday."

Justin chuckled. "You win. What Bridey saw in my tea leaves is a bit of a mystery to me. She told me, 'At the center of the storm is a stillpoint, and that's where your heart is.'"

Gianessa sat back, put down her cards and contemplated. "You left the storm behind when you came back here, I thought. Or was home a stormy place for you at one time?"

"Both, I think. My life's been stormy wherever I've been. I don't want that anymore. The high stakes, the drama, the glitz, the over-the-top lifestyle."

"She said the stillpoint is at the center of the storm. Maybe you can't just turn your back to the storm. Maybe you have to confront it to make peace with it."

"I never thought of that."

"Have you found a stillpoint?"

"I believe so." Justin held her gaze.

"And at that stillpoint, is your heart present?"

Justin saw no mocking in her face, no pretense, simply peace and happiness. "Yes, it is. What about your heart, Gianessa? Is it here, too?"

She blinked and smiled into his eyes. "Yes."

Justin watched as a slow, sexy smile appeared.

He sensed a twinkle in his own eye. "If we finish out this hand, you'll win."

"And if we don't finish it out, you'll win by default." She picked up her hand again. "That's not happening. I'm going to trounce you, Justin Cushman." She wiggled back in her chair. "I'm playing four hearts, and I'm two tricks away from trouncing you."

He sat back and assumed a casual pose. “We should play together, with other people. There are some friendly games, I’m told, among some of the college people.” He led the eight of clubs from his hand.

“I would like a friendly game with you as my partner,” Gianessa said as she scooped up the trick with her queen. “Wouldn’t you prefer something more cutthroat?” She led off the last trick with her king of hearts.

Justin set his two of spades on the table and let her collect the trick. “No. I’d prefer to play with you and to make it a friendly evening with a few others.”

He watched her shuffle the deck. A smile spread over her face.

When she met his gaze, her eyes were a warm, smoky violet. “I’d like that. Let’s do it, Justin.”

“So a frittata starts like an omelet, but instead of folding it over, you pop it in the oven?”

Gianessa nodded. “Basically, that’s it.” She was in teacher mode this morning, the last Sunday of March. She stood across the island from him, observing and coaching him step by step.

“And you had me whisk it more than an omelet. Will that make it puffier?” He struggled to understand why the frittata was on the menu instead of their favorite omelets.

“Exactly, and remember, for an omelet we would have let the egg set up a bit before adding the toppings; for the frittata, we sautéed our favorite add-ons right in the skillet then poured in the egg.”

Justin shifted his weight and puzzled, “But we set aside the avocado and cheese.”

“We’ll wait until it’s set a bit to add those kind of toppings. You’re a quick study, Justin. Of course some people sprinkle the cheese on just before it sets up and then switch on the broiler to give it a golden, crispy top."

"Do you?"

"Me? I keep it simple. No crispy top."

He leaned against the counter and looked her in the eye with a knowing smile. "You're teaching me the frittata so I can save face, aren't you?"

Gianessa blushed. "Whatever do you mean?"

"I mean, if someone, not saying me, is really bad at letting the egg run under to set an omelet or really clumsy at folding . . ."

"Or both." Her musical laugh brightened the rainy April morning.

Justin grinned. "You are busted." He stretched across the island and gave her a kiss. "This could become my signature breakfast dish. No more broken, lopsided omelets."

"Yes, it could. I would like that."

They watched as the surface of the egg mixture began to congeal.

"Is it ready for the oven?"

"Ready. See, you have good judgment, Justin."

He muscled the skillet into the hot oven. "How long?" He shut the oven door.

"About five minutes, but you really have to watch it."

He set the oven timer and rested his oven mitts on the island.

Gianessa asked, "I enjoyed the bridge with your friends last night. How do you think it went?"

"I think you were a hit. They'd like to do it again."

"Would you?"

He nodded, studying her face. She was the picture of serenity, he decided. Content, untroubled, looking forward to the next step and enjoying the present.

"I'll get the table ready," he offered.

She flashed a smile, gathered the bowls and utensils, and carried them to the sink where a dishpan of sudsy water waited.

As he set out plates and mugs next to dishes of fruit, Justin watched her work and wondered if she felt, as he sometimes did, that they were in a holding pattern. Not just the five minutes while the frittata set up, but in their relationship. She seemed content, as he was, with their Saturday night sleepovers, hot sex, Sunday cooking dates, and long walks whenever the weather let them venture out. Yet he wondered how long that would satisfy her.

Knowing how deeply her heart was broken by the loss of her little girl, he thought she must want to marry and have more children. Perhaps he should step aside and let her find a younger man eager to have a family with her. But part of him wished he could step into that role himself. Why did he feel so unsettled in himself and so unsuitable as a long-term partner for this beautiful, captivating woman?

"You're really tense, Justin," Gianessa observed.

Do I dare say what's on my mind?

The timer spared him. He bounded back to the oven, reached for the mitts, opened the door a crack and saw that the egg was not quite set. He switched on the oven light, closed the door, and squatted down to watch the progress.

The frittata was "delicious" according to Gianessa. He agreed.

The massage she gave him after their meal to ease his tension was "divine" in his words.

His clumsy effort to give her a massage led to playful sex that ended abruptly when Gianessa pushed at his chest and said, "No, stop. Stop, Justin. It hurts."

He sat back in alarm. "What's happened?"

She curled on her side, and he covered her with a throw from the foot of the bed.

"How can I help? What do you need?"

"I just need to stop for now. You were really deep, which you know I love, but today it hurt. I don't know why." She managed a half smile and met his eyes. "I'm sorry, I was enjoying that so much."

He looked around for his clothes. "Rest a minute," he told her and got dressed. "I'll make tea, unless you need me to stay here with you."

"I'll be fine. I'll be out in a minute for the tea."

As he set the kettle over, she called from his bathroom, "Do you have Tylenol or something?"

"Yes, in the medicine cabinet. Need help?"

"I'm good. Thirsty for that tea."

When she joined him, she was fully dressed with her hair in a ponytail and her arms folded across her middle as if she were still hurting.

"I'm worried about this. How bad is the pain? What do we need to do?"

"It's nothing. Really," she insisted.

"You're holding onto yourself."

"I'm chilled. Fallout from the bad surprise." She gave him a sexy smile. "And the disappointment at having our pleasure cut short. Forgive me?"

"There's nothing to forgive. I want you to see your doctor."

"If I have even a twinge after the Tylenol kicks in, I will call her first thing in the morning."

"And you will let me know one way or the other."

She bit back annoyance. "I will. Please don't worry."

He could see, from the way she avoided his eyes and the determined set of her mouth, that asking any more questions would escalate into an argument.

Chapter 10

Justin maneuvered the Saab to a smooth stop at the curb just as Manda and her older sister breezed through the double doors, each dragging a bright pink suitcase.

Gianessa sucked in her breath, and Justin reached for her hand and held it protectively. "Trouble."

Joel had implored Justin and Gianessa to come with Manda today, worried that the much-anticipated reunion of the sisters could be a disaster.

The sisters were both five foot eight and slender, with long legs and cheekbones that turned heads. Manda was a dark-haired, blue-eyed, natural beauty. Lyssa was a mess. She had teased her lifeless red hair into Texas Big Hair, ringed her eyes with kohl, and smudged the eyelids with garish green eye shadow.

Justin speculated, "That's more than alcohol. Her body is vibrating, and I doubt it's nervousness at meeting us."

"Manda joked about a marijuana maintenance plan. Look at how pasty her skin is, Justin. Either she's not eating well, or she's not eating."

"Darling, she's killing herself."

Gianessa turned to face him.

"Sorry about the 'darling.' It slipped out."

She pressed his hand. "No, I know you're upset. I am too. Somehow we need to handle this so Manda and Joel have a beautiful wedding."

"Yes, and we will." Justin switched off the motor. "Maybe we can do something to help Lyssa, too." He popped the trunk, and swung out of the car.

As he approached Manda, he saw three little worry wrinkles in the center of her brow. He hadn't seen them since the day he'd met her, when Joel's condition was still a dark unknown for them. Justin renewed his vow to do all in his power to erase those worry lines and keep them away.

"Justin, meet my sister, Lyssa," Manda said, her voice straining to be cheerful.

Lyssa snapped her hand out for Justin to shake.

His humor took over. "Quick Draw Doughty, is it?" He gave her a firm handshake.

Lyssa laughed and told him in her adopted Texas twang, "Hey, Uncle Justin. My little sister has been tellin' me all about y'all." She waved wildly to Gianessa in the front seat. "Hey, Gianessa."

Gianessa's smile was frozen on her face. Lyssa didn't seem to notice.

Justin busied himself with Lyssa's suitcase and carry-on bag, grateful he could escape into his role as chauffeur for the next fifteen minutes.

At the canal side restaurant, he stayed behind Gianessa and Manda as they climbed the wide stone steps. Gianessa had her arm around Manda's shoulders. Manda looked like she would burst into tears.

"We'll have a delicious, healthy salad and iced tea right now," Gianessa told her. "We can tell Lyssa all about your gown and the plans you have for the ceremony. How does that sound?"

Manda gave a wooden nod. "I can do that." Her toe caught on the top step, and she would have stumbled if Gianessa hadn't steadied her. "Thank god you and Justin are here."

"Of course we're here. We'll help you figure this out. You and Joel are going to have a beautiful wedding. We'll see to that."

Manda rushed ahead to tell the hostess there were four of them and they wanted a table on the upstairs porch.

Gianessa turned to Justin and reached out a delicate hand.

He squeezed it in support. "You take care of Manda, I've got Lyssa." He stayed at the entry until Lyssa caught up, then steered her through the tables and onto the porch, held her chair for her, and drummed his fingers on the back, waiting for her to sit.

"You know what?" Lyssa said. "Can y'all order me a soda and a salad with chicken? I'm going to stretch my legs a few minutes."

Justin waved his arm back toward the front door. "Just don't fall in. You wouldn't want to ruin Manda's wedding now, would you?" His tone went beyond sarcastic to menacing.

Lyssa glared at him and flounced out.

Manda squeezed her eyes shut.

Gianessa drew a waiter with her magnetic smile and arranged for ice water all around, three iced teas, and one ginger ale. "And we'll be ready to order when you come back with those." She gave him a wink that mobilized him.

Justin nodded his agreement, although the waiter took no notice of him. He made a mental note of the young man's name. Gregory.

He relaxed for a moment, knowing that he and Gianessa were a good team. Together they would help Manda find her way out of this nightmare.

He took heart that Lyssa's spring break came early enough for Manda to rethink her wedding party. That detail was easily fixed. The emotional toll on Manda and the impact of addiction on Lyssa were not so easy.

Gianessa put a gentle hand on Manda's arm.

"If you need to cry, Manda, I have plenty of tissues in my tote bag." Gianessa pressed a few into Manda's hand.

Manda choked out, "Gwen tried to tell me this could happen." She held the tissues to her eyes and sobbed. "And she was right."

Justin's gaze follow the canal path beyond the benches and shops busy with families. Near the bridge, he saw Lyssa's red hair, a puff of smoke, and a shaking white hand that sheltered a toke. He debated a moment then decided that if she were arrested, he would not bail her out.

He watched the scene until their waiter approached, straining under a heavy tray. He hesitated at the drama and looked to Justin for direction.

"Good man, Gregory," Justin told him. "That's exactly what we all need."

Gregory lost no time distributing the water and drinks. He tucked the empty tray under his arm and looked directly at Justin's nose. "What can I bring you folks?"

Justin gave him the order for four salads of varying descriptions, knowing what he wanted, what Gianessa usually ate, what Lyssa had requested, and what Manda would ask for in her sunniest mood. "And these women are starved," Justin said in a conspiratorial tone.

"I'll get that order right in for you, sir."

Justin reached across the table for Manda's hand. "Good lord, what a mess."

Manda grabbed onto his hand and implored him, "What am I going to do?"

"One solution is to buy your sister a beautiful dress and make a backup plan. I'm sure Sara would serve as your maid-of-honor or Gwen or Gianessa, all reliable women who love you and honor your marriage to Joel."

Manda sat up straighter and reached for her iced tea. She met his eyes over the rim of her glass and gave him a little nod.

Gianessa followed suit, and Justin joined them.

Gregory delivered their salads, and Gianessa beamed her thanks.

Justin spotted Lyssa coming back up the path. She concentrated on every step. "She's on her way now, and she's high. I say we eat our salads, perhaps go for a stroll after lunch, and then what? Do we want to shop for dresses today like we planned?"

Manda stiffened.

Gianessa looked doubtfully from Manda to Justin and back again. "I just need to eat something right now," she told them.

"Agreed."

When Lyssa appeared in the entryway, Justin stood up and motioned her back to their table on the porch. He held her chair, and Lyssa stumbled into it. She set about devouring her salad without a word to anyone.

Justin ended his phone call and turned to Gianessa. "She's been admitted. She passed the intake, which is good news and bad news." He thanked her and took the cup of hot chocolate from her hands. They sat on stools at the island in his kitchen.

Their after-lunch stroll on the towpath had heated up when Lyssa chided Manda for planning a sober wedding reception, not even champagne for the toast. The argument escalated until Manda screamed that she wouldn't let Lyssa come to her wedding, let alone be her maid-of-honor. At that point, Justin and Gianessa intervened, pointing out the effect of Lyssa's addiction on her sister and her sister's wedding plans.

"It was a nightmare, Justin. How did you ever keep your cool?"

"I was shaking inside, sweetheart. It was all I could do not to throw her in the canal."

"This was supposed to be the weekend that Lyssa and Manda reunited after six years and Lyssa got her gown as maid-of-honor for Manda and Joel's wedding. How could it go so horribly wrong?"

"Manda had unrealistic expectations. Denial, I suppose, forgetting how the disease turns us into monsters."

“Us? Why did you say that?”

He didn’t know why he’d included himself. He shook his head. “She knew Lyssa was still drinking and using. Yet she pinned her hopes on Lyssa coming here, reconnecting with her, helping to plan the wedding and standing up with her on the most important day of her life.”

“A setback like this is the last thing Manda and Joel needed.”

Justin put his arm around Gianessa and kissed her temple. “They’ll be fine. Tony and Phil are with Joel, and Manda is at a meeting with her sponsor Gwen, which is exactly what they both need.” He rubbed her back with calming circles. “And Lyssa may or may not accept the help she’s given at the rehab. But an intervention was the right thing to do, don’t you think?”

“Short of throwing her in the canal, yes.” Gianessa’s laugh was full of irony. “We couldn’t just go shopping for a bridesmaid gown and pretend everything was fine.”

“You do know I suggested that simply to show the absurdity of it?”

She looked up at him through her eyelashes, a smile curving her lips. “I’m catching on to your strategies.”

“And I’m wondering, did you have the rehab on speed dial?” Justin teased.

Gianessa looked at him like a child who’s been caught snitching a cookie. “I—yes, I have the hospital number in my phone, and I knew they could connect me with the rehab. We were just lucky they could take her today.” She closed her eyes with a sigh, possibly of exhaustion or relief or both.

Justin gave her a covert glance and, from the peace on her face, concluded she did not even suspect his sudden, generous contribution to the hospital, which had gone a long way toward making an intake counselor and a bed available. He said heartily, “Yes, before she changed her mind.”

Gianessa frowned suddenly and covered her ears. “I

can still hear Manda shriek at Lyssa and see those cyclists swerving off the path to avoid running into them."

He stroked her arm. "That's enough drama for one day. How about a stroll along the lakeshore?"

Gianessa looked at him with a question in her eyes.

"What is it? What would you like to do?"

"I'd like to climb up to that spot on the Cushman grounds, up near the birches where you can see the whole lake. Would you like to?"

Justin's smile radiated from his heart as he reached for her hand.

Gianessa stood utterly still, gazing at the lake, allowing its strength and permanence to soothe her troubled thoughts. "I love it here," she said to Justin.

"I do as well. I'd like to enjoy this view every morning and every evening."

"You know, until you brought me here, I'd look at our lake—Chestnut Lake—and think, 'It's not my ocean.' Now I can see its beauty, and I love it, whatever mood it's in."

She drank in the sight of the deep blue water. A cluster of islands crowded together in the northeast corner of the lake, each one a little mound covered with evergreens. The shore curved gently south from there, as far as she could see. "I didn't give it a chance. It is gorgeous."

Years of living by the Pacific had trained her eye to see the vast ocean, not to appreciate this pristine lake in a finger-shaped valley carved by a glacier. That life by the Pacific was gone, and she had come around to giving this life her full attention. Intuition prompted her to meet Justin's gaze. "You're going to build your dream house here, aren't you?"

He blinked. "I—yes, I am. First, though," he said with a nod toward the old mansion, "that's coming down."

"You're really going to demolish it?" She wasn't surprised. She'd actually wondered what the holdup was.

Justin nodded. "They've just assigned the crew. They'll start next week."

"It's a big job," she guessed.

"Wrecking ball, asbestos abatement, a horrible job. People who are in that business know what they're doing."

She gave him a smile. "It's a sure thing. Not like rehab."

He pursed his lips. "We can hope for Lyssa's recovery. I hate seeing Manda in so much pain. I caused her pain like that when I couldn't be found after Joel's accident."

"Justin, you were in the hospital for a serious condition that—thank god—turned out to be treatable."

"Thanks to you. Between my illness and my bankrupt spirit, I thought I was dying."

"You've come a long way in a few months." She looked admiringly at his physique. "You've worked hard, and it shows."

Justin touched her cheek and reached his fingers into her hair. "You are a wise woman and very good for me. Do you know I've fallen in love with you?"

Gianessa's breath caught. Her emotions fell all over each other: happiness, love, a touch of fear, faith. She met his kiss and let him enfold her with his strong arms.

"What do you suppose we should do about this?"

"I want to enjoy it a day at a time," she told him, hoping he wanted more, not daring to say she did.

He nodded. "Let's come back here after the mansion is gone," he proposed.

She could tell from the flush on his cheeks and the heat in his eyes that he wanted her in his bed.

A smile warmed her whole being. "Let's."

"How's your young man?"

The coffee caught in Gianessa's throat, and she coughed, helpless to end the tickle.

"My timing has always sucked," Carol joked. "Put your arms straight up over your head.

Gianessa did as she was told. The spasm slowly passed. She smiled and nodded but did not attempt to talk.

"That wasn't a hard question, was it?"

Gianessa shook her head, put her hand on her sternum and tested her voice. "He's well," she croaked. She told Carol about the drama with Manda's sister and the hope they all had for Lyssa's rehab.

"You know, I hear a lot of respect for this gentleman when you share about your time with him."

Gianessa tried another sip of coffee. "He's a good man underneath it all," she said.

Carol chuckled. "Underneath what all?"

"He's used to having his own way and wielding a great deal of power."

"I'll bet you don't let him get away with that in your relationship."

Gianessa regarded her thoughtfully. "You're right."

"As you've opened up these past few months, I've seen surprising strength in you."

"Why do you say 'surprising'?"

Carol tapped her perfectly manicured fingernails—dark plum this month—against the ceramic mug. "Fair question. When I met you, you had that lost little girl look, remember? And you're so slender and ethereal, I didn't expect to find the resilient core that you've developed over the years."

"Thank you."

"Where do you think that strength came from?"

Gianessa flashed a happy smile. "My pop. Have I told you about him?"

"Your father? No, we haven't talked about your family."

"Pop is the greatest. I miss him like crazy."

"Has he passed?"

"No. He and his sister—twin sister, my aunt Ariella—moved

back to Italy last year. That's part of why I made the decision to move here. I had no more reason to stay in California."

"Your father can't be old enough to retire?"

"You're right. Actually he took his talent back to Italy and opened a restaurant there. In Milano. He caters to the fashion community and calls it Ariella's American Restaurant."

"You're giving me a sly smile. What's the joke?"

"It's basically the same menu he used in San Francisco at Gianni's Italian Kitchen."

Carol laughed and took another swallow of her coffee. "That's unusual, isn't it, to move a business back to one's home country?"

"I suppose so. There was something going on in San Francisco, and he wouldn't tell me what it was, but he was more and more worried. For a while I thought he was worried about my addiction and my divorce but, once I cleared up, I realized it wasn't about me. I think he stayed as long as he did to be near me, but that wasn't the reason for his business decision. I asked Ariella once, and she said, 'Baby girl, you don't want to know and you don't even want to ask. We will be fine once we're away from it.'"

"Some criminal element pressuring him?"

"I don't know, and I don't ask. They both wanted to be back home in Italy, so that's where they went. They are fine, the restaurant is catching on, and Pop's got a girl."

"A lady friend?"

Gianessa nodded. "I think if the business does well, he'll marry again."

"What's the story with your mother?"

Gianessa shook her head. "There were never two people so completely different. They were passionately in love, I think, when they first met. They married, I came along, and then they grew apart. Totally apart. My mother is brilliant, and she has a distinguished career in high-tech. She's made millions in start-up companies in the Bay Area.

They split up when I was very young. Ariella moved from Italy to help Pop raise me."

"Did you see your mother or have a relationship with her?"

"A little. She always fussed over my birthday, which is early in July. Every August she'd take me to New York City for a huge shopping spree—clothes and accessories and shoes and purses." Gianessa gestured at her outfit—form-fitting designer jeans topped by a silk T-shirt and an artfully arranged scarf. "I don't have a big budget for clothes, but those lessons never left me. These pieces are from consignment shops and thrift stores that my roommate Sara knows about. If I had the budget, I'd probably be wearing Italian leather boots and an obscenely expensive belt." She kicked up one foot shod in a hiking shoe with deep tread on the sole. "End of season sale at Bean's."

"Smart choice for Upstate New York. Do you have a relationship with your mother now?"

Gianessa hated Carol's persistence. "No. Her work has always been an obsession, more so every year. She is completely focused on the competition and maintaining her edge."

"Did she remarry?"

Gianessa shook her head. "She has her fortune and her reputation." She winced at the anger in her own voice.

"Sad. It must have been hard being her daughter."

"Pop and Ariella are my parents. They're the best."

"Would you say your young man is more like your father or your mother?"

Gianessa thought about it. "A bit of both. He has money and power, but he's also a terrific cook and he's got an infectious sense of humor."

"I look forward to hearing more. We're coming up on meeting time. Let's not be late."

As Joel swam his warm-up routine, he watched her move around the pool area, humming as she gathered the floats and belts and weights for their workout. She was more graceful than last week, if that was possible, and far more beautiful and womanly than she'd been when they met at the retreat center last fall. He thought the fling with Justin had brought her home to her beauty, but intuition told him the womanliness was something else.

Gianessa looked up and caught him spying. "You look like a man who doesn't want to tell a woman her panty line is showing." There was no self-consciousness in her statement.

"It's not," he told her with a big smile. He hoisted himself onto the ledge of the pool, pivoted his hips into a sitting position, and accepted the hand she reached out to help him stand.

"You're much stronger. Your arms are nearly equal when you reach forward in the modified crawl. How was the twist today when you sat on the ledge?"

"Still sore, but I know it's improving."

He balanced on his right leg while he dried the left and noted with satisfaction how solid his stance was now. "It's encouraging to see progress. You've thought through every move, haven't you?" he quizzed her. *Every move except one*.

"That's what you're paying me to do. And I'm thrilled with how quickly you're improving. Fess up. Are you in this pool at night by yourself?"

"I like being in here at night, but I'm not that foolish to come alone. Manda swims with me a few nights a week after work. I think it's the only time she relaxes."

"That's good. I need your promise you won't try anything you're not ready for when I'm not here."

"It's a promise," he vowed.

She pointed to the weights in the adjoining space, and he looked questioningly at the props she had gathered by the pool.

"Would you rather try some weights today? I think you're ready, and I won't push you too hard the first time."

"Let's do it."

She moved him through a short routine, using the lightest settings for just a few reps at each station. Even so, Joel reached his limit with the last leg press. "That's enough," he told her.

She nodded. "We're done here. You're way ahead of where I expected you to be." She handed him a full bottle of water, and he drank thirstily. "You can shower or cool down in the pool first. Your choice."

"I'll get a shower in a minute. Let me take you to lunch today."

She raised an eyebrow, and then smiled at him. "Something on your mind?"

Joel nodded, drilled her with a look, and asked her, "Does he know yet?"

Gianessa frowned at him, puzzled.

Genuinely puzzled. "I'll take that as a 'no'."

She laughed at him. "Either I've exhausted you to the point of insanity, or I've missed something entirely." She took a deep breath and asked patiently, "Does who know what?"

Joel stalled by taking a long pull on the bottle of water. "I have the uncomfortable feeling you don't know yourself."

"Joel, what are we talking about?"

"I could swear you're pregnant."

Her mouth opened.

Joel watched emotions chase each other across her face. Her breathing became uneven and the blood drained from her face.

"Sit down," he ordered. He slid his stronger arm around her waist and helped her to the bench. "Put your head between your knees." He placed his hand at the back of her head for a moment. "Stay there until the dizziness passes." He sat next to her, stroked her back and encouraged her to take belly breaths. When she nodded, he eased his hand back.

She lifted up partway, resting her forearms on her knees and her head on her arms. She turned her face toward him.

"Did you even suspect?"

She shook her head. "How could I not know? The clues were there, but I didn't see them."

"Denial maybe?"

"Tell me how you knew."

"I must have a little of my grandmother Bridey's intuition."

"But something must have clued you in."

"There's a womanliness about you that's new. A softness in your face and eyes, a fullness in, well, you know. It's like your body is preparing for the child in your womb."

A shudder—or was it a thrill?—coursed through her, and she wrapped her arms around her middle. "Joel, Justin will hate me. What on earth am I going to do?"

"You're going to have lunch with me, and we'll stop at a drug store on the way to get a pregnancy kit."

She sat up straight and rubbed her hands on her thighs. "Not in Tompkins Falls, we're not. The whole town will think you and I are pregnant."

"Rochester," he said. "We'll swing through Victor for the kit and have lunch along the canal in Pittsford. And we'll talk about it."

She looked at his face then, and he saw in her clear, peaceful gaze that she would be all right with this. "You're a good friend, Joel."

"So are you," he told her.

She exited the ladies' room, stopped in confusion, and looked blankly at the dozens of lunch-goers who had crowded into the restaurant in the last five minutes.

Joel stood and waved to her. Relief flooded her face. He pointed out a clear route back to their table in a quiet corner.

She settled into her chair, and he asked, "Confirmed?"

She nodded, unable to speak.

"Bottle of wine for you folks?" a cheerful waiter announced himself.

Gianessa covered her face with her hands.

Joel told him firmly, “Just ice water for us for the moment, and we’d each like a pot of green tea as soon as you can manage.”

“And are you ready to order?” he asked.

“I’ll wave when we’re ready to order,” Joel told him sharply.

The waiter sniffed and turned away.

“Sorry,” Gianessa whispered. “Thank you for sending him away.”

“I’ll order for us when you’ve had a chance to choose.”

She breathed quietly. “He’s going to hate me for this.”

“I have a few questions,” he said, “but they can wait.”

Gianessa gave him a shaky laugh. “It would be easier to deal with questions than to come up with a coherent thought of my own.”

He squeezed her hand. “Can you eat?”

“I think I need to eat, even though I have no appetite.”

“What will work with your food plan?” He handed her a menu open to the salads.

She read the offerings and scanned them a second time as though she couldn’t make sense of them. “The chicken and pear over mesclun with Greek dressing on the side, no croutons or onions. Entrée size.” She laughed. “I guess I do have an appetite.”

“Good.” He signaled to the waiter, gave him a big smile along with their order, and asked him not to bring bread to the table.

“You are beautiful,” he said. He had brought this woman to Tompkins Falls, to the Manse, and now she was carrying his uncle’s child. A new generation of Cushmans. He wondered what Bridey would think of that.

“Thank you for saying that.”

“I mean it. And I want you to know, whatever happens with Justin, you’ll be supported.”

She put her hand on her belly and smiled down.

"This is your cousin, baby. He is the finest of men, and he is our friend."

"You do want the baby?" Joel asked.

She nodded and smiled across the table at him.

"Any idea how far along you are?"

"I'm thinking I probably got pregnant when we were in New York City at the end of January."

"So three months or so?"

Gianessa nodded.

"You haven't had any symptoms?"

"Now that I think of it, little signs, nothing more. No morning sickness, thank god. Of course, no periods, which I didn't even notice. I've never been regular." She closed her eyes. "Sorry, TMI."

"No protection? Did either of you even think of it?"

She shook her head. "I stopped using birth control a couple of years ago because I didn't need it and couldn't afford it. I just never started again or even thought of it. How irresponsible is that?"

"There's no doubt this is Justin's baby?" His tone was sharper than he intended.

She jumped a little and looked him squarely in the eye. "No, there's no question. Would you want me to have a paternity test?" There was an edge in her voice.

"No, not for my sake." *I can't guarantee Justin won't.* He reached for her hand. "I have no right to say this, but I really hope you'll stay here and let me be part of this baby's life, regardless of how things work out between you and Justin. I'm just putting that out there for now. I trust you to do what's best for you and the baby."

She nodded and gazed at her hands on her belly.

The waiter returned with their teapots and mugs. Gianessa dunked the teabag up and down in the hot water, lost in thought. When she tried to lift the pot, it was too much for her shaking hands.

Joel poured her tea and then his own. “It’s hot,” he warned when she picked up the mug.

She set it down again. “I think the next right thing is to call my doctor and get in to see her as soon as possible.”

“Why don’t you call her right now?” Joel encouraged. “I’ll be right back.” He left the table for a few minutes to give her privacy.

When he returned, their salads sat on the table, and Gianessa jotted notes in a tiny notebook.

“She’ll see you?”

“This afternoon. Two o’clock.”

“Where is she?”

“Clifton Springs. That doesn’t give us much time to eat. Joel, when do you need to get back to the Manse?”

“I need to support you right now. Let’s eat our salads, and while we’re eating, tell me what you want me to do.” He was glad to see her perk up a little as she ate. When she didn’t suggest a course of action, he said, “I can wait in town, in the car, in the waiting room, wherever you’re most comfortable.”

“It’s complicated,” she said with a sheepish smile. “I’m thinking.”

“What would you really, really like me to do?”

“I’d really like you to help me talk with the doctor after the exam.”

He swallowed against his nervousness. “This will be good practice for me when Manda gets pregnant.”

“Okay. Here are my questions.” She tapped her finger on the notebook. “You tell me what else I should be asking.”

Gianessa asked Joel to take the wheel on the drive home from Clifton Springs. “I am shaking again,” she told him. “God, I could never have done that alone.”

He reached over and covered her hand. “And you won’t do any of it alone. Manda and I will help you all we can. And you have friends in the program that will be there for you. Give some thought to who you want to tell and when.”

“Please don’t say anything yet. Not even to Manda.”

“I’m prepared to keep it confidential as long as you want. Manda is consumed with classwork and wedding plans, so she’s not going to guess a thing on her own. And it’s not for me to tell Justin.”

“God, Joel, what am I going to do? How can I go to him and tell him?”

“Tell me what you’re afraid of.” Glad the car was automatic shift, he drove carefully through the parking lot.

“He will think I seduced him to get him to marry me, that I am after his money.”

“Why would he think that?”

“You know how suspicious he gets.”

“He’s capable of better.” He turned left at the traffic light and breathed a sigh of relief that they had the road to themselves.

“I can’t imagine he wants to be a father.”

“I’m inclined to agree with you about that one, but he did say something off the wall when I first came out of the coma. I don’t think he had even met you yet. But either way it stunned me.”

“What was it?”

“He was urging me to propose to Manda, which I already intended to do. And to have a family, which I had already come around to wanting.”

“You hadn’t wanted to have children?”

“No. I could never see myself as a father. But I started to see myself in that role the more Manda and I fell in love. There was a moment when I looked at her and imagined her pregnant with our child, and it felt so right. And I realized, by watching her grow and change in recovery, I really enjoyed being part of that development, and I knew I wanted to be a dad and to have children with her."

"I'm so glad you told me that."

"Even though it's not exactly what I started out to say."

"Which was?"

"That, after I came out of the coma and Justin realized I was serious about marrying Manda and having children, he said he intended to beat me to the first Cushman heir. And I laughed at the time, thinking it was just that old competitive streak between us, or maybe it was his way of telling me he thought it was an outstanding idea for me to produce an heir and raise a family. But I can't help thinking he was serious."

"Serious about having a child of his own?"

"Yes." It was giving him a headache to nod and to turn his head, so he kept his eyes on the road.

"It's hard to believe."

"Why do you say that?"

"I have the impression he would like to have a long term relationship with a woman, but marriage and family have never been in his plans."

When he pressed the brake at the stop sign, pain shot into his knee. He made the left turn onto a road that would take them into Tompkins Falls, still a few miles ahead. "You may be right, but I wouldn't count him out."

"Why?"

He heard the hope in her voice and said carefully, "He had no desire to take over the college, and yet he stepped up to the job. And people are following his lead. He has potential in the father department, whether he knows it or not. He was an amazing father to me when I was at my worst."

"He told me, the first time we cooked together, that you were his greatest achievement."

A smile spread over Joel's face. "Like I said, I can't help thinking he was serious about having a child. It takes two, and obviously neither of you otherwise intelligent adults thought to use protection."

Joel steered abruptly into a shallow turnoff and pressed the parking brake with his left foot.

Gianessa touched his arm. "You weren't ready to drive, were you?"

"No. My right leg is shaking. I need you to take it from here."

When she dropped Joel at the Manse, he tried to convince her he was all right but she ordered him to rest for the remainder of the day.

"I will, if you promise you'll tell Justin right away. You'll know what to say. Don't wait."

Justin answered her call and buzzed her in. She focused on her breathing as she climbed the stairs. *Give me the words. Give me the courage*. He had the door open and waited for her with a warm smile.

Gianessa blurted out, "Justin, I've spoiled everything, and I can't undo it." She took one look at his stern face and the courage drained out of her.

She forged ahead. "I'm pregnant." She closed her eyes swayed with sudden dizziness. "I'm sorry."

"Sit down before you faint."

Gianessa jumped at his harsh tone.

"Please, Gianessa," he said gently. He steered her to the sofa and fluffed a pillow for her.

She sank down and willed herself not to cry.

"I never meant for this to happen."

"Are you unhappy that it has?" He squatted next to her and touched her hand.

Gianessa's eyes opened wide. She searched for some sign of hope, but she was too dizzy and too filled with anxiety to see his face clearly or make sense of the expression in his eyes. But he was not smiling. "Not for me, no. I want this baby, our baby. But I know it's not what you had in mind for our relationship and for yourself. I know—"

"How can you know what I want?" He rallied a weak laugh. "I'm not sure I know myself."

A weight lifted from her chest. She breathed deeply and her head started to clear.

"When did you find out? Have you seen your doctor? Are you all right?"

"Yes, Joel went with me this afternoon."

"Joel?" he yelled and rose to his full height.

Gianessa watched helplessly as Justin's fists hardened and his handsome face distorted with rage. "What has Joel to do with this?" he roared.

"Nothing. He knew before I did. I was in shock. I asked him to come with me to the doctor. He was kind enough to—"

"Get out." He took two steps back and swept his arm toward the door. "I won't take the fall for Joel's mistake. You and he will have to deal with this yourselves."

"Justin, Joel and I never—"

"Never what?" He spat the words. "Never meant to hurt me? Oh please."

"Listen to me." Her shock turned to anger, and her voice shrilled. "I love you. I've never slept with Joel. We've never been anything to each other except respectful friends and professional allies." She could see from the flash of his eyes and the set of his jaw that he didn't believe her.

Has he has lost his mind?

"How dare you try to put this on Joel. Justin, how can you even think that he—?" Her hands went to her belly, and she tried to calm her breathing. "This is our baby, Justin. Yours and mine."

"I would be a fool to believe you." His voice was hard, menacing. "Get out of my house and out of my life." His features twisted into a caricature of the handsome man she knew. Fear gripped her heart.

"Justin, you're insane." She whispered it. When she tried to stand, though, the blood drained from her head. She fell back into the embrace of the soft blue pillows.

Justin said something. Though it didn't sound threatening, she was too dizzy to make it out. The front door slammed.

In the silence that followed, she prayed. *God, I don't know what to do. Help me. Protect my baby.* She stretched out flat and raised her legs, one at a time, onto the back of the sofa to make the blood flow to her head. She counted breaths until the dizziness passed. The tick-tock of the old grandfather clock made her feel less alone.

Lowering first one leg, then the other, she sat up slowly and counted the seconds as the clock ticked them off. At sixty, she stood up. No dizziness.

In Justin's kitchen, she poured a tall glass of water and stood drinking. *If I could take back the sentence about Joel helping me . . .* Her eyes turned to the lake, gray and dull this afternoon.

"Isn't it a good thing that Joel supported me?" she said aloud, although no one was listening. "Shouldn't Justin be glad of that? Isn't it insane to think what he's thinking?"

Her heart ached for him, for his rage and the agony behind it. Afraid for him, for herself, for their baby, Gianessa grabbed a towel, buried her face in it and screamed until tears came. *God, help him, he has lost his mind.* Her breathing came in ragged gasps, and her head pulsed with pain.

A woman's quiet voice said, "This is not good for the baby." *Who said that?*

With a deep inhale, Gianessa took control. She felt the comfort of a loving arm around her shoulders. Another deep breath, and she knew it was time to leave. She needed to go home and take care of herself and her baby. She found her purse and cautiously descended the two flights to the street.

Cozy in her little blue car, she made a promise. "Baby,

it's you and me, and I will take care of us both. We will be happy and healthy together, no matter what."

I have to tell Sara. I need her support. Gianessa put the car in gear, wheeled around the cul de sac at the top of Lakeside Terrace, and headed downhill and around the marina to Sara's.

One glance at her pale face and shaking body was enough to make Sara gasp. "Ohmigod, you broke up with Justin. What can I do?"

Gianessa nodded. "I need to talk to you very seriously. I need you to keep a confidence. Really keep a confidence. You cannot tell Manda or Remy or Grace or—"

"Ohmigod, you're pregnant."

"Yes."

"And he threw you out?" Sara screeched.

"Yes."

"I can't believe this is happening." Sara flailed her hands. "What can I do?"

"Help me fix some sugary tea before I pass out."

"Sit down. No, not there, in the kitchen so you can coach me."

Gianessa hugged her. "I love you. You always know how to lighten me up."

"Thanks, roomie." Sara drew her into the kitchen. "It will be okay. You'll see. Tell me what happened." Gianessa told the story, leaving out Justin's accusations against Joel.

When their tea was ready, their talk shifted for a few minutes to work and gossip, safe subjects.

Gianessa's spirits rose with the sweet, hot drink and the girl talk. "I'm getting a little hungry."

"That's a good thing, right? We'll get you a good mom snack." Sara rummaged in the refrigerator for a block of cheese and put it on a plate with a knife. She set it in front of Gianessa. "And I'll make us supper, if you tell me how."

"Deal." Gianessa grinned. She nibbled a hunk of Colby-jack cheese and sipped tea while she directed Sara to assemble a salad. Between each careful step, Sara jabbered nervously about her customers that day at the spa.

Gianessa didn't register a single name or detail, but it helped her to stay present and to soak up Sara's caring and concern.

"You love every one of your people, I can tell."

"Well." Sara made three syllables of the word. "I let them think so, and they almost always come through with good tips."

"But you like some of them, don't you? I like quite a lot of my customers. And it feels good when I can help them feel better. Don't you like making them look better?"

Sara stopped with the olive oil poised over the salad. "Speaking of that, are you going to get a mom haircut now?"

"Watch what you're doing there." Gianessa tried to distract her from the haircut topic. "How about a lesson in making a simple lemon vinaigrette? Start with our third smallest glass bowl." She pointed to the stack on the counter.

Sara dutifully reached for the bowl while Gianessa slid off her stool and removed a few ingredients from the cupboard. She found a lemon in the refrigerator.

"You're going to mix a quarter cup of the oil with the same amount of rice vinegar."

"In the glass bowl?

"Yes."

Under her watchful eye, Sara made painstakingly exact measurements with a metal measuring cup.

"Now I'll squeeze this lemon into the your dish." She sliced the lemon in two and squeezed each half. The strength she sensed in her hands helped her feel stronger for the road ahead.

"Now you'll add a pinch of these herbs." She pushed a container of salt-free garlic-herb blend in front of her roommate. Sara's fingers moved in slow motion toward the short, squat bottle of herbs. She pinched a tiny amount and looked up hopefully.

"Maybe twice that amount," Gianessa encouraged. She drew in a calming breath.

Sara tried again, got a big smile from Gianessa this time, and deposited the herbs in the bowl. "What's next?"

Gianessa handed her a tiny whisk.

"Now you whisk it together lightly."

Sara did it. "Okay." She waited for her teacher's nod. "That's all there is to it?"

"Good job. You see, you're a cook already. I'll start paying you rent, and you'll be the cook. What do you say?"

"In your dreams. But I would love for you to teach me to cook."

"Really?" Gianessa smiled at the idea but felt dizzy again. With Justin, it had all started with cooking lessons.

"Are you going to pass out? Don't pass out. I don't know what to do."

"I'm okay." Gianessa braced her hands on the counter. "I just need to sit down again." She reached for the stool and slid onto it. "And I'll be proud to give you lessons. We'll have fun."

Sara raised her eyebrows skeptically at the salad. "You may change your mind after this."

"This is a beautiful salad with healthy dressing. Suddenly I'm starved. Pull up a stool, and let's eat here."

Sara set two bowls on the counter and fished two forks out of the drawer. She consumed half the salad before asking, "I can't tell Manda why?"

"Every time I think about this, I know I'm right. Joel and Justin will be angry at each other about this. I won't try to explain that, but it's very serious. If Manda gets in the middle anytime soon, everyone's anger will explode. Joel cannot handle that stress under his own roof at this point in recovery. We need to buy him some time and let things cool down before Manda finds out. Can I count on you for that?"

"You're totally right." Sara turned frightened eyes to Gianessa. "This will be really hard for me, but I'll keep your secret. I promise. I'll do my very best. Honest."

Gianessa grabbed Sara's hands and hung on hard, so hard Sara winced.

"I wouldn't have burdened you like this, but I need a friend very badly right now. If you want me to move out, I will."

Sara squawked. "No way. Certainly not before the baby comes. I know you'll probably want your own place then." She jumped off her stool to hug Gianessa. "Ohmigod, you're having a baby." She squealed. "This is so cool."

"You're right, it is cool." Gianessa laughed through a sudden rush of tears. "Even though it's a disaster, I'm really happy about it."

Sara smoothed back Gianessa's hair. "Well, in spite of everything, the dad is wicked impressive."

Wicked impressive. "That totally sums up Justin Cushman."

Chapter 11

Justin pounded on the front door to the old garage. He gave Joel thirty seconds before hitting his speed dial.

"What?" Joel sounded exhausted and defeated.

That made Justin pause. He hadn't heard defeat in Joel since the two of them had confronted Joel's addiction many years ago. Joel had worked hard in recovery, and defeat was not part of his makeup anymore.

Hearing it now in Joel's voice, Justin's fear for his nephew trumped his anger. He calmed his voice. "We need to talk, Joel."

"I know. There's a key under one of the flowerpots. I'm in the bedroom, and I'm good for two minutes."

Justin ended the call. Rage simmered below the surface, but he knew it had no place in this discussion. What he needed were answers.

He heard himself murmur, "Don't let me hurt this nephew that I love more than myself." *Where did that come from?* He'd never been one to pray. Reading scripture was one thing, but asking God for help was not something Cushmans did. Still, it felt right. *Maybe I should have prayed before I blasted Gianessa.* His breath came out in a whoosh. *God, I've screwed up.*

He let himself in and moved through the silent, dim living room into the bedroom. Joel sat unmoving in one of the chairs by the window in the bedroom. His left hand lifted an inch to acknowledge Justin's presence. As Justin came beside him, he saw that Joel's face was gray, taut with pain, his eyes closed. If he couldn't keep his eyes open to the lake that he loved so much, Joel's pain was very serious.

Justin stood between Joel and the windows so Joel would not have to turn his head. "I can see that you need rest, but I need some answers. What is your part in this pregnancy?"

"I took her to Rochester for lunch, and we picked up a pregnancy kit on the way. She was able to get in to see her doctor soon after. I drove us most of the way home from Clifton Springs, which was foolish. That's my part in it."

"This is not your baby?"

Joel's eyes flew open and locked with his. "No," he shouted. "Are you insane?"

"You brought her here." Justin's voice rumbled. "You warned me away from her. You set her up with an exclusive job." He opened his hands. "What am I to think?"

"I sent her a bus ticket."

Justin lowered his eyes and relaxed his stance a fraction.

Joel continued, his voice tight. "She's a talented, recovering alcoholic-addict who needed a break and who had the skills and brains and credentials to transform my little spa into a place of healing. The fact that I destroyed my body in an accident made it imperative that I employ someone with her credentials for my rehabilitation and that we build a therapy suite way ahead of schedule. And thank you for seeing to that."

Justin lifted his gaze, but Joel glared him into silence. "I am committed to Manda. You know that. I am not now and never have been involved with Gianessa sexually." He grew louder and stronger with each sentence. "You obviously have. You and she are having a baby, uncle. Face it. And I'm fucking pissed at you for fucking with her when I warned you not to. She had enough to deal with already, without an unplanned pregnancy."

Justin reached out to Joel, wanting both to calm him and to hold on to him like a lifeline.

"No!" Joel shrieked.

The alarm on Joel's face made Justin back up until he bumped against the windows. *Dear God, he thinks I mean to harm him.*

"Get out." Joel's voice was icy with disgust and dismissal.

Justin went cold with fear. His head lowered with humility. He heard the echo of his own command to Gianessa to get out of his life. Now he understood why Gianessa had fallen back on the sofa as if she'd been struck. Had his anger been as forceful as Joel's just now? *Yes.*

His anger and suspicion had just destroyed his relationship with Gianessa and now with Joel. *And with others before this, and it will happen again. I have no power over it. I cannot fix it myself.*

Joel's hands gripped the arms of his chair, and his breathing was labored.

God, I need you to help this man, whom I love more than myself. "I will leave."

"Get help, Justin." Joel implored him. "Call Gwen Forrester."

Justin read censure in Joel's eyes, mixed with something that might be pity. Every ounce of bravado went out of him, along with his self-respect.

Joel closed his eyes again, and his face creased with pain.

"I'm sorry," Justin said to his nephew as he walked away.

Justin trudged to his car, beeped it open, and sat fiddling with his phone. He had keyed Gwen Forrester's number into his contacts when Gianessa gave it to him months ago. Gwen was one of the two therapists Gianessa knew in AA who could work through the twelve steps with him if he wanted. Why hadn't he called her then?

Arrogance. Pride. Look where that had gotten him, gotten all of them.

"Gwen Forrester," her voice answered.

Justin started. "Yes, Gwen, forgive me, I was sure I'd get your voicemail."

"Darn," Gwen teased and followed it with a little laugh.

Justin wanted to join her in a lighthearted exchange, but he was on the verge of tears. He struggled to find his voice.

"Levity not appreciated, I see. I don't recognize your phone number, sir. I don't even recognize the area code."

"Chicago. It's Justin Cushman. I need to see you professionally."

He heard her tapping keys on her computer.

When she didn't answer right away, he urged, "Would that be possible?" His voice shook. "Soon?"

"Yes. I have an opening tomorrow morning. Can you be here at eight o'clock sharp?"

"I can. Where?"

"My office is in my home, on the east side of the lake. Four and a half miles past the park, watch for the yellow sign with Forrester at the start of the private road. And it's a killer road. Drive with care."

"Thank you." Justin didn't know what else to say.

Gwen asked, "You'll be all right until then?"

"Yes."

She ended the call.

Justin pocketed his phone. His head throbbed.

Not knowing what else to do, he drove to the park at the top of the lake and set out on the gravel path. Perhaps fresh air would stop the pounding.

Why did I think this baby was Joel's? His insecurity went all the way back to their exchange in Joel's hospital room just after he'd met Gianessa. What was that phrase Joel used? She was "artfully arranged." Joel was fully aware of Gianessa's beauty, and he'd said she was "off limits" or something like that. Justin had always taken that to mean, "She's mine" or "She's taken."

He'd gotten it all wrong. Joel's warning not to "mess with her" was not the warning of a jealous lover. Joel was simply being protective of Gianessa. He'd said something about "devastating losses," which Justin now knew referred to her failed marriage, her lost child and her ruined career. Joel had brought her here—by bus, good god—to restart her career by remaking his spa. That was all. And then hired her for his physical rehabilitation.

How could Justin have imagined there was anything more to Joel and Gianessa's relationship? It was obvious to everyone who knew them that Joel and Manda were devoted to each other.

You were jealous of that. He, too, wanted an exclusive, passionate relationship, one that weathered the storms and basked in sunny days. He'd dreamed of that with Gianessa. Dear God, he'd had that with Gianessa.

And now he'd destroyed it with his jealousy and suspicion. *And rage*. Even Sydney had warned him not to bring his paranoia into the relationship, and he'd snapped at her for even suggesting he was capable of such a thing.

A baby. His baby. Their baby. He'd been delighted to hear Gianessa was pregnant and puzzled that she was distraught about it, that she'd "ruined everything."

When she'd said Joel took her to the doctor's, he'd leapt—vaulted in a superhero leap—*no, a villainous leap*—to the conclusion the baby was Joel's. *They're both right. I am insane*.

As Justin trudged the gravel path along the lakeshore, he forced himself to deeper honesty. His explosion of anger that blasted Gianessa back onto the sofa came just as he decided, in his twisted mind, that Joel had gotten Gianessa pregnant in California and brought her to Tompkins Falls, and the two of them had been searching for a way to cover up her pregnancy when the trip to New York City materialized, and Justin was the perfect fall guy.

That's exactly what I thought.

He stopped on the path and jammed his hands in his coat pockets. He stared out at the whitecaps and wondered how an otherwise intelligent man could harbor such despicable, twisted thoughts. This was his beloved nephew Joel he was maligning—the very person he knew to have deep personal integrity. Joel, who was the model for the changes he wanted to make in his own life.

And Gianessa who had persuaded him to adopt a healthy lifestyle and food plan, who'd taught him to cook his own meals and stay on course through business meetings and lunches out. Gianessa, who'd listened and advised him on college affairs, who'd graciously accepted his friendship with his old lover Sydney. *Why didn't I listen to Syd about my paranoia? Why did I let it poison my love for Gianessa?*

Tears rolled down his cheeks as he remembered Gianessa in his kitchen, mourning the loss of her little girl. Gianessa in his kitchen forgetting to put an oven mitt on her hand before reaching into the oven for the hot pan of hors d'oeuvres. And failing to use protection when they made love. Perhaps she'd chosen not to. Perhaps she'd manipulated their friendship to get pregnant. Perhaps, like him, she'd not given protection a moment's thought.

He was grateful now that Joel had intuited the pregnancy and accompanied Gianessa today to see her doctor. The pregnancy was probably why she'd had pain lately when they made love. He had urged her for weeks to see her doctor but she'd waved away his concern. Was she in denial? Or afraid? He'd pick denial.

Joel had been right all along. Gianessa needed protecting. Instead of respecting that, Justin had muscled in, started a passionate affair, and gotten her pregnant.

And he intended to bare his soul about all of this to cute little Gwennie Forrester, Doc Forrester's daughter, who was at least a dozen years younger than he? He would sooner escape back to London. Even the old life was better than the wreckage he was piling up in Tompkins Falls.

Two cyclists passed him from behind, and their wake swirled dust around him and into his eyes. He blinked it away and thought about Lyssa and Manda on the canal path, the two cyclists swerving to avoid their screaming match. He and Gianessa had persuaded Lyssa to enter treatment, and she'd had the courage to follow through.

If Lyssa could find the courage, so could he.

"So"—Gianessa paused for a deep breath—"now you have the whole sordid story. You cautioned me not to get pregnant or get my heart broken, and I did both."

"Well, you didn't drink or move to Timbuktu," Carol comforted.

"Morocco." Gianessa squeezed her eyes shut. "Sorry, same thing. I've let you down." She stole a glance at her sponsor.

"I'll survive, but you've certainly complicated your life. I'm sorry that the gentleman—"

"He's not." Gianessa snapped the words.

Carol sat taller and continued her statement in a firm voice, "Sorry that the gentleman in question is not stepping up to his responsibility. And you need to give up that resentment if you're going to move forward in a healthy way. You know why our program warns against resentments."

"There are no justified resentments." Gianessa parroted the words she so often heard at meetings. "They lead right back to a drink, I know. But I have to tell you, this one's going to take a while."

Carol said, with a dry laugh, "It's going to take praying your butt off."

Gianessa gave up a laugh. "I do want to move forward in a healthy way. I want this baby, and I want to be a good, sober mom. I will take care of us both."

"You've complicated your finances big time."

"I know. I have a cushion, but figuring out child care and—oh god—the whole career picture." She could never be part of Justin and Manda's holistic rehab center now. She put her head in her hands and sobbed for a bit. Then she shook her head and wiped away the tears. "But I will find my way. With a lot of help from my friends."

"Didn't your friend Joel say you could count on him for support?"

Gianessa gave her a grateful smile. "Yes."

"And here's a thought: If you can prove the father's identity, you can require some level of child support. A lawyer can help you with that process, if it's something you want to pursue."

"How would I find someone to guide me through that?" Her hands trembled, and she placed them flat on the table.

Carol took out her phone, scrolled through her contacts and wrote a name and phone number on a sticky note. "She's in the program. She's a lawyer and she specializes in women's issues."

Gianessa grabbed for the piece of paper. She met her sponsor's gaze. "I need to do this."

"Time to play hardball, Gianessa."

"Nice to see you after all these years, Gwen," Justin announced.

Gwen squinted at him from behind her desk. What was different about him? He was thinner. And older. There was more, though, something important.

In the face of her silence, he added, "I feel like the specimen in Prufrock, pinned and wriggling on the wall."

At that she gave him a smile. "Junior English. T.S. Eliot, wasn't it?"

"'The Love Song of J. Alfred Prufrock.' How fitting I should pick a line from an unlovely love poem."

Gwen came out from behind her desk. "I didn't intend to analyze you standing up."

Justin's eyes swept over the spacious room and came to rest on the two chairs angled toward each other at the window. "Yet you don't have a couch."

"I'm not a shrink. Thanks for coming, Justin." She held out her hand and they shook perfunctorily. "Right after you called yesterday afternoon, I had a call from Joel, making sure you contacted me. Sounds like we have a lot to talk about." She motioned him to the chairs.

He chose the farther chair, the one with the straight-on view of the lake, and sat down with a heavy sigh.

"Do you know how this appointment came about?" Gwen began their first session.

"Of course I do. Joel and I had words. When I reached toward him to bridge the gap, he was terrified I meant to hit him. He believes I'm insane. He insisted that I get help, and I agreed."

"A-plus for that answer," Gwen confirmed. "What do you think about what Joel said?"

"About your expertise as a therapist?"

She shook her head. "That's not in question. I meant about Joel's fear."

"That I'm insane?"

She nodded.

"I think he's right." He looked pensively out the window. "I think anyone who in the space of one hour can threaten, terrify and hurt beyond recall the two people who mean the most to him in this world must be insane, yes. And I would add that I am the most baffled and terrified of us all."

Gwen shifted in her chair. "That's actually an excellent starting point for some serious and, I suspect, long-overdue therapy. Are you game?"

He had the eyes of a man who is broken and lost and clueless about how to proceed. That, she realized, was the difference she'd seen as he stood in her office doorway. The arrogant, puffed-up, entitled, master manipulator was absent today. She rather liked the new, clueless Justin Cushman. This lean, handsome man sported well-fitting blue jeans and a muted green cotton Henley that showed his intelligent, gray-green eyes in their best light—she'd like to help this man.

"I am game, counselor. I warn you, I will probably bawl my eyes out."

She produced a box of tissues. "I get a lot of that in this office." She pulled several tissues straight up out of the box, made a nest of them and placed it on top of the box. "A good handful at the ready," she told him. "I want to start with your argument with Joel that nearly led to violence, or so he thought."

"Thank you for not mincing words."

"My perspective first, if I may?"

Justin nodded.

"Manda suspects from things Joel has said that you and Joel sometimes argue with F-bombs, swearing in general, angry words, angry tone, all out shouting. Correct?"

"Yes."

"And do you engage in that behavior with colleagues?"

"No, I wouldn't dare."

"With loved ones?"

"No, although swearing and name-calling have occurred, with no good result."

"Violence toward loved ones?"

He narrowed his eyes as he met her gaze. "No."

She thought he was being honest about that.

"Have you ever wanted to slug a woman, a lover?"

"I wanted to wring Alexa's neck when I learned she'd been cheating on me, but I didn't act on it."

"Alexa?"

"The woman I loved and lived with in Switzerland for five, six, seven years, around the time Joel and I lost our family, back when Joel was at his worst."

"I will need to hear more about Alexa, but I need to get us back to the point we've strayed from. Remember what that was?"

Justin looked out at the lake for a moment and nodded. "Am I willing to give up the aggressive Cushman method of processing disagreement? Yes, I am. However, I'm clueless how to do that."

"I'm very glad to hear that."

"That I'm clueless?" Justin chuckled.

She nodded. "That you're willing and that you're aware you're not able, on your own, to change it."

"And that last bit pleases you why?"

"In AA we have two steps that talk about our shortcomings. Step six says we're ready for God to remove our shortcomings, and step seven says, we ask with humility to have them removed."

Justin was deep in thought, maybe putting something together for himself.

"Does that mean you're willing to work through the twelve steps with me, even though I don't seem to be an alcoholic?"

"Yes. Tell me where that idea came from," she said, "about going through the steps with someone."

"It came up when . . ." He took a steadying breath and blinked moisture from his eyes. "Gianessa came to my apartment, Joel's apartment which I had appropriated, to give me a cooking lesson in gluten-free eating. Our first cooking lesson. I had no idea why she would put herself out for me that way, but she did, and I appreciated it and enjoyed it. We talked about why I had come home."

"Which was to help Joel?"

"It was actually more than that. I had lost my way, had lost my soul, and needed to find my heart and seemed to think Joel was the key." He reached for the nest of tissues and buried his face in the soft, beige tissues. Sobs shook his shoulders.

Gwen left the room without a sound. When she returned with a glass of water, he was looking out at the lake, tears still falling from his eyes.

"Thank you. Most kind," he said. "I was thinking, 'What kind of monster destroys the very people he knows are put on this earth to save him?'"

"I would say a very sick one who forgot he was in need of saving."

"I agree with that. Is it arrogance?"

He turned his green eyes to her, and she felt she was seeing into his soul. Yes, this was a very different Justin Cushman. She might be able to help this one.

"A lifetime of arrogance, I think, and denial and being in charge," she answered him. "As you have discovered, meaning to change and doing it are not the same thing. How much do you want to change?"

"It is—I think it has to be my highest priority. Even more than being a father to my baby, the baby Gianessa is carrying. More than being an uncle to Joel. Because I've demonstrated that without changing, I can't be a father or an uncle or anything else that is dear to me." He exhaled and managed a ghost of smile. "It's good to know there are some people and some responsibilities that are dear to me. I could not have said that before I came back here a few months ago."

"Do you drink, Justin?"

"No, not in many years. Six or seven, I think."

"First homework assignment," she announced.

Justin looked up obediently.

"For next week I want you to figure out, on paper, exactly how long ago you put the drink down, and why, and what happened after."

"All right."

"Do you do any drugs, Justin?"

"No, never."

"Power drinks, energy drinks, marijuana?"

He shook his head and held Gwen's eyes as she went down her mental list.

"What do you drink when you go out?"

"Perrier, espresso, tea."

"Do you smoke?"

"No, not since a bout with pneumonia in college."

"Do you have sex with women you don't know?"

"I gave that up in the Middle East when I caught sight of myself in the mirror, naked, with a very young escort who'd been provided by my hosts. I could see she was probably fourteen and trying very hard to hide her terror and revulsion. I gave her more than her fee and sent her home and never accepted another escort."

Gwen was aware of her leg jumping, displaying her anger at human trafficking. "Was that the end of it?" Her voice was hard.

"Yes, and I would add it was the beginning of my journey here. After that, I saw so many ways my life was . . ."

He looked out at the lake again, lost in thought.

Gwen used the time to get her breathing back to normal. "Justin?" she prompted.

He turned at her.

"You were saying that incident with the teenage escort opened your eyes to something about your life?"

"Yes, to the corruption of the systems and people I was doing business with. I started questioning my work, my purpose, my profession. I was making millions upon millions for a few people, but how was that benefiting the millions of people who lived in those countries? I'd become someone who made money for the sake of making money, and I'd crossed over to the dark side somewhere along the way without realizing it or intending it."

"How did you know you were on the dark side?"

"I saw myself corrupting that beautiful young girl as though it was a normal part of doing business, and the truth was I was being pandered to, pimped to, at the expense of this beautiful young girl and all the others like her. They had few if any choices about their lives. And exploiting them was not what I wanted to do with my life."

"How long ago was that?"

"A few years, I think."

"Again, I will need a chronology of these key insights. I need you to do your best with that for next week. I don't pretend it will be easy."

"I suspect it will be humiliating," Justin said. "Just as this is."

"We use the term 'humbling.' I think you'll find there's a difference. And it will be worth your while to do the inventory and the chronology. Some advice," Gwen said, "you might find it easier to do this work at a retreat house, away from your routine for a few days."

"Since no one in their right mind is speaking to me, the time is right to go away for a few days." He gave her a grim smile.

Gwen took a pad of paper and a pen from the lower shelf of the table. "Here are names and phone numbers for two retreat houses nearby who offer private rooms for individuals. I'll want to know where you are."

"Are we done for today?"

"Not by half. I need to get some insight into why you went off on Gianessa when she told you she was pregnant."

Justin recounted all that he'd thought about during his walk along the lakeshore after seeing Joel.

Gwen nodded during the telling. When he finished, she said, "I'm glad you can see all that. It sounds like a big dose of honesty to me. One of the unanswered questions is how and why you started down that mental path. Some of it may come from unresolved anger toward Alexa. But quite often, the way we regard and act toward a spouse or lover has its roots in the relationship we saw between our parents. Did your parents drink, Justin?"

"Both of them drank. Father had his work and mother had her cocktails."

"Meaning?"

"I think if he hadn't been obsessed about making money, father would have been an alcoholic. There's no question my mother was an alcoholic."

Gwen hadn't realized that. "She hid it well."

"They were both very practiced in the art of deception."

"What do you remember about your parents' relationship with each other?"

"I remember that it was nothing I wanted to repeat in my own life."

"Specifically?"

"They were all about wife swapping and sleeping around and multiple affairs. If my sense of history is correct, they were married just after birth control was legalized, and just before abortion was legalized."

"And that behavior characterized your parents?"

"Yes. Why does that surprise you?"

She shrugged. "They were the epitome of propriety, as far as I knew."

"They could act the part, no question. Behind closed doors was another matter."

"Did they argue about the affairs? Did either object to wife swapping?"

Justin shook his head. "Not that I ever heard or sensed."

"Did it bother you?"

"The hypocrisy bothered me. As you say, they seemed to be so proper, and mother espoused waiting until marriage for the girl and protection for the boy."

"The double standard."

"I'm curious. Why didn't you marry?" she asked him.

"I'm curious, too. I don't have much of an answer. I loved Alexa and enjoyed our life together until she cheated on me. After that, I was very focused on making money. I had no interest in having children, settling down, raising a family. Women were friends, business partners, lovers."

"Did anyone try to talk you into marrying them?"

"Who'd want to?" Justin said with a dry laugh.

"Someone who loved your money," Gwen said sharply. She worded it in a way that could be about Gianessa, though she had no way of knowing the truth of Gianessa's motives. "Someone who saw you as a handsome, wealthy man who was away a lot and who didn't care what she did when you were away."

She was surprised Justin didn't show any response.

"Someone who would bear your children, divorce you, and then leave with the children and a fortune for herself."

"Are you suggesting I would want to marry a woman like that?"

"I'm suggesting a woman like that would want to marry you and would go to great lengths to make sure it happened. Is that a chapter from your life?"

"No."

Gwen was fairly sure he was not seeing Gianessa in that role, which had been her point in asking.

"If I were you and I were an alcoholic, those facts of life would be the perfect excuse to drink my way through life, avoiding attachment, moving from one empty affair to another, cynically believing there were no genuinely loving and lovable women in the world."

"I don't know that I felt much of anything for a long time. Perhaps when I'm on retreat I will remember and will see how it fits."

"Or not. I've given you a lot to think about. There

is one more thing I need to address with you before we wrap up for today."

"Your fee?"

Gwen smiled easily. "That comes when we wrap up. Right now I want to go back to something you said about Joel having the key. You came back here because Joel had the key, I believe you said. Do you know what you meant by that?"

"Yes, I think it's because of the way he uses his money to benefit others. Even more than that, the way he lives his life. In my mind Joel has integrity. It startles me sometimes, the things he comes out with, the way he thinks."

"How would you describe it?"

"I would describe his thinking as moral, ethical, in tune with his community, disciplined, warm-hearted. No Cushman I ever knew, including Joel's father, my brother Josh, ever had those traits. If it was genetic, he got it from Bridey."

Gwen brightened. "Bridey who read the tea leaves?" She'd forgotten about Bridey.

Justin nodded as he laughed from his belly. "Joel's mother's mother. She was grand. I'd have liked to marry a girl like Bridey. And Joel is marrying a girl like Bridey. But to get back to your question, I had it in mind that perhaps I could find my way to my heart and my soul by being around Joel."

Gwen studied his face. "You may be right," Gwen said, "though you need to give Joel a lot of space right now. I think you know that. Let me ask you this: How do you think Joel got like that, if it wasn't genetic, from Bridey?"

He turned back to her and shook his head. "I only know that getting sober was the beginning of it for him. I think that's why I stopped drinking some years ago. I saw that I needed to change as radically as Joel was changing, and being sober was the beginning."

"Good. We will work through the same process Joel used, the twelve steps. There's one key I haven't heard you reference, and it's important that you think about it on your retreat."

"What's that?"

"The notion of a God or a power greater than you. One that will guide you if you seek it. Do you have a higher power?"

"I heard myself mutter a prayer yesterday. At least I think it was a prayer."

She gave him a minute to recall the only time in their conversation he'd made reference to a power greater than himself.

Justin looked clueless again.

"I think you have a kernel of a god in your thinking. I heard you say—and I may have the words wrong, I apologize—'What kind of monster hurts the people that are put on this earth to save him?'"

Justin nodded but seemed even more puzzled.

"It's the idea that Joel and Gianessa were put on this earth to save you that makes me think you have faith in something watching over you, working toward your redemption as a human being."

His face brightened. "Redemption, yes. That's what I am searching for, and I don't seem to be able to get it for myself. It's not something I can buy or demand, I know that. It comes—I'm not sure how it comes, to tell you the truth, but it's what I need. It's why I'm here, why I came back to Tompkins Falls."

Gwen reached out her hand. "Welcome back from the dark side, Justin. Time to do the hard work."

"I'm surprised you didn't get that denim jacket," Sara said to Gianessa as they left the bargain back room of her favorite shop in Aurora.

"I might go back for it."

"What were you thinking when you decided not to buy it?"

Gianessa grinned. "You are getting good at making me talk. I'm not sure I like that."

Sara gave her waist a squeeze. They mounted granite steps, side-by-side, to an elegant lakeside inn. "Are you as hungry as I am?"

"Starved."

"You don't get morning sickness, do you?"

"Thank god no. And so far no cravings. I'm eating pretty smart, and I've only gained a couple of pounds. But today I could go for a juicy burger and fries and a hot fudge sundae."

Sara chortled. "This I've got to see."

They asked for a table on the porch and were seated by picture windows that framed the dark blue lake. One intrepid sailboat plied the choppy water. Its big white sail bent with the wind.

When Gianessa learned the burgers had breadcrumbs in the mix, she settled for a grilled chicken salad with sweet potato fries. Sara indulged in a Reuben with extra dressing and steak fries.

"Spill, roomie," she said after the waiter left. "Start with why you didn't get the denim jacket which, by the way, was wicked cute on you."

Gianessa toyed with her linen napkin, pleating it with sharp creases. "I realized when I saw myself in the mirror that I need maternity clothes really soon, and I don't have any."

"You could wear the denim jacket pregnant."

"True. But not these jeans, and maybe not even my dozen white T-shirts, which are already tight on my boobs. I want to be beautiful pregnant."

"Cool. For that you need a haircut."

"You're right."

"What?" Sara yelped, without thinking, then held up her hands in apology to the ladies at nearby tables. "Sorry. Just got a little excited." She scooted her chair closer to Gianessa. "You're serious? You're going to let me cut it?"

Gianessa nodded and bit her lower lip. “Soon. I think you’re right about the beautiful pregnant damsel-in-distress.”

“You’ve given up on him, haven’t you?” Sara slumped onto one elbow on the table, her jaw rested in her hand. “You really don’t expect him to apologize and woo you back.”

“Not after he gets the letter from my lawyer, no.”

“What letter?” Sara’s voice was deep with foreboding. “What lawyer?”

“I got a sample of Justin’s hair, I won’t tell you how, and I’ve had DNA testing done to establish he’s the baby’s father. And my lawyer has written a letter requesting him to support the baby, including braces, health care, education, the whole works. And to support me for five years until I can establish myself professionally.”

“Holy cow, roomie.” Sara’s eyes widened with incredulity. “Way to kill a romance.”

“The romance died when he accused me of being pregnant with Joel’s baby.”

“He said what?” Again, she raised her hands in apology to the ladies nearby. She mimicked locking her lips with a key. “How could he even think that?” she hissed.

“He’s a little insane. Joel says he’s gone into therapy, which is a good thing.” Gianessa leaned in and whispered, “You cannot, cannot say anything to anybody about this. Especially Manda. Please promise me.”

“Okay, I promise.” She squinted toward the kitchen and warned Gianessa, “He’s bringing our food.”

“Good. I’m so hungry I was going to eat your hand.”

Sara bit off a laugh.

“I really need to hash over the whole career thing with you,” Gianessa said. Her eyes grew round as she surveyed the huge salad and the oval dish mounded with sweet potato fries. “And I need you to eat half these fries.”

“Got my own big pile. We can take them home. Let’s chow down for a minute.”

When they'd both consumed a third of their meals, Gianessa sat back for a break.

Sara reminded her, "I thought you were going to be a star in the holistic rehab thing Manda has going on."

"Guess who's putting up the funding for it?" Gianessa's eyes met Sara's.

"Ohmigod, Justin?"

Gianessa nodded and took another mouthful of salad.

"Kiss that good-bye. What are you going to do?"

Gianessa shrugged. "I've applied for my PT license in New York, but it's a long process, and I don't know what all they'll require. That's why she, my lawyer, wanted me to ask for financial support."

"Of course. She was right."

"Thank you." Gianessa reached for her water glass, but her hand was trembling so much she didn't try to pick it up.

"Hey, you don't need my approval." Sara covered Gianessa's hand with her own warm one.

"I really want to know what you think."

"I think you're acting brave and smart. I'd probably be a total wreck."

Gianessa fingered the vase on their table filled with fragrant yellow carnations. "Pretty. We should get flowers sometimes. Anyway, I'm going to do my best to build a career without depending on Justin's support. If I can't get my PT license, it's hard to say what I'd do."

"Well, you can probably do a hundred more things, just with your doctorate—like teach college. Or manage a clinic or a spa. Or do research with any of the PT programs around here."

Gianessa brightened. "Thank you. Thank you, for getting me unstuck."

"And I'll be done with my MBA this December. We could open our own spa together."

"Cool idea. Or maybe you and Randy will get married."

"Not going to happen. It's time for me to meet some new guy. Randy just wants a buddy, and I'm ready for more."

"You sound very sure about it this time." Gianessa pointed with her fork. "And you're using protection, right?"

"Yes, Mom."

Gianessa groaned.

"Oops, sorry, that wasn't a slam."

Chapter 12

Sara and Gianessa strolled barefoot across the sweep of green lawn, sandals swinging in their hands, arms brushing as they made their way toward the new terraced garden on the grounds of the Manse.

"I'm so glad you're Manda's maid-of-honor," Gianessa said.

"Instead of Lyssa? I forgot about that. That must have been a nightmare."

"No one needs that much drama for their wedding."

"You know I'll do anything for Manda. She's like a sister to me. You are, too, Gianessa. My very own big sister." Sara reached her arm around Gianessa's shoulders and gave a squeeze.

Gianessa laughed. "Just don't follow my example, little sister."

"I love the way the grass feels between my toes." Sara giggled. "You've got me tuned into the Universe, into so many little things."

"Do you think they'll guess I'm pregnant?"

"They'll guess you're anemic because you're so pale. Have you made that doctor's appointment? I don't want to keep bugging you about it."

"I will. I feel okay. I just keep forgetting."

"I think we could be twins in our long flowery skirts and bright T-shirts."

"That's sweet. There's Grace." Gianessa pointed to the cart path and waved.

Grace gave them her signature one-pass wave that swept left to right and ended in a little finger wave. "You look like spring flowers, ladies." She put an arm around Gianessa's waist. "You're so pale, Gianessa. Are you taking care of yourself?"

Tears brimmed in Gianessa's eyes.

Sara signaled Grace to back off.

Grace changed gears. "Sara, has Manda explained what Gianessa and I will be doing at the ceremony? I don't think she expects all three of us to stand like bridesmaids, but I'm clueless what she's thinking."

"Other than being gorgeous, I have no idea. I think that's why she wanted us here this morning. Since Joel isn't up for a rehearsal or a rehearsal dinner, this is our run-through."

The three swept arm-in-arm onto the lower level of the garden and spotted Manda waiting for them under the rose arbor.

Manda did a pirouette of pure joy. "You three are so beautiful. My wedding is going to be the most beautiful little garden wedding ever."

"Your wish is our command," Grace said with a curtsey.

Manda told her entourage, "Let's do a run-through, and then we can have lunch together."

Gianessa spoke up. "Thanks for the thought, but Grace and I have to start work in an hour."

"Okay. Well, it's easy," Manda said. "Sara and I rehearsed the whole procession, but just once, this morning with Phil. We practiced our formal step-pause and those tricky turns before and after the steps."

"Let's show them how good we are," Sara suggested.

Manda beamed.

The two climbed, giggling, to the top level of the garden and passed through a waist-high holly border onto the lawn.

"I am so happy," Manda told her maid-of-honor. She had tears in her eyes. "I love Joel so much. I can't believe in five days I'll be Mrs. Joel Cushman."

Sara gave her a fierce hug. "You are perfect for each other."

"Thank god Phil is giving me away. He is my rock."

"We'll pretend Phil is here, just like he was this morning." Sara lifted Manda's arm as though Phil had offered his elbow. "Take his arm and hold your bouquet."

Sara stepped in front of Manda and faced the holly hedge. She cupped her hands as though she carried her fragrant bouquet of pastel and periwinkle flowers. "Ready? On three. One-two-three."

Sara made a graceful entrance into the garden and caught her breath as the panorama of the lake unfolded for her. Between the upper and lower terraces, hostas unfurled beneath oriental maples, and bright blue phlox mounded between evergreen shrubs. The fragrance of Lily of the Valley filled her senses.

"Sara, what's wrong?" Manda asked from a few inches behind her.

"I was enthralled for a minute. This garden is gorgeous."

"It is, you're right. Don't you love that the phlox is almost the color of your dress?"

"Totally. Okay, I'm good now." Sara pivoted to the right, traversed the upper terrace, turned, stepped down to the lower terrace, turned, and smiled at Grace and Gianessa.

Their eyes, though, were riveted on something over her left shoulder.

Sara swiveled to see Manda shaking at the top of the steps.

Gianessa hurried across the terrace, up to Manda's side. As she murmured comfort and encouragement, Manda slowly recovered.

"Nice steady breaths," Gianessa breathed with her.

Manda nodded.

"Think about Joel and how excited he is and how beautiful you are."

Sara marveled. With all the uncertainties in her life, Gianessa was focused on helping a friend achieve her dream. *She's going to be a great mom.*

Manda gave a shaky laugh. "I know it's only three steps. Phil avoids stairs, so we did just one practice run this morning, and he decided he'd be fine. I was so focused on him, I didn't realize how scared I am."

"Tell me why you're scared."

"What if I fall? I could hurt Phil and make a fool of myself and ruin the wedding."

"Think you really will fall?"

Manda shook her head and demonstrated how easy it was by taking the stairs in three nimble steps. She turned, raced back to the top of the garden, and executed the procession once more, with grace and dignity.

Sara, Grace, and Gianessa clapped and hooted.

"I should probably practice in my heels, too, so I won't panic Saturday morning."

"Smart idea." Gianessa gave her a thumbs-up.

Manda's smile turned dreamy. "And when I get to the bottom of the steps, I'll turn and see Joel, and I'll know exactly what to do. He'll be so handsome in a morning coat."

"I can't wait to see Tony wearing one," Grace said.

"And driving the golf cart," Sara chuckled.

"I can't wait to see Tony and Joel together," Gianessa said, "standing tall, less than six months after the accident. Who would have guessed that was possible?"

"Joel wanted to get married in the hospital, and I freaked. For once in my life I cared about what I'd wear and how I'd look—not just to Joel, but to everyone who knows him. Wait till you guys see my gown."

"It's magnificent," Gianessa said. "We need to hustle. Teach us our jobs, Manda. What is this 'Shepherd' thing you've got Grace and me doing?"

"Yeah, what's up with that? We're not wearing head wraps and carrying crooks, even for you, Manda."

"Okay." Manda stepped in front of them. "There are twenty honored guests at the ceremony—the big wigs, Joel calls them. Our friends will join us after, at the reception. Possibly including my sister, Lyssa, and nobody give me grief about that, okay?"

Manda's glare silenced them. Shrugs and eye rolls were the only responses.

"So, here's what the shepherds do." She started at the rose arbor and moved to the far end of the terrace, slicing the air six times as she went. She explained, "Six rows, four chairs in each row, except three in the first and last rows. Gianessa will sit in the first chair in the last row. Tony with be right behind her in the big golf cart."

"Cool, I get Tony," Gianessa said with a grin.

Sara saw the relief on Gianessa's face. *Thank god Manda listened to me and put Gianessa away from Justin.*

"Grace will sit in the first chair in the first row, right next to where Sara will stand."

Sara did the math on her fingers. She nodded, satisfied that it added up to twenty guests plus the two shepherds.

Grace urged, "Let's go to our places."

She and Sara raced each other to the rose arbor. Gianessa floated toward the far end of the terrace where she pretended to sit in her chair.

"When the ceremony is over, Justin will direct everyone up to the Manse to start the reception ahead of us, while we stay here for photos. And this is when the shepherds do their thing. When Justin finishes speaking, Grace and Gianessa will stand, very beautifully." Manda gestured for them to stand.

Grace stood tall and imitated Manda's arm waves.

Gianessa and Sara laughed.

Manda continued seriously, "The shepherds direct the people in each row toward the golf cart or the gravel path, or the lawn leading up to the Manse. You work your way row by row and wave everyone away from the terrace up toward the Manse." She shooed the imaginary guests away from the rose arbor. "The main thing is not to let anyone move in on Joel."

"Oh," Gianessa said, "we're protecting him. Like his body guards, but gracious and happy."

"Exactly. You're crowd control wearing smiles and gorgeous dresses. Tony will make as many trips as he needs to, and he can take four or five at a time."

"Let's do it, Gianessa," Grace enthused.

Grace and Gianessa moved slowly toward each other, row by imaginary row, smiling and shooing their imaginary flock up toward the Manse.

They met in the middle and gave each other high-fives.

Sara laughed. "Wait a minute. Who came up with 'Shepherd'?"

"Isn't that cool?" Manda said. "Justin's into biblical references. It just fit."

Gianessa turned away, but not before Sara saw the pain on her face.

"Justin, you've mentioned several times that you're done with running. We need to talk about what you're running from. Do you know?"

"Probably guilt. When I try to pinpoint it, it's mixed up with self-worth. But I do know when it started."

"Really?"

"Is that unusual?"

"It's a big plus. Let's hear it."

"It came to me when I was in New York in December talking to Sydney, my old friend and lover. We talked about the fact that one of the reasons we didn't marry was that we had different agendas on different continents. She reminded me I went to London and never came back. And I said something like, 'Yes, I ran and now I'm done.' And I had a flashback to that phone call about the crash."

"What crash?"

"I was nearly done with my doctorate, and my parents came to London for a visit. Their plane went down in the Atlantic."

"I'm sorry. I'd forgotten how they died."

"They'd given my name as the contact for the insurance. Remember when people did that? Bought flight insurance for a big payout if the plane crashed?"

"Yes. And they'd bought one of those insurance policies and named you as the beneficiary?"

"Exactly. When the call came, I had no idea it was about money. All I heard was the plane had gone down and both of them were killed. I couldn't bear the pain of never having had a relationship with them. Right on the eve of having some acceptance from them for who and what I was."

Gwen struggled to draw in a deep breath. It wasn't often a client opened a treasure chest of insights in the first five minutes of a session. She wasn't sure which gem to pick up first.

Justin didn't give her a choice. "Actually their acceptance was only about the professional position I was assuming in the family tradition of high finance, but it was, at last, something they approved, and I was absurdly proud of that. In the face of such devastating loss, that bit of approval felt like the key to the future. I grabbed it and ran with it. For two decades, Gwen, I ran with it. Straight to the depths of hell. What was I thinking?"

"Before they died, what had you envisioned for your career?"

"I saw myself as a venture capitalist with a primary interest in seeding businesses for innovators. Creative thinkers who could turn around the status quo when it had stagnated or who had solutions to problems like hunger and disease. And, instead, I allowed myself to be courted by the energy firms and cartels that wanted my genius for sniffing out the promising ideas among the dross."

Gwen said the words before she knew she was thinking them. "It sounds like you lost your mind out there, along with your soul."

"I did."

"I'm not sure why that popped out of my mouth."

"It's the truth. Let's be glad it came out."

The man is full of surprises today.

"I'm curious. Did you ever give yourself the chance to work with any of those creative thinkers who wanted to improve the status quo?"

"Perhaps a few. I would have to think hard to recall their names or their ideas."

Gwen shook her head. "Pity."

Justin hung his head. "Yes."

"The bright side is you can turn that around now."

"Thank you. I mean to. Somehow. And is that the way out of the guilt and the grief I've never dealt with?"

"Possibly. Let's talk about the guilt some more. Were you blaming yourself for their deaths?"

"Yes, the truth is, they'd normally have gone directly to Amsterdam or Berne or wherever father's business was. That was their pattern. They'd invite me to join them, rather than come to London to visit me."

"Seriously?"

Justin nodded and averted his gaze, but not before Gwen saw the pain written on his face.

Had she really known these people? *What kind of parents operated that way?* "I'm speechless."

Justin cleared his throat. "Thank you for that. Others reinforced the guilt. Chief among them, Josh."

"Your brother? Why?"

"I can tell you what he said, but what was behind it is anyone's guess. He was furious about the insurance money coming to me."

"Surely that wasn't his opening line when you reported their deaths to him?"

"Actually, the airline reported their deaths to him, as the eldest son and next of kin. He called me to break the news, and I had just ended the call with the insurers. I blurted out something about already knowing because . . . If ever I could take back my words, that would be the one time I'd pick."

"We say stupid things when we're in shock. But I can see how that would start the conversation down the wrong path."

"Exactly. There was always animosity between us."

Justin and Gwen talked about the sibling rivalry, the differences between the sons, how those differences were twisted and used cruelly against them by their parents.

Justin summed it up. "Josh was not ambitious. He was content with his position as the son of a wealthy family, happy in his role as husband to a wealthy woman, and delighted to be the father of bright, charming children."

"He sounds like a happy, contented father. I don't see anything wrong with that picture."

"Of course you're right, but I'm sure he took a lot of heat from mother and father, and they'd probably been rubbing it in about their visit to me in London and how proud they were of my promising career and blah, blah."

"Ouch."

"I suppose, hearing I'd drawn the lucky number being the beneficiary of that particular flight insurance policy, he was worried about coming up short in their will. As their first son he had nothing to worry about, of course. I suspect they took out policies like that every time they flew, alternating the beneficiary. Suffice to say, he was upset about the insurance and outraged at anything that smacked of favoritism. I suddenly seemed the fair-haired boy, and that added fuel to Josh's fire."

"He blamed you for their death?"

Justin nodded. "Loudly and at every opportunity."

"Say more."

"I brought their remains home. Arranged the funeral. Stayed long enough to sign off the probate papers, and escaped back to London. Josh kept up a barrage of blame. If I hadn't been working at the London campus instead of in Chicago. If they hadn't flown to London. If they hadn't taken out the insurance."

"That's magical thinking, would you agree?"

"Of course, but that's where his head was."

"So he blamed, and you ran."

"Exactly. Josh became bitter, even with his inheritance and the relative peace of mind once they were off his back. And I blamed myself for his bitterness. I should have been able to change his thinking, bring him back to the reality of the situation."

"Did you try?"

Justin sat pensively, looking out at the lake. "I did try. Yes. Every effort was thrown back in my face. Gwen, I remember the children's faces—Joel and Christie—as they listened to us arguing. I was no help to them at a time when they'd lost their grandparents. My brother and I were adding bewilderment to their pain. And I couldn't bear it." He shuddered once and took a cleansing breath, before continuing. "So I left."

"I wrote to Josh a few times, but nothing I said could penetrate his bitterness. I gather he could never quite enjoy the gifts of his life with Maireid and the children after that. Bridey—Maireid's mother—kept in touch with me, let me know how the children were doing. Josh drank heavily, she told me, and got worse all the time. I half suspect he was drinking when their SUV went off the road and killed them all except Joel."

Gwen sat without moving.

Justin's breathing grew shallow as his own words sank in. "God help me, I think that's the truth of it."

When he met her eyes, Gwen let her sadness show on her face. It was the truth. He must have heard it at the time of the automobile accident—it was all over the papers—and stuffed it down with his grief.

"You're not going to talk me out of it, are you?'

Gwen shook her head. She swallowed hard but still could not speak. Her eyes brimmed with tears.

Justin turned to the lake, fading from view now in the darkness of early evening. "The alcoholism didn't skip a generation, as I always thought," he said.

Gwen said quietly, "Denial makes things easier for a time."

"As does alcohol. I used it for many years to escape all the feelings that overwhelmed me through that horrible storm of guilt and blame and grief after our parents' death. God, the children's faces!" He choked on the words and reached for the tissue box. "I was useless to them." He choked with sobs for a time, then blotted his face and said, "So I used alcohol to manage the pain and remorse, until alcohol stopped working."

"Think you're an alcoholic, Justin?"

"Yes. I've known it for some time. I think I couldn't say it without accepting that Josh was too. And now I've said it."

Gwen offered a compassionate smile. "You're in good company."

"Or would be if I joined AA, you mean."

"It wouldn't hurt, you know. Perhaps you can start on that this week."

"Is time up already?"

"Yes. Are you all right?"

He nodded. "Where would I find an AA meeting tonight?"

"Big Book Study at Phil's, seven o'clock. He lives right next door, you know, still has the old house on the lake. Look for 'Phillips' at the start of his drive. Maybe I'll see you there."

"Will Gianessa be there?"

Gwen shook her head. "But Manda might."

Justin's smile broke through the gloom. "I could use a good dose of Manda tonight."

Justin hung his coat on a peg in the foyer.

"Hey." Manda smiled at the happy surprise and came out to greet him.

"Hey, yourself."

"Did you need to see me?"

"I, uh, needed a meeting, and Gwen said there was one here and you might be, too."

Manda searched his face, disbelieving and accepting at the same time. She stood up a little straighter and asked him, "What are you saying?"

"I'm saying I belong here. I'm an alcoholic." His eyes teared up and he forced a chuckle. "It took me about twenty-five years longer than you to know that about myself. Think it's too late?"

Manda shook her head. "I think it's about time. Does Joel know?"

"Probably. I think he's been waiting for me to figure it out."

"You need to cry, don't you?" She flung her arms around Justin's neck, and he hugged her to him like a lifeline.

"Yes, child, I need to weep." He let the tears flow.

Manda cried, too, and held him like a brother. When her tears subsided, she snuffled and offered the same words of comfort and encouragement she'd heard in her early days of sobriety. "You're home now. You don't ever have to feel this bad again."

Phil handed her a box of tissues. She pulled out a bunch for Justin and another for herself.

When Justin's tears came to an end, Phil clapped him the shoulder and held out his hand for a firm handshake.

"Welcome, Justin. There's coffee, tea, and cider in the kitchen and a lot of good cookies you probably can't eat."

Justin nodded, unable to trust his voice.

"We don't usually have newcomers at this meeting, but tonight we'll read out of order, from the very start of the Big Book. I think you'll identify with what Dr. Silkworth had to say."

Justin nodded again.

No one seemed to mind the drama in the foyer of Phil's lakeside home. The meeting got underway in the usual manner.

Justin hung back. Manda put a glass of cider in his hand, and he gave her a smile. She grabbed his other hand and led him to the sofa by the big stone fireplace in Phil's living room. He sat beside her.

Justin expected to feel out of place or under scrutiny. Instead, as he listened to the readings and discussion, he felt like he was among friends, as though he'd come into a room full of people who knew exactly what he'd been dealing with for the twenty or so years that he drank and the dry years since he stopped drinking. He let go of defenses that had stopped serving him a decade ago.

Near the end of the meeting, Phil asked in his gravelly voice, "Would you care to share with us, Justin?"

Justin opened his mouth, paused, and shook his head. "Thank you for— Thank you."

Manda touched his hand and whispered, "Welcome."

Her gesture and her voice invited Justin to look her in the eye. He smiled at the sparkle he saw there. Then, one by one, he made eye contact with the other eight people in the room. Each of them smiled back or waved or saluted with a coffee cup.

Gwen had joined them late, without his realizing it, and he saw tears in her eyes. She gave him a thumbs-up.

"Stay a minute and I'll find you a meeting list," Phil said. "We'll close tonight with the Serenity Prayer."

As the group spoke the words of the prayer, Justin focused on the phrase "courage to change." How would he ever find the courage to make things right with Gianessa? Was it even possible?

Joel glanced at the phone lying beside his hand, then gazed a while longer at the lake, brilliant blue today with puffy white clouds scudding across the sky. He picked up the phone, set it down again, and watched the shadow of a big cloud cross the lawn and darken the lake on its passage toward the far shore.

He picked up the phone once more. Phil's voice echoed in his head, as it had all morning.

"Just call him. You'll know what to say."

"Don't you think we should meet with him together, all three of us?"

"You don't need me in the mix, Joel."

"Why are you so sure?"

"I can't tell you. I just know. Call him."

Joel hit speed-dial, and his uncle answered on the first ring.

"You'll excuse me now," he heard Justin say. Evidently he was in a meeting. Probably with the college administrators or with the attorneys.

It pleased Joel that Justin regarded his call as more important than business.

"I'm so glad you called, Joel."

"Phil's been on my case."

"He told you I came to his meeting last night," Justin guessed.

"What? No. What are you talking about?" *Phil's meeting is closed. Only alcoholics are allowed to attend.*

Justin had not answered his question, so Joel took a side step. "I just wanted to ask you about the apartment you're renovating for Manda and me at 14 Lakeside Terrace."

"Why don't I show you how it's coming?" Justin said heartily. "I'll be by for you in, what?, fifteen minutes?"

"Good." Joel snapped the phone closed and realized he'd done it all with this right hand. It was shaking, but not out of weakness. He smiled and went in search of his ebony-headed cane.

Justin held the car door for him.

"You could be an independently wealthy chauffeur," Joel said, and Justin laughed. "Or a college president with impeccable manners."

"President? I hope you don't know something I don't know."

"Just saying you're dressed for the part. Maybe you should consider it. I hear people are supporting your moves to save the college."

"Thank you for saying that. Right now I want to talk about us."

"What's there to say?" He clicked the seatbelt, and they rolled ahead.

"A lot. I've been a huge ass, and I wouldn't blame you for cutting me out of your life, starting with your wedding."

"You know that's not going to happen."

"Thank you. I'm not sure I deserve that, but I'm grateful for it."

Justin maneuvered the Saab down the drive of the Manse, onto the state highway and north toward the city limits of Tompkins Falls.

"I owe you much more than an apology, Joel. I want to know how to make things right between us."

Joel sat stiffly and stared straight ahead. "You need to make things right with Gianessa." His hands fiddled with the head of the cane.

"Yes, I do, and I mean to. But I also need to make things right with you."

Joel nodded once. He stayed silent the rest of the way to Lakeside Terrace.

Even with the cane, it was difficult to negotiate the two stairs up to the porch. “A ramp would be helpful here. Maybe just a temporary that fits over the granite steps.”

“We’ll take care of it for you.”

Justin handed him the key to the front door. Joel tried it with his right hand and quickly switched to his left.”

“I’ll look into making that easier.”

Joel changed the subject. “We’re planning to honeymoon in our suite at the Manse, did Manda tell you?”

“No. It’s a good idea.”

“Ireland a year from fall. She’ll have graduated, and I want to climb some of those hills with her. Maybe kiss the Blarney Stone.”

Joel took a quick look at Justin’s face and saw a twinkle there.

“Say it, uncle.”

Justin held up his hands. “I wasn’t going to say anything about blarney or the gift of gab. You already have both, of course.”

Joel chuckled, “You kissed it when you were twelve, probably.”

“I never,” Justin blustered comically.

Time for the truth. “You went to Phil’s Big Book meeting Wednesday?”

“Manda didn’t say anything?”

“Neither did Phil. It’s an anonymous program.”

“Yes, I went.”

“They let you into a closed meeting?”

“I’m an alcoholic.”

Joel waited a beat. “It’s about time you figured it out.”

Justin nodded. “Gwen is the right therapist for me.”

“Good.”

“I’m very grateful you made the suggestion.”

"The suggestion?" Joel's eyebrows raised. "You mean when I *ordered* you to get help and *insisted* you call Gwen?" His eyes twinkled.

Justin barked a laugh. "That suggestion, yes."

"So show me around this place." Joel took a few steps inside and surveyed the space.

Justin pointed to the left. "Manda's old studio apartment has been swallowed up by all this."

"She loved that little place. We'll have to warn her."

Justin pointed to the bones of a gourmet kitchen at the far end. Joel limped eagerly toward it, and Justin scuttled ahead of him, shoving aside random hunks of wood and nails and drop cloths in his path.

"Hardwood floors, unless you say otherwise."

Joel nodded silently.

"I didn't want this kitchen to go too far without your input," Justin said.

A straight line on the floor separated the living-dining space from the kitchen. Straddling it, a makeshift table held the construction plans.

Joel studied the design. "I like how open it is and how bright." He turned toward the bank of windows on the north side. "No upper cabinets on that wall?"

"Exactly. Possibly shelves, maybe a rack for pots. We can use the other walls for as many cabinets as you need. With the windows, you have a view of the marina, the north end of the lake and the willows along the park. You can even see a couple of the islands if you stand at the sink."

Joel squinted at the drawing and moved to the spot where the sink would be. "You're right. This is great."

Justin relaxed.

"How many bedrooms?"

"Two the same size as yours on the third floor. We're thinking in terms of a master suite and a guest room. We could make the guest room into office space, if you prefer."

"The side-by-side alcoves you gave us at the Manse are perfect. There's room here in the living area for something like that. Then the guest room could double as a getaway place. Do both bedrooms have porches?"

"Yes."

"Nice detail." Joel gestured to three graceful archways that separated the living area from the bedroom hallway.

"We had to respect the load-bearing elements, so we made curving archways.

"I heard you're bringing down the Cushman monstrosity."

When Justin blanched, Joel clarified. "I meant the pink mansion you inherited."

"I thought you were talking about my therapy again. The Justin Cushman Monstrosity is being dismantled, rest assured. It will take more time and effort with Gwen and AA—much more. But, to your point, the Cushman mansion is gone. They finished the cleanup last week. Did I go against your wishes?"

"God no. I hated that place, you know that. Let's sit down. I'm not good at standing for much more than ten minutes."

Justin muscled two folding chairs into the master suite, and they sat looking out at the lake.

"To be honest," Joel told his uncle, "Manda and I went over there a few times last fall, and she really loves the grounds. We dreamed about getting rid of the eyesore mansion and building a place on that level area over by the tennis court. Do you know where I mean?"

The statement warmed Justin's heart. "Yes, and I can picture you there. When Gianessa and I first saw it, she said she imagined your children playing on the lawn." He dipped his head for a moment and got control of his emotions. "I love the area up by the birches. I'm planning to build a house up there. I had hoped to share it with Gianessa."

"Don't count it out, Justin. I'd love for the four of us to live on that property and raise our children there—you and

Gianessa, me and Manda. Start a new Cushman generation and a new legacy. What do you say we work toward that?"

"You don't think Gianessa and I are a lost cause?"

"No, I don't. You're in recovery now, and that was the missing piece, though neither of you knew it. Gianessa went to the trouble of establishing the paternity of her child. She knows she needs a father for this baby, and if you're willing to step up—just as you have done at the college, and as you did with me after my family was killed—she'll find a way to set aside her anger and her badly damaged pride."

"And I'll spend the rest of our lives making it up to her."

"I think she just wants your love and your partnership. With you in recovery, and with the work you're doing in therapy with Gwen, you have a chance. Don't blow it."

Justin nodded. "Care for a meeting tonight?"

"Tony and Phil are bringing one to me at the Manse. Join us. Six-thirty."

"I will. And this place will work for you and Manda for a year or so?"

"Until I'm able to walk down to the lakeshore and back. Then we'll build on the Cushman grounds with you. It might be a couple of years. Things take as long as they take."

Justin saw the signal from Phil. The women were in place, and the ceremony would begin as soon as Joel took his place.

Justin sat in the chair next to Joel. "Sure you want to stand for this?"

"Are we ready?"

"We are, and it's your wedding, so play it however you want. These two chairs are here for you and Manda whenever you choose."

"I'll stand for the ceremony and sit for most of the photos. No procession out. Hors d'oeuvres and refreshments are ready for the guests in the Fireplace Room. No reception line until then."

"I'll see to it."

"You have the two rings?"

Justin showed them to Joel. Joel touched each of them as if to convince himself this was all real. Justin watched as emotions played across Joel's face when he looked from the rings to the rose arbor and up at the opening in the holly hedge.

He stood from his chair with no assistance, moved fluidly to his place under the rose arbor and turned to smile at the guests. The pastor signaled the string quartet to play the processional.

Justin stepped to his place near Joel's left hand. His heart soared when Joel leaned toward him and said quietly, "I would not be here except for your love and determination."

Justin met his gaze and nodded. "And I as well."

Sara stepped into view at the top of the garden, a smile lighting her lovely face. Her hands trembled a little with the bouquet of creamy gardenias, blush roses and blue periwinkles. She processed gracefully across the upper level of the terrace, stepped down the three steps to the lower level, and paused. Justin spied Gianessa in the last row smiling encouragement at Sara.

When Phil stepped into the garden with Manda on his arm, Justin heard a rush of breath from Joel and the single word, "God."

Manda was a breathtaking bride, from her elegant silk gown to the flowers sprinkled through her dark curls to the profusion and cascade of blooms in her bouquet—cream, blush, and periwinkle. As they stepped across the upper level, Manda turned toward Phil, and they shared a lighthearted exchange. They paused just a moment at the top of the steps. At the next bar of music, Sara came forward, and behind her Phil and Manda made their descent—smiling and confident—to the lower level. Gianessa reached a hand to Manda as she passed, and their fingers brushed. The guests focused on Manda as she and Phil processed toward Joel.

Justin focused on Gianessa, her radiant amethyst eyes, the soft, familiar planes of her face, her slender body that carried their child. Her breasts were fuller now, and her waist had just started to thicken. His eyes devoured her.

Gianessa looked straight at him, and he saw a warning in her eyes, with pain just behind it. When he did not turn away, her forehead creased with annoyance.

Phil cleared his throat and said, "I represent Manda's family this morning."

Justin had not heard the pastor's question, "*Who gives this woman?*" He dutifully returned his attention to the ceremony. Manda kissed Phil's cheek.

Manda and Joel shared a long, loving look.

When they turned to face the pastor, Joel did not falter nor wince. Justin felt sure he could stand for the remainder of the ceremony.

The formalities and the exchange of vows went quickly, just as they'd planned. On cue, Justin offered the rings. Manda's voice was steady, while Joel's shook with emotion. With their wedding bands on their fingers, the couple joined hands.

Justin felt their devotion as a force that flowed from them and beyond to fill the garden. His heart warmed. This was what his nephew had worked toward on his quest, and it was what Justin sought for himself.

When Joel and Manda shared their first kiss as a married couple, the guests cheered and clapped, and Tony let rip a whistle that raised a few eyebrows. Sara and Grace laughed and turned to each other for a quick hug.

Joel whispered to Manda, and she nodded to Justin. Everyone was on the same page with the plan. Justin faced the guests while Joel slid onto the nearest chair and Manda took her place protectively at his side. He heard Manda ask Joel if he felt strong enough to continue with the photography session, and he gave his assent.

Justin kept his smile in place and raised his hands to the honored guests for quiet. He announced, “At this point in the festivities, Joel and Manda and the wedding party will stay here for formal photographs and will join you very shortly. The reception is in the Fireplace Room, where light refreshments are waiting for you now. Please feel free to take your time on the return to the Manse and enjoy the grounds. We’re so pleased that each of you has joined us here for the wedding ceremony.”

Grace handed back Sara’s bouquet and waited for her cue. Justin nodded to her and to Gianessa. The shepherds directed their flock, touching an arm or grabbing an elbow as needed, smiling with charm, while Tony, a dashing figure in a morning coat, welcomed guests to the golf cart. Justin gave him a wave of thanks.

When Justin turned back, someone had shifted the bride and groom’s chairs so the rose arbor made a backdrop. Joel sat in the groom’s chair, his arm braced along the back of Manda’s, his face pale but relaxed.

“Are we ready?” Justin asked and motioned the photographer into place. Relieved, he stepped out of his director role and stood near Joel to await instructions. For the first time, he caught the scent of the roses and let his head fill with their promise of love.

The photographer circled his finger to direct Phil and the pastor behind the couple, under the arch of roses. The flash fired, and the tableau changed around Manda and Joel, who stayed in their periwinkle, cloth-covered chairs, as different groupings assembled behind, beside, and in front of the couple.

Finally Manda stood alone under the arch of the rose arbor, and Gianessa fussed with the hem of Manda’s dress and the angle of the bouquet. As Gianessa stood to take a step back, Manda saw the truth. She blurted, "Ohmigod, you're—"

Gianessa saw it coming and rushed her into silence. After a hug and a whispered conference, Manda turned accusing eyes on Justin. Gianessa squeezed Manda's hands and coached her into a glowing smile. Joel stood up and beamed a smile at his bride. Gianessa stepped out of the picture.

Justin knew the right thing was to muster a proud smile for Joel and Manda, but he turned away in shame. With his gaze on the lake, his mind replayed the scenes from the weekend in New York—in the bridal shop, in Henri's jewelry shop, at their restaurant, in their suite—and the nights of passion with Gianessa since then.

Manda was right to censure him. He was every bit as responsible for this child as Gianessa was, and he'd had the audacity to act like the aggrieved party. Gianessa hadn't tried to trap him into marriage; she'd only insisted that he take financial responsibility for the child. And she'd had to retain a lawyer and finagle DNA testing to insure that he did. *What an ass I am.*

How could he have thrown away all the tenderness and excitement and dreams they'd shared? He thought of the moment they'd stood near the birches on the Cushman grounds, when she'd realized—made him realize—he wanted to build a house and a future there. Knowing there was a child on the way, he should have formalized his commitment to her and shortened whatever timetable he had in his head. Instead he'd sullied their love and their relationship and all they'd been together.

Phil's gravelly voice behind him brought Justin back to the present.

"Justin, Joel would like a shot of the two of you."

Justin couldn't trust his voice, so he nodded, put on a smile, and turned to find Joel. At the far end of the terrace, he saw Gianessa, Sara, and Grace step into Tony's golf cart. With a *putt-putt*, they headed uphill.

The photographer motioned Justin to take his place beside Joel, who was on his feet, but pale and strained. Justin met Joel's eyes and saw doubt and concern. Justin nodded his shared concern. The two Cushman men turned to the camera, their smiles grim. Justin knew this photo would not make the wedding album. Instead, it would always remind him of the many ways he had diminished the joy of Joel and Manda's wedding.

Chapter 13

She knows who I am. Lyssa's stomach flip-flopped. A beautiful pregnant woman in a creamy linen dress floated toward her, the same woman who was with Manda and that man at the restaurant. What was her name? Vanessa or something like that. Gianessa, that was it. *Is she going to throw me out? I should have brought my invitation.*

Gianessa smiled like the Mona Lisa, but that didn't mean anything. Who knew what the Mona Lisa was thinking?

In spite of her fear, Lyssa put on a smile for Gianessa, and something made her reach out her hand. She stammered. "You look beautiful, Gianessa."

"Thank you, Lyssa. I needed to hear that today." Gianessa amped up her smile. "And you are a million times healthier than when we met."

"I'm clean and sober." Her voice caught. "By some miracle."

"We're all miracles in AA."

"You, too?"

Gianessa nodded.

Lyssa blurted out, "I'm so ashamed of how I acted and how I ruined Manda's happiness. I don't know how I can ever make it up to her." She brushed at a few tears.

"Let's see." Gianessa gave her a quick hug. "You didn't crash her party, did you?"

"You're kidding, right?"

"Kidding. Manda invited you to the reception because she wants to heal the rift between you. And you showed up, clean and sober." Gianessa gave her the once over. "You couldn't be more beautiful for your sister's special day. You're here for her, and you love each other."

"So I'm already making amends, you're saying?"

"Yes."

Gianessa's eyes shifted.

Lyssa followed the direction of her gaze to the reception line. *He's the man who drove that day, the rich one.* "Your husband is very handsome in his morning coat."

Gianessa's gaze flew back to Lyssa's face.

So much anger and pain. Lyssa was unnerved by the way it twisted Gianessa's features.

"He's not my husband," Gianessa informed her in a cold voice.

Lyssa stammered. "But you're pregnant." *Just shoot me.*

Gianessa's hands fluttered to her face, and Lyssa saw her struggle against tears.

"I am so sorry." Lyssa reached out a hand and touched Gianessa's arm.

"So am I, believe me." Gianessa shook her head. "Not about being pregnant. I'm very happy about that. But Justin and I are not meant to be."

"He can't take his eyes off you."

"That would be his problem."

Lyssa worried about the mercurial changes in Gianessa's mood. Maybe hormones played a part, but she was pretty sure she was seeing a resentment. A serious, unhealthy one. She had a bunch of those herself, and it scared her to see how ugly Gianessa's resentment made her previously beautiful, serene face. She said a silent prayer—something she was doing a lot lately—that she could help Gianessa somehow.

She opened her mouth and said, "You know, I really appreciate the way you forgave me just now. I believe, from everything I saw when we met, that Justin loves you with all his heart. Whatever he's done, I hope you can find it in your heart to forgive him. I think you're meant to be together. And I think your baby needs its father as much as it needs you."

Gianessa stood with her fingertips pressed against her forehead.

"I'll shut up now and get in the reception line, since there are only two people left and Manda's giving me the eye."

She gave Gianessa's arm a gentle squeeze and edged toward her sister's wedding party.

The girl in the pretty blue gown held out a delicate hand. "Hi, I'm Sara."

"Lyssa," she mumbled, "Manda's horrible sister."

Sara giggled and shook her head. "I know she's really excited that you came. You look gorgeous, Lyssa. That shade of green is so perfect with your hair. I do hair, you know, and I love the way that short, natural style shows off your curls. Like Manda's, only copper."

"You're a sweetheart. Thanks for being a wonderful friend to my sister. You're a beautiful maid-of-honor."

Sara shook her finger playfully back and forth. "And I *will* catch the bouquet, so don't even think about getting in my way."

"Trust me, I won't be anywhere near it."

"Do you know Justin Cushman, the best man?"

Sara handed her off, and Lyssa licked her lips nervously.

Justin gave her a stern eye. "Lyssa."

Taking a cue from his formal tone, she said, "Sir, I want to thank you for getting me into treatment. I don't deserve the compassion you showed me, and I'm deeply ashamed for the way I behaved toward you and Manda and Gianessa."

To her surprise, Justin had a twinkle in his eye. "You rehearsed that speech?"

Lyssa let out a laugh and teared up at the same time. "But I mean it, from my heart. Thank you."

"We're all glad you're here today, healthy and, if I may be so bold, clean and sober?"

"Yes, and it feels good." Lyssa smiled with happiness.

Justin patted her arm and turned to his left. "Manda is more beautiful than any bride I've ever seen, don't you agree?"

"Yes." A smile bloomed on Lyssa's face. Her sister radiated love and happiness.

Manda said goodbye to a bosomy blonde then pulled Lyssa into a tight hug. "I'm so glad you're here, Lyssa."

The sisters rocked back and forth. Over and over, Lyssa said, "I'm so sorry. I love you so much."

Lyssa felt a hand on her shoulder. Justin informed them, "The reception line is finished, ladies, so do what you have to do. I'll move the festivities along."

Someone put a bunch of tissues in Lyssa's hand. She held them to her face as the musicians switch from classical to swing.

An arm came across her shoulders. "Welcome, sis," a husky baritone voice said.

She saw a younger version of Justin, standing with a protective arm around her sister's waist.

Lyssa trembled. "Are you Joel?"

"I am."

They eyed one another. This was the hottie that won her sister's heart. Lyssa saw the sharp mind and inner strength behind his eyes. She blurted out, "Thank you for taking care of her and for loving her."

"It's my pleasure." A smile played around his lips. "Glad you could be here today to celebrate with us."

"Joel's got to sit down," Manda said, "and I'm a little shaky, too. At least half of the guests are sober in AA, so just introduce yourself and you'll feel right at home. I want you to enjoy the food and the fun."

Lyssa looked around and wondered how she would tell who was in AA and who was not.

A big hand clapped her on the shoulder. "Heard you might be a friend of Bill W."

Lyssa laughed. “I guess that’s how I’ll find my people.” This one was wearing a morning coat, and his arm was around a perky blond with big boobs.

“Tony P.,” he said, “and this is my good friend, Sunny. How about joining us at our table? It’s all AA people.”

“I’d really like that.” She turned to Sunny. “I’m Lyssa, Manda’s screw-up sister.”

Halfway through a slow number, Tony swung Gianessa around, and she landed in Justin’s arms. Her smile froze.

Justin drew her close. “I need you to listen for half a song. Please.”

When she didn’t fight him, he bent his head close to her ear. “If this is the last time I hold you, so be it. I need you to hear that I love you with all my heart. I want you to have abundant happiness and good health. I intend to do everything I can for our baby, and I am honored that you are the mother of my child. I know you will be a wonderful mom. Gianessa, if you can ever find it in your heart to forgive me, I want us to marry and make omelets and tromp all over the Cushman grounds with our children.

“I’ve been working very hard in therapy. I am so deeply sorry for the way I behaved, for my insane thoughts, for doubting you, for accusing you of things you would never do. I mean to be healthy and whole, and it will take much more work. I’m in AA now, too, where I should have been for the past seven years.”

He held her until the song ended. She looked torn. “Please tell me what you’re thinking.

“I need to be able to trust you,” she said. “And I can’t right now.”

Justin let out an agonized sigh of surrender. “Please be happy, sweetheart, and know that I love you. Perhaps in time?”

She searched his eyes for the briefest moment, before her tears brimmed over. "I love you, Justin, but it hurts so much right now. I need to take care of myself and the baby, for now. Please let me be, just for now."

Justin felt a wrenching in his chest as Gianessa ran from him, slipping through the partygoers, fleeing with his heart and their baby and all he had dreamed about for their future together.

He started after her but paused when Sara caught up to her, wrapped her in a sisterly hug and led her toward the parking lot. Justin wanted to be the one whose arm wrapped around Gianessa's shaking shoulders and comforted her and took her home, not the one who caused her pain.

A flash from the bar grabbed Justin's attention. The bartender flourishing a bottle of something amber that captured and spun the light and made the crowd laugh. He remembered there were three receptions today, and only Joel's was a sober wedding.

Out of the corner of his eye, he saw a summery green dress move toward the bar. Lyssa. He watched her halting steps. She took in the jovial crowd in the bar, just as he had, then glanced around nervously, and spotted Justin watching her. He gave her a knowing smile. She lowered her head, came up with a half-smile and sauntered in his direction.

"It looked good for a minute," she admitted as she came nearer. "I'm really nervous and uncomfortable here today, even though it's a lot of AA people."

"Let's grab something non-alcoholic and amble down to the water's edge. What do you say? I'd enjoy getting to know you, now that we're family."

Lyssa studied his face. He was careful not to show any censure or animosity. He was, after all, just another drunk, and she'd saved him from a drink just now.

"You're not going to throw me in the lake?"

His face split with a grin. He remembered his threat back on the canal path when they'd first met. He gestured to a table with deep blue, quart-size, chilled bottles of Saratoga water. At her nod, he grabbed one for each of them and ushered her out the French doors and across the veranda.

“Did you know,” he asked her halfway down the lawn, “I, too, have a doctorate in economics?”

“No shit?”

“God’s honest truth.”

“So we have something in common.”

“How did your defense go?”

“It was pretty rough. My committee was disgusted with me—no surprise. But the work was solid, and in the end they signed off with no revisions.”

Justin gave a whistle of admiration. “What are your plans?”

She hesitated two steps behind him.

He turned back. “Is the lawn a problem?”

She kicked off her heels, one at a time, and hitched up her dress a few inches. “Not any more. Let’s go for that bench.” She pointed across the lawn to the only unoccupied bench at the water’s edge. “Did you know the garden and the benches were my sister’s idea?”

“I did not.”

“Everyone was thinking gazebo, but Manda knew how talented the gardener is and how much Joel likes nature, so she suggested a terraced garden and a few picturesque stopping places along the shore. And today they got married in her garden.”

“Sounds like you admire her.”

“I do. I love my little sister. I’m glad she didn’t cut me out of her life, even though I almost ruined her wedding.”

Justin knew how that felt. “Yes, that was quite a scene a couple of months ago. I’m glad you took us up on the rehab. Not everyone would take that step.”

“And I guess not everyone gets it when they’re given the chance. It’s a good facility, you know.”

"So I've heard." He raised his bottle to her. "And you did the work, Lyssa. You made the commitment to be sober."

Lyssa clinked her bottle against his. "But I almost blew it today. I almost forgot what my sponsor says."

"What's that?"

"That you have to do the work every day. If you want a good life, it's one day at a time."

"And do you want a good life?"

She paused, took a long pull on the bottle of Saratoga water and laughed. "That's not a hard question, I know. It's just hard to imagine what it will look like. I've been so obsessed with being my father, keeping his memory alive. I don't know how to think about my own life."

"Your father's gone?"

Lyssa nodded and heaved a sigh. She sat back and crossed one leg over the other. Her top foot kicked a nervous rhythm.

Justin saw grass stains on the hem of her dress and the bottom of her bare feet.

"He and our mother were both alcoholics, and they died in a drunk driving accident when Manda and I were almost finished with high school. I never accepted their death. I was a lot like my father, and I couldn't stand it that he was gone, just like that." The snap of her fingers was so loud, two little birds flapped out of a nearby bush.

Justin watched their panicked flight and saw them settle quietly in a tree a few yards away. "Tell me about him. How were you like him?"

"Dad was a college professor—economics—at a small college where we lived."

"Which was where?"

"Olean, down near the Pennsylvania border."

Justin nodded.

"He was wicked smart, and he loved theories about money, but mostly he loved the psychology of why people buy things they don't need and get into trouble with money and worry about money and care about money more than about people."

"Those are radical ideas for an economist."

Lyssa nodded and took another long pull on the blue bottle. "He was happy to work at a college that emphasized values. He could have been rich, I guess, but he didn't care so much about that."

"What about you?"

"It's funny you should ask. I thought I cared more about money than anything else, but every time Manda and I talked, which wasn't very often, I knew I cared more about her than anything else in the world. And when I screwed up with her, in front of you and Gianessa, it's like everything came crashing down. In detox, and after, in treatment, I started to clear up. Like wake up and smell the coffee."

She turned to see if he was still listening, and he nodded.

"I realized finally that my committee wanted me to fail because I was so high-maintenance. I thought Manda would never want to see me again. I knew for sure our parents were never coming back. And I couldn't stand what I had become. I'll never be my father, except I'm a drunk like him, and I've got a Ph.D. in economics like him."

Ah, to be so self-aware at twenty-five. It had taken him another twenty-one years. "And what do you care about now, Lyssa?"

"I care about making it up to Manda and Joel." She stole a look at Justin. "And you and everyone else I've smashed along the way. It's overwhelming to think about how many people I used and ticked off and abandoned in the last eight years."

"That's how long you drank?"

"And did pot. Yes." She uncrossed her legs and rested her elbows on her knees.

Justin offered some reassurance. "I think you'll be

all right if you stick close to your meetings and let your sponsor guide you."

Lyssa let out a sob and tried to bite it back.

He squeezed her shoulder and told her, "You know your sister is the queen of crying jags."

She laughed and rubbed the back of her hand against her nose.

He handed her a clean handkerchief.

"Thank you."

He sat quietly while she cleaned up her face and composed herself.

She gave one final snuffle. "It's beautiful here."

"Yes, it is."

"I'd like to live someplace like this."

"In a mansion?" Justin teased.

"No." Lyssa laughed. "In a college town on a lake."

"Would you teach?"

"Honestly, I'd like to, but mostly what I want to teach is personal money management and financial literacy. I get the theories, and I'm qualified to teach much more and at a higher level, but . . ."

"Go on, I'm really interested. You've lost your accent, by the way."

"Really?

"Really, no more Texas twang. It's easier to talk to you this way."

"Well, I'm glad then."

"So you know theory but . . ."

"Oh yeah. Manda and I had to make it on our own after our parents died. I mean, it turned out there was an inheritance, a really decent one, but neither of us knew about that until Joel made inquiries last summer. So we both had to find ways to finance college, and, for me, a doctorate, and earn money to live on, and all that. If our

Dad hadn't taught us how to do that, we'd probably be flipping burgers now. Nothing against flipping burgers, but it wasn't what we saw ourselves doing with our lives. We both finished our degrees debt free, which is really unusual, and it gives us a head start. So many people I know have huge loans and credit card debt."

"You could blow your advantage pretty quickly if you got heavier into drugs."

Lyssa lowered her head. "Yeah, you're right, and I need to work my program to stay out of that hell. And I don't mean to short-change that, but what I started to say was I think it's important for college students to get savvy about their finances right away, regardless of how much money they want to make or what career path or what major or any of that."

Justin smacked his hands on his thighs. "Now I'm hearing your passion."

Lyssa turned a worried face to him.

He praised her. "That's good. Passion will see you through many rough patches and set backs in your career. And *your* passion is timely and important. Financial literacy is essential. Dr. Lyssa Doughty, I challenge you to use your first-hand knowledge and your degree, fired by your passion, to build a satisfying career."

Lyssa looked hard at him and seemed to satisfy herself about his sincerity. She sat tall and said decisively, "Okay then. I will. Can I teach it? In a college?"

"If you're any kind of a teacher, you can teach it to high school, college, recent grads, full-blown adults, retirees, widows, anyone who will listen and maybe some people who won't. Is there a college teaching job in it? It depends on the college. At Tompkins College we're working hard to revitalize the curriculum, and it will contain all kinds of literacy, including financial. Watch the web for jobs at the schools you're interested in, do research on those schools, do your networking, and, most important, work your AA program every day."

"Thank you. I owe you." She took in a deep breath and blew it out forcefully.

He wagged his finger. "First you owe Manda and Joel and Gianessa. You make things right with them, you'll have paid your debt to me."

Lyssa held out a slender white hand that trembled only a little. From nervousness this time, he thought. He remembered how it shook from her disease when she snuck a toke on the canal path.

"Deal," she said.

"Deal." Justin clasped her hand and was pleased with her firm, professional handshake.

"I'll go back to the reception and see if I can be useful." She stood up and collected her shoes. "Are you coming, too?"

"I think I'll enjoy the view a few more minutes."

He sat on their bench and watched the little birds they'd disturbed. They fussed with some berries, twittered when half a dozen of their species flew in to join them, and eventually moved on with the group. At a loss for another distraction, he stood up, stretched, and welcomed the chirping of his phone.

"Joel and I are getting ready to vanish," Manda told him. "You're too late to catch the garter, but Joel wants to say goodbye and thank you."

"On my way."

Sara helped Gianessa out of her linen dress and hung it carefully on a hanger.

"I don't ever want to wear it again. Lyssa guessed I was pregnant. I'm not even five months."

"Don't worry about it for now, Gianessa. Just rest. How's the baby?"

"I wish she'd start moving."

"Are you worried?"

"No, just wanting to know she's there and we're in it together."

Sara stroked her arm. "Do you know for sure it's a girl?"

Gianessa shook her head and lay back on her bed. "Just a hunch and a wish." She smiled with her hand on her belly. "I still need to tell Pop and Ariella."

"Who's Ariella?"

"My aunt, Pop's twin sister. She came from Italy to raise me with Pop after my mother divorced him."

"Why did she divorce him?"

"He wanted a wife, she wanted a career. They had grown apart, and once I started walking and talking that was it. She didn't want to be a mother."

"So why did she get pregnant?"

"A moment of passion, I guess." *Like me and Justin?* "They were passionate people."

"Suppose it's a boy?"

Gianessa patted her belly. "Maybe it is."

"You could name him Justin."

"I'll name him after Pop."

"Pop's a really bad name for a boy." Sara giggled and Gianessa joined in.

"My father was Gianni, short for Giovanni."

"That's how you got your name."

Gianessa nodded. "Gianni, and my mother was Vanessa. So, Gianessa was my name."

"Gianni means John, right? You could call him John. Keep with the Cushman tradition of men's names starting with J."

Gianessa gave her a sly look. "You really want it to be a boy, don't you? Why?"

"I think the baby needs a father, and you'd be more open to Justin parenting with you if it's a boy."

Gianessa covered her eyes with the back of her hand. She smiled. "How did you get so smart?"

One of their phones rang.

"I don't want to talk to anyone. Except I'll call Pop later."

"That's my phone anyway. You rest. Do you need anything before I go back to the reception?"

"I'm good for a while. Thanks for bringing me home. You're the best, roomie."

"Syd, I've destroyed my life, do you hear? I've utterly destroyed my relationship with Gianessa."

"My dear, I hope that's not the case," Sydney said. Her brow furrowed. "This baby needs a father, and I want you to make it right with her." She sank down on the sofa in her plush living room in midtown Manhattan and tucked her legs under her. "Talk to me. Tell me what she said and did that makes you think it's beyond repair. Where are you? You're not at a bar, are you?"

"I'm standing at the French doors to Joel's porch, debating if I should stay in the cool of the air conditioning or go out in the warm night air and feel the breeze off the lake."

"Go outside and get comfortable somewhere."

"Why?"

"Do it, Justin."

She heard him grumble, heard the squeak of the hinges as the door swung open and shut again. A *whoosh* told her he'd settled into a cushioned chair, and she thought the two *thunks* might be his feet coming to rest on a railing or a stool.

"Are you comfortable?"

"You're right, it's much better out here. Thank you."

Sydney chuckled. "You see, you're able to say things like 'I'm sorry' and 'You're right' and 'Thank you.' That's all new. There's hope for you, Justin."

"But I'm still such an ass, Syd."

"Stop moaning. Tell me everything she did and said when you talked to her."

When Justin had recounted the entire two-and-a-half-minute conversation on the dance floor, he sighed. She expected him to say more, but he just sighed again.

"I counted at least one 'I love you' in her side of the conversation."

"Yes."

"And about half a dozen 'just now" and 'right now' and so on. Didn't you hear that? Don't you see that she loves you and just isn't ready to take you back?"

"But she'll never forgive me for the horrible, despicable things I said, Syd. Why would she?"

"If and when she does, it will be because she loves you and wants to work things out with you. And she'll tell you what that means, and you'll either hold up your end of the bargain or be out on your ass."

Silence. She let him think about it.

"So, you think there might be hope."

"Might be," Sydney said. "And you can't rush it. It's her timetable."

"What can I do?"

"Give her time and give her incentive."

His voice brightened. "What kind of incentive?"

"Well, didn't you say you'd received a request from her lawyer?"

"Yes. She asked for support, as she should. For the baby and for herself while she builds her career."

"And have those requests been attended to?"

"Mostly. My attorney is waiting for me to give the go-ahead. Now that I've spoken with Gianessa, I suppose I should do that."

"And what exactly are you directing him to do?"

"Well, provide generous child support, of course."

"And her request for support while she gets her career on track?"

"He said to ignore that."

Sydney sprang to her feet and let out a howl of disgust. "Who is this idiot? And why are you listening to him? He sounds like a divorce lawyer. You're trying to woo this woman back, not alienate her for life."

"He handles familial disputes of all kinds."

"He's a glorified divorce lawyer. Justin, dummy, listen to me. You're trying to give her incentive to give you a second chance.

"Syd, we already know Gianessa won't be bought."

"I get that, Justin, but there are other ways to use your money as incentive."

"Like?"

"First, triple whatever figure he has for child support. Do you hear me?"

"All right. I will. Why?"

Syd breathed through her teeth. "Because you are this child's father and you want Gianessa to know this child means the world to you and you want it to have every advantage you can offer. You do, don't you?"

"Of course, I do. I'm starting to get what you're saying. Now what about financial support for her personally as she establishes herself professionally? How do I frame it so she knows what's in my heart?"

"Justin, this is the love of your life you're talking about. She is precious beyond measure. Think. Big."

"Yes, but she can't be bought. She's apt to turn it down, and I don't want her to do that. How do I get her to take whatever I offer?"

Syd paced the living room. "Okay, think of it this way. This is your one chance to provide for her the way she should be provided for, if the two of you must live separate lives. If you were making out a will, what would you want to guarantee her, personally, for the rest of her life?"

Silence. She waited. She heard his two feet thunk back to the floor. The cushion sucked in air. "Justin?"

"Thinking. Writing."

"Sounds like you're back in the game. Listen to me. Are you listening?"

"Listening, Syd."

"You decide that figure and dictate it *exactly* the way you want it to read. Dictate it to that idiot lawyer and make him read it back to you, word for word. When he's got it all and got it right, go down there and read every detail of the letter before you sign it. Then hand-carry the letter to her house and deliver it, or slip it through the mail slot."

More silence. "Justin?"

"Yes, I'm here. Playing with the wording."

"Dear god, you've got a smile on your face, don't you? What's happening?"

"I've got to call the idiot lawyer, Syd. I'll keep you posted."

"See that you do." She chuckled. "I'll be watching for a wedding invitation or a baby announcement, whichever comes first."

On Friday afternoon, Sara heard Gianessa's gasp and turned to see envelopes fluttering from her hand to the floor. Gianessa's hands shook as she struggled to open one official-looking envelope.

"What is it? Who is it from?"

Gianessa had one hand against her mouth as she read through the text. Her face reflected fear followed by satisfaction followed by comic disbelief. She held out the letter to Sara. "Justin's attorney."

Sara grabbed the letter and scanned the lines. Gianessa had been so stressed about going to a lawyer. "This is really good," she said when she saw the dollar amount Justin was proposing for child support. "And educational expenses, medical, dental . . . What's 'enrichment'?"

Gianessa waved her hands. "Like ballet, piano, summer camp, non-school sports. Keep reading."

"Are you freaking kidding me?" Sara screamed. "He's offering you, personally, a million a year?" Sara collapsed cross-legged on the floor.

Gianessa sank down on the ottoman. "What do you think I should do?"

"Geez, roomie, take it."

Gianessa took a few slow breaths.

"You're all hunched over. Are you okay?"

Gianessa made an effort to sit up straight, and her hands went automatically to her belly.

Sara grabbed her arm. "Is the baby okay?"

Gianessa nodded. Her face was full of doubt.

"Justin has rocked your world again, right?"

Gianessa nodded. "I don't know what it means. It sounds like he's buying me off."

"What?"

"That wording around the million dollars. It's like he wants to be done with me."

Sara went back to the letter and read aloud, "'Also to be paid to Ms. Dupioni, the sum of one million dollars per annum, for her personal disposal, without limitation, in perpetuity.' That means forever, right? And you can do what you want with it?"

Gianessa's nodded, her eyes brimming with tears.

"I don't see that as buying you off. Why do you think that?"

"I think he's going to move on to someone else now. And I'll be 'that woman he got in trouble when he came back to town.'" She jumped to her feet and planted her hands on her hips. "I don't want to be 'that woman.'"

"You could move."

Gianessa cried in earnest.

Sara enfolded her roommate in a warm hug. “I’m sorry, I don’t want you to move. I’m just trying to help. It will be okay, Gianessa.” She said it over and over until the crying turned into hiccoughs. “I’ll fix us some tea and we’ll talk about this. Okay?”

Six tissues later, Gianessa joined Sara in the kitchen. She set two mugs on the counter. Sara poured their tea.

Gianessa held the fragrant tisane close to her puffy red nose. “Jasmine. Thank you. What do you think of the child support?”

“Sounds like his lawyer is on the ball about current costs,” Sara offered.

“I’m sure Justin has no clue.”

“It seems really generous.”

“I’m trying to figure out where he came up with the million-a-year idea. What do you think?”

“Would the lawyer really be the one to suggest that?”

“It doesn’t make sense.” Gianessa set down her mug. “Oh.” Her eyes grew round.

“What?”

“I’ll bet he talked to That Sydney Woman.”

“Who?”

“Sydney. The woman in New York he had the rendezvous with after we found the wedding dress. You remember, he dropped Manda and me at Radio City Music Hall and went on to see some college administrator he knows, who turned out to be a woman and an old friend and probably an old lover. Then he met Manda and me for dinner.”

“I don’t think you ever told me this story. But if he met you for dinner a couple hours later, I doubt if they’re still lovers.”

“You must be right.”

Sara noted a little smile at the corner of Gianessa’s mouth.

“So, you think Justin and Sydney also talk about your relationship. Besides professional stuff?”

“I’ll bet. In fact, I’m sure of it.”

"Spill, roomie, this sounds juicy."

"I'm thinking about how he was before dinner that night and how he was at dinner and how he got me to stop being pissed at him. I think she probably coached him." Gianessa chuckled. "And it worked."

"Fill me in here. I think I missed a whole chapter."

Gianessa recounted the sequence of events in New York City the day Manda found her gown and told Sara about Justin's need for a college advisor because of his work at Tompkins College on Joel's behalf.

"And I probably shouldn't have said so much, but I know I can trust you."

Sara had tears in her eyes. "You do? You trust me?"

"Of course I do, Sara." Gianessa grabbed her in a fierce hug. "You've been so careful about all the stuff I've shared with you. It means so much that I can trust you, and it must be really hard for you. Thank you for being a true friend to me."

Sara choked out, "That's the coolest thing anyone's ever said about me."

"I couldn't have gone through this without your support, roomie."

"Okay, so you're going to take the money, right?" Sara wiped away her tears. "You know he's not trying to buy you off?"

"I'm not sure. I feel better knowing, sort of knowing, the idea came from Sydney and not from some lawyer. But I'm still not sure how I feel about it."

"Well, come at it another way. If it's not a million dollars you want, what *do* you want from Justin?"

Gianessa drew back her hair and sighed. "I don't know."

"Well I know one thing."

Gianessa eyed her with caution.

"You're a few weeks overdue for the Devastating Damsel in Distress haircut," Sara told her, with a firm nod.

Gianessa gave her a long, slow smile. "You are a genius."

Sara squealed. "Let's sneak into the spa and do it. Right now."

Sara really needed coffee, but it was way too quiet in the kitchen. Gianessa usually hummed as she made breakfast. Today there was just the occasional rustling that sounded like pages turning. Sara poked her head in the kitchen. Her roommate flipped slowly through a baby magazine.

Gianessa sensed her presence and looked up with a bright smile. "Is my genius hairstylist roommate ready for coffee?"

"No regrets?"

"I feel beautiful." Gianessa fluffed one side of her new do.

Sara examined the waves curving along Gianessa's elegant cheekbones. "Turn, please."

Gianessa tossed her head to the right and to the left.

"I am a genius, aren't I?" Sara did a happy dance.

"Allow me make Your Genius the breakfast of your dreams."

"Seriously? I would love an omelet. Wait, can you eat omelets?"

"Absolutely. Mushrooms? Tomato?"

"And bacon."

"Coming up. Have a seat," Gianessa said, "and relax."

Gianessa took out bowls and utensils and ingredients, cracked eggs, sautéed vegetables, microwaved bacon. When she swirled the egg in the omelet pan, Sara sighed. "You're going to teach me that someday, right?"

"Absolutely. We'll do it. First lesson tomorrow morning. Do you want toast?"

"English muffin. I'll get it."

"Uh-uh." Gianessa wagged her finger and clucked her tongue. "Genius needs time off, you know."

Sara laughed. "You really like the haircut?"

"I love it. I feel pretty and desirable and in charge of my life."

"That's exactly how you should feel."

"Hah. Five months pregnant, single, and soon-to-be unemployed. That's exactly how I should feel. Pretty and desirable and in charge."

"Why not?"

They tucked into the meal. Sara devoured her omelet and the bacon.

Gianessa chuckled at her roommate, nibbling at her English muffin.

"What?" Sara said. "I love it when the butter drips through my fingers. That's why English muffins are my favorite. You have to go slow if you want every finger to drip butter."

"The secrets of true genius." Gianessa sipped her tea and took another bite of her omelet.

"Have you decided what to do about Justin's offer?"

"I think so. But first, tell me what you think I should do."

"I think you should take it all—the child support and the million for life. I mean, why not?"

"I guess."

"What were you going to do?"

"I was going to turn down the million for life part."

"Tell me why."

"Because what I really want is Justin."

Sara started to smile but stopped. "Even though he trashed you to your face when you told him about the baby?"

Pain washed over Gianessa's beautiful face.

"I'm sorry. I don't mean to be hurtful, but I need to know you're thinking about both sides of it. It's important. I don't want my friend married to a man who's going to go off on her."

"You're right. It is important. I think he knows that now. He's in AA now. Neither of us knew he was a dry drunk. And when we danced at the wedding, he said he's working hard in therapy. And I know it's Gwen he's working with."

"Gwen who knows Manda and Joel?"

Gianessa nodded.

"What does Joel think about this?"

"I want to ask him. And I would do it today, except he's on his honeymoon."

"Manda was back at work late yesterday for a couple of hours."

"Awesome haircut. Very chic. Very sophisticated."

Gianessa gave him a dimpled smile and then squinted "You're sure I'm not interrupting your blissful retreat?"

Joel shook his head and gave her a brotherly hug. "I was glad you called. Manda worked a couple of hours this morning and then went off with Gwen on a bike ride. I'm ready to get back to the weights. Most important I want to know what's happening with the baby."

"I have a doctor's appointment next week." Her tone told him not to pursue it just yet.

Joel noticed again how pale she was. "Routine?"

She nodded with her Mona Lisa smile.

He would wait, but he would get it out of her before she left today.

"Tell me what you've been doing for exercise. Edited, please."

He blushed. "Edited, yes."

"Any workouts in the pool or with the weights?"

"The usual pool routine every day. No weights. Some short strolls on the level paths through the woods. With cane, of course."

Gianessa beamed at him. "Terrific. So let's do a little bit with weights to start and see how you feel tomorrow. I need you to promise you won't do anything more with the weights at all, not later today or tonight or tomorrow, until I see you again. Deal?"

"Deal."

"I also need to talk over something with you."

"Anything," he agreed. "I can't advise you, but I can give you my take."

They focused for twenty minutes on a simple routine in the weight room.

"Surprised you broke a sweat?"

"Yeah." He reached for a towel. "Let's get some water and talk over your agenda."

Gianessa took two bottles of water from the kitchen. Joel grabbed his cane and led her to a weathered bench in shade-dappled sunlight at the edge of the woods.

"This is peaceful, thank you."

"I could see you were tense all of a sudden. Is it the baby?"

"It's Justin. He told me at the reception he's in AA and in therapy. I want to know if you think he's sincere about working on his issues."

"I do. He's working very hard. What's the context for the question?"

"Now you're stressed, and there's no reason to be. Use your breathing routine for a minute."

Joel took a few deep breaths, and she waited for him to signal he was ready.

"Joel, when I first knew I was pregnant, I asked a lawyer to write him, asking for child support and also support for myself for a few years while I got on my feet professionally. I don't know if you were aware of that."

"I was not, but I'm glad to hear it. I only knew that you established the baby's paternity." He waited, holding his tongue, hoping she would share Justin's response.

"I heard from his lawyer yesterday. He's offering a very generous allowance for child support and other services for our baby, like medical and educational. Very generous. And I mean to accept that."

Joel turned sideways on the bench to see her face. She was biting her lower lip. "That's all he's offering?" Joel prompted.

Gianessa breathed out a laugh and shook her head. "I don't know if it's a grand gesture or buying me off or what, but he's offering me a million dollars a year for life, no conditions."

Joel laughed from his belly.

She was shocked by his response.

He held up a hand. "Sorry." When he'd sobered, he said, "I cannot believe what he comes up with sometimes." He shook his head, and another laugh escaped.

Gianessa pressed her fingers to her forehead and chuckled. The chuckle turned to a laugh. They laughed together until tears came to their eyes.

"Seriously, he offered you a million a year?"

"Seriously."

"Now that you've had a good laugh, what do you think it means?"

"I think everything about the child support probably came from the lawyer, but the personal money, I don't know. It might have come from That Woman Sydney in New York, the one he talks to about the college. But no matter. Joel, I don't know how to proceed. I'd really like some support while I figure out the career thing. I can't be involved with Manda's holistic rehab if Justin is backing it. But this is over the top."

"You think?" Joel snorted.

"Okay, Justin's over the top, we know that. I don't want to take it, Joel, but I don't want to use the baby's money to make ends meet. I'll be okay for a year, given the proceeds from the sale of the necklace, but I'd really like your take before I decide how to respond."

Joel contemplated her face for a moment then gave her an honest answer. "I agree the million would never have come from a lawyer, particularly since you made a very specific request for support for a finite number of years. I believe it's several things." He raised one finger with each explanation. "It's a grand gesture, a test, and a statement that he holds you in the highest regard."

"You're right, it does feel like a test. But a test of what?"

"Well, first, when I said 'grand gesture,' what did you think I meant?"

"I thought he wanted me to take the money and go away like a good girl and not bother him again." Her eyes filled with tears.

"If you were divorcing each other, that would be the lawyer's idea. Pay the lady off and be done with it. Since it wasn't the lawyer's idea, it's Justin being over the top, making a grand gesture."

"I see now. And that's all you think it is?"

"No, it's a test, too."

"Of what?"

"What do you think?"

"I— Maybe if I take the money, he'll believe I was only interested in his money all along."

Joel squeezed her hand. "No, that's not it at all. He got the message a long time ago that you don't operate that way."

"Hmm, so what's the test?"

Joel grinned. "He's baiting you. He wants you to ask him what he's up to."

That sparked her anger. She jumped from the bench and put her hands on her hips. "Well, that stinker. Of course you're right."

Joel laughed and tugged on her arm.

She plunked down next to him.

"And I mentioned a third part. Remember?"

"You said it means he holds me in the highest regard. Does he?"

"Yes, he does. He loves you, and you're the mother of his child. If you take the money, he'll know you're protected for the rest of your life, and that's very important to him. If that's the best you'll let him do for you, he can go forward without worrying about you."

Gianessa's gaze was probing. After a full minute, she seemed satisfied he was being completely honest with her. "Why couldn't I see that, Joel?"

Joel pressed her hand. "You're still pretty angry. That can blind you. And remember, I've known him all my life. I mostly get him."

"I just thought of something."

"What?"

"Suppose my baby is just like him?"

"Could happen. But Justin didn't have a reliable, spiritually fit mom. You'll do fine, and so will your baby." He drew her into a hug. "Decided what you're you going to do?"

"I'll definitely take the baby money." She drew back and winked at him. "But not yet."

"Why the delay?"

"It's a test. If he wants to talk to me, he knows where to find me."

"He'll want to talk to you, bet on it." *And he's going to flip for the haircut.*

Chapter 14

"How have you been feeling?" Dr. Bowes asked Gianessa after the ultrasound.

"Why? What's wrong?"

"Nothing's wrong," the doctor assured her. She placed a hand on Gianessa's arm. "That's a standard question five months into a pregnancy."

"Is it?" Gianessa asked nervously.

"It is. Your pregnancy is becoming obvious now. Any day now, the babies will start kicking. They'll keep you busy."

Gianessa nodded. "Manda and Lyssa both guessed I was pregnant at Manda's wedding, over a week ago."

The doctor reminded her, "I do need to know how you've been feeling lately."

"Tired."

"You're pale, probably anemic. The blood tests will tell us more. Are you able to work?"

"I'm functioning. Joel is taking it easy with his therapy after the strain of the wedding. I'm doing more massages at the spa. I'm concerned about what comes next professionally."

"Did you enjoy the wedding?" the doctor asked cheerfully.

"Manda was a gorgeous bride. Her gown was stunning. It reminded me of our shopping trip to New York City for the gown. That's when Justin and I made this baby. Manda flew back early, and Justin and I stayed another two days and screwed our brains out."

"Sounds like fun." The doctor laughed.

"Actually, it was," Gianessa admitted.

"But you don't see yourselves getting together for the sake of these babies?"

Gianessa shook her head sadly. "I don't see that happening." Belatedly, she heard the plural in the doctor's question and raised her eyes.

Dr. Bowes smiled broadly.

Gianessa sank back on the exam table. She placed both hands on her belly.

"You're having twins," Dr. Bowes said. She patted Gianessa's belly. "We have a boy and a girl in here. I was fairly sure when we did the amnio, but I wanted to see how things developed before I sprung it on you. And when I say 'how things developed,' I didn't just mean the babies' development. I meant your relationship with the father."

"I can't," Gianessa said plaintively. "I can't do this alone."

"I agree, Gianessa. Having financial support is important, but raising twins as a single mom is daunting, particularly when you're not established in a workplace with childcare and health benefits and don't have family you can call on. It's foolish for you to let your pride stand in the way of your happiness and the babies' welfare."

"Oh, dear god, what am I going to do?"

"I suggest giving yourself sixty seconds to finish moaning. Then get up, get dressed, and call the babies' father for a serious talk. Meet him and show him the stills from the ultrasound that we're sending home with you. See what happens when you and he both fall in love with them."

Gianessa heard the wisdom in her doctor's words. She thought about her pop trying to raise her alone and calling Ariella to come all the way from Italy to help. She thought about Lyssa telling her to forgive the man who loved her with all his heart. She thought about Justin asking for the same. She thought about Joel explaining why Justin offered her the million. *Ohmigod, he is too much sometimes.*

Joel believed in Justin's recovery. Maybe she needed to do the same. For the babies. So they would have their daddy, too. Could she and Justin really make a happy marriage and raise a healthy family together? One day at a time, with both of them in recovery.

"Yes." She sat up, let her head adjust to being upright, swung her legs over the side of the exam table, and nodded decisively. "I will do this." Still, she couldn't launch herself from the table.

The doctor added, "Gianessa, it may help to know he has called here several times checking on you and the pregnancy. Of course, we've refused to give out information about you because of the privacy laws. He's forceful, as you know, and he's looking for a way to be part of this pregnancy."

"I didn't know." Gianessa sensed a softening inside of her.

"We didn't tell you, because you were dealing with enough stress as it was. We hoped the two of you would talk to each other, without our interference. And now the time has come." Dr. Bowes reached out a hand and helped Gianessa down from the table.

She steadied her and directed, "Get dressed, use the conference room at the end of the hall and make your call while you're here with us. We'll talk after to make sure you can get home safely."

Justin answered on the first ring. "Are you all right?" he asked. He must have seen her cell number in his caller-ID window. She could tell he was at work. Voices surrounded him, debating, arguing.

She breathed out. "Yes, I'm all right, but I need to see you. I need to talk to you." She heard a door close, and there was quiet. "Are you there?"

"I've just left a meeting. Where are you? I'll meet you or pick you up."

She exhaled in relief and then drew in a big breath. "I want to make a pizza with you for supper," she said. Suddenly her plan sounded so silly. She kept her voice light. "Can we do that together?"

"Gluten-free pizza?" he asked with a laugh, his voice skeptical.

"Yes, of course. It will be delicious. You'll see. What toppings do you like? I'm stopping at the store on the way home."

"From where?"

"The doctor's office."

"You're in Clifton Springs?"

"I am."

"You can drive all right?"

She took a steadying breath. He was caring, not criticizing, she decided. "Yes. Yes, I'm okay to swing by the store and come to your place. About an hour?"

"Call me when you get to Lakeside Terrace, and I'll come down to help you."

"Thank you," she said, touched. She reminded him, "Toppings?"

"Whatever you like, sweetheart. I don't care."

"Please care. It matters what you want."

She heard him turn the impatience into indulgence. "Mushrooms. Some kind of cheese. Maybe two kind of mushrooms and two kinds of cheese. Spinach or something green. You decide. I'm too befuddled right now," he confessed. "You'll be careful driving?"

"I will. I promise." *Where did that come from?* She laughed at herself with disbelief.

"And call me when you arrive."

"I will." She ended the call and sat still for a moment. She liked it that he sounded excited. She liked hearing his concern for her, for them. *Does he know it's twins?* She checked her watch. Just enough time to swing by the Canandaigua

Wegmans. She'd get a packaged gluten-free crust this time. Next time she'd plan ahead, get some buckwheat flour and learn to make crust herself.

"Next time," she said out loud. "Please, God, let there be a next time. Don't let me mess this up. You know I'm terrified."

A tap sounded at the door. Dr. Bowes entered. "Sounds like it went well?"

Gianessa nodded.

"Vitamins with iron," the doctor told her, holding out a giant bottle of organic capsules. "They are gluten free," she said in anticipation of the question. "And the first photos of your twins." She held out an envelope with the images. "Wait and open them with the father. Have you been eating well?"

"Yes, out of discipline."

"Good. Keep it up. Watch the sodium with that pizza," she said with a wink.

Gianessa laughed. "This was supposed to be a private conference room."

"I never said it was private." Dr. Bowes gave her a hug. "We're all concerned about you, Gianessa. You call us anytime, even if you have the silliest question or the tiniest twinge. We're in your corner, and we want your man to be there with us."

"I do, too," she said. "We need to make this work."

"Then you will. Believe it," the doctor said decisively.

"That's usually my line."

"I know. I borrowed it. You need to start applying it to your own life."

Why was it harder to call from the street outside 14 Lakeside Terrace than from the doctor's office? Gianessa sat for a moment looking out at Chestnut Lake, thinking about the last time they climbed up to the birches on the Cushman property. She wanted to channel the love and promise of that moment, to make it work for them all—her babies, their daddy, Justin, and all of them as a family.

She pressed his speed dial and waited. After two rings, she began to worry. Someone opened her car door, and she whirled around in fear. "Oh, my god, I'm sorry, I was frightened," she said and let Justin draw her out of the car into his arms.

"I'm sorry I scared you," he murmured and held her close.

Gianessa rested in his arms and felt how right it was, how well they fit together with two babies between them.

"How is the baby?" he searched her face.

He doesn't know. "That's what I need to talk about."

Fear filled his face.

She touched his lips with caring fingers. "No, don't worry. Let's get these things upstairs and have some privacy."

But his hands were already tangled in her shorter hair, and his mouth was on hers. She lost herself in the kiss, hungry for him.

"God help us," she said when his lips moved to her neck and one hand caressed her belly.

A movement caught her eye, a neighbor coming from the parking area, trying to slip by unseen on the way to his own Lakeside Terrace apartment.

"We have an audience," she said to Justin. "Can you help me with the bags? I forgot about salad."

"Not to worry. Can you manage the stairs okay, or do you need a hand?" He smiled into her eyes. "Or a carry?"

She laughed. "I'm doing well with stairs. Thanks for taking the groceries."

Comfortable in her favorite kitchen, she took ingredients out of the bags and assembled them on the island. Justin rummaged in the cabinet next to the oven. "Doesn't a pizza need a flat, round pan of some kind?" he said, puzzled.

"Yes, or a stone."

He glanced up from his crouch. “A stone?”

“A thick, flat stone.” She squatted next to him. “I’m serious,” she said when his eyes crinkled in a grin. “Do we have anything like that?” She peered into the next cabinet. “Maybe Joel doesn’t do pizza.”

“That would be my bet. We’ll improvise.”

“Exactly.” She felt his hand at her back as she reached for a jellyroll pan standing behind everything else. She got a hand on it and slowly maneuvered it over the top and out. “This will have to do.”

He stood, and she passed it to him. He placed it on the island and reached a hand down to her. “Thank you.”

Justin held her close. “I need to say that I love you, Gianessa. You are precious to me, and I want to make pizza with you every night of our lives if that will make you happy.”

She laughed and put her arms around his neck.

“Let’s see how this one goes for us.” She planted a kiss on his cheek and told him, “I love you, too.”

“There’s no tomato sauce,” he said, as he surveyed the ingredients on the counter.

We’re all over the place. “I’m not a fan of tomato sauce on pizza. I might use fresh tomatoes, but not sauce. Northern Italian cooking does not use marinara the way most Italian restaurants in this country do.” She held up her hands. “Not that you wanted a cooking lesson. I’m a little nervous here.”

Justin looked at her with a twinkle in his eyes. “This is our crust?” He held up the packaged crust. “In this package?” She let out a laugh when he sputtered “package.”

“Aren’t packaged foods loaded with sodium? What are you, a pregnant woman, doing with a packaged crust?”

Her hand was on her belly as she laughed away her tension. “Hush. I had to start somewhere, and I didn’t have the time or the presence of mind to make crust from scratch tonight. So I’m . . .”

"Compromising?" He drew out the word and raised his eyebrows. "Say it, Gianessa. Compromising."

She swatted his arm playfully. "I'm compromising my very high standards in the interest of getting food on the table. Come on. Help me out. We need olive oil and garlic."

"Coming up." He produced a gallon can of the finest olive oil along with a decorative stopper bottle half full of olive oil. "Your choice," he said.

She took the bottle.

"And do you want the garlic as a paste or pressed or chopped?"

"Someone's been practicing. Let's have it chopped, but not too much for me."

"How about your half and my half, because I'd like lots of garlic tonight?" He looked at her. "Unless you mind?"

She shook her head with a happy smile and finished preparing the crust with a thin layer of oil. While Justin attacked the clove of garlic, she set the oven temperature, opened the packages of cheese and took the mushrooms to the sink. They worked in silence for a few minutes.

We have our rhythm back. She breathed a sigh of relief.

Justin switched on the radio to a jazz station and turned the volume low. After opening the door to the balcony a crack to let in some fresh air, he coated the sauté pan with oil and started slicing mushrooms. "How's my technique?" he asked her.

She stopped to give him a sexy once-over and then pretended to study what he was doing with the mushrooms. "You're doing very well," she approved.

Justin tossed the mushrooms into the sauté pan. "How does one slice a portabella?" he asked.

"Thin strips." She opened the spice drawer. "Pepper, oregano, and what else?"

"That will do it for me." He distributed the garlic and mushrooms on the crust, then placed the rounds of mozzarella

Gianessa handed him. "Is that fresh asiago?" He pointed to a dish with grated cheese.

"Fontina. The spinach was dreary today. We'll use some fresh basil."

She tucked basil leaves around the mozzarella, and he finished with a heavy sprinkle of the fontina.

"Like snow on a Christmas tree. Tomatoes would add color another time," he remarked, "but I don't have any."

Gianessa wiped her hands and cleaned the island. Justin removed a bowl of fresh-made salad from the refrigerator, along with a dish of homemade Italian dressing.

"You're a prince among men, thank you."

"I needed to keep busy while I waited. I knew we'd both want a salad."

Gianessa could wait no longer. "Justin, I need to know if you were serious about being a father and helping me parent?"

"Completely. Scared but completely serious. Please tell me what's wrong with—?"

"We're having twins."

Justin was speechless, his mouth open, his eyes round.

"A boy and a girl."

His mouth curved, and his eyes softened.

"I need you, Justin." Without warning, she burst into tears.

Justin wrapped her in his arms.

"I need you to do this with me. I love you, and I need you to do this with me."

"Of course we'll do this together. We'll make it work, Gianessa. Somehow, God help us, we'll make this work." He stroked her back and kissed her forehead. "Please don't cry. It will be all right."

She nodded and pressed her hot cheek against his cool one. "I believe it. I believe you."

"But I insist we get married."

"Is that your best proposal?" She winked.

"It's worse than Joel's first proposal to Manda. We love each other, Gianessa, and I am committed to being sane and sober the way the program wants. I know we can be good together—good partners, good parents, good friends." He laughed and shook his head. "Stop me, I'm babbling."

She touched his lips.

He knelt and held both her hands in his. "Gianessa, will you do me the honor of marrying me and spending the rest of our lives raising these babies and cooking and compromising and—"

"I will do all of those things with you, and love you and support your work, and be the kind of wife you are proud of."

The oven signaled its readiness. Justin slid the pan onto the rack and set the timer.

"Let's enjoy the evening air for a few minutes and talk about a wedding and about you and me." He motioned her out to the porch.

Gianessa sat in one of the tall white rockers and let the soft evening breeze cool the heat in her face. She watched sailboats moving in and out of the marina. When Justin joined her, he held two tall glasses of sparkling water, each with a wedge of lime.

"I like these rockers." She accepted one of the glasses from him.

"And I like sitting next to you, talking and enjoying the lake." He gave her a kiss before settling in the next chair to hers. "Our lives will be very busy in a few short months." He reached for her hand, and she gave his a squeeze. "I want us to be married soon. I know I need to earn your trust, and I mean to do that."

"Justin, are you going to AA meetings regularly?"

"Every day. There's a noontime near campus that I especially like, but I'm trying different ones so I'll have options, whatever my schedule is."

"And you're still working with Gwen in therapy?"

He nodded. "For now she's acting as a sponsor as well as therapist for me. I see her once a week with homework between. She's tough and smart, and that's what I need. It's hard work. And humbling."

"Thank you for doing that and for sticking with it."

She let the peace of the evening relax her, and she felt Justin relax a little beside her. "Justin, should we see a couples therapist, too?"

"I'm open to it. What made you ask?"

"I was thinking of that phrase we hear in the rooms, be 'willing to go to any lengths'. I am willing, if we find ourselves struggling."

Justin was quiet a while and then asked, "Are you as scared as I am to raise these babies?"

Gianessa turned to him with a warm, happy smile. "That part isn't so scary to me. Pop and Ariella were great parents to me. I know if I'm sober and working my program I'll be a good mom." They held hands, and she ran her thumb across his knuckles. "I know you will be a good dad. I want you to believe in yourself, trust your instincts and don't spoil them. And accept that you'll get it wrong at least once a day."

"Pizza critique," Gianessa declared. "What worked, what didn't?"

"Keep the portabella. Next time spinach or broccoli. Fresh tomato for color. Great cheese combination. Fontina, you say?"

"And mozzarella. But the crust was too salty. Think it's worth trying again with a homemade crust?"

"How about tomorrow?" Justin said with a grin.

"We're a good team."

He said softly, "Yes, we are. We can take on any project together. Raising beautiful babies. Building a pizza. Remaking a college."

Gianessa reached across the table for his hand. “Tell me how the college is going.”

“There’s hope for it,” he answered. “The bad actors have packed their bags and left for new territory. The trustees are on board with a complete overhaul of the curriculum. The faculty have sent the consultant packing and are clamoring to take charge of the new curriculum.”

Her eyes sparkled. “They sent your consultant packing? Isn’t that a bad thing?”

Justin grinned and squeezed her hand. “You knew that was the plan all along, sweetheart, and it worked perfectly.”

“You knew he was a fool, and you used him to unite the faculty.”

“The fact that they united and took ownership is what I hoped, but it’s not possible to guarantee such an outcome. They might have united against me, sent me packing and continued their dysfunctional existence.”

“In which case you’d have closed the college?”

He cocked his head. “If they didn’t put themselves out of business in a year, yes, I would have.”

“It was a gamble.”

“I’d say it was a chess match, and I played a skillful game, with your inspiration. We’re all fortunate that the faculty stepped up to the job. They’re a fine lot. However, I do need to talk one thing over with you.”

Gianessa smile warily.

“There’s talk of my becoming the next president of the college. It may not go anywhere, but I need to know how you feel about that.”

“I feel proud about that.” She sat up straighter. “Do you want to do it? What does a college president do?”

“I want to do it, yes. It is mostly a fundraising position in this day and age. In the past, most presidents came from other, high-profile administrative roles in a college, but today some are coming from outside academia. It’s critical to have credibility with the trustees, which I have, and it helps to have credibility with the faculty, which I have, because of my long-term faculty affiliation with the University of Chicago. The fact that I have ties to the global economy and understand new ventures and funding sources is seen as a big advantage. But I wouldn't do it if you didn't want to be a president's wife."

"What does a president's wife do?"

"Charms, entertains, watches for trouble, goes on trips with the president, and advises him on every aspect of the work."

"That says we probably can't live in Joel's apartment very long." She laughed.

"We'll need a home for our family and a home suitable for entertaining."

"You're not suggesting we open the Cushman mansion, are you?" She shuddered.

"It's been leveled and cleared away, and there are plans on the drawing board for a house up by the birches. I hope to start construction in a month."

Gianessa gave him a radiant smile. "Let's build something we love, and something suitable for the job.

"Since the two may not be compatible, we need to make decisions soon."

Gianessa reached for his hand. "Thank you for consulting me. Yes, I will be a president's wife, if you want the job. Can we sit down with the plans one day soon?"

"Yes, very soon. This week. Tomorrow if we can manage it."

"What are you going to call your college? Still Tompkins College? I don't like the way Cushman College sounds, do you?"

Justin made a face. "We could have a name-that-college contest, what do you think?"

"Very wise, President Cushman. How about letting the incoming freshmen organize it?"

"Yes, good, or advertise to donors. Put your name on a new concept in higher education for a hundred million."

Gianessa murmured a reminder in his ear. "You and I need to name a couple of babies."

"And plan a wedding. Unless you want to elope?"

Gianessa shook her head. "Very simple wedding with Joel and Manda and a handful of others."

"Agreed."

"Can we manage a short trip to Italy to meet Pop and Ariella?"

"How about a honeymoon trip to Italy?"

Joel leaned closer and told his uncle, "You'll make a great father, you know."

"I hope you're right. I am scared to death."

Joel's smile told him he understood that feeling. "Glad you can admit it, uncle."

"I'm determined to be a good husband, Joel. Gianessa is everything I could want in a woman, and for some crazy reason she loves me." He looked around the garden and noticed that the chairs were filled now. He wanted just a moment longer sitting beside Joel, drinking in the love and acceptance his nephew offered.

"And you love her?"

"I do, with all my heart, and I didn't know that was possible before I met her. But I wonder if I'm equal to the task of loving her," Justin said humbly. His heart beat a little faster at the thought, and his cheeks flushed.

"I think it's something we grow into. I'm still learning how to love Manda the way she needs. It's probably a lifetime job," Joel assured him.

Justin braced himself, hands on his knees, arms straight. "You're saying there's no formula?"

Joel let out a laugh. "I wish. No, there's no formula. I had to learn early on to listen to her tell me what she needed. And take it seriously, even when it sounded silly."

"Such as?"

"Well, there was the time she came to visit me in the hospital after a shopping trip and wanted to know what kind of lingerie I liked. The fact that I prefer her naked was not an acceptable answer."

Justin chuckled along with Joel.

"We tried to talk about styles and fabric and colors and yada yada. Finally she produced a bag and showed me what she'd bought, and it was nothing I ever thought of as lingerie, but I dug it and she loves it and that was the end of the discussion."

"And I can tell from your smirk that you were rewarded for your dedication to the task and have been enjoying the lingerie ever since."

"Well, yeah, come to think of it. Just having that conversation was really important to her, although I have no idea why."

Justin clapped him on the shoulder, the good shoulder, although there was little visible difference now. Joel's muscles were well developed again on both arms. "I think I get what you're saying."

Joel distilled it, "I went with it and it made her happy. If I'd said, 'You decide, honey,' she would not have been happy."

Justin heard someone clear a throat. He glanced up and stood tall to shake the minister's hand. Joel's generous tip from his own wedding six weeks ago was all the incentive the pastor needed to officiate at Justin's wedding on short notice.

"Justin, Joel, good to be back here with you for another wedding. Everyone is assembled. Are we ready for the ceremony?"

Justin nodded, although his breathing was suddenly a little shallow.

"Rings?"

Joel stood, produced the rings, and put a calming hand on his uncle's shoulder.

"We'll do the standard ceremony. Anything I need to be aware of?" the minister asked.

Justin filled him in. "My best man, Joel, and the matron-of-honor, Manda, will both be seated during the ceremony. Our friend Phil will walk the bride down the aisle."

"Coming down from the upper terrace again?"

"No, we're using just the lower terrace this afternoon, keeping everything simple."

The pastor inspected the assembled guests. "Most unusual to have everyone in casual dress. Except that lady in the first row wearing the expensive silk suit. Is that the bride's mother, I suppose?"

Justin looked where he pointed and saw a raven-haired woman with an aura of power. She wore a Paris original made of deep rose silk, with an abundantly flowered scarf and heavy gold jewelry at her earlobes, left wrist, and two fingers of her right hand. "I have no idea who that is. Nor do I recognize the woman with her." The two fifty-something ladies were deep in conversation.

"Friends of the bride, evidently."

Justin shrugged. "We'll meet at the reception, I'm sure. Pastor, we'd be honored to have you join us for the reception. I hope your wife will as well."

"We wouldn't miss it. Now, if we can assume our places, I will cue the bridal party."

"Deep breath," Joel said.

They exchanged a handshake and broad smiles before turning to the guests.

Today the terrace accommodated sixteen friends in four pairs of chairs on the left, four on the right. On the groom's side were Sydney Shorey and her husband Danny, the trustee Patrice from New York with her husband, the president of Tompkins College with his wife, and the provost with her husband. On Gianessa's side were the mystery women in the first row, Gwen with an open seat for Phil, Sara and Grace, and, behind them, Tony and his girl, Sunny. Just off the terrace at the far end, Justin spied Manda peeking from behind a screen of evergreens.

In response to the minister's cue, she stepped onto the terrace wearing a long blue sundress the color of her eyes. She carried a bouquet of Stargazer lilies, deep lavender roses and baby's breath. She walked slowly—step-pause, step-pause—down the aisle between the chairs. When she pried her eyes away from Joel for a moment, Justin gave her a warm smile and a wink. She winked back and flashed him a big smile.

As soon as Manda reached her position, Phil and Gianessa stepped onto the terrace and paused for a moment. Gianessa squeezed Phil's arm and bent close to whisper something to him. Phil blushed with pleasure. He had consented to wear a polo shirt and chinos, just like Joel and Justin. Justin's polo was gray-green. Joel's was dark green. Phil's was deep purple to coordinate with Gianessa's violet sundress.

Gianessa had never been more beautiful. Her toffee hair was artfully arranged—thanks to Sara—in layers around her face, and a violet ribbon wove its way through. Her simple sundress was nearly to her ankles but allowed him just a peek at the sandals on her slender feet and the violet ribbons that criss-crossed up her calves. If she let him, he'd undo those ribbons later, very slowly, one shapely leg at a time.

Her face radiated happiness and contentment. Her bouquet, a cascade of the same blooms Manda carried, rested easily on her belly. She showed off her baby curves today. His mouth stretched in a silly smile, a mix of disbelief and joy beyond measure.

When she arrived at the rose arbor, she stood facing him and gazed deep into his eyes. Time stopped for a moment. Justin felt himself shift to a place he'd never been. He saw their children playing on the lawn at the house near the birches, saw quiet mornings on their lakeside porch, evening strolls down to the water's edge and back, and nights filled with love and sharing.

The minister intoned, "Dearly beloved."

Justin's heart sang with joy as Gianessa spoke her vows. He spoke his own vows to her with a steady voice. When he envisioned them loving and cherishing each other from this day forward, he added, "One day at a time."

When the moment came to kiss as husband and wife, Gianessa stroked his cheek and whispered, "I love you."

He tipped up her chin and kissed her lips lightly before whispering in her ear, "I will love you all of my life and beyond." He had no idea where the words came from, but they healed something in him, that soulsickness he'd suffered from so desperately when he had first arrived home.

Their guests cheered and clapped. Sydney and the young women on Gianessa's side of the aisle dabbed at their teary eyes.

Joel shook his hand and Justin clapped him on the shoulder. There was no need for words.

Amid more hugs and handshakes, two big carts *putt-putted* up to the terrace. A quick trip to the Manse took the guests to a catered cookout Joel had arranged for them.

Gianessa was deep in conversation with Phil and Tony when she saw Justin embrace the bosomy blond with salon-styled hair. She was sure it was That Sydney Woman.

"Excuse me," she said quietly and made her way across the porch to her husband. As she approached, she heard Justin say, "We'll never stop being friends, Syd. You'll always have a little piece of my heart."

"Nonsense, Justin, I never did." The woman dabbed at her eyes.

"It's true, and I value your counsel in this new role of mine."

Justin's eyes cut to a handsome gentleman, who could be an ad for athletic wear for the middle years, making his way toward them.

"Is your husband going to deck me?"

Sydney chuckled, "No, but Gianessa might." She reached out a hand to the bride. "My dear, you are beyond beautiful. Justin is a lucky man."

Gianessa took her hand in both of hers and said softly, "Yes, and he knows it." She lifted her cheek for Justin's kiss. "Sydney, we're so glad you and Danny could make it to the wedding. You're a very important friend to my husband, and I hope that will continue. You're welcome here any time."

"How gracious."

Justin put his arm around his wife and held out a hand to Danny. "Mr. Shorey. Pleasure to meet you."

"Danny, please, and it's Brennan, by the way. Congratulations to you and your lovely wife." Danny shook Gianessa's hand and raised his eyebrows. "Strong arms. You work out?"

Gianessa rewarded him with a musical laugh. "I do a yoga routine every day, and I'm a masseuse and physical therapist. That builds strength. I see you keep fit, Danny."

He shrugged, but his flushed cheeks signaled his pleasure. "Played basketball at Notre Dame, and that discipline stayed with me, I guess." He gave her a conspiratorial wink and eyed Justin and Sydney. "I can't tell you how glad I am about your marriage, Jessica."

"Gianessa." She placed both hands on her belly. "The twins are glad, too."

Sometime later, Justin stood by himself with a fresh glass of sparkling water, surveying the smiling guests. He felt a touch on his arm and turned to see the raven-haired woman in the pink Paris suit.

"Justin, nice to see you again after all these years."

"I don't believe I know you. Have we met?"

Gianessa moved toward them, her forehead set in an angry frown.

Justin opened his arm to welcome his wife.

The woman continued speaking, "We'd have been famous together if Netscape hadn't beaten us to it."

"Sweetheart," he greeted Gianessa and pushed a wave back from her brow.

Belatedly he registered what the woman had said. He dredged up a name from twenty-plus years ago. *This must be Van Russell*. He had financed a high-tech venture for her that was subsequently trounced by a once-famous product.

Gianessa zeroed in on the woman. "Good of you to come, Mother." Her words were gracious, her tone clipped. "And to bring Aunt Roseanne. You're both looking well. I hope you're enjoying the cookout."

Justin's mouth opened. *Van Russell is Gianessa's mother?*

"Your husband is an old friend," Van simpered. She reached one hand to claw Justin closer to her. When he did not budge, she dropped her hand and told her daughter, "We were business partners, as he's probably told you."

"No." Gianessa feigned disinterest.

Justin noticed one eyebrow cock as soon as Van's attention shifted away from her daughter's face.

He skewered the high-tech maven with, "Not at all, Van. Gianessa and I never talked about her mother. Did you know we're honeymooning in Italy and visiting her Pop and Aunt Ariella? Or perhaps you weren't aware they've returned to Italy?"

In Gianessa's eyes, he saw unbridled admiration for the way he'd added two and two, taken her side and squashed her mother's attempt to sully her happiness.

Justin said heartily, "Can I buy you and Roseanne a drink, Van? We find that Californians don't always like our local wines. What's your poison?"

"Marvelous idea." Van turned briefly back to her daughter. "How nice that you've found someone to rescue you, Gianessa."

Gianessa let out her breath in a laugh. "I'll let Justin explain who rescued who."

Justin hailed a passing waiter and deposited a twenty-dollar bill onto his tray. "Young man, you and your crew are doing a stupendous job for my wife and me. See that this lady and her sister, the woman in black coming toward us, find their way to the bar and order whatever they like." He slipped a tip, another ten, into the young man's palm.

"Van, it's been lovely seeing you. You and your sister have a good time now." He pointed Van toward the bar and gave her a bow of dismissal and a little push.

Sensing that his bride was on the verge of tears, he used his body to block everyone's view of Gianessa and said loudly enough that anyone nearby could hear, "Sweetheart, may I have a moment in private?"

Gianessa let him wrap an arm around her and spirit her away to the patio. She was sobbing before they came to a halt in the privacy afforded by a screen of potted palms.

"I can't believe the way she treated you, Gianessa. Why is she even here? I didn't invite her. I had no idea who your mother was. You never said her name, did you?"

Her arms came around his waist, and she let him rock her and soothe her with his voice. When she reached the end of her tears, he handed her a handkerchief and reached for a chilled bottle of water on a nearby table. They sat side-by-side on a cushioned loveseat facing the lake.

He squeezed her knee. "Are you all right? What can I do?"

She nodded, licked her lips, and managed a weak smile. "Thank you for getting me out of there for a minute."

"Just relax now. We don't have to go back if you don't want. I can make excuses if you want to take a break or leave altogether."

She pressed his hand. "I'll be okay in a minute." She laughed. "My makeup may never recover, but I will. You were magnificent, Justin."

"We're a good team, sweetheart."

"So, how did you know her?"

Justin explained what little he remembered of his business dealings with Vanessa Russell.

"Please tell me you didn't sleep with her?"

"Oh god no. It was a cardinal rule of mine not to sleep with a client, but I wasn't even tempted in her case." He heard what he'd said. "No offense, sweetheart."

Gianessa let out a belly laugh, and he squeezed her hand.

"Justin, I didn't fully appreciate how quick witted and socially adept you are until this happened. You should be president of the college, no question."

He reached for a cloth napkin, poured some of the water onto it and handed the bottle back to her. He attended to her face, dabbing away the two streaks of mascara.

Gianessa drank the rest of the water and set the empty bottle on the patio.

"I invited her," she said, "and Aunt Roseanne. My sponsor suggested it. And now we know it was a bad idea. Except that this is the first time in my life I've stood up to her." She took a deep breath and puffed out her chest. "That felt good."

"You were forceful. Her face fell flat when you brushed off her snarky comment about being rescued."

"Thank you for helping me do that."

"You're wearing a saucy smile." He placed a tiny kiss on the side of her mouth. "What's that about?"

"I love you more each day, dude." She welcomed his next kiss with willing, parted lips.

As the kiss ended, Justin spied Sara waiting behind the potted palm. "Someone needs to interrupt us," he said in a playful tone.

"Who?"

"Sara." His voice was full of merriment. "She's holding something—a box. She's pointing to it and pointing to you. Now she's pointing to her eyes and lips and pointing to you."

Gianessa's laughter filled the patio.

"She's mouthing something. I can't make it out." He motioned Sara to join them. "Give me a clue, pretty lady."

Sara giggled. "Silly man. There's only one reason I'd interrupt a bride at her wedding."

"The emergency makeup repair kit." Gianessa wiped happy tears from her eyes.

Justin gasped. "Good lord, I don't belong here." He gave Sara a wink and kissed his wife's cheek. "I'll check on the Tompkins College people."

Gianessa reached out a hand to her friend, "Ohmigod, you always know what I need, Sara."

Sara set up her makeup kit and got her giggles under control. She turned Gianessa's face to the best light and made deft repairs to her foundation, mascara, eye shadow, and lipstick. "So who was that overdressed witch anyway, and who invited her to the party?"

"I did. She's my mother."

The brush suspended its arc. "Sorry, I forgot you still had a mother somewhere. Vanessa, right?" She wrinkled up her nose. "Seriously, she used to be passionate?"

Gianessa's face softened with compassion. "I'm sure she's forgotten the passion. To be honest, I think she'd forgotten me. It was probably Justin's name on the wedding invitation that drew her here. They did business together way back when. It failed."

Sara held out an open tube of lipstick. "Hold this while I brush it on. Then you'll be good to go."

When Sara had finished her artful job, Gianessa told her, "I'd never say this to Justin, but all the ways I had to stand up to him this year made me strong enough to hold my own with her today. I'm proud of myself."

Sara focused on packing her kit.

Gianessa reached for a brush that had rolled off the table and handed it to her.

"Thanks. I'm going to miss you, Gianessa, but I'm not going to worry about you."

Gianessa touched her shoulder and drew her into a gentle hug. "If we cry we'll ruin your artistry. Justin has started working out with Joel Saturday mornings. We should cook or do a thrift shop run some Saturdays."

"Until the babies come," Sara said, her smile a little sad.

"Justin and I are going to find a nanny to help out so I can keep working and cope with twins. We can make sure she's willing to work on Saturdays."

Sara brightened. "Now you're talking. I might even know someone." She tucked the kit under her arm and offered Gianessa a hand. "You're getting bigger. How are the three of you doing?"

"Jack and Jill are kicking up a storm right now. I'm a little tired but very happy."

Sara giggled. "You're not really naming them Jack and Jill, are you?"

"You're my key people next year," the president told Justin and the provost, Lydia.

Justin smiled and curbed his impatience. *Doesn't he know this is a wedding?*

"Justin, I expect you to get the curriculum defined. It needs to be excellent, current and challenging, and it needs the buy-in of all the remaining faculty. Lydia, it's your job to recruit and hire new faculty so we're staffed and ready to roll out the new curriculum the following fall. I have a few administrators left who will work with me to tighten the policies and procedures and review the budget."

He turned to Justin. "And if you pull this off, I'll gladly hand over the keys to the college."

"I'll do my very best, sir."

"Patrice, would you agree?" the president asked as he took a step back to let the longest-serving trustee join their circle.

Justin spotted Gianessa and motioned to her to join them as well.

"I not only agree, I'm betting on it. Justin, am I out of line to ask if you and your beautiful wife are planning a family?"

Justin threw back his head and laughed. "Women know these things, don't they, Patrice?" He reached out a hand to Gianessa and drew her into the group. "We thought we'd start with twins—a boy and a girl. My wife is partial to naming them Jack and Jill. I have to admit I like the sound of it better every day." He gave his bride a kiss and put a protective arm around her shoulders.

"Patrice, did your children come to Tompkins College?" Gianessa asked.

I would never have thought to ask that.

Patrice's face brightened, and she launched into the story of her two daughters' experiences at Tompkins College the previous decade. Justin watched the dynamic, noting the animation on Patrice's face and the excitement in her voice. *Women know these things.* He was certain Gianessa would be comfortable in the role of president's wife, if it came to that.

Sunny returned to the porch with Manda close behind. She spotted Gianessa and called to her.

Gianessa welcomed her hug. "Did Joel give you a tour of the therapy suite?"

"Yes, just now. I love it. Justin did a fabulous job, didn't he?"

"He did. He made it so easy for all of us. So you're all set to take over Joel's therapy while Justin and I honeymoon in Italy?"

"All set. We'll work together four days a week, and he's committed to keeping up his routines, as prescribed, the days in between. And I'll study for my certification exams on the off days. I can't thank you enough for making this happen. It will stand out on my resume."

"I'm so grateful for your support with my application for my PT license in New York State."

"Have you heard anything?"

"Not yet. I'll take it as it comes and do whatever they require to prove myself."

"When are you going to throw the bouquet?"

"In two minutes. Be there."

"So, Dr. Forrester," Phil said to Gwen as they sipped iced coffee on the patio, "we have two newly married couples under our wings. How do you feel about that?"

Gwen stretched out her legs and laughed. "I think they'll need some help."

Phil chuckled. "They do have a lot going for them. They're in love, they have each other, they have us, and they're sober today." Phil speculated, "Fate seems to have brought Gianessa and Justin together, and I think it's meant to be a fruitful and happy marriage."

"I agree. What about you, Phil? Are you wanting a soulmate?"

Phil placed his hands on his knees and said, "I married Edie for life, and it won't be long before we're together again in the next life."

"That's sweet. But don't leave us too soon. Promise."

"I promise to leave in God's time. And you, Gwen, will you look for another love?"

Gwen sat up straighter and drew in a deep breath. "I'm only thirty-two, and I'd love to have a child. It's time I got back in the game and met a good man for myself. When Jeb died, I thought I'd never recover. But lately, my dreams tell me, 'Time, Gwen. Time for you to dive back in.'"

Gianessa climbed the first three steps of the curving stairway at the Manse. For just a moment she admired the polished mahogany banister, the white marble stairs, and the thick, lake-blue carpet runner. She let her left hand rest on the banister and imagined Joel's grandmother Bridey trailing her hand on the same wood decades ago as mistress of this elegant home. A smile spread over her face as she felt a gentle current flow into her hand. It left as quickly as it had come, after filling her heart with hope—hope for her marriage to Justin, for their children and the new generation of Cushmans. *Bridey has given us her blessing.* Gianessa remembered what her neighbor Linda said on the day she'd met Justin—that those who lived at Lakeside Terrace found their true love quickly and were happily married soon after.

Manda touched her arm. "We have a disturbance." Amusement and concern showed in her sparkling eyes and angled eyebrows. "Look behind us. Our wedding friends have been joined by every female who happened to be at the Manse tonight."

Gianessa turned to the sea of faces. At least two dozen young women stood in the center with a ring of gentlemen around them. In front of the pack were Sara and Grace, each trying to step in front of the other for the best chance at the bouquet.

"Good, you have your flowers, too," she said to Manda. "I hope you're okay with this."

Without explaining what she meant, Gianessa called to the crowd. "Ladies, your attention, please."

The crowd quieted. Gianessa beamed a smile. "Thank you for sharing our excitement. Because so many of you are here, both Cushman brides will throw their bouquets this evening."

She squeezed Manda's hand and continued. "As most of you know, my treasured friend and matron-of-honor Manda Cushman married my new brother-in-law, Joel, a few weeks ago.

"There is no doubt our marriages are blessed by Joel's very romantic grandmother Bridey O'Donohue Tompkins, who I understand is a legend in Tompkins Falls."

She saw Joel wave to her. Justin gave her a proud smile. She blew a kiss to her handsome husband.

"We think these two bouquets are touched with Bridey's magic. Manda and I will toss them to two lucky ladies who want to marry their true loves."

She turned to Manda and quietly added, "Please hold tight to Bridey's banister. You give me the countdown."

On the count of three, the two bouquets of lilies, roses, and baby's breath sailed from the graceful stairway over the waiting pool of arms. Manda's went wide and landed in the arms of a willowy woman dressed in a brilliantly colored sari. Her escort cheered and gave her an enthusiastic kiss.

Just as Gianessa's bouquet reached the top of its arc, she turned to the crowd and noticed someone's elbow jostle Gwen Forrester. Gwen was propelled from the sidelines into the pool of eager young women. Faces full of hope and excitement surrounded her. Arms reached up around her. Hers reached up, too.

The bouquet glided past Sara and Grace. They turned away, disappointment written on their brows.

Gwen's eyes widened in disbelief as rose petals caressed her fingers and the bride's bouquet settled in her hands. A collective "Ah" rose from the women.

Gwen gaped at the delicate blossoms. Then she looked beyond, surprise and delight on her face, and met Gianessa's gaze.

The bride blew her a kiss, and Gwen touched her hand to her heart.

While Manda pushed through the crowd of women to embrace Gwen, Gianessa floated down the stairs and threaded through the crowd to Justin for one more kiss on their magical day.

Also by **Katie O'Boyle** and **Soul Mate Publishing**:

Stepping Up to Love

Miracles happen when romance is higher-powered.

A lakeside porch in the Finger Lakes is the perfect spot for a quiet moment or a heart-to-heart with your special someone. Joel and Manda's first heart-to-heart on the breakfast porch at the Manse Inn and Spa is anything but romantic. Joel the owner of the Manse is furious with his junior accountant for using one of the spa showers. If Manda didn't have a desperate story and a spectacular body, Joel might not be feeding her breakfast and falling in love. Can Manda get sober, clean up her act, and open her heart to her rich, hunky boss? Fall in love with Joel and Manda in *Stepping Up To Love*.

Available now on Amazon: http://tinyurl.com/olr2yfg

Coming Soon from **Katie O'Boyle**
and **Soul Mate Publishing**:

Find the Way Back to Love

Author Biography

Born in the Upstate New York village known as the Birthplace of Women's Rights, Katie O'Boyle loves the Finger Lakes in every season. She enjoys lunch with friends on many a lakeside porch, and she cherishes the lakeside porch as a place for intimate sharing, laughter, and inspiration. By day, she is a tech-savvy college professor and, after hours, a passionate author of warm-hearted romance. She is hard at work on Book Three of the Lakeside Porches romance books and novellas.

Meet Katie O'Boyle:
on Facebook as "Katie O'Boyle Author"
on Twitter as "TompkinsFalls"

CPSIA information can be obtained at www.ICGtesting.com
Printed in the USA
BVOW05s1410280715

410639BV00001B/1/P

9 781619 358386